Pain of Death

Adam Creed was born in Salford and read PPE at Balliol College Oxford. He abandoned a career in the City to study writing at Sheffield Hallam University, following which he wrote in Andalucia then returned to England to work with writers in prison. He is now Head of Writing at Liverpool John Moores University and Project Leader of Free To Write.

Pain of Death is the third novel in the D. I. Staffe series, which also includes *Suffer the Children* and *Willing Flesh*.

ADAM CREED

Pain of Death.

faber and faber

First published in 2011
by Faber and Faber Ltd
Bloomsbury House
74–77 Great Russell Street
London WC1B 3DA

Typeset by RefineCatch Limited, Bungay, Suffolk
Printed in England by CPI Mackays, Chatham

A CIP record for this book is available from the British Library

ISBN 978–0–571–24524–6

2 4 6 8 10 9 7 5 3 1

FOR

Ada
Gertrude
Marie
Ruth
Stefanie

All wonderful mothers

PART ONE

One

Staffe sinks to his knees, the ground surprisingly warm, here beneath the City. The ponding water leaches into his trousers and he leans close to the face of the dying woman. In this false light, her skin is the palest blue, almost neon, and her broken lips are strangely bright, like burst plums. He searches for a glimmer of life but there seems to be none.

Then she moans.

He could swear she does, so he puts his ear to her mouth, but feels nothing, just his own drumming life, within.

Water drips. The deep vaults echo the constant murmur of the small generator. A camera clicks and the crime-scene lights buzz. On each of her wrists, he sees a ring of red pressed into the skin, like thick bracelets.

A paramedic asks Staffe to move away and another stands over the woman, drapes a red blanket over her. It covers her body, not the face.

'No,' says the photographer. 'I need to see all of her.'

Beneath the blanket, the woman is as she was: naked from the waist down, a cotton dress hoisted up around her stomach and breasts. No underwear.

A scene-of-crime officer in plastic overalls removes the blanket and looks away as the photographer tries to capture the scene.

'We have to move her,' says the doctor, who wears patent purple, chunky heels. Her hair is done up in a swirling twist and her plastic suit rustles in the subterranean mêlée. The night she had dressed for was in a different, brighter world.

'Then take her,' says Staffe, snatching the blanket from the SOCO. As he replaces the blanket, he sees the smears and clusters of blood, some dried, some fresh. It is all over the down curve of her stomach, and her legs, and between. He beckons the paramedics.

'We need more time,' says the crime-scene photographer.

Staffe says to the doctor, 'I'm sorry. Please take her away.'

The paramedics lift her onto a stretcher, as if she were a Fabergé egg. Written on all their faces is the doomed concentration of people who wish to save lives, who often as not tend the new dead.

The doctor places a hand on Staffe's elbow, grips it lightly, saying softly, 'She might be all right.'

They smile weakly at each other.

He watches everybody leave, taking their kit with them: the SOCOs and medics in separate groups.

The inspector remains in this tunnel the Victorians earmarked as an underground railway. But it never made it.

His chest tightens.

Far away, at the bottom of the shaft that delivered them here, the last light disappears and for a moment all Staffe can hear is his own heart. In the dark, distant, a light flickers. As it slowly grows larger and closer, Staffe sees it is a man approaching. He looks like something from a Hammer film, his eyes intent and narrowed. His bearded jaw juts and his thin lips are dark; there is blood on his hands and his shirt front, too.

This is Asquith, Secretary of the Underground Victorians and an amateur historian. He found the dying woman and called the police. Staffe knows he will have to question him, will have to search for a link between Asquith and the woman but killers don't call; and if they do, they don't stick around.

'Strange,' says Asquith. 'All my days, I have peered into the past, but this is now. They will come here, to the scene of this murder.'

'She's not dead.'

'This will become history.'

Staffe watches Asquith disappear down the tunnel, towards the streets and libraries, the hospitals and homes. A fat drop of water hits him on the forehead, runs down his face and a rat scuttles across his shoe. They say you are never more than twelve feet from a rat on the London streets. Beneath, God knows.

He tries to imagine what it would have been like for the woman down here. How long had she been below ground? Who had brought her and why had they done what they did: the blow to the head, the scratch marks on her arms and all the blood – down *there*, caked on the tops of her thighs and smeared on her stomach. Her lip was lacerated, too. The doctor reckoned the woman had probably bitten through it herself.

Staffe shivers, pulls his jacket tight as the tunnel becomes coffin-black once more, the light from Asquith's torch fading completely. The iron door slams shut again and he turns on his torch, its batteries weak. The failing beam stutters as he casts around the scene, flickering on the dark stain of blood, where her legs had made their confluence.

He makes his way, piecing together a critical path to follow, but catches his boot on a paving slab and falls, into the harsh darkness. The wet stone floor rips his hand. He turns the torch on a flap of skin, loose on the soft pad of flesh by his wrist. It stings and he wonders what might get into the blood. He pushes himself up and walks gingerly towards the iron door but his torch fails. Staffe gropes for the latch, grazing his fingers and knuckles, eventually heaving open the door. Daylight falls through the shaft, like weak water, and for a moment, it blinds him, then he remembers a promise he had made for today.

Above ground, it is a fine spring day, a pleasant surprise after the long winter; the city folk are out in shirt-sleeves, bare legs. Staffe carries his jacket slung over a shoulder, past the Earl Marshall, stolen away between the Old Street roundabout and the Limekiln estate. The daytime drinkers are at it, leaning against the pub wall and drawing on their fags, flicking ash and looking the girls up and down. He pats down the loose skin on his hand, grimaces.

Jasmine Cash clocks Staffe as soon as he walks into the Limekiln's dirty cloister. Some kids are kicking a ball against a wall. Others skulk on the steps up to the low-rise tenements in the shadow of the Limekiln Tower. Jasmine holds her baby on her hip and waves to him. The infant Millie copies.

When Staffe gets to Jasmine's flat, mother and daughter have gone inside. He lets himself in and sees Millie jabbing her fingers into the stereo. She stands with her legs wide apart, still in nappies. She chunters to herself in a private language and her mum joins in, as if she understands.

'Tea?' says Jasmine.

'How do you keep this place so fine?' says Staffe.

'This is Millie's world. It doesn't have to be S-H-I-T in here.' Jasmine smiles, winking at Millie. 'We'll get out of here, soon, but until we do, I can make it fine.'

Staffe bends down and picks up the child, lifts her right up to the ceiling and Millie chortles, 'Ma sconce pantalililly,' down at him.

'Not now, Mill,' says Jasmine. 'Jadus will sort us out. He will get it, won't he?'

'You've got to prepare for the worst.' Staffe lowers Millie down, holds her close. She smells of oatmeal.

'No way. I prepare for the best. It's how it's going to be.' She holds out Staffe's tea and he places Millie on the floor. 'For sure, and all thanks to you.'

Staffe considers his role in the trial of Jadus Golding – those years ago – and the tribulations since. He must shoulder some blame for the mess that is Jadus's life. 'You've put him on your rent book?'

Jasmine produces the book, beaming all over her face. 'He's coming home, I tell you, and we're going to be a family.'

Staffe takes the book, together with the offer of employment from Jasmine's cousin who runs an eel and pie shop in Bethnal Green.

She says, 'He wrote to that post office man just like you said. And he got a letter back. That man's so bitter, still. He's got no idea how my Jadus has changed. No idea.'

Staffe can't think what to say to Jasmine, without bursting this bubble. Jadus was in the gang that pulled a gun on that post office manager, ruining his life and his business. Two years on and the man still can't sleep nights. He can't ever be a father or a husband the way he was. No surprise that Jadus's letter from the blue left him cold. But that isn't to say the world can't be a better place; Jadus reforming himself. The crime is in the past, the victim with it. Staffe knows the world has to be made better, whatever way we can.

'You remember what you said, Jasmine?'

She nods. 'If he steps one foot out, you'll know. I promise. But he won't.'

Staffe places the documents in the plastic wallet that Jasmine has given him. 'I'll call you when we're through,' He slides in the latest photographs of Millie, too. 'It might be bad news. It really might, you know.'

'He's learned his lesson. He's ready to be a father and a husband. He's ready to work,' says Jasmine, totally unprepared for the parole of her loved one to be denied. How could the board disappoint her?

Two

'How did Golding's parole hearing go?' asks DS Pulford, late in the day.

'What are her chances?' says Staffe, looking past his sergeant to the woman in bed. Against the brilliant white starch of ward linen, the woman seems in a far worse state – as if you can now hear the sub-audio screams of her bruises and cuts in this harsh and clean environment. In the tunnel, it had seemed she might be saved by something like apothecary or faith.

'Touch and go. More go than touch.'

'Has she said anything?'

Pulford shakes his head. Both men angle towards the woman. 'We have had the ID confirmed, sir – from her prints.'

'She's got a record?'

'Strange, isn't it, sir?' Pulford's young face looks puzzled, almost cherubic. 'When they're naked and beaten up, put between those sheets and fed on a drip, their history counts for nothing. Could be hooked on the crack pipe or pulling in a million a year in the City.'

'What kind of record does she have?'

'Benefit fraud. And ABH.'

'ABH?'

'Against the dad.'

'The dad? There's kids?'

'Oh, yes. But the kids are in care. And the doctors reckon there's another one. They reckon she's had a baby, just.'

'What!' Staffe looks at her, remembers the smeared blood and what he thought were wounds. 'She had a baby down in the tunnel?'

'Forensics say there was no sign at the scene.'

'Christ! We've got to speak to her.'

'The doctors can't say when that might be.'

'What's she called?'

'Kerry. Kerry Degg.'

Staffe sits beside the woman, takes her hand in his, careful not to disturb the tubes that tunnel their way into her veins. Life dripping into her, dripping away. 'What kind of animal would take her down there?'

'Perhaps she went in herself. Forensics say she could have been down there a couple of days. But no more. There's no, you know . . .'

'Excrement,' Staffe sighs. 'And when did the baby happen? Can they say?'

'They say they need to keep her stable. They can't go into that. Not yet. Not until she's better; or . . .'

Staffe tries to imagine what might make a woman go to such a place to have a baby. 'And the husband?'

'Sean. They've been married six years, since she was seventeen. He's thirty-six and clean as a whistle.'

'We'll see about that.' Staffe reaches out, squeezes her hand, as firmly as he dare, to see if her eyes will flicker or her pulse change. But she is dead to his attentions, for now.

He studies her, and something stirs inside him. Stripped bare of all make-up and her jet-black hair combed, he thinks he might know her.

'How did the parole go, sir? The Jadus Golding thing. Is he coming out?'

Staffe looks at Kerry Degg, clinging onto life, having issued life; having had cause to attack Sean Degg, her husband of six years; having been deemed unfit to hold onto her own children. He turns his gaze to his young sergeant. 'Do you ever doubt what we do is for the best?'

Sean Degg hunches by Kerry's hospital bed, whispering constantly into his wife's ear under the watchful gaze of a uniformed police officer, a nurse and DI Will Wagstaffe.

He keeps his hand flat and gentle on her stomach. Tears pop from his eyes and run freely down his cheeks. He doesn't sob, or wail, but when he is done, he says to the nurse, 'I came here thinking she would be gone, but she's not. You think she'll be all right, don't you?'

The nurse is young with golden hair and a constantly cheerful face. She looks at Staffe, then at the uniformed officer, making her smile as thin as she can.

Sean says to the nurse, 'Am I wrong?'

'She's been through a lot.'

Staffe says, 'And what about the baby, Sean?'

The nurse says, 'You come with me, Mr Degg. You look all done in. We'll have someone take a look at you.'

'I'll need a word, first,' says Staffe.

Sean says, 'I don't know about a baby. Is there a baby?' He

looks confused. Or is he afraid? 'I haven't seen Kerry for months.'

'You deserted her?' says Staffe.

'The other way round. With Kerry, it's always the other way round.'

'I am taking him to see a doctor,' says the nurse, raising her eyebrows and crossing her arms under her breasts. 'He needs attention.'

Staffe looks at Kerry Degg, splayed on the bed with only tubes drawing the line between her and a fast, certain death. He rues her silence, says to the nurse, 'No. He's coming with me. I'll bring him back to you as soon as I am done. He'll survive.'

'Did you want another baby, Sean? I don't suppose you did. Already got two in care,' says Staffe in the interview room at Leadengate station, just a stone's throw from the City Royal Hospital, and in the company of duty solicitor, Stan Buchanan.

Buchanan says, quite mechanically, 'You have already been advised that Mrs Degg left my client months ago when she was still pregnant and he hasn't seen her since. He can account for his actions and his whereabouts ever since she departed the marital home on . . .' Buchanan leafs wearily through his notes.

'It was the sixth of January. I was taking the Christmas decorations down and she had someone to see.'

'Why did she beat you up, Sean?'

Buchanan nods at Sean, who says, 'It wasn't the first time. Sometimes, she's not herself.'

'Why didn't you keep the children, Sean?'

'I chose Kerry. I love her. I always have. Nobody else can look after her.'

'And the children can look after themselves?'

'I could only do so much.'

'Not so much, if you left her.'

'She left me.'

'Oh, I'm sorry. And what exactly did she leave you for?'

Sean shrugs.

'If you love her as much as you say, you'd have bloody well found out where she went. She didn't stray far, by the look of things.'

Sean Degg looks Staffe straight in the eye, says nothing. His lip quivers.

Staffe can tell one kind of fear from another and he senses that this is a man who does not fear for his liberty. Sean Degg looks like a man who knows something but can't be harmed any more. 'I'll get to the bottom of you. Believe me. In the meantime, can you confirm that you are still living on Flower and Dean?'

He nods.

Staffe immediately registers who, living in that vicinity, is in his debt, says, 'And you'll remain there and co-operate fully with our enquiries, and fill out this log of your whereabouts, morning, afternoon and night since the sixth of January?'

Sean nods, utterly resigned.

'You can return to the hospital. I have to advise you to seek medical treatment when you get there. Your wife's nurse will arrange it for you.'

'Thank you, Inspector,' says Sean Degg, standing.

'The children, Sean – are they yours?'

'I raised them as my own – as far as I could. But no, they're not.'

'You are registered as the father. Are you saying that Kerry has been having an affair throughout your marriage?'

'Not an affair, and it doesn't mean I can't love her.'

'And this latest baby – was it yours?'

Sean Degg looks away.

Staffe puts down the phone and scribbles 'The Earl' on his blotter, then looks at the pile of papers that his accountant is screaming for: management figures for his property portfolio. A part of him wishes he had sold up when his City friend of old, Finbar Hare, had urged him to do so – but what would he do with the money?

'Have you got a minute, sir?' Josie Chancellor helps herself to the chair opposite Staffe and begins to read the preliminary forensic findings from the tunnel. As she reads, she winds strands of her shoulder-length, smooth brown hair around her fingers. 'Only one blood type. Kerry Degg's.'

'And no signs of a placenta?' says Staffe.

'. . . Not a sausage. There's no sign of a birth down there. The scene was cleaned up, spick and span. We're checking all the hospitals. But what Sean said is true, sir. Kerry Degg is on our missing-persons list. From the tenth of January.'

'That doesn't make what he said true. I assume he was the one who reported her missing.'

'He did.' She pushes the papers across the desk and leans back, brushing her hair from her face. 'Why've you got it in for Sean Degg?'

'I've got it in for whoever put that woman down there. For whoever knocked her up and abandoned her. I've seen nothing to tell me he didn't do those things. Unless you know who else might have.'

'She's the promiscuous one – by the sound of it. She's the mother who let her kids go into care and got herself knocked up again.'

'If there's two sides to this story, let's hope she gets to tell hers.'

'She's a victim. It doesn't mean he can't be, too.'

Staffe smiles, stands up. 'Where d'you get all that wisdom from, Chancellor? Let me buy you a drink.'

'Have you forgotten?'

'What?'

'It's Pulford's party tonight. His new place.' Josie shakes her head slowly, smiling. 'You should know, you used to be his landlord. Surely you're coming.'

'Of course I'm coming,' says Staffe, lying. 'Doesn't mean we can't have a quick sharpener, though.'

'Where are you suggesting we go?'

'You'll see,' said Staffe, dialling reception. 'Jom, have you got that search warrant for the Deggs's place? Good.'

'You said a drink.'

'And I meant it.'

'But Sean won't be there. He's gone back to the hospital.'

On the way out, Staffe picks up the pile of paper for his properties, tugs out the bottom drawer of his filing cabinet with the toe of his Chelsea boot, dropping in all the accounts and leases and variations. It makes a metallic thud and he kicks the drawer shut, fast. As he leaves, he feels life flutter in his chest. The prospect of the ordeal ahead makes him glow, like a chance meeting with someone you secretly adore. This reaction is not something he admires in himself.

The Earl Marshall sits as proud as it can in the shadow of the mid-rise, late-Victorian Limekiln tenements. The Limekiln Tower looms above. The pub hasn't been knocked about with any vigour in over a hundred years. The rooms are separated by etched-glass panels and the spring sun floods in through smeared, ceiling-high windows. The swagged, heavy drapes look like they haven't been cleaned since they buried Queen Victoria, and the red-topped, veneered tables are sticky with glass rings and weeks of spilled beer. There is a smell of dog and the punters are sitting down, rather than standing at the bar. They sit on their own and look into their pints and chasers, or at their shoes, or into the racing pages.

Sean Degg, however, is talking animatedly to a tall, sharp-dressed man ten years his junior, Ross Denness. Sean Degg doesn't know that in a recent phone call, Ross fingered the Earl as Degg's local. And to preserve this deceit, Denness takes his leave, edging away from Degg, towards the door. He will wait for Staffe in a car down on Jellicoe, the other way from Degg's place on Flower and Dean.

Josie says, 'How did you know he'd be here?'

Staffe nods towards the man leaving the pub by the side door.

'Aah. Ross Denness. You've still got your paw on his tail?'

Staffe takes a step towards the bar and everyone looks up. The side door slams shut. Sean Degg clocks Staffe, who takes the warrant from his pocket and waves it at Degg. 'Thought you were desperate to get to the hospital, Sean? Finish your drink and take me to your place.'

'You're harassing me.'

'I'm protecting the public, and that involves going through your home. If your wife doesn't recover, it'll be murder, according to our legal department. Whoever took her down there left her to die and we won't be settling for anything less. There's a baby's life here, too.'

'I haven't seen her for three months.'

'Eighty-eight days, by my reckoning.' Staffe puts his hand heavily upon Sean Degg's shoulder and Kerry's husband tenses up, blinking. Staffe knows everybody in the pub has him down as a copper, so he leans right up against Degg, whispers in his ear, 'I'll see you back at yours in ten minutes. Get the kettle on, eh?' And he pushes a folded twenty-pound note into Sean Degg's shirt pocket – for everyone to see.

Denness is in the driver's seat of his Audi A4, dragging on a Benson's and listening to some high-revving dance music.

'Nice motor, Ross. Things must be rosy for you just now,' says Staffe, sliding into the passenger seat, turning down the music.

Denness turns the music back up, says, 'That's my business. We had an understanding.'

'I'll be the judge of that. What can you tell me about our friend Sean?'

'He's a fucking loser, man. He loves that slag and if you ask me, he wouldn't harm a hair. But he did say something.'

'What's that?'

'Are we even?'

'I guess so – if it puts him on the hook.'

'What if it gets him off the hook?'

'Let's have it, Ross.'

Denness powers up the engine and toys with the accelerator. The throaty surges of power clash with the dance beats. 'He was desperate for her to have that baby. Reckoned it was his. You know the other two aren't.'

'How'd he know it was his?'

'She beat him up. Proper mashed him. Used a wheel-nut spanner on him when she found out she was knocked up. Said it was his fault. She must have given herself a coupla months off from sleeping around, or stuck to giving head, or . . .'

'All right, all right. I get the picture.'

'Muppet reckoned the social would let them keep this one on account it was botha theirs. He's in pieces, man. I kinda feel sorry for him, you know. And he loves her. You'd better believe that. Sad fucker.'

Sean's house on Flower and Dean is a modern, urban-infill house from the eighties. Inside, Kerry Degg is everywhere: framed and posed, black and white portfolio photographs, colour shots of her on stage with jet-black hair and showing silk and flesh.

Staffe walks across to the laminated kitchen pier and lifts his mug of tea, delves into Sean's shirt pocket for the twenty-pound note.

'They all think I'm in your pay now,' says Sean.

'You're going to have to tell the truth, then. Don't want both sides of the law holding it against you.' Staffe picks up one of the many framed photographs of Kerry. She pouts into camera with her face tilted up and a hand gripping her head; one foot up on a piano stool, showing her legs off. She wears a tight-bodiced, slit dress. The look is unmistakably burlesque.

'Kerry's a singer.'

Staffe looks around the flat. Its interior contradicts the building it is in, and its locale. Hippy scarves hang from light fittings and theatre prints and record sleeves adorn the walls. Patchouli is ingrained and all the LPs are alphabetised, from Oleta Adams to Frank Zappa. An eclectic mix of blues and soul, jazz and vaudeville. In the kitchen, an optic rack holds Pastis, Tanqueray and Havana Club. Over the years, Staffe has been in many houses and flats, bedsits and squats. None quite like this.

He pulls open a drawer and suggests to Josie that she makes a start on the bedroom.

'These things are precious to us. This is our life,' says Sean.

Staffe picks up a flyer for a show last October at the Boss Clef. 'Lori was her stage name?'

'That's right.'

He does know her.

On the flyer is written, LORI DOS PASSOS. Below the photograph of Kerry, pouting, *DOES* BURLESQUE. And, for sure, Kerry's performances were risqué. Staffe had seen for himself, in that drunken hinterland of the final break-up from Sylvie.

Josie calls down from the bedroom and he goes up, telling Sean to sit down and keep his hands off everything.

Standing in front of a whole wall of opened wardrobes, Josie says, 'This lot doesn't come cheap. Christ. Why do they live in a place like this?'

'Because they spend all their cash on Kerry's career?' says Staffe, running his hand along the rails of sequined, brilliantly coloured silk and satin dresses, skirts and blouses. Above, hats and scarves. Below, neat pile after neat pile of corsets and knickers, bras and belts.

'And it might have been about to pay off,' says Josie. 'That burlesque is all the rage, you know. Look at this. It was in her bedside drawer.'

Staffe takes the letter, an acknowledgement of receipt of contract from Rendezvous Enterprises. Phillip Ramone runs the two most successful clubs in Soho, and has seemingly offered Kerry a residency at Rendezvous. Fifteen hundred quid a week.

'What a shame,' says Josie. 'Just as she was about to break through.'

'Into motherhood again,' says Staffe, storming back towards the lounge. He takes a deep breath before going in, walks slowly towards where Sean sits. He wants to lift him up by the throat and launch him into the wall, see what the weasel would say under real duress. But he forces himself to concoct another way.

'Were you going to look after the baby, Sean?'

'How d'you mean?'

'Different, when the biological father's intent on giving it a home. And things picking up, too – with Kerry's career. This one was yours, wasn't it?' Staffe sits alongside Sean, puts his big hand on Sean's small, bony knee. 'You'd make a good dad, Sean. That's my guess. And all the support you've given Kerry over the years. She was growing away from you, wasn't she?' He looks around the room. 'Getting too big for all this.'

'I don't know what she's done with the baby. Honest, I don't.'

'There is no baby, is there, Sean? Kerry had her career to think about.'

'I helped her every inch. Not that I got anything out of it. But she's worth it. She's special.'

'I know. I've seen her.' Staffe takes the Boss Clef flyer from his pocket. 'I was there, that night. Some show. You wouldn't have guessed she had your child inside her.'

'Shut up.'

'And I wouldn't have guessed she'd have beaten up her husband – so bad he had to call the police.'

'I asked for it.'

'What exactly did you ask for, Sean? You said you didn't get anything out of her. Why should you?'

'I curated her. I found her and developed her. I saw what nobody else did – before it was even there.'

'You *curated* her?'

'It's what I do. I just wanted her to love me. That's all.'

'They say you should never marry too good.'

'That's shit. You've got no choice who you love.'

'But Kerry did.'

'She loves me, all right. In ways you'll never understand. We'll always be together. She knows that.'

'I'll understand, Sean. Don't worry about that.'

Josie comes in, swinging a clutch of clear plastic bags. 'Driving licence, passport, bank details. She hadn't planned to be away for long. Not exactly doing a runner, was she?'

'You could have told us that, couldn't you, Sean? But you decided to withhold on us.' Staffe stands up, looks down at

Sean Degg and holds out his hand. Josie unclips the cuffs.

'I never touched her. I never could. I never could!' Staffe goes down onto his knees and takes a hold of Degg's chin with finger and thumb. 'If that's so, there's nothing to worry about. And nothing to fear from the truth – which you'd better start spewing up. Because if you don't, and if Kerry never comes round to give her side of the story, you'll be going to a dark place.'

'Don't say that,' says Degg. 'I can't do time. I can't.'

Three

As soon as the uniformed officers had arrived at Flower and Dean to take Sean Degg back to Leadengate station, Staffe walked back to City Royal to see how Kerry Degg was progressing.

He sits alongside her, hoping with everything he can muster that she pulls through. Lying there, with her greasy hair combed straight and her skin deathly white and her broken lip butterfly-stitched, you could not compute that she lives her life upon a stage, that her house is adorned with such exotica, that she can estrange her own children.

'Her chances are slim.'

Staffe turns quickly as a dark-haired nurse pulls up a chair. She has olive-coloured skin, smooth as Wedgwood, and dark eyes. She is solemn.

The nurse says, soft and northern, 'How on earth will you find the baby?'

'We have alerted all the hospitals and clinics.'

'How did she get down there, after she'd given birth? Your sergeant told me about the tunnel.'

'My sergeant should watch his tongue.'

'He seems a decent sort. He said he was having a party.'

'And no doubt he invited you.'

Now, the nurse smiles. 'As a matter of fact he did.' She looks at Kerry Degg. 'It doesn't seem right. Not tonight.'

23

'You can't have that attitude in your job, surely.'

'Sometimes, it gets to you. It's awful, to see a mother and no child.'

'A party might take your mind off it.'

'Are you going?'

'I have to.'

'You make it sound like a chore.'

'What's your name?'

'Nurse Delahunty. Eve.'

'I'm Staffe.'

'Aah. I heard,' says Nurse Eve.

Pulford's flat is in the eaves of a Victorian town house and Staffe is pleasantly surprised at the turnout. Pulford has never been the most popular of sergeants, on account of his fast-tracked progress, courtesy of a degree in history, but there is a smattering of officers from Leadengate and a couple of dozen others who are patently not police.

He has laid on an impressive spread, with a full range of spirits and a dustbin full of beers on ice. Some kind of Northern Soul morphs with House. The young people represent a side of Pulford he never saw when the young sergeant lived at Staffe's flat in Queens Terrace.

'We've brought Degg in,' he says to Pulford as he gives Staffe and Nurse Eve a tour of three small rooms.

'I never said, not properly –' Pulford is the worse for wear, has lipstick on his face. '– how grateful I am, sir.'

'Shut up.'

'No.' He turns to Nurse Eve. 'He took me in when nobody else wanted to know. I was up to here.' He raises a hand to the ceiling. 'But I'm over all that shit now. I'm all set, and it's thanks to him. Have a beer, sir.'

'Just one,' says Staffe. Nothing worse than being amongst the half-cut. He thinks this might be the first party he's been to since he split with Sylvie.

He sits on the edge of the bed, alongside Nurse Eve, and Pulford brings their drinks, gets pulled away by a drunk girl who looks about eighteen. 'She was into burlesque,' he says. 'Kerry.'

'I've never been.'

'You should.'

'It's strange. When they come to us, in states like that, they could be into anything and we'd never guess.'

'They could be guilty of anything.'

'Cynic,' she says, laughing. When she laughs, her eyes glisten and the flesh between her eyes crinkles.

Staffe thinks, Nurse Eve should laugh more. He thinks she has a good spirit, has sadness close by. He also thinks that she is unlike Sylvie, that she lacks Sylvie's confidence. And he wonders if he has a type.

'I should leave you alone. You look as if you have some thinking to do.'

'I have. But I don't want to.' He raises his bottle, clinks it against her wineglass. 'So, you've never been to burlesque. You should try it.'

Josie turns away from Sean Degg who is disconsolate in the holding cell. She says to Jombaugh, 'Do you want me to do it?'

'You look done in. Leave him to me. It's a withholding charge, you say?'

25

Josie beckons Jombaugh outside, keeping an eye on Sean Degg, who looks as if he might be coming down from something. She whispers, 'Staffe wants to leave him a few hours. Keep Buchanan away from him and let him stew. He knows more than he's letting on.'

Jombaugh looks into the cell. 'Is he on something?'

'Could be.'

'I'll run a piss test on him. That'll buy some time. You get yourself home. It's been a rough day.'

Josie lets herself out the back of the station, into the car park. She thinks she hears something. An animal or possibly something human. She can sense a presence. She sniffs the air, thinking it might be a crafty fag being had. No smell. But something is moving in the car park. She can feel it, and peers into the corner of the yard, where the bins are kept, listening intently.

This time of night, the car park is less than half-full. Josie makes her way slowly to the far wall, which adjoins Cloth Fair. She shines her torch along the gap between the parked cars and the wall and hears a shriek, then a scamper of padding feet. Her heart pounds, then stops. The cat jumps onto a ledge, up onto the high wall and beyond, into the night. Josie's heart starts up again and she laughs to herself. Pure relief. She switches off her torch and makes her way towards the pedestrian gate.

A car draws along Cloth Fair, its headlight beam sweeping towards Josie, then away. She sees it. She isn't going mad.

At the foot of the railings, wrapped in a tea towel, the baby seems blue. Its eyes are shut, tight. Its lips are white. The silence of the tiny creature makes Josie's heart pound harder this time, and for several moments she is frozen.

She kneels down, the ground sharp on her bare knees.

Her hands shake as she lifts the baby into her breast. She presses her cheek to its head and whispers into the baby's ear, soft as skin, 'Please God, please don't. Please God, please be all right.'

She rocks and holds her breath and searches for the baby's temple with her finger, holding her breath still deeper, that she may sense a pulse or feel the whisper of breath. But nothing.

Her stomach yawns. She wants to scream and curse whoever did this. She holds the baby tighter, struggling to her feet and walking towards the back door not knowing whether to go fast or slow. And then it happens.

The baby screams. Into her ear. Deep and hurt, the baby screams with every surge of blood and well of air from its egg-sized lungs. A last, despairing cry to be saved. Josie slumps to the ground and rocks back and forth, back and forth, holding the baby's head in the palm of her hand.

When they come, Jombaugh kneeling beside her and trying to prise the baby away, Josie won't let go, simply says, over and over, until the ambulance arrives, 'For the grace of God, for the grace of God . . .'

And even then, she won't let the paramedics take the baby without her going too, quite convinced that this baby will surely die if it is taken from her sight.

The wine has made Eve loose. Her hair is ruffled and her eyeliner is smudged – as are her words. Her smile comes easy and she speaks faster, her northern accent thicker now. She toys with her glass and supports her chin with the palm of her hand, looks up at Staffe as if he is the only person in the room. But she had done the same with the doorman and the waiter. On the way, she told him how she came to London four years ago with a friend. She hated it, but it's not so bad now, and she can't imagine herself ever going back.

Staffe watches the act up on the stage. They are at a small table in the Boss Clef. The audience is hemmed in to the stage by a horseshoe of red drapes. He thinks, how refreshing, that she knows he is a copper but hasn't delved at all into his job, or his life.

At the end of the song, Eve spins on her seat, joins in the applause and leans into him, her lips on his ear and whispering, 'We haven't talked about you at all, have we? But I know.' She pulls away.

'Know?'

The applause subsides and Eve picks up her glass and finishes her vodka and soda. 'Your sergeant told me all about you.'

Staffe's instinct is to tell her that he's really not got his head round his ex, that he's actually not made love since then and has barely had the inclination. Suddenly, he knows he should see Sylvie. It's the least she deserves – an explanation. Perhaps she deserves to never see him again. What does he know?

'He told me about your ex.'

'Sylvie?' He likes the word in his mouth.

'Let's not talk about her.' She finishes her wine.

He wants to tell Eve he is too old for her. Suddenly, in his battered leather jacket and his boot-cut jeans and his grown-out hair and his day's growth, he feels the full weight of his years.

He looks at his mineral water and Eve's empty glass, and gestures to the waiter, asks for another vodka and a Laphroaig. 'A large one.'

'Don't drink on my behalf,' she says, straight-faced. 'Not unless you want to.' Her face cracks into a smile and she slaps his leg, says, 'Let's dance.' She nods to the small gap between the stage and the front line of tables – enough room for a few people to shuffle. Nobody is dancing.

Eve stands and holds out her hand towards Staffe. His heart sinks and he looks around the room. He knows what he would think of a man like him dancing in public.

She tugs him and he surrenders to it. He lets her lead him between the tables and he smiles apologetically, in case anybody cares to look. He feels the heat of the stage lights on him. The singer raises her hands and claps, smiles at Eve, whose hips draw figures of eight. Staffe doesn't know where to put his hands, what to do with his feet, but Eve reaches out and takes his hand and winds herself around him, under his hand and twirling in his grasp. By the end of the song, there are a dozen people on the dance floor.

When they get back to the table, the drinks have come. Staffe pours some water into his whisky and feels his phone vibrate.

He should ignore it.

'You're ringing,' says Eve. 'You should answer. I understand.'

Four

Even in the dead of night, Keller ward is bright and clean. It smells of talcum powder and warm milk. Brightly coloured animals romp across the walls in primary colours and the distant reprise of cartoon soundtracks swoons through the halls of new life, like lullabies. It is a world away from Kerry Degg's small room, just a couple of corridors away.

However, in a room built for one tiny human, a row of glum people huddle along one wall: a uniformed officer, a doctor and a nurse, who Staffe recognises from Kerry's ward – the one with the golden hair.

DC Josie Chancellor sits by the plastic-domed cot. Within the germ-free bubble is the baby they have called Grace. The DNA has been sought and is being analysed, but the outcome is widely predicted: Baby Grace is the daughter of Kerry Degg. The father? That remains to be seen.

'I found her, sir,' says Josie, looking up with wide eyes, her kohl bled black in gothic zags down to her cheeks.

'I'm sorry, Josie. I should have dealt with Degg myself.'

'No!' says Josie. Her eyes are glazed and her lips are plump, blood red. 'If anything had been different about tonight, I wouldn't have found her. She might . . .'

'She won't go home. We keep telling her,' says the nurse.

'She was so light, like lint. And she screamed for me. It was the most beautiful thing.' Josie turns towards him and Staffe wraps her up in a tight embrace. 'Sir, it was the most beautiful thing.'

He thinks, he must smell of drink and the club and maybe scent. 'Thank God you went out when you did.'

'Jombaugh got a call, sir. About two minutes after I found the baby. It sounded like a woman, but he couldn't be sure. They were talking through some kind of device. We're having the tape analysed.'

'Where was the call made from?'

'A prepaid mobile. No chance of a trace.'

'They told Jom about the baby?'

'Described the exact place. Said to call an ambulance, that the baby wasn't taking its food properly and she was ill.'

'Why wouldn't they take it to a hospital?'

'A police station's the next best thing? You know how quiet the City is at night. They must have passed her through the railings. Might even have been on their way here and lost their nerve, or got spooked by something.'

'And Sean Degg was here. He couldn't have brought her. Not personally.'

'I thought she was dead but she screamed. Another few minutes . . . They say she may die, still. Who would leave her like that?' Josie pushes Staffe away and turns to the plastic bubble, staring intently at the baby, naked save a nappy that swamps her. Her eyes are shut, tight; her tummy swollen and her ribs push against her blue-white skin. She has a swirl of matted black hair that winds around the crown of her head. 'She has nails. Have you seen, sir? She has nails and she can kick her legs and she held onto my finger. She made a fist.'

31

The nurse says, 'Her brain is growing. Even in sleep, babies learn about their world.' She smiles, beaming. 'It's proven.'

In the corridor, the ward sister tells Staffe that the baby's depositor had ensured the baby was fed and wore a disposable nappy of the Mamapapa range. The doctors reckon she is a couple of days old and is very weak, quite probably premature. The baby has a chest infection and her heart is weak.

'Consistent with being born in a cold, damp environment?' Staffe says.

The sister nods. 'I've heard about the woman Degg. If she's the mother you will find the bastards that did it, won't you?'

We might already have them, he thinks. Staffe can't get his head round what might possess Sean Degg to be involved in treating his only child in such a way. He decides he needs Pulford, that his party will have to be interrupted. He makes the call, tells his sergeant to pour some coffee down and to get a taxi to Flower and Dean, meet him there in an hour. And he makes his way to Leadengate, to get the key off Sean Degg.

In the corridor, a commotion erupts outside Baby Grace's private room. A doctor runs past them and when they look back, Josie is being led from the room in the clutches of a nurse. In the clean and brittle hospital air, a silence descends, into which the high-pitched squeal of a cotside monitor begins to soar.

Sean Degg is beginning to look as if he hasn't slept in a long time. The skin under his eyes sags. His face is grey and he stares into his clasped hands. Stan Buchanan comes in and sits alongside him. He chews on gum, but the stain of the night is still thick in his air.

Sean Degg says, 'They told me a baby was found. A girl.'

'We'll be needing your key, Sean.'

'Why?'

'I don't need to give you a reason. We have the warrant.'

'Something has happened,' says Sean.

'The baby might not survive. She has an infection.'

Sean puts his head in his hands, says, 'What do you know about the baby?'

'We'll check her out. Someone will be in for your DNA.'

'Is she mine? Mine and Kerry's?'

'All I know is we won't rest until we find who left Kerry down in that tunnel and who dumped that baby. So you'd better tell us now, everyone she knows. Anyone who hated her.'

'Nobody hated her.'

'Then who loved her?' says Staffe. 'You can love someone too much, can't you, Sean? What about family?'

Sean looks at his feet, looks cagey. 'You want me to do your job for you?'

'You want us to find who did that to Kerry, don't you?'

'And you'll release me – if I help?'

'He should be with his wife,' says Buchanan.

'Tell us,' says Staffe.

'She has a sister, Bridget,' says Sean.

'Maybe Kerry went to stay with her, when she left you.'

'They don't get on.'

'Where does she live?' Staffe hands him a piece of paper and a pen. 'And what about any friends Kerry has? Special friends.'

Sean shakes his head. 'I'd be the last to know. I always was.'

'Why did you stay with her?'

'Because I can't leave her. I tried once, but I can't be without her.'

'My client has co-operated fully,' says Buchanan. 'His wife is in hospital and there is no evidence that he has had any contact with her since he reported her missing nearly three months ago. He hasn't had a proper meal . . .'

'So take him, Stanley,' says Staffe. 'Take him for a pub breakfast in Smithfield Market. Jom will sign him out.'

Staffe looks at the address for Kerry Degg's sister, Bridget Lamb: 16 The Green, Thames Ditton. 'Shit,' he says. He knows the house, less than half a mile from where he grew up. It is a smart place. A different world from Flower and Dean.

As he drives to Degg's house, he rings Josie. Her voice sounds gluey and he can tell she has been crying. 'How is the baby?' he asks.

'They've put her on life support. They say they can't increase the dosage for the infection. She can't take it.'

'Try and get some sleep, Josie.'

'Good night, sir.'

It is a bright spring morning.

Staffe flips through his notebook, runs his finger down to the name of Paul Asquith of the Underground Victorians. He calls the number, apologises for the hour, but needn't have worried. When he asks if Asquith would mind terribly helping him with a further investigation of the Smithfield tunnel, the amateur historian actually gasps with uncontained pleasure.

* * *

The deeper Staffe scratches at Sean's house, the more he realises that he isn't close to understanding Kerry Degg, née Kilbride. Apart from her book collection, which includes first editions of Philip K. Dick and Angela Carter, he soon uncovered notebooks full of poems and sketches; untravelled charts of life-affirming journeys, by foot, across the continents of Africa, Asia and South America. There were self-scrawled vocab books for Spanish and French, and he flicked through the Spanish one, gleaned from the familiar shapes of the foreign words that she was of an intermediate standard.

He sits cross-legged by her desk in the bedroom and reads her poems, soon gathers that they follow two themes: the futility of the search for a perfect love; and the loneliness of her childhood.

Staffe doesn't know how long he has been here, reaching into this dying stranger's life, but when he hears a creak in the hall, he looks at his watch, realises he will be late for Asquith. Without looking up, he says, 'You done, Pulford?'

The springs on the bed behind him heave and when he looks up, he sees not Pulford's long legs or trendily sculpted hair, but the hunched and emaciated frame of Sean Degg, who talks to the floor: 'She never let me into her notebooks. And I never looked. I could have, but I didn't. Nobody knows her like I do. Does she write me in a bad light?'

Staffe closes the book. He can't work Sean Degg out. To look at him, you might think he is a low-life loafer, scruffily dressed and unkempt. But the things he says suggest someone else. 'In this job, it sometimes pays to think ill of people. It's an instinct.'

'So she did write ill of me?'

'She writes ill of herself and of love and her childhood. If it is her wish that you don't read them, you wouldn't want me to say any more than that. But I wouldn't say she wrote ill of you.'

'I couldn't ever harm her.'

'Before, you said you "curated" Kerry.'

'I have always worked in performance. I went to university, you know. I studied stage design.'

'Where do you curate?'

'Residencies, tours, one-off nights.'

Staff tries to disguise his scepticism, says, 'Tell me about her father.'

'Because I am older than her?'

'She was sixteen when you met.'

'And I was twenty-nine. You think that's sick, do you?'

'It's unusual, but not sick.'

'I couldn't stay at the hospital. It was too much.'

'You think this baby is yours?'

'They said she might die.'

'The baby, or Kerry?'

'I have a feeling one of them will be taken from me.'

'I asked you about her father.'

'I don't know him.'

Staffe watches as Sean looks away. He can tell when a man is lying but has a lesser instinct for the truth. He gathers together what he feels he needs and makes a list, hands it to Sean, returning the rest of Kerry's possessions to her desk.

Degg looks at the list: *notebook, red; notebook, blue; school records; doctor's notes; sundry photographs x 12*. He doesn't look up or reply when Staffe bids him farewell.

* * *

'What exactly are we looking for?' whispers Pulford, to Staffe, straining to see beyond the twenty-foot beam from his head torch. Paul Asquith marches ahead, carrying a larger lamp, casting a wider beam far into the dark. He strides confidently into the Spitalfields tunnel where he had discovered Kerry Degg. 'We'll have to watch him,' Staffe whispers.

'You don't think . . . ?'

Staffe raises a finger to his lips and glares at Pulford. The ethanol afterburn of the sergeant's party is strong.

As they follow Asquith, Staffe ponders quite what sequence of events might have brought Kerry Degg to this place, having had her baby already. Could that be possible?

When they reach the spot where Kerry Degg had been found, with its dark stains illuminated by Paul Asquith's powerful torch, Staffe says to the historian, 'Where would you hide something – from here?'

'There is a series of spurs – some were trial tunnels, others to accommodate machinery. We haven't actually finished mapping them. The documentation isn't what it might be.'

'But you have maps?'

Asquith smiles, proudly, and holds up a clipboard, to which he has taped a plastic envelope. He shows it to Staffe. 'The red-hatched areas are what we sourced from the original documents.'

'And the yellow?'

'That was our mission. To verify these minor tunnels and spurs.'

'And we are here?' Staffe points to a red area.

Asquith nods, sagely.

'Knowing what you do of the system down here, and if you had brought someone down here, say, a week ago, and wished their presence to be untraceable, where would you store the provisions – and secrete the traces of life?'

'Food and water and ablutions? I can't be sure, but there is a link a hundred yards or so to the west. It is in some documents but not others.'

'Is it safe?' asks Pulford.

'This could have been a station. That's what I think. But they chose Aldgate.'

'Is it safe?'

'We shall see.'

Pulford takes a step away from Asquith's arc of light, holds Staffe's sleeve and tugs, waits until Asquith has advanced beyond earshot. He hisses, 'They could be down here, still.'

'Who?'

'We have an officer on the door. Nobody has come out. If they were down here when you answered Asquith's call, doing whatever they were doing with Kerry Degg – they could still be here. They would have to be.'

Asquith turns, thirty yards ahead, says, 'I'm willing to take my chances.'

'And so am I,' says Staffe, who turns to Pulford, says, 'Go back above ground, start phoning around everyone in Kerry's address book. And check out all the Underground Victorians. I'll be up when we're done here.'

'Are you sure you want to go further down there?'

'I'll be fine, Pulford. Go on.'

Staffe feels his chest tighten as he watches the shape of his sergeant fade to nothing, his light dying. Just him and Asquith left. One map, two torches and God knows how many tunnels.

Five

DCI Pennington slaps his rolled-up *Telegraph* in the palm of his hand, with a steady beat. He has a smile on his face as he approaches Pulford's desk. Opposite, Josie's desk is empty. She is at the hospital, but must have left Baby Grace at some point the previous evening because, as is proven by the unfolding of Pennington's newspaper, the national papers had photographed her, palpably worn by events. She looks straight into camera, beneath the headline 'Blue Angel. WPC saves abandoned baby'.

'For once, the press regards us kindly,' says Pennington, ever aware of the political aspects of his job. A smile forms on his gaunt face.

'It's wrong, though,' says Pulford. 'The baby is not saved yet. She is on life support.'

Pennington turns the pages, trails a finger along the columns, and taps the newsprint where his own name is writ. 'As I say, had DC Chancellor not found the baby and acted with such professional instincts, Baby Grace would be dead now. She gave that baby a chance.'

'But I know her, sir. She'll blame herself if anything happens to the child.'

Pennington reinstates his resolute exterior. 'We'll have a chat with her. Now, how's the investigation going?' He looks around the room. 'And where's Staffe? He's not in his office.'

Pulford feels a pang of dread, having left Staffe down in the tunnel with that spooky amateur historian, Asquith.

Pennington sits in Josie's chair, looking across the shared desk at Pulford. 'I hear the husband is the father – not so for the other kids. If she was going to get rid, he could have held her, against her will. You can tell this Degg that if he confesses, he will not get a rough ride. The public will be with him. It's a saved baby we're talking about, and he played his part. Do you understand?'

'Have you spoken to Degg, sir?'

'No.'

'I don't think he could harm Kerry Degg.'

'I've read the notes. He was saving the baby, not harming the mother. Think positive, Pulford. Now, where did you say Staffe was?'

'I don't know, sir.'

Staffe lies in the dark. He is flat to the cold, damp ground, imagining what it would have been like for Kerry Degg. Rats scuttle and he sniffs at the putrid air, wonders how long you could stand it down here – let alone with new life growing inside you every second, every minute, getting closer to that moment when another human pushes and strains and finally punches their way out of you and into the world.

He is at a low, tight dead end within the petering network of tunnels. According to Asquith, the engineers may have decided the geological substructure was wrong here. Asquith had suggested that money, or lack of it, might have had a part to play in abandoning plans for a station on this part of what became the Metropolitan Line, a line along which they generally cut and covered rather than burrowed.

Staffe's breathing is constricted and he twists over, looks across at the array of plastic bags. He can't help sniffing. The bags hold the detritus from weeks, maybe months: drink cartons, vitamin supplements, rotted fruit skins, takeaway dishes – and shit. Human shit.

He is exhausted and slides his way out of this low enclave. From what they have discovered, he is certain that Kerry Degg didn't have the baby above ground and then come down here.

Staffe picks up the plastic bags, trying not to inhale the smell as he makes his way out. The uniformed officer at the entrance to the tunnel looks at him oddly as he passes, watching Staffe put the bags in the footwell of his Peugeot, then open all the windows.

He places a smaller bag on the front seat. It holds what looks like dried-out offal. He suspects it might be the placenta – from the little he knows of such human biology. And they found an iron loop, low down on the wall at the dead end of the furthest tunnel. It could have been used to restrain Kerry. It would account for the bracelet marks on her wrists. What must it have been like for her? She is strong. He thinks she will survive, speculates as to what kind of a tale she will tell.

Jadus Golding sits in a wing-backed chair looking out across the Limekiln estate and sips from a can of Nourishment drink. In his left hand, a half-smoked spliff burns away. He is all alone in this room full of people: family and friends.

When he sees Staffe, his eyes brighten, temporarily, then close down their hoods, as if he is struggling not to surrender to sleep. Jadus's way.

Staffe had gone back to his flat in Queens Terrace and cleaned up. He'd rustled up some coddled eggs and munched down an entire cantaloupe melon, washed that through with two cans of Red Bull, then dropped the bags off at Forensics. Two blocks away in a £5 car wash, a youth had given Staffe's car the third degree. The youth had tied a West Ham scarf around his face to guard against the smell and quoted twenty quid for a quick valet. Danger money, he had called it.

He kisses Jasmine on the cheek and she says how nice he smells. She introduces Staffe around the room and he shakes the hands of Jadus's family. His father is absent, which is a cause for relief. The last time Staffe saw him, Mr Golding spat at him; the day Jadus was sentenced to seven years. Partly because of Staffe's efforts, the boy, now a man, had served less than half.

Jadus's grandmother grips Staffe tightly by the hand and thanks him. The grandfather turns his back.

Jasmine puts some music on: calypso, he thinks. An uncle and an aunt get up and dance, gliding across the floor, hips undulating to the beat. The grandmother serves some punch. Jadus, unmoved in his winged armchair, catches Staffe's attention, beckons him. 'Didn't think you'd come.'

'I said I would,' says Staffe.

Jadus smiles, doped. 'Thought it'd be all crack pipe and Cristal and pussy, right?'

'You have a good family, Jadus. You're lucky.'

'Oh, I'm lucky all right.' Jadus looks around the room, a serious expression establishing itself. 'Got my Millie to tend for now.' Suddenly, Jadus looks sad.

Staffe doesn't know why this twenty-one-year-old isn't more pleased to be free once more.

'You *are* going to be all right?'

'That job's not there. Jasmine's cousin with the pie shop is a prick. I can't work for him.'

'When's your first session with probation?'

'If I can't get a job, the whole thing's fucked, man. I got no chance.'

'Why did you lie?'

'Who's going to give me a job?'

'Plenty of people. You're an intelligent man, you're prepared to work.'

Jadus feigns a weak smile and raises the spliff to his mouth, takes a long drag. 'You know, I don't understand why you chose me.'

'Chose?'

'Visiting me. You said you wanted to help me turn my life around. Your words.'

'In my job, people like you and people like me . . . it's a battle. We win, we lock you up. You win, you do it again. I just wanted to try the middle way.'

'You really don't think I'll do it again?'

Staffe looks across at Jasmine Cash, beautiful and happy and surrounded by family in the home she has made from the sty; baby Millie on her hip. 'I'll see what I can do.'

'Maybe I could walk the fucking beat, hey?'

43

Staffe sneaks a look at his watch, but Jadus catches him. 'There's somewhere I have to be. Sorry.'

'I guess there'll always be another me, waiting to fill the empty bed, right. You go catch the poor motherfucker, Inspector. Don't let me stop you.'

Staffe mulls what Jadus had said, and, true enough, by the time he is caught in traffic, where Old Street meets City Road, his mind is turning towards the hospital, the bed of Kerry Degg. Will he get to talk to her, ever? Would she have known her captor?

A uniformed officer guards the door to Kerry's room and the doctor brings Pulford up to date. They can't prescribe any stronger doses of antibiotics even though the infection is spreading. Kerry isn't strong enough to withstand an operation, but if she doesn't improve in thirty-six hours, they will have to employ the knife anyway.

'Will she make it?' asks Pulford.

'She's very poorly,' says the doctor.

'If you had to say one way. If you were a betting man.'

The doctor looks at Pulford as if he is unclean. 'We may well have to gamble, Sergeant. But I'm not a betting man. These conversations are worthless.'

Pulford sits with Kerry and is still there when Staffe arrives. He watches as his DI reads the spreadsheet analysis of all the Underground Victorians. Of the contacted members, none of the cells (address, employment, dependent profiles, performance, criminal activity) tally with Kerry's.

Staffe looks at Kerry Degg. She appears calm, almost serene. Her eyes are closed, her limbs laid straight: still as a windless night. He tries to recall her bursting with life and theatrical allure, on stage back in October in the Boss Clef. He wonders if she knows she has a new baby daughter; and will she ever sing her a lullaby or see the baby's father ache with worry about her?

He eventually says, 'I found new evidence. Forensics have got it all, but I'm pretty sure the bastards kept Kerry down in the tunnel for weeks. And she had the baby down there, too.'

A knock at the door and the uniformed officer comes in, says to Staffe, 'You're needed, sir. Up at the station. It's DCI Pennington. Said it was urgent. Apparently, he's been after you for a while.'

On the way to see Pennington, Pulford says to Staffe, 'How did you get on with your nurse the other night? You left early.'

'You told her about Sylvie.'

'She was asking about you. It was a party; I'd had a bit.'

'I'd rather you keep out of my private affairs.'

'Is that what it is?'

'Shut up, Pulford.'

Staffe knocks on Pennington's door and the DCI beckons them in. He is frowning. 'Well, it didn't take long for this to go tits up,' he sighs.

'How, sir?' said Staffe.

'The DNA results came through. It's Sean and Kerry Degg's baby all right.'

'But that's good news. And it consolidates his motive.'

'You'd think. But I got this half an hour ago.' Pennington passes an A4 piece of paper. Staffe reads it quickly, says, 'Oh, God,' then reads it again, slowly, before handing it to Pulford.

On the letterheading of a group called Breath of Life – which carries neither address nor telephone number – the letter briefly introduces Breath of Life as an independently funded community of Christians who 'enforce the sacrosanct rights of our Unborn Population'.

It explains that their sources had advised them that Kerry Degg had attended a consultation at City Royal Hospital and had requested a termination which had subsequently been denied on the grounds of the unexpired term being too short.

Acting on reliable information regarding Kerry Degg's intention to pursue her proposed termination through a 'Private Murdering House', Breath of Life felt they had no choice but to treat Mrs Degg themselves, providing an 'Assisted Childbearing' on a 'Secluded Site'.

'Is this right?' says Pennington. 'About her consultation at City Royal?'

'I don't know, sir.'

'Well, you should.'

'We'll check.'

'I already have. And it's confirmed. She went there at the beginning of her twenty-fifth week. The sixth of bastard January.'

Staffe takes the letter back from Pulford, squints at the signature.

Pulford says, 'I think it says "Lesley Crawford", sir. I'll get onto it and search for the group, too.'

'Call themselves bloody Christians,' says Staffe. 'We have evidence that she had been held down there for weeks, sir. Forensics are checking it out, but we found food and drink debris down there, and faeces, too. There was tissue, or organs, as well.'

'Christ alive,' says Pennington. 'We have to foreground the positive in this case, the Josie Chancellor angle.'

'What will the press make of Lesley Crawford and her mob?' says Pulford. 'There's plenty of people will see it as a life saved, sir.'

'That's nothing to do with us,' says Staffe.

'Exactly,' says Pennington. 'Let's hope that mother and daughter both survive and we can pin this on Crawford sharpish.'

Staffe rereads the letter, examines the wording closely and fears the worst.

Six

Staffe drives through Richmond Deer Park and picks up the river road at Kingston, passing Surbiton with its tree-lined streets of Victorian villas that run down to the Thames. He parks up on the Green at Thames Ditton. The daffodils are out and the schools must have broken up for Easter because mothers sit in clusters, forming rings and watching each other's children play, cajoling excellence from their offspring. An old boy in a panama makes measured progress, stick in hand. He checks his watch and veers to a bench, knowing the Angel will not be open for another half-hour.

16 The Green – the home of Bridget Lamb, née Kilbride, sister of Kerry Degg – is just how Staffe remembers it: a double-fronted, stuccoed, Georgian residence with a perfectly tended garden and a freshly painted, racing-green front door. He presses the bell. It rings brilliantly in the spring morning.

A man of similar age to Staffe opens the door. He is dressed for retirement, though, with thick brogues and mustard cords, a Bengal shirt and hair oiled with pomade. 'Mr Lamb?' he says.

The man nods, looks at him, inquisitively. For a moment, he appears to be taken aback. Beyond, the hallway is tiled, after William Morris. The house is shiny and silent. 'Inspector? She's expecting you.' Lamb shows Staffe into a room at the back of the house. The french windows are open and a woman sits at a table on the patio, a fresh cafetière yet to be plunged and a crystal pillbox piled with Parma violets.

Bridget Lamb wears sunglasses. She has fine, blonde hair in a bob and ruby-painted lips. She looks ten years older than her sister, maybe more. When she speaks, it is a child's voice. She holds out a hand and Staffe takes it, mindful not to be too firm. Her hand is cold, the grip firm. She says, 'It's terrible, what's happened to Kerry. I would visit, but I don't want to upset her.' Her breath is strong and floral from the violets.

'You don't get on?'

'It wouldn't take a policeman to discover that we are chalk and cheese.'

She plunges the coffee and it takes all her might. Slowly, as if recalling the lines of a poem from prep, Bridget elucidates the ways in which Kerry had made different choices. She makes it sound deliberate, can't mask her disappointment.

'I've seen her school reports,' says Staffe. 'Was there a point when she lost interest?'

'She was a woman very young. I'm two years older, but Kerry was first to most things. I've had analysis.'

Staffe looks back, into the house, then checks the garden out. 'You don't have children?'

'You're here to talk about Kerry, aren't you?'

'Her social workers say she didn't have the emotional strength to be a mother, but she appears to love the children.'

'She loved the fathers more.' Bridget looks away from Staffe as she says it, ashamed, as if she had bitten into something unexpectedly foul.

A device within the house pings.

'You and your husband . . .'

'I must go in now.'

As they pass through the house, a smell of something freshly baked drifts from the kitchen.

Bridget fusses in the kitchen, struggling with the Aga, using oven mitts. Crouched, and with her back to Staffe, Bridget says, softly, 'I find it upsetting to talk about Kerry.' She waits for Staffe to come closer. 'My husband said I should co-operate.' She lifts a tray onto the top of the oven. It bears two small, golden cottage loaves and Staffe wants to rip into them right now, while they are hot.

'Your sister is very ill and it is none of my business, but if anything happens – which is quite possible – I would hate to think you had missed an opportunity to see her a last time.'

Bridget gasps, swallowing her own breath and puts a hand to her throat. She shakes her head and steps away, knocking into the open oven door and blinking, her eyes watery. 'You should go,' she says. 'Please go.'

On balance, Staffe decides to comply. But as he gets to his car, Bridget's husband appears from nowhere, rag in hand. He had been crouched behind his car, supposedly waxing it. 'You don't remember, do you, Will? Malcolm Lamb.'

Staffe squints, feigning incredulity. 'Malcky?' He remembered him from the minute he clocked Bridget's married name, put it with the address.

'I remember your parents. Always very decent to me. Such a terrible shame. Did they ever catch those people?'

Staffe shakes his head, recalling that he hadn't always been decent to Malcky Lamb. On close examination, he sees how little that shy boy, who now lives in his parents' house, seems to have changed, and as he drives away, he is transported to the day his own parents died – the aftershock from that Biscay bomb.

Josie's eyes are dark and hollow, her shoulders sag. She stares vaguely at the collected monitors and sacks of liquid that stand beside the confined cot that holds Baby Grace. Tubes and wires feed life through airlocked holes into the incubator.

Staffe draws up a chair and sits beside Josie. After a minute or so she holds out a hand. He takes it, puts an arm around her shoulder and draws her to him. She rests her head against his neck and he feels her breathing slow down a little. Shortly after, her body jolts. In her dreams, she must have fallen. He stays with her until Sean Degg arrives. Then, he whispers in her ear, 'The father has come. You'd better leave him alone with the baby.'

The jolly nurse with the golden hair is with Sean. As Josie blinks from sleep, she says, 'Can he be trusted?'

Sean says, 'You're the one who found her? I can't ever thank you enough. She is a gift from God. Truly a gift.'

'You should have done more,' says Josie.

'She doesn't know what she's saying,' says Staffe.

Sean says, 'I can't believe she is mine. I can't believe she survived.'

Staffe watches the way Josie looks at Sean, unable, in her stripped-bare state, to see him with anything other than contempt.

Sean kneels beside the cot, his hands clasped together, looking intently at his flesh and blood; there is a zealous strain of contrition in the way he rocks back and forth, saying, over and again, 'My gift.'

Staffe asks the nurse if someone will be staying with Sean.

'He *is* the father.'

'I will send someone. Until then, please keep an eye on him. Every second.'

In reception, Staffe urges Josie to go home. She consents, but says she'll be in tomorrow – to catch the bastards: 'That witch Lesley Crawford. I'll see her burn – if she's the one who left Grace.'

Pulford arrives, says, 'I've got what you wanted, on Breath of Life.'

Staffe takes it. 'Now, check up on Bridget Lamb. Bridget Kilbride as was. She lived in Kingston after she left school, then when she married, she moved to Thames Ditton. Look out for any mention of church groups she might be involved with.'

'This is Kerry Degg's sister?'

'Exactly. Now, what's the latest on Kerry?'

'No better, sir.'

'So tell me about Lesley Crawford and Breath of Life.'

'She lives out in Southfields.' His sergeant hands Staffe a wad of paper. 'The internet's got some stuff on her, but the latest thing, before this, was a letter she wrote about the private member's bill being brought by a backbencher, a guy called Vernon Short. It's to reduce the threshold for terminating pregnancies to twenty weeks.'

'And she's in favour of this?'

'You'd think so, but it looks like she's got it in for this bloke Short. She calls him a collaborator.'

'I'd better go and see her.'

'Not a problem. When I spoke to her on the phone, it sounded as though she couldn't wait.'

Outside, the remnants of the warm day linger. The evening draws in, but people are staying outside and the bars and pavement cafés are effervescent with office workers, drinking and chatting. It is a day to cling on to and as they get into Staffe's car, he says, 'Read me that letter of Lesley Crawford's that the *Guardian* published.'

Pulford taps away at his BlackBerry, begins to read:

'It remains one of the most incomprehensible crimes of modern Britain, that we expend so much time and energy preserving the rights of all manner of minority groups, that we are immobilised by political correctness and bibles of legislation from Brussels; that we engage in wars in far-flung corners of the globe to protect foreigners against tyranny, and write off billions upon billions of pounds of debt from the so-called developing world, yet on our own doorstep murder is sanctioned every hour of every day. It is time to address the genocide of an Unborn Population and the Rt Hon Vernon Short's proposed bill simply doesn't go far enough. In fact, it further legitimises these crimes. This is a question of murder and morality, not simple arithmetic.

'And she goes on, sir. She seems pretty militant.'

'Not half. Sounds like a bloody Mitford sister. Should we expect blue stockings and a revolver in her handbag?'

In her art deco lounge, Lesley Crawford says, 'You expected me to be a nutter, did you? Well, you may be right.' She steps out of her court shoes and leans back into a Macassar ebony chair that looks as if it might be a Paul Kiss. She wafts an arm for Staffe and Pulford to sit.

'How did you do it? Get into the tunnel, I mean,' says Staffe, weighing up the room, trying not to concentrate on Lesley Crawford and her slow, confident mannerisms.

'Whatever makes you think I did?' Lesley gives them a superior, withering look.

'What about the letter you sent?' says Pulford.

Staffe interjects, shooting a chastising, sharp glance at Pulford. 'Of course, *you* didn't. The "you" was plural. Your hands are for letter writing, not dirtying on the common business of kidnap and murder.'

'The child would have died,' she says. 'The organisation had no choice.'

'How long did you have her down there in the tunnel?'

'How long does a child have to live in this world before you are stopped from killing it?'

'I'm not here to talk politics, Ms Crawford.'

'I'm a miss. And I'm talking about murder, not politics. Murder is police work, isn't it, Inspector?' She leans forward, elbows on her knees, chin raised and resting on a single, extended index finger.

'Whoever delivered the baby had a reasonable knowledge. And they knew how to clean up a crime scene.'

'This was an act of kindness, not crime.'

'So I'll need a list of all your members.'

'There is no such thing.'

'Your church will be a good place to start. And a thorough search here, of course.'

'You can't do that.' Crawford looks directly at Staffe and smirks.

He slowly pulls an envelope from the inside pocket of his jacket. 'This is a warrant, to search these premises. You could give me the list of your members, to save time. And to avoid any mess.'

Lesley Crawford stands, takes a mobile phone off the mantel, and says into it, 'You can come through, Jasper.'

Staffe watches her intently as she sits back down, untroubled. Together, they look at the door as it opens. A tall, elegant man enters, wearing a finely tailored suit with a high-collared, open-neck shirt. He is about as smooth as the legal profession gets.

'Inspector, this is . . .'

'Yes, I know. Jasper Renwick. Come on, Sergeant, we're going,' says Staffe.

'Don't you want to search my home?'

Staffe approaches Crawford. In heels, she would be almost as tall as him. He hisses, 'I will nail you for this. The law is a sword, not a shield.'

'What murderous metaphors you choose, Mr Wagstaffe. I'll see you in court – if you wish to waste police time.'

On the way out, Staffe notices how many books Lesley Crawford has, in cases lining the hallway, all the way to the kitchen at the back of the house, and he wonders what madnesses people might become capable of when they spend their lives drowning in words.

As they drive away, he says, 'She wants front pages out of this. Well, she'll get nothing from us.'

'Jasper Renwick, he's quite famous, isn't he?'

'He's a prick who'd do anything to get on television.'

'But he's good.'

'We won't give him the chance. He wants us to go after Breath of Life. So we won't.'

Pulford says, 'Because it's the individual we need to get.'

'Exactly. Breath of Life just collates the publicity. We can't put an organisation, a letterheading, in the dock. It's not even a charity.'

Staffe's telephone rings. The screen says 'Josie.'

He answers and, immediately, Staffe can tell she is upset. 'What's happened?'

'Kerry Degg has been taken into theatre. Twenty minutes ago.'

Staffe knows that Lesley Crawford wouldn't bat an eye, would quite possibly draw her thin lips into a smile.

Kerry's face is all he can see of her as a surgeon works intently. From the look on the nurses' faces, Staffe concludes it is a forlorn matter.

A man in a suit, masked and gloved, sidles to Staffe, says, 'The prospects are poor.'

Staffe looks at Kerry, focuses on her eyes, hoping they will flicker, might impart some clue. He will find the killer, anyway. Won't he? It seems to him that something moves. And her lips – they seem to have parted. He thinks it the slightest semblance of a smile.

A high-pitched, electronic whine comes from beside the anaesthetist. He moves into action, putting an oxygen feed over Kerry's face, and Staffe closes his eyes. The man in the suit says something that Staffe doesn't hear. He feels something leave the room, pictures Lori Dos Passos beguiling her audience with movement and voice, flesh and life.

Seven

The press are having a field day with the Kerry Degg story. Baby Grace is in a critical but stable condition. Sean, by her bedside, has been staring transfixed at his daughter ever since the nurses told him that his wife had passed away. He shed not a single tear, which made Staffe think that, if Sean did crack, he would break altogether.

The red-tops have somehow acquired a picture of Sean by Grace's bed, but the editors haven't dared to come down one way or the other on the subject of Lesley Crawford: devil or do-gooder. It doesn't help her cause that, despite the fact that she is the signatory for Breath of Life, she looks so calm and assured; nor that she is a childless spinster; nor that Jasper Renwick, smoothest of all the slippery lawyers in London town, has kept the law from her door.

The *News* dared to say, in its editorial, that no matter what you think of Vernon Short's upcoming private member's bill, the saving of one life – if you accept that is what it was at the time of Kerry Degg's abduction – can never justify the taking of another. Conversely, though expressed with the lightest of touches, the *Post* said that an innocent was saved and that nobody could ever call Kerry Degg innocent. They carry a picture of her two children with their foster parents, John and Sheila Archibald. The children smile into camera with gap teeth. The foster parents look glum.

The broadsheets focused on the story's gothic unusualness. Any political analysis was even-handed. Certainly, Vernon Short was transformed from a backbench nobody to a daring crusader. Some church leaders hailed him as a potential future Home Secretary, or even Prime Minister.

Pulford shakes a newspaper, angrily. 'Breath of Life and Vernon Short are both getting exactly what they want.'

'I'm going to see Nick Absolom,' says Staffe.

'At the *News?* I thought you loathed him.'

'And then I'm going to pay Vernon Short a visit.'

Vernon Short is perfectly happy to tell Staffe about his upcoming private member's bill. He repeats his statement of regret, to Staffe, as if his every word will be committed to history. He says that everything that is incumbent upon us as a responsible nation should be achieved through discourse and legislation, not direct action. What happened to Kerry Degg was reprehensible. However, let Baby Grace be a shining testament to the value we should assign to life; the virtue of his bill is illuminated by this sorry tale.

'Save the speech, Mr Short. It's wasted on me,' says Staffe. 'I'm not here to cast a vote. What do you know of Lesley Crawford?'

Vernon's smile shallows, in the finest degree. 'We both believe in the rights of our unborn population. Our methods are different, of course.'

'In what respect?'

'I wouldn't ever . . .' Vernon stops himself and presses the intercom on his telephone, asks his secretary to make some coffee and bring through biscuits.

'You wouldn't ever . . . ?'

'I really don't know anything about Lesley.'

'You clearly think she is capable of murdering somebody, to further her ambitions.'

'I said no such thing. You should be careful what conclusions you draw, Inspector.'

'Lesley's press statement and Kerry Degg's baby daughter have lengthened your day in the sun.'

'I don't care for your tone.'

'The pollsters reckon so. A few days ago, nobody had even heard about your bill. It was doomed. A backbench flirtation.'

'It is good law. The argument will speak for itself.' The door opens and Short's secretary comes in with a tray. Short stands and hitches his trousers, motions with the slightest dip of his head for the secretary to take the coffee and biscuits back where they came from, which she does. 'I have another appointment.'

'No point in good laws if they're not enforced, Mr Short. Now, tell me what the Home Secretary makes of your bill.'

'It is common knowledge that she is publicly against it. We are a broad church and Cathy is pretty much on the centre left.'

'Political suicide for you, then, I'd say.'

'There comes a time when you have to stand up for what is right.'

'The government doesn't want this debate, does it? Especially Cathy Killick.'

'The government embraces debate, especially the Home Secretary.'

'You can amend your bill. You can change it any time in the next week.'

'Short regards Staffe with renewed suspicion. 'You've done your homework. But I do not intend to.'

'You "do not intend to". You could have said, "I will not." But you didn't.'

'I do not intend to.'

'You're a career backbencher, eh, Vernon? Not even the sniff of a junior ministry, and you're what? In your fifties? These young guns with their spin-doctoring ways tearing past you. It would crown your career, wouldn't it, if you were to be offered something. Stepping into the old man's shoes at last.'

'You have quite an imagination. You should exercise some restraint, Inspector.'

'When did you take up the cause of the "unborn population" as you call it?' Staffe takes out a single sheet of A4. From it, he begins to read a list of bills that Vernon Short has voted for and against – provided courtesy of Nick Absolom, of the *News*.

When he is done, Staffe says, 'Hardly a coherent pattern of voting behaviour; not the actions of a moral crusader.'

'I judge each case on its merits. You have to take voting into its wider context. You are being a little naïve.'

'You have always gone where the Whip blew you. Until now.' Staffe places the sheet of A4 on Vernon Short's desk. 'And you, Mr Short, are the naïve one, if you think I won't find out exactly what you do from now on – and what you have been up to, all the way back to the sixth of January.'

'The sixth?'

'Ask Lesley Crawford. Ask Sean Degg. Ask the baby when she grows up and can answer you. Because I'll have to answer to her, when she asks who murdered her mother.'

Josie carries the drinks into the room where Sean Degg sits beside his daughter's incubated cot. A dark-haired nurse had sat with him but leaves as soon as Josie returns.

She hands Sean his black tea and sips from her own machine-made mocha. 'You were going to tell me how you and Kerry met. She was much younger, right?'

Sean sips his black tea, pops a pill into his mouth. Soon, he looks relaxed and he talks, low, almost to himself. 'Kerry was sixteen when we met. I was booking gigs. I had a couple of clients but I never made much money. Too soft, I suppose.'

'You met her at a gig?'

Sean stands and looks down on his baby, her eyes closed and her skin still pale. He mumbles, 'She was adopted. Never even knew her dad. And when Kerry was six or seven, her new father was killed in a crash. I tried to get Kerry to see someone about it, but she wouldn't.'

'What about her sister, Bridget?' says Josie. 'Maybe you should go and see her. It might help both of you.'

'Kerry wouldn't want that.'

Josie knew the answer to her next question, asked it anyway. 'Have you seen Kerry – since she . . . passed away?'

'She wouldn't want that.'

'And what about you?'

'The first time she performed for me was an open mike up at the Angel. She could make herself anything on that stage. I saw it from the first look, the first sound of her. I saw it.' He is transfixed by the motionless baby. He looks at Josie, then quickly away, as if afraid of her response. 'Do you believe them, when they say Grace's chances are good?'

Josie reaches out with her hand and Sean takes it. He grips Josie hard. Together, they sip from their drinks.

Staffe settles into his nook in the Hand and Shears, drinks lustily from his pint of spiced-up tomato juice. He eyes up the Adnams.

April catches him at it from behind the bar and throws a tea towel over her shoulder, laughs, 'I don't know why you deny yourself, not when Dick's beer is so good.'

'Some of us have work to do,' he says.

'Oh, dear. Someone's in for it, then.'

'Hopefully,' he thinks, breaking open the early evening edition of the *News*. He scans the front page and sees no outcome from his earlier conversation with Nick Absolom. Flicking through, he spots it on page seven, a two-column piece.

He has another draught of the Virgin Mary and takes in a cube of ice, sucks on it as he reads.

New developments in the Baby Grace case suggest that police are looking beyond the claims that members of the Breath of Life Group are responsible for the kidnapping of Grace's mother, Kerry Degg. No official statement has been made by City Police, but we have cause to believe that the claim, by Lesley Crawford, a member of Breath of Life, that Kerry was kidnapped by their members, is simply a smokescreen.

The upcoming private members bill, presented by backbencher Vernon Short, has gained a dramatic surge in support following the saving of Baby Grace.

Our reporters attempted to seek clarification that Vernon Short condemned the actions of Breath of Life, but the MP was unavailable for comment. After four days, and even in the light of the death of Kerry Degg, no arrests have been made in relation to what the organisation calls 'Assisted Childbearing'.

Carole Aimes, spokesperson for CHOICE, an organisation fiercely opposed to Short's bill, reiterated that Lesley Crawford should be arrested. Aimes condemned as irresponsible any possibility that City Police were treating Breath of Life claims lightly.

The condition of Baby Grace remains critical but stable and her plight has served as a rallying call for religious groups throughout the country who represent the interests of 'The Unborn Population'.

Staffe rereads the piece and folds the paper back down. Lesley Crawford will have to make the next move if she wants the world to believe that Breath of Life were behind the Kerry Degg murder.

He finishes his tomato juice to within two thick fingers of the bottom of the glass and catches the attention of April, mimes the pulling of a pint. She laughs out loud and wags a finger at him, then pulls his Adnams.

He texts Pulford to get back down to Southfields, to monitor the comings and goings of everybody who visits Lesley Crawford. Under no circumstances is he to be seen, though. It is imperative that she believes the police are looking elsewhere for Kerry Degg's killer.

The narrow doors to the snug swing open and Josie comes in, takes his pint from April and sits alongside Staffe.

'You talked to Sean?' he says.

Josie picks up the glass of tomato juice, finishes it and says, 'Hmm. He let something slip. Said Kerry was adopted. Her new dad died when she was young. And he told me how they met. I don't see that Sean could have taken Kerry down into that tunnel.'

Staffe puts down his pint, untouched, says, 'Adopted? Bridget didn't say anything about that.'

Eight

In his office, Staffe reads Kerry's school reports again, and her small volumes of poetry, handwritten in an immaculate, leaning hand within slim, hard-backed volumes, tied with mauve ribbons.

She had been a B student who did not apply herself in the least and was both easily led and a distraction to others. None of her teachers thought anything would come of her, save a Mr Troheagh who took Kerry for English and in the last two years of her education, urged her to stay on for the sixth form and to push herself to get into university. He said Kerry had a unique voice in her writing and a natural grasp of the power of words.

Staffe read one poem again, entitled 'Blood on the Thorn', about loving an older boy, possibly a man. The closer she got, the more it hurt, until finally the love became unbearable. It scarred. The symbolism of a girl changing into a woman, too fast, and still trapped in the body of a girl, is obvious.

Staffe wonders who the Thorn might be. Sean? Troheagh himself? Possibly. He makes a note to look up the teacher, but then drifts back to that night, maybe seven years after she wrote that poem, when she stood on stage and captivated a decadent audience with her bawdy songs and sultry voice, her tight bodice and bared secrets. And she would be discovered, too, by Phillip Ramone who would offer Kerry her chance in life.

He makes a tick under 'Document removed' and signs for it, slips the volume into his pocket and returns the rest of the documents to the box, takes it down to Jombaugh.

In the City, it is another mild day, after the long, hard winter. He calls Pulford, to see whether there have been any comings and goings at Lesley Crawford's house.

His sergeant – displeased and tired and failing to see the point of his vigil – says nobody had come or gone, and asks if somebody else could take a turn. Staffe tells him 'No', hangs up, and turns to Josie. 'Fancy a ride down to see Kerry's sister, in Thames Ditton? I'll treat you to lunch, by the river.'

'You used to live down there.'

He can't remember when he might have told her that.

Bridget Lamb gives her husband a chastising sideswipe of a look as he stands in the drawing-room doorway, looking at Josie a second too long. He asks if they want coffee or something a little stronger.

'There's no need for you to be involved in this,' says Bridget. 'There's that shopping to do.'

Staffe says, 'I think it would be good for Malcolm to sit in.'

Malcolm nods, sheepishly, and sits down beside Bridget.

'Sean tells me that you and Kerry were adopted.'

'How is that relevant?' says Bridget.

'Perhaps it's not. But what interests me is why you didn't tell me.'

'Because it has no relevance.'

'I'm trying my damnedest to understand her. You know that.'

'So now you know.'

'And we know she had been offered a residency at the Rendezvous in town. Are you *au fait* with the place?'

Bridget nods, crinkles her nose.

'How would that make you feel?'

'I don't see how what I might feel has anything to do with what happened to Kerry. And it's no business of yours.'

'I need to understand you too, Bridget.'

'You make her sound like a suspect, for God's sake,' says Malcolm.

Bridget shakes her head, disdainfully, at Malcolm.

'I've been reading Kerry's poems – from school. There was a teacher – a Mr Troheagh.'

Bridget looks at Malcolm again and her hands clasp tight.

'When was the last time you saw Kerry?' says Josie.

Bridget regards Josie with suspicion. 'Not in a long time. She is in my prayers, of course.'

'Did you go to the hospital?'

'It wouldn't have helped.' She looks at Malcolm, who nods. 'But Sean did come to see me, when she left him, in January. He thought she would be here. He said he was sure the baby was his this time and he said she was going to get rid of it.'

'You would have been dead against her not having the baby?' says Josie.

'Wouldn't anybody, who knew right from wrong? It was for her career. You can't kill just to get a step ahead.'

'Especially as you aren't in the position to have a family,' says Staffe. 'That must make Kerry's decision hard to handle.'

Malcolm glares at Staffe, tries to restrain himself, but can't. It seems that a suppressed force has been released. He takes a step towards Staffe. 'What gives you the right to pry so? You are a guest in my house, my parents' house. They knew your parents and you might have deemed yourself superior to me, but we are adults now. Do you have no common decency? My wife has lost her sister and you come snooping like this. Not an ounce of decency, not an ounce!' Malcolm is shaking. His chin is weak, trembling.

Staffe stands, looks slightly down on Malcolm. He recalls him as a frail boy, but dismisses that. 'There'll be no stone unturned here and let's all pray that if we ask enough questions and look under enough stones, we might unearth some decency, for the sake of that baby. If she lives!' He scribbles in his notebook for a minute, allowing the silence to stretch. He has a notion that Malcolm had a disease, a condition, at least. 'I hope your wife is what she seems, Malcolm. I really do.' He looks at Bridget. 'You see, I know. Sean told me.'

Bridget looks quickly away and begins to shake. Malcolm puts his hand on her shoulder and she shrugs him away, says, 'He told you what?'

Staffe takes a step towards Malcolm, puts a hand on his shoulder and says, looking at his watch, 'Perhaps that drink might be in order. DC Chancellor and I will have tea.'

Staffe waits for Malcolm to go, then sits beside Bridget. He says, softly, 'You have to tell your side of it.'

Bridget looks up, fierce determination in her eyes, her jaw set firm. In a clear, unwavering voice, she says, 'I don't have to do anything. Their lives don't touch me. I'm not like them. Whatever he has said, take it with you. You'll get nothing from me.'

'Then we'll do it the hard way. Shame, for Malcolm.'

'He's a good man,' says Bridget.

69

'We'll see.'

On their way out, Staffe and Josie meet Malcolm coming out of the kitchen, carrying a tray. Nothing is said and each man looks as if he doesn't have anything to be ashamed of.

As they get in the car, Josie says, 'What did Sean Degg tell you, sir?'

'Oh, nothing. But Bridget did.'

'What did she tell you?'

'That she and Sean have a secret. And she can't have children.'

He drives them to the Alma, as he had promised, for a ploughman's on the river, looking across to Hampton Court. Henry and all those wives and unborn heirs.

Sean has pulled his chair right up to the cot where Grace is lying, enclosed in a plastic dome against the germs of the world.

'You need to tell me all about Bridget, Sean,' says Staffe.

'What would I know about Bridget?' Sean Degg sighs, turns towards the baby's monitors.

'I've been thinking about why you would lie like that.'

'Like what?'

'Telling my constable you've not seen Bridget in years.'

'Did I?'

'But you called round to see her when Kerry disappeared.'

'I was only there ten minutes.'

'It's not looking good for you, Sean. You need to stop lying to us.'

'All I can say is, I'd never harm Kerry. Why can't you believe that?'

'There's something else you need to tell me.'

Sean stands up. He goes to the cot and puts his fingers to the glass bubble. He stoops, says to Grace, 'I won't be long, my darling.' He turns to face Staffe and blows out his cheeks and smiles. 'Let's get some air. How is Bridget?'

'You wouldn't think she had lost a sister. I know they didn't get on, but Kerry was her sister.'

Sean stops in the corridor, and a trolley is pushed by. He crouches, messing with his bootlaces. He curses. When he stands, he says, 'Siblings can be like that. Bridget wasn't the baby, not once Kerry came along. You got any fags?'

'Gave them up.'

'I used to roll them for Kerry. I miss that.'

Outside, they pass a newsagent and Sean says, 'I'm going to get some bacca.'

Inside, Sean checks what he has in his pocket and keeps a fiver and loose change back. He offers the newsagent sixty quid, whispers, 'You have a back way, don't you? It goes onto the estate.'

'None o' your business.'

Sean looks back, sees the inspector looking up and down the street.

'Sixty quid for you. Let me out the back. That bloke out there, he's looking for me. I was with his wife, see. Look at the size of him. He'll kill me.'

'Maybe you deserve it.'

'I didn't know she was married. She's a tart. Honest.' Sean proffers the money and the newsagent shakes his head. 'Somebody once fucked my missus.' He smiles. 'I beat the shit outa them both.'

71

'In that case –' Sean reaches carefully into his pocket. '– I'll keep my money. Treat her to dinner, maybe.'

'What?'

Sean pulls out the scalpel he had lifted from the trolley in the hospital corridor. He makes the smallest gesture towards the newsagent, who flinches. 'Got it from hospital. It's used. I'm a male nurse and this has plenty of germs. It's not the cut that'll do for you, it's the disease.'

The newsagent nods, wide-eyed, sidles from behind the counter and goes into a passageway, unlocks the back door. Sean pushes the newsagent outside and follows him. 'Lock it,' he says, and the newsagent does. 'Now, lie on your stomach and count to a thousand.' Sean bends down, lifts the keys from the newsagent's hand and jangles the bunch. 'I can slip in the back any time I want. So don't you say a fucking thing.'

Sean puts his boot on the newsagent's wrist and nicks the fleshy pad at the base of his thumb with the scalpel. He presses with his boot and watches the blood come.

Nine

Staffe can't believe that Sean Degg has slipped his net and he can't quite fathom why he would do that, when he wasn't even under arrest. He has replayed the conversation they were having about Bridget, but it only leads him back to his own bluff. There is no point going back to Bridget until he knows more about Sean, until he has spoken to Sean. In the meantime, he has come to see Kerry's children.

The foster parents, John and Sheila Archibald, are more than enough to scare the bejesus out of any child, standing in the porch of their inter-war semi on the outskirt sprawl that is the Finchley Road. All they need is a pitchfork and a pig out back to be straight from Hopper's Midwest.

'You don't look like a policeman,' says Mr Archibald, squinting at Staffe's warrant card, his beige-coloured tongue poking out between his fat, wet, ox-blood lips.

'The sooner they're in, the sooner they're gone,' says Sheila. 'And you won't be dragging our name in no mud. Those poor children, they can't choose their parents. Nobody can.'

'We can choose the children,' says John Archibald, a proud grin spreading. 'But not their parents.' He stands aside, waves Staffe and Josie into his home, as if it were the primest waterfront.

Staffe knows the Archibalds' situation. According to Carly Kellerman of Social Services, they are serial fosterers. Their track record is untarnished and they take all ages. They are in it for the money, according to Carly, and, apparently, it's not necessarily a bad thing for their itinerant and ever-changing subjects. They are pros.

'This is Miles,' says Sheila Archibald, passing the palm of her hand across his suede head. Miles looks up, glum. He wears short trousers and a polo shirt. His cheeks shine and his eyes don't. Staffe thinks he looks like an evacuee.

'Hello, sir,' says Miles, avoiding Staffe's eye. Not an ounce of sincerity.

Miles's little sister, Maya, clutches onto Mrs Archibald's perma-creased slacks. Sheila swirls the child's ponytail in her fingers, absently. But she catches Staffe's eye and says, 'We brush it every night, don't we, Maya?'

Josie sits on her haunches, eye level with the children. 'It's lovely here, isn't it? Aren't you lucky?'

Miles shrugs and Maya scuttles round the back of her temporary mum, buries her face between Sheila's knees.

Staffe takes a pound coin from his pocket and crouches alongside Josie, winking at Miles. He extends one arm, places the pound coin on his downturned hand and with the other, flicks it up his shirt cuff. It is disappeared. 'Where's it gone?' he asks Miles.

Miles shakes his head, shows a gummy smile.

'Maya, do you know where it is?'

Maya peers out from behind Sheila's legs.

Staffe reaches across, letting the coin slip into the palm of his hand, putting it behind Maya's ear and withdrawing his hand, holding the coin between his thumb and finger. 'In Maya's ear, all the time.'

'Again!' shouts Miles.

''Gain!' shouts Maya.

Staffe repeats the trick, pulling the pound from down Miles's nose, then out of Josie's mouth and finally from behind the ear of an unimpressed Sheila Archibald. 'Now, you show Josie your toys while I have a word with Mum and Dad.'

'They call us Sheila and John. And it doesn't do to get them excited,' says Sheila.

Staffe watches the children go with Josie and says, 'Does mum come round ever?'

John Archibald shakes his head. 'Good thing, too.'

'But the children must ask about her, if they know you're not their parents.'

'This isn't *Little House on the Prairie*. We can't get attached.'

'You mean the children can't.'

'She came round once,' says Sheila.

'Just the once,' says John, a hint of disapproval in the look he shoots at his wife. 'She was in a state.'

'Drunk?'

'Worse. She ended up crying and the children heard. We didn't let them see her, of course.'

'Would you say she loved them?'

'I don't know what you mean by that,' says Sheila. 'She had another one on the way. That's all I know. Women like her, they should be . . .'

'Sheila.' John Archibald goes to his wife, puts an arm around her. 'We have been told she is dead. The children don't know. I guess they'll be up for adoption now.'

'What about the father?' asks Staffe. 'You ever see him?'

They shake their heads in unison.

'Or hear about him?'

'Far as we know, there isn't a father. That's right, isn't it, Sheila?' says John Archibald.

'I was talking about Sean Degg, Kerry's husband.'

'Aaah.'

'Have you seen him recently?'

'I'm not sure we ever have.'

The Archibalds are clearly uneasy on the subject of the children's father and Staffe can't clearly recall if Sean ever mentioned visiting the Archibalds. Surely he must have. And if he did, why would they deny it?

'What about the real father? Sean wasn't the real father.'

'We know,' says Sheila.

'We don't know,' says John, his lard-coloured face beginning to blotch. 'Not exactly.'

'Did Sean tell you he isn't the father?'

'No,' says Sheila.

'He's not been here. That's why. We don't know anything about a father.'

'I'll need to ask the neighbours, show Sean's photograph.'

'We're respectable people,' says Sheila.

Staffe's phone rings and he sees it is Jombaugh. He calls up to Josie, who comes to the top of the stairs, carrying Maya and holding Miles's hand. Staffe says goodbye to the Archibalds, waves to the motherless children.

Outside, he calls Jombaugh back.

Jom says, 'We've had the analysis back on the phone call we got, reporting the baby in the car park. It's inconclusive. They can't even tell the gender of the caller – it was

76

heavily disguised and might have been warped on a tape machine or even a mobile phone. Apparently they can do that these days.'

'Was it was recorded or live?'

'Probably recorded.'

Staffe hangs up, thinking that a recorded message reinforces the level of premeditation, the professionalism of the crime.

On the drive back to the City, he thinks about what the Archibalds had said, and how. He says to Josie, 'They know the bastard father. I know they do. Why wouldn't they tell us?'

Staffe catches up on his texts as he has a cup of tea with Jombaugh in Leadengate's reception. One is from Jasmine Cash about Jadus, saying he's got a formal warning from probation for a failed employer's report. She says he has a week to find a job, otherwise his parole will be in breach. Staffe curses, thinks of the home Jasmine Cash has made for Millie and her dad. Good intentions amount to Jack Shit if you haven't got a job and a house and a family. You need all three to get straight – and stay that way. He feels an idiot for thinking he might be able to help.

Jombaugh takes a call of his own, nods across to Staffe with an upward jolt of the head.

'Pennington?' whispers Staffe.

Jombaugh nods, making a theatrical glum face.

Pennington isn't wearing a jacket. A piece of A4 in front of him has a list of names and numbers on it, in his handwriting. On the face of it, it would appear that this DCI has spent at least some of the day tending to police work.

'You can forget Sean Degg for a while, Staffe. Jesus Christ, how could you let him get away like that?'

'I'm more interested in why he'd want to get away. But I'll catch up with him soon.'

'Not any time soon, you won't.'

'Has something happened?'

'Bet your arse it has. Christ, this is getting nasty.'

'What's happened?'

'Just had a call from a DI Flint of South Liverpool CID. There's another pregnant woman missing. You're going up north, my man.'

'My case is here. I need to talk to Phillip Ramone, and to all Kerry's friends.'

'Twenty-four weeks pregnant they reckon. It made the evening edition of their local rag.'

'You think it's related? How could it be?'

'Half an hour ago, we got another letter from Breath of Life. They knew all about the woman. She's called Zoe Bright.'

'And what about the husband?'

'Forget it, Staffe. He loves her to bits, apparently.'

'Sounds familiar.'

'She nearly died having their first baby. It didn't survive.'

'He loves her as much as Sean loved Kerry Degg?'

'You make sure your team stays all over Lesley Crawford while you're up there.'

'There's a couple of things I have to do first,' says Staffe, thinking of Phillip Ramone.

'There's a train from Euston in an hour. They'll be waiting for you at the other end.'

'There's a couple of things . . .'

Pennington leans forward and in his softest voice says, 'Please, Will. Just this once, be a good lad.'

PART TWO

Ten

In no time, and with a rackful of reservations, Staffe is transported to Liverpool. The railway tracks have magicked him with their tittle and tattle, and along the way he spoke to Pulford about staying on Lesley Crawford's case. Then he had called Josie, to tell her to follow up on Kerry's list of friends.

Now, the daylight is almost gone and the train jolts, slows. People press their faces to the windows. As the carriages draw towards Lime Street station, the tracks breathe in and the train is sucked along a narrow chasm in the sandstone bedrock. Anybody who has travelled into this Celtic city will know that its gates open like rock thighs, as if it were delivering you into a new world.

And then it is dark.

In the vaulted, glass-roofed station, he steps down, valise in hand, and looks for a uniformed welcome. There is none.

A tall, beautiful woman approaches him. She has layered red hair, cut to her shoulders. She is, in fact, very tall. 'Inspector Wagstaffe?' she says.

'How would you know?'

'You have to be able to spot your friends as well as your foes.'

'You're police?'

She offers her hand. 'How else would I know you were coming?'

He takes her hand, finds a firm grip. She looks him in the eyes. Hers are the palest green.

'I'm Flint,' she says.

'Christ.'

'Charming.'

He expects her to smile, but gets the reverse and she spins on her heel, shows him her back and walks off at a fine clip.

Anthony Bright's house was a model for modern living when Lord Salisbury gave the land up for artisans and clerks in the preamble to the First World War.

Now, on a tree-lined street of immaculately coiffeured gardens and ringing birdsong, Staffe walks up a gingerbread path and has the front door opened for him by a bright-eyed constable who looks about twelve.

In his back room, sitting in a modern Swedish chair, Anthony stares into his garden. Staffe has read all the case notes and the interview transcripts. He wants to like Anthony but all he gets is a scowl. Nonetheless, he introduces himself, pulls up a dining chair.

'She'll be back. There'll be some explanation, but if you lot are here, she'll never call. She'd hate the fuss. I should never of called.'

'It's a serious matter, Anthony. I'm from London and we have had an abduction similar to this down there. We need to know everything about Zoe; everyone she saw, ever since she was pregnant this second time.'

Anthony stares at the trees at the bottom of his garden. Through the windows, you can't see any other property.

'Did she bring anybody new to the house in these last few weeks?'

He shakes his head.

'Anyone new in her phone or her address book?' he says as much to Alicia Flint as to Anthony.

'I would never pry,' says Anthony.

'We're having her phone analysed,' says Flint.

'She didn't take her phone?' Staffe takes the address book from Alicia Flint and scans quickly, looking for new names – in bold ink or interposed between old names. Zoe Bright is clearly very orderly and all the names are alphabetical. In four cases, names have been squeezed in, between lines.

'Is this a new book?'

'She spent all night copying everything across.'

'Where's the old one?'

Anthony walks, round-shouldered, to a small pine sideboard and hands Staffe a dog-eared notebook. In turn, he gives it to the constable, along with the new book. 'We need a list of all names that are in the new book, but not the old one.'

Alicia Flint hands Staffe a typed list of three names. 'These are they,' she says, smiling.

'You said in your interview that Zoe likes to read,' he says, looking around for bookshelves. 'Where are her books?'

'She takes them to a charity shop when she's finished them. She only keeps ones that are on the go. They're upstairs.'

On the landing is a small bookcase: photo albums and an atlas below, half a dozen paperbacks above. In the front of each book is a stamp which says 'The Curious Cat'. On it, the outline of a cat in a fireside chair, legs crossed, reading.

He checks in the bedroom and even in the loo. 'What was the last book she bought?' he says, coming back into the sitting room.

'*Beloved*.'

'Toni Morrison?' says Flint. Her eyes flit as if she thinks she might have missed a trick.

'It's not here. We'll leave you in peace, Anthony,' says Staffe.

Anthony nods and on the way out Staffe thinks how peculiar, that a missing woman would take a novel with her but not her mobile phone.

Pulford watches Lesley Crawford leave her Southfields home. She looks furtively up and down the street of mid-sized, late-Victorian terraces with modest bays and front gardens the size of picnic blankets.

Staffe had warned him not to take any risks, just to monitor who came and went, but he has been here, off and on, for the best part of two days and the boredom has got to him.

He calls Staffe and curses as the screen of his phone tells him the call has been ignored. He gets out of the car and locks it up, loiters out of Crawford's eyeline behind a tree, waiting for her to reach the corner and then he catches up, going up onto Replingham Road towards the Tube.

Pulford rummages in his pockets, pulls out his travel warrant and follows her across Wimbledon Park Road and into the station, which is like something from Betjeman's England, red brick and with tall, mock-Jacobean chimney stacks.

He picks up the evening edition of the *News* and gets into the same carriage, sits on the same side as her so he can monitor her reflection in the window from above his paper. He looks at her as she stares right ahead. She has an exotic face: a hook to her nose and dark eyes. He knows from the case bio notes that she was educated at Queen Elizabeth Grammar School, Blackburn, then studied Greats at Cambridge. She did some lecturing but abandoned her DPhil and worked in Papua New Guinea with the VSO before doing a PGCE. From what they can gather, she hasn't had a full-time job in five years.

At Embankment, she stands up and moves smoothly to the doors. She is the first to step down. The train is not crowded and he waits as long as he dare, feels a tingle around his heart and a slow fold in his belly as he follows her onto the platform. She carries a hessian eco Waitrose bag. Did she have it before? He thinks not. He is sure of it. He lets the gap between them extend. The carriage doors close and the train jolts.

As it moves out of the station, Pulford tries to clock anyone who was in her locale. A middle-aged man and a small group of foreign kids. He tries to picture her coming out of her Southfields house again. Did she have a bag? When he turns around, she is gone.

'Shit!' he says, too loud, and checks to see if anyone has heard him, but he is alone. He quickly calculates what connection she might make and realises there is only the Bakerloo or the Northern Line. He walks as briskly as he thinks you can without looking like a nutter – or a copper.

He chooses the Bakerloo, because he hates the Northern Line, and as he approaches the platforms, with steps down, dividing, he opts for north because there are more options. A train-gathered gust builds and the rattle of the train gets louder. He bowls onto the platform, which is mainly full of twenty-something folk. Again, he tries not to move quickly or look concerned and waits, not seeing Lesley Crawford anywhere.

There is a final push. He steps on and the doors close behind him. He works a pocket of space. There is little room and although he is tall, in the two minutes it takes to reach Piccadilly Circus, he can't spot her, despite his surreptitious looks and adjustments of stance. The doors open and he takes the opportunity to step out, to allow people off. Seeing nothing, Pulford steps back into the thinned carriage and the doors close behind him. The train jolts and stutters out of the station. As it goes, he scans the platform for signs of Lesley Crawford.

There she is, with a straight back and a high head, turning into the tunnels that will take her above ground or, more probably, further along on her journey.

Pulford curses and tries to calculate where Lesley Crawford is most likely to be going. Before he knows it, the train is slowing again as they enter Oxford Circus. He could chase to the opposite platform and get the next train back, but he knows there is no point, so he sits on a seat and lets the long ribbon of travellers wend past him, into their night. He looks at their shoes and their faces and wonders where they might be headed. He looks at their clothes and the bags they carry, decides to get back to Southfields to at least glean how long Lesley Crawford stays out for.

Then he sees it. A hessian eco Waitrose bag. There must be

thousands of them, but he can't recall ever having seen one before tonight.

When she left, was Lesley Crawford carrying hers? He doesn't think so, but he is already up, following the man with the bag. He is young and lean. He walks quickly and climbs the moving escalator. The neon mayhem of Oxford Circus meets them. The lean man barely wavers as he strides out through the hordes of late shoppers. Pulford struggles to keep up, but then the man slows, goes into the Argyll.

Pulford follows him in, carries straight on through, clocking, in a panelled and paned snug on the right, who the lean man is here to see.

This is a pub for tourists, but there is an upstairs bar, which is where the man and his companion go, sipping from their pints as they climb out of sight, achieving a further degree of privacy.

Ten minutes later, when the Rt Hon Vernon Short comes down and leaves the Argyll, he is alone, save for his hessian eco Waitrose bag.

Staffe sees he has a missed call from Jasmine Cash. He trousers the handset and gives his undivided attention to the conversation between Alicia Flint and the doctor with whom Zoe Bright was registered at the Waverley Park Medical Centre for Women. Doctor Fahy looks at her watch repeatedly and punctuates her speech by blowing out her cheeks. She is homely with freckles and bright blue eyes. 'I'd love to be able to tell you exactly what we talked about, but we're not at that stage. All I can do is confirm that Zoe had an appointment that day and she attended.'

'This woman is undoubtedly in a situation which compromises her well-being,' says Alicia Flint, for the umpteenth time.

'Then get your court order.'

'It's coming.'

Staffe says, 'What proportion of your consultations are related to terminations? This is a generic question.'

'A significant percentage.'

'A hundred per cent?'

'Not quite.'

'Anthony didn't accompany her?'

'Like I said . . .'

'I'm telling you, he didn't attend. She was twenty-four weeks and you saw her about a termination. Fair to say, you set her up with a date for the deed just an hour or so before she went missing.'

'That's what you're saying,' says Doctor Fahy, blowing out her cheeks for the longest time, staring at her watch. 'In fact, it would have been only our second consultation. And I shouldn't even be telling you that.'

'You do a difficult job and I'm sure there's good achieved here in some ways. I don't give a toss about that. I'm here to do my job.'

'Then we're peas in a pod, Inspector,' says Doctor Fahy.

'Not quite,' says Alicia Flint. 'The lives we save are cut and dried. We have to do what we can how we can. Are you a partner in this practice?'

'Yes.'

'You wouldn't want it to be closed down, indefinitely.'

'Of course not. I hope . . .'

90

'You have had a patient abducted and a national organisation, vehemently opposed to what you practise, has claimed
responsibility. I'm not sure we wouldn't be derelict in our
duty to the public if we allowed such a situation to persist – at
least until we have found Zoe Bright.'

Doctor Fahy sucks her cheeks in and stares at Alicia Flint.
After a long while, she nods, looks at her watch. 'I have an
appointment which I simply can't miss.' She clears her desk
into a drawer, save for one file. She logs off the computer,
says, 'I'm sorry I can't be more help. Please show yourselves
out.'

All three of them look at Zoe Bright's file, on the desk.

When Doctor Fahy gets to the door, Alicia Flint says, 'You
should think about security. I could send an officer down, to
take names and addresses of everyone entering, and log
vehicle registrations, too.'

'That's very kind, but we started doing that ourselves as
soon as we heard about Zoe. We are a professional operation,
Inspector Flint, we just don't have quite the same access to
double standards as some. Thank God.'

She closes the door and Flint says to Staffe, 'We got there
in the end.'

Staffe is reading the first sheet of the file. 'Christ,' he says.
'What is it?'

'Zoe Bright signed up for a termination. It was going to be
today. And Anthony was in the consultation with her.' Staffe
continues to read, sees Doctor Fahy's handwritten notes 'pre-
scan required. Patient dates dubious.'

Eleven

Staffe and Alicia Flint have discussed what to do about Anthony Bright and, for the moment, DI Flint has won the argument. Given that the information they have procured is by no means admissible, they will bide their time to use his deceit against him.

Now, they are in the ten-foot-square front room of Teresa and Michael Flanagan on Gladwys Street. Teresa and Michael are Zoe's mother and father. This is Toxteth and dusk has gathered. The kids are playing football in the street, watched over by adults. The women are already in pyjamas, ferrying fish suppers from the Chinese, and the men are in Everton and Liverpool replica tops. Never far away is the searing siren of a pursuit car.

Teresa Flanagan dips into her box of Bestco tissues as if they are a dish of peanuts, constantly wiping her eyes and blowing her nose. Michael Flanagan sits silently as Teresa bemoans her daughter's disappearance. On the floor, all today's papers are piled. Teresa has given up on her daughter, says, 'I don't know what happened to my girl. All she ever wanted was a family like her sisters. They lead proper lives, but she had to go off to *that place* and she never was the same again. I lost her. She was never the same again.'

'What place?' asks Flint.

Teresa addresses Staffe, as she has done throughout, and

Alicia Flint quietly fumes. 'That university. None of us have ever gone and it done us no harm, so what made her think she was any better?'

'You see her regularly,' says Staffe. 'Anthony said she came round once a week.'

'Anthony, now there's a lad. I thought the first time she brought him round he might sort her out. A lovely lad, sees his mum all the time. She's in Old Swan and he goes every Sunday teatime to see her. But oh, no, I don't know why he said that. We don't see Zoe one month to the next.'

'Teresa,' says Michael Flanagan. 'It's not like that.' He talks into his lap and stirs his mug of tea.

'It is and you know it is. I'm fed up of giving that girl chances.'

'Why would Anthony say she came round if she didn't?' asks Alicia Flint.

'He wouldn't lie, that lad,' says Teresa, to Staffe.

'You're not proud, that Zoe is an educated woman?' says Flint.

'And I bet you don't know that's not her name. Changed it, she did. She was Anne-Marie and one Christmas, that first Christmas she came back, she said she was Zoe. Disowning us, that's what she was playing at.'

'How did she meet Anthony?' asks Staffe.

'Had to come home, didn't she? Tail between her legs when she couldn't get a job with that fancy degree that got her into all that debt. And we put her up without a word.' She looks daggers at Michael, mutters, 'Soft lad.' Teresa stands up. 'They went together at school and she dropped him. But when she came back . . .' She collects the mugs on a tray. 'He did the right thing, like a shot. Loves her to bits, he does.'

'Zoe was pregnant, so they got married?' says Staffe.

'What do you think?' says Teresa, leaving the room to get more tea on the go.

As soon as the door closes, and without looking up from his lap, Michael says, 'She's the baby, you know. My baby and always has been. She's a lovely girl. Different from the rest, but I love them all the same.'

'How often did you meet up with her, Mr Flanagan? Once a week?' says Alicia Flint in a softer voice.

'I never said that.'

'She didn't even tell her mum she was pregnant again, did she?'

He shakes his head. 'She would've made a wonderful mum, you know.'

'She will, still,' says Alicia Flint, putting her notebook into her briefcase and slipping Michael Flanagan a business card. 'You should come to see me, Michael. On your own. We'll find Zoe, don't you fret. If there's anything we can do, it'll be done, but we can't be having all these lies. Every hour counts. Every hour, Michael.'

Staffe follows Flint out. Back on the street, the kids flock around them.

'I need a drink,' says Alicia Flint.

'Where do you suggest?'

'I have no choice. I've got to get home, it's only round the corner.'

'There's a pub over there.' Staffe nods at the Empress, recognising the tall and slim, embossed early-Victorian hostelry from the cover of a Ringo Starr album.

'I have a child,' says Alicia. 'My mum puts him down for three hours in the afternoon so I can bath him. You go to the pub if you want.' She gets in and revs the car and Staffe turns back to the house, sees Michael Flanagan's face in a chink between the nets. His wife must catch him because he flinches and the curtains quickly close.

Josie checks her watch and looks down the list of contacts that Staffe had distilled from Kerry Degg's phone records, address books and her old Christmas cards, and from the interviews on the neighbourhood knock. This one is Cello Delaney, a club singer, who sent Kerry a card on her birthday and was in her phone and was also mentioned by another singer she had interviewed the day before yesterday – describing Kerry and Cello Delaney as 'thick as thieves'.

The house is a tidy little terrace off the New North Road, by the Regent's Canal. When the door opens, a smell of cooking oozes from the darkened hallway, and Cello Delaney looks put out. She says, 'Police? I was wondering when,' and steps aside, showing Josie in, not bothering to scrutinise the warrant card.

The blues is being sung from the kitchen and Josie listens, thinks it might be Billie Holliday – not her bag, though, so she asks.

'Bessie Smith,' says Cello. 'Kerry loved her. I miss her already.' Cello looks at Josie with wide eyes and smiles, as if touched by a good memory. 'She always came on a Wednesday and I would make soup.'

'That explains the smell,' says Josie. She thinks Cello might be out of it. She looks more intently, sees her pupils are dilated. 'It's a bit late for lunch.'

'Is it? I don't believe in time.'

Josie wants to ask how she gets to her gigs on time and what would happen if her audience didn't believe in time. 'Tell me about the fathers,' says Josie. 'The fathers of Kerry's children.'

'She loved them. I never met them, of course, but Kerry would never have slept with anyone she didn't love and when she had Maya, she absolutely wanted her. But she just couldn't cope. It's a responsibility, isn't it? I remember we went shopping in the market up Dalston and we got stuff for goat curry and some saucy pants and some other stuff and then went to the Nags and I said, "Where's Maya and Miles?" And Kerry said, "Shit! Not again." And Maya was in a pushchair. I mean, how can you forget you're not pushing a pushchair?' Cello laughs, fondly.

'And Sean? Where was he when she was with her men?'

'Sean? She was better than him. I don't know why she kept going back to him – but she did. She never loved him. She loved the others.'

'So the two children have different fathers?'

Cello shrugs. 'They're both the spit of Kerry. How would I know? It's not Kerry's style to bang on about that sort of thing. She lived in the moment, not the past.'

'Did she want this latest baby?'

Cello shrugs again.

'What do you make of Sean?'

'Don't you know, he doesn't have friends. Not any. Only Kerry. I've got to stir my soup.'

Josie follows Cello into her kitchen. The units are hand-painted in thick oils: bright colours and abstract. The tiles are multicoloured and jars are everywhere. Vegetable peelings litter the work surface.

Cello bends down and opens the oven door. The draught of heat is fierce and Cello reaches in. Before Josie can call out, Cello takes a hold of the bread tin. When she hears Josie's voice, Cello turns round, the piping hot tin in her hand, and then the pain must prick whatever narcotic bubble she has around her and Cello screams, but doesn't drop the tin. She places it onto the worktop and then wrings her hand.

'You should put it under water,' says Josie.

Cello nods, her eyes wide; she holds her hand under a rushing tap and begins to stamp on the ground, moaning. 'Shit! I have something for this upstairs.'

'Shall I go?'

'No!'

Which arouses Josie's curiosity. She watches Cello go up the stairs, then rushes back into the kitchen, unlocks Cello's phone handset and clicks through the last numbers called, all the way back to the last time Cello called Kerry, just a week ago, but the call history tells Josie it was not answered. Then she reads the texts, shuffling along the hall and listening for a tread on the stairs.

Earlier today, a number not assigned had texted Cello to meet at the Half Moon – tomorrow night.

Josie hears Cello on the landing, above. She goes back into the kitchen, noting the number that texted Cello, and locks the handset, puts it where she found it.

'You say Sean had no friends, but he must have been well connected, to be in that game.'

'What game's that?'

'He's an impresario. A curator, he says.'

'A dodgy cunt is what he is. I don't know how he's got through life without someone having a right pop at him. Well, I do . . .'

'Go on,' says Josie, trying not to appear overly interested.

'I need to sort this soup. I really do.'

'Sean had somebody to look out for him. That's what you're saying.'

'I'm not sure I'm saying anything.'

'You said you knew why nobody had taken a pop at Sean.'

Cello suddenly looks more alert. 'No, I didn't.'

Josie nods upstairs, says, 'Do I get a tour?'

'No.'

'Never mind.' She knows Cello has clammed up, and knows also that there are Half Moons all over London. But she knows for a fact that the one in Putney is known for its music.

Alicia Flint's mother has left and her daughter is bathing her son, Ethan. Before she disappeared upstairs, in the duplex apartment she owns overlooking Princes Park, Alicia had tossed a wad of takeaway menus onto the ornate, far-eastern coffee table and given Staffe a bottle of Amstel without even asking, had said, 'You decide. I'm starving. Anything spicy.'

He feels the beer hit his throat and leans back in the sofa, swallows, then takes out his phone, sees he has a missed call from Pulford. He makes the call.

'Crawford hadn't left the place or had any visitors for nearly two days,' says Pulford. 'But today she went on the Tube.'

'How do you know?'

'I followed her.'

'I told you not to take any chances.'

'She didn't see me. And I lost her because I didn't get too close, but she had this bag. Or, she didn't have this bag but someone gave it her on the Tube and she gave it to someone else.'

'You saw it?'

'No. But I saw another man with it.'

'What?'

'And he gave it to Vernon Short.'

'How do you know?'

'They met in the Argyll in Oxford Circus, and Short had the bag when he left the pub.'

'The same bag?' Staffe hears Alicia coming down the stairs.

'It must be. What are the chances?'

Staffe smiles at Alicia and raises his eyebrows, to give the impression it is an unwanted social call.

'What should I do?' asks Pulford.

'Things are fine up here,' says Staffe. 'You take it easy.' He hangs up, thinking how it suits them, for Lesley Crawford to know Vernon Short, for there to have been contact.

'What did you order?' asks Alicia Flint, now in a running vest and jogging bottoms, her hair in a high-up ponytail and all her make-up scrubbed away. Her skin sings.

'Don't you cook?'

'You've got to be joking.'

'I'll do us something,' says Staffe, standing up, going into the open-plan kitchen area which has a window overlooking the park. Way down below, it is getting dark. A group of youths with straining killer dogs loiter by the gates, exchanging something barely disguised. 'Can I?'

'Go ahead.'

He opens a cupboard.

'I can't wait till we can hit Anthony Bright with that appointment at the clinic. Why'd he lie to us?' says Alicia, beside him in the kitchen. She pulls a beer from the fridge. 'I don't know what you'll find to cook. Rusks and baby jars is all I buy,' she laughs, swigging from her bottle. She bends down, reaches into a cupboard and plonks a butternut squash on the work surface. 'I don't know what to do with this. Mum brought it round.'

'Do you have any garam masala?'

'What?'

'It's OK,' says Staffe, finding some cumin and chilli powder at the back of the spice cupboard. He toasts the cumin and puts the oven on; dices the squash and thinks about whether to tell Alicia Flint about the connection they might have established between Lesley Crawford and Vernon Short. He roughly measures out the risotto rice and pops the kettle on to make an instant stock.

'What's happening your end? Any news about Sean Degg or that bloody Crawford woman?' she says.

'How spicy do you want this?'

'Is there something you're not telling me?' she says.

'As soon as I know anything, you'll know. I need to make a quick call.'

'What did your DS do to piss you off?'

'My DS?'

She frowns. 'Don't take me for a fool, Inspector.'

'He followed Lesley Crawford and lost her.'

'Could she be tied up with the private members bill of that idiot Short?'

'It'd be nice,' he says.

'Very nice,' says Alicia. 'You'd better make your call. And as much chilli as you like, for me.'

Staffe shakes up the roasting squash and puts the boiled water to the bouillon, then calls Finbar Hare, his old friend and string-puller. It is no surprise that he gets no response. At this hour, Fin will either be sleeping off a long lunch or having an aperitif – either with his beautiful wife, or somebody else's.

He says, into that message board in the ether, 'It's Staffe. Just wondered about getting together some time. Give me a call. And, oh . . . I'm looking for a job for someone I know. He's pretty desperate, just something menial. It doesn't matter, really, just to keep him occupied. Better if it didn't involve a police check. He's a good lad. Love to Flick and let's hook up some time.' He blows out his cheeks, trousers his phone and gets a raise of the eyebrows from Alicia Flint who is pulling out another pair of Amstels from her fridge.

The light flicks off and her heart hurdles a beat. After hour upon hour of nothing happening, just the slow arc of the sun and the pale fading of the weather against the Welsh hills, Zoe is nervous of change. The man and the woman who come, in masquerade masks and black raincoats, keep telling her she need not worry. They asked her about the baby and gave her a vitamin supplement. It will be soon, she thinks. It feels soon; sooner than the dates she gave the doctor. The last baby was too soon: too small, too weak.

She closes her book in the dark. She has been reading it slowly and deliberately, so as not to be without it. She has tried to get inside the mind of Toni Morrison, to distinguish her from the narrator. The task stretches the book and exercises her mind, something she has learned to do in private.

Zoe undresses and slides between the sheets on the mattress which she has moved to beneath the window. Last night the moon was unobscured. Not so tonight. The shapes within the room emerge slowly from the dark as her eyes adjust.

She passes her hand across her belly in slow circles. The baby hasn't kicked since after lunch. She wishes it would. She closes her eyes, remembers the look on the doctor's face as they agreed upon a termination. The woman was insisting on a final scan, but there was no smear of emotion, no hint of the right and wrong of it.

And before she finds sleep, in those bulrushes between the conscious and the not, Zoe wonders whether, if this one dies, it will find its brother. And she dreams that when she wakes, she is crying. She begins to dream that she is between the leaves of a book, listening to this stupid woman cry.

Twelve

A sea fret comes up from Albert Dock and drifts around the sandstone monolith of Liverpool's Anglican cathedral which broods high above cobbled Huskisson Street. Below, the city slopes away from Staffe. Above the seam of mist, he can see the sun glint on the hills, which must be Wales.

Staffe has stopped by the entrance to a bail hostel – fashioned within a grand neo-classical house. He looks behind him, up to the beautiful, stately Falkner Square where the brass is already out, tricking, or buying their daily dose. Boys in black track suits and black trainers skulk with their hoods drawn up. Somewhere, a peal of laughter smooths through the mist. It is the sound of students. He checks the address he jotted down from the stamp in Zoe's books, and carries on.

Before long, he sees the large Chinese arch and carries on past, down Duke Street. There are more junkies in these streets, just one block off the main drag, and even though it isn't yet ten o'clock in the morning, they are carrying cans of super-strength lager as if they were styrofoams of coffee.

The Curious Cat is no ordinary bookshop. Tucked away between a done-up boozer and a fancy Japanese restaurant, it is in a double-fronted, rickety Victorian building that opens out into a small bazaar. The sandwich board at the entrance to the indoor market tells you these are shops for the socially aware, funding the victims of government crime. It says, 'IF YOU CARE, SHOP HERE'. Above the entrance, on a cracked plastic banner, in red letters: 'ALL PROCEEDS TO THE VICTIMS OF GOVERNMENT CRIME'.

The Curious Cat is opposite a tattoo parlour called Free Ink. Behind its counter, chewing on an unlit roll-up and reading the *Guardian*, is a dreadlocked woman aged thirty, or thereabouts. She smells of cat and Staffe wonders if this could be deliberate.

She looks up and frowns at Staffe, sussing him for precisely what he is. 'I ain't done nothing wrong,' she says.

Staffe ignores her, clocks that a final demand for her council tax is lying on the *Guardian*: 'Ms Petal Broome' of 102 Devonshire Road. He mooches around the bookshop, winding up and down between the shelves which go back and back. The books are mainly fiction and travel but there are good sections on politics and biography, too. They are alphabetised and fairly priced. Every now and then he takes a book down, flicks through, thinking about the lives the books have had before. It makes him wish he had more time to read.

Ms Broome comes up to him, says, 'I'm going for a fag. Don't nick nowt.'

'Don't you want to know why I'm here?'

'Couldn't give a toss. I'm clean.'

'There's a woman shops here, mid-twenties, smartly dressed. She comes regularly. Called Zoe.'

'Zoe. She won't take no money for them. The deal is, we buy our books back. We pay half what they paid if they bring them back, so long as they're in good nick. We sell some dozens of times. It's a good cause.'

'Who do you give your profits to?'

'It's a co-op. There's plenty causes – political, like. We're very political.'

'When did you last see Zoe?'

The woman shrugs.

'She's missing, Petal.'

'How d'you know my name?'

'I want to help her. We're not all bastards, you know.'

Petal shrugs. 'She's nice enough. Sometimes, she brings me ginseng tea. Proper stuff. Not Starbucks shit. What's happened to her? She was having a baby.'

'Do you believe in a woman's right to choose, Petal?'

'Up to the woman to decide if she's a right to choose. She'd be due soon. She'll have finished that Toni Morrison, and an A.L. Kennedy.'

'Do you have another *Beloved*?'

Petal slinks away and comes back with a dog-eared copy. He gives her a fiver. When Petal gives him the change, he leaves a quid for her, says, 'Have a ginseng tea.'

'Week or so since she's been in. She's not come to no harm, has she?'

Staffe gives her a card with his number on, can practically hear Petal's cogs whirr. 'She's in trouble. That's for sure. Do you have anything to tell me?'

Petal shakes her head.

'You ever see her with anyone else? A fella?'

'A fella? Nah.'

'A woman, then. Or women?'

Petal shakes her head.

'If she's a friend of yours, you should tell me if Zoe said anything unusual. If she was planning a change.'

'She can't change. She's got a baby coming, hasn't she?' Petal says this with a disapproving gurn of her face. 'Look, I hope she's OK, I really do. She's a good woman, an intelligent woman, but I've nothing to say about that girl.'

Pulford says to Josie, 'I could go in on my own, you know.'

'You think it's too risqué for me, David?' She gives him a knowing, sidelong glance and looks up at the Rendezvous. 'You should know better than that.' A distant memory wafts through the unilluminated glass doors. Tonight, the curious will queue beneath the pink and blue neon, waiting for their fix of Phillip Ramone's taste of old Soho. He was here before they cleaned it up. And he's still here.

Pulford raps on the glass and they wait.

Josie came here with a hen party, years and years ago, and then just a couple of years since, on a weird date. She should have known better. The Rendezvous is no place for a second date.

Nobody comes and Pulford raps again.

The bloke who brought her here was a doctor, for crying out loud, and he had tried to show her the middle toilet: one for girls, one for boys, and the middle one for the unsure or inquisitive. Doctor Finney had certainly possessed an enquiring mind.

Inside, the light flickers on and a big man comes. He walks slowly, wide-gaited, as if he has a problem 'down there'. He mouths something through the glass and his face is angry. He has black stubble all over his head and a low hairline. Pulford takes out his warrant card and holds it to the glass. The big man talks into his lapel, squints at the warrant card as he speaks.

He unlocks the door, and as he heaves it open, he breathes heavily, smells of garlic. 'What you want?'

'Mr Ramone.'

'What you want?'

'It's about a woman called Kerry Degg.'

The man turns his back which pushes out against his chalk-stripe jacket. He has haunches like a bull and a small waist. He talks into his lapel again, turns and says, 'You lucky.'

They follow the man in, through the lobby with the ticket office on the right and the cloakroom on the left. The place smells of too many humans and bleach. However, when they make their way past the three toilets and round along the raised dining area opposite the stage, the smell evolves into a blend of booze and greasepaint and cologne. The lights are dim, but you can almost hear the echo-garble of good times: a bodiced woman, or man, in a spotlight, crooning, seducing the willing.

Phillip Ramone is in an office off the first floor, up a winding stairway and past a raised mezzanine with six small tables, tight up against a gold-speckled balustrade which overlooks the stage.

The proprietor – and this is only one of six businesses he runs in this parish – is waif thin and has his legs crossed like a forties Hollywood dame, talks with a cigarette drooping from his lips, which appear to have a tattooed outline, so that they can be distinguished from the rest of his grey face. He has a pencil moustache which Josie thinks must be to draw his gender. His hair is silvery thin and back-combed into a candy fluff that almost covers his skull. The light is low and his voice disarmingly so. The big man sits down next to him.

'You offered Kerry Degg a residency,' says Josie. Ramone has a standard lamp on behind him and she has to squint. Plumes of smoke curl around him.

'Kerry? You mean Lori. Lori Dos Passos.'

'That's her stage name,' says Pulford.

'And you have come to that stage. This is her world.'

'Was.'

'Yes, I heard. A tragedy.'

'When did you last see her, Mr Ramone?' asks Josie.

Ramone shifts, square to Pulford. He might have taken a shine to the tall young policeman. 'I thought I had done something to upset her. Either that or her idiot husband had her shipped away onto a cruise. Have the child at sea, perhaps. The shame of it.' He laughs, unconvincingly, at his own joke.

Josie says, 'Would you say Kerry was upset at the pregnancy?'

Ramone leans forward, presses a button on his telephone. 'Not upset. Pissed off, more like. Her career – her blooming life – was about to take off. She was going to get rid, that's for sure.'

'And you encouraged her?'

'Me? I love children.' He laughs. 'It was really of no consequence to me.'

'But what about the residency?'

'We have a very mixed clientele, but they're decent people. Nobody would have objected to a pregnancy – except maybe the last month or so. That would have been her pigeon.' He laughs again, louder, lights another cigarette.

An elderly woman appears through the door, stands beside Ramone and reads from a diary, as if it were sacred text. 'Miss Dos Passos was last here, officially, in December. The twenty-eighth. But if I recall, she did come to the Hoot-a-Fanny.'

'Of course,' says Ramone. 'New Year's Eve. Oh my, that is some time ago. Has she been gone *so* long?'

'You replaced her residency?' says Josie.

'I have a public, miss.'

'Have you seen her husband since then?' says Pulford.

'An irascible little scrote.'

Pulford smiles at Ramone. 'I wouldn't have put her with him. Still, it was Sean's offspring this time, apparently.'

'You surprise me.'

'He calls himself a curator.'

'He's nothing more than a pimp.'

'A pimp with connections. Tell us about Sean's connections,' says Josie.

'What do you mean?' Ramone regards his cigarette, takes a deep drag, as if it was his last, and stubs it out. He smiles at Pulford. 'I don't know his connections. I doubt you'll find anybody does. If I were you, young man, I would let that sleeping dog be. Now, if you wish to talk further, you can arrange an appointment with June here, but I must tell you I have little to add.'

Josie says, 'We know for a fact that someone looked out for Sean.'

Ramone smiles at her. 'I liked Kerry and I'm sad she's gone, but I don't make the world we're up against. I have to try to survive it.'

'And we are only trying to make it easier to survive. We're not on opposite sides, Mr Ramone. Are we?'

He smiles at Pulford and pulls two tickets from his desk, hands them to the detective sergeant. 'These are good for any night. Come along. I have nothing to hide, but I am a *terribly* busy man. *Terribly.*'

Thirteen

Staffe climbs up to Alicia Flint's flat. When he gets to the second floor, her place is open. From the door, he watches Alicia hold her boy tight, his head nestled into the shallow of her collarbone. With her free hand, she takes his meal from the microwave. 'You hungry, young man?' she says to her boy, Ethan.

The flat is two-storey, but the whole of this floor is open-plan. Three large windows look out onto Princes Park. Every now and then, Alicia checks her watch whilst she feeds young Ethan. Staffe reckons he is eight months or so. He can't walk, can't talk. Staffe wants to ask what happened to dad, but doesn't. Ethan pushes the food from his mouth with his tongue.

'You enjoying our fine city?' she asks Staffe, looking at Ethan.

'I like it. It's more a big village – after London. I even went to a second-hand bookshop yesterday. The Curious Cat.'

'Lucky to have time to read.'

'It's where Zoe Bright got her books.'

'How d'you know that?' Alicia looks up at him, accusingly.

'I wonder if you could check up on someone called Petal Broome. She runs the shop. Be nice to have a carrot to dangle.'

'Or a stick. Petal's holding out on you, is she?'

Staffe goes to the windows, looks out across the park. The sky is big here and gulls squawk. He wonders where Zoe Bright might be, and is she reading her *Beloved*, her baby inside her?

The entryphone buzzer goes and Alicia lets them in without talking, and says, 'It's odd, chasing down Anthony Bright and the Flanagans and having this political angle, too, especially when you've practically got a confession from that Crawford bitch.'

'We can't touch her,' says Staffe. 'And the politicians are only people, too. The same urges and regrets and broken homes.' He stops himself. He and Alicia look at each other, and he wonders how well he will come to know her.

Alicia's mother comes in and seems startled to see Staffe. She raises her eyebrows and Alicia says, 'Don't start, Mum.' She hands Ethan across and whispers something to her mother, which makes them both laugh.

As they make their way down, Alicia bemoans the fact that they can't haul Lesley Crawford in and give her the third degree.

Staffe thinks twice, says, 'Don't you have mixed feelings? You're a mother. A part of you . . .'

'No. Absolutely not. We work the law, don't we? There's nothing but violation going on here.'

'But if we were to find Zoe Bright now. Right now . . .'

'That's what we have to do. It's all we have to do.'

'I know. But I'm not a mother.'

'You ever get close?' laughs Alicia, popping the locks to her car.

He watches her get into the car, thinks he might enjoy

spending the day with her. As he gets in, he says, 'Let's think politics, then.'

'Ahaa. You're on my wavelength, Inspector. Let me introduce you to a friend of mine.' She pulses the accelerator, indicates, looks over her shoulder and tears out into the road, cutting up a cab and keeping it in second all the way to five thousand revs.

It takes them six minutes to get from Alicia's flat to Declan Hartson's office in the centre of town. They park up on Water Street and Staffe looks up at the civic glory of Liverpool's central business district, its aspic wealth.

They are shown straight to Hartson's office, where the councillor sits behind a six-foot partner's desk. He doesn't get up. Staffe can tell the time by looking at the dial on the Liver Building through the window behind the diminutive, cheeky chap. Staffe recognises him, vaguely, and Hartson must clock this.

'We had our moment in the sun, back in the eighties. Didn't we, 'Leash?'

'Speak for yourself,' says Alicia Flint. 'I was a child.'

'She believed, too. And then she joined the police. A great loss.'

Alicia Flint helps herself to a glass of water and takes a seat. 'Do you have that list, Declan?'

He hands her a sheet of paper and Flint puts on her glasses, reads, turns over the paper. Meanwhile, Staffe gets the feeling that the cut of his jib isn't to Hartson's liking. If he recalls correctly, Hartson was once an MP, involved with the far left. He has a slender recollection of scandal. 'Nice office,' he says.

'Bourgeois spoils. I'd rather the money went to those who need it, but what can I do? We rage and we rage but the machine just gets stronger. See anything you like, 'Leash?'

Flint hands the list to Staffe, says, 'This is every political group with an official presence on Merseyside.'

'No Breath of Life?'

'There's plenty of right-to-life organisations here – as you'd expect. We're Dublin's eastern suburb, so some say. The Church isn't what it was, but even so.'

'Did you ever come across Vernon Short when you were in Westminster?' says Staffe.

'We overlapped. He loved it. Always in this bar or that, supping on the cheap.'

'He's having *his* time in the sun.'

'He's a bastard. Doesn't believe in anything apart from himself. I don't know who put him up to that bill of his.'

'Put him up to it?' asks Staffe. 'His own party's against it. Isn't he just being bloody-minded – a final throe?'

'He's his father's son. We have to do better than our fathers, don't we? I'd say he was trying to gain some leverage with the PM or the Home Secretary, but that would take balls and Vernon isn't overly endowed in that department. He'll be acting from fear, if I know him.'

'Fear?'

'Or cash, of course. That's a common cause.'

'Does he have hidden depths?'

'We *all* have hidden depths, Inspector. Even me,' laughs Declan, too chirpily for Staffe's liking.

'The Ropewalks Caucus, Declan. Do you know them?' says Alicia.

'A few charity shops. We extended their council tax exemption the other month. All in a good cause.' He looks quite pious, now. 'They have a good bookshop.'

'You come across a woman called Petal Broome?'

'Aaah, Broome. Her mother's an old SWP mate of mine.' He taps his nose. 'We go back. Virginia Broome. Hmm.'

'Did she have any particular bees in her beret?'

'The usual. Palestine mainly, and CND.'

'Right to Choose?'

'Of course, but she had her girl when she was young and on her own. I wouldn't have thought . . .' Councillor Hartson seems to drift into a private space. He plays with his lip, with finger and thumb. 'This is to do with that Zoe Bright. Am I wrong? They kidnapped her.'

'Not for me to say, Declan.'

'Direct action – sounds so archaic now.' A nostalgic glaze forms upon Hartson's face. '. . . Got to take your hat off.'

'You're just an old traditionalist,' says Alicia Flint, standing.

'You'll scratch my back some time, won't you, 'Leash?'

'What do you have for me?'

'Virginia Broome is on the dragon's tail.'

Baby Grace seems to look straight at Josie. Could this be the first time she has opened her eyes? She is stock still, pin-cushioned with her nutrient tubes. Josie rubs her eyes, knows she should get some sleep. Grace's eyes close.

A nurse comes in and Josie says, 'Can she see?'

'It'll be a blur for her, my love. It's early days.' The nurse smiles at Josie, as if she is a child. She cheerily jots on the board that hangs from the side of the monitor, then flicks each of the tubes that lead from the plastic sacks down into the baby's blood and stomach.

When Josie has to leave, she seeks out the nurse – the jolly, golden-haired one called Natalie – to make sure she has her mobile number in case anything happens, but she can't find her. In a recess down the corridor from Grace's room, there's another nurse she has seen before. This one has sad, dark eyes. 'Can you give this to Nurse Natalie?' says Josie, handing her number across.

'Who are you?' The dark nurse's eyes flit. She looks as if she might burst into tears at any moment. Her name card says 'Eve Delahunty'. Josie takes the card back, not wanting to burden her.

As she goes down the corridor, she looks back and Nurse Eve makes her way towards Grace's room.

Outside, it has turned cold in the City and the early breath of summer seems to have expired. The sky is black and full of rain.

Josie thinks about the people she has met since she found Grace. Sean Degg and Cello Delaney and Phillip Ramone, and even though she is dead on her feet, they all pull her west, to the Half Moon.

Vernon Short tucks in his shirt, precisely buttons up his flies. He thumbs up his braces, then shifts the way he is dressed. He regards himself in the mirror and, for some reason, finds himself recalling the day he gave his maiden speech to the House. He takes his jacket from the hook on the back of the stall door. His heart beats fast and he considers where all the years and the hope went. He shoots his cuffs. He can still see the young man, can still feel the principles even though they were trampled into the Westminster earth a long time ago. He wonders what might be in his blood.

Are they finally going to see what he has to offer? He looks at his notes, writ small in his fastidious hand on a business card. According to the *Telegraph*, sixty per cent of the people are now with him on the bill. Today, Baby Grace had been relegated to page five. The Liverpool woman hasn't caught nationally. It will, if there is a baby – but that's not now. Not today. Politics is a twenty-four-hour game, these days.

He checks his watch. A minute late, already, for the Home Secretary. Who would have thought it? Vernon breathes deep, thinks of his father, once a vociferous backbencher and universally regarded as one of the last of the House's true characters: a landed, fuck-them-all free thinker. That look in his father's eye – when he visits him on the farm in Sussex for the monthly Saturday lunch – dismounting after the drag hunt, four sheets to the wind and evaluating his son: no disgrace, but not nearly a match.

'Bastards,' he says, aloud, opening the door, stepping out into the halls he always dreamed he would bestride. They think he is a fool, but he got a double first and salvaged the family firm in the late eighties. In his time at Westminster, he has body-swerved all the scandals. No mud stuck to Vernon – somehow – but he was born just beyond his time. Until now. He looks up the corridor. It is a five-minute walk from here. 'Bastards,' he says again, striding towards Catherine Killick, Home Secretary.

Killick opens the door herself, shows Vernon in, even though she has people to do that for her. The modern way. She is ten years his junior and it's an airbrushed, widely known secret that Killick was militantly pro-choice when she first cut her teeth on politics. Since Blair and the bland new Clause Four, though, it has been a relentless drift towards the centre for Cathy, especially after she was made a parliamentary private secretary to the PM, when he was in Trade.

She pours Vernon's tea. Vernon: a man, a type, she has always despised. She beams the best smile she can at him. But she won't fuck about. 'We can't be having this turn into a circus, Vernon,' she says.

'Serendipity,' says Vernon.

Cathy Killick puts down his tea on her desk and goes behind, rests her feet up on a stool to the side of her desk and interlocks her fingers on her swollen, pregnant tummy. 'Serendipity is a wanky shop for hippies that sells Indian scarves and moonstones up Camden Market. Been going for years. There's nothing real about serendipity. It's just what we're dealt and, as you know, we can change what we're dealt.'

'The baby is still in the papers.'

'All this Whole Family claptrap.'

'I thought that was our claptrap, Home Secretary.'

'Word is, your bill would pass if it went before the House today,' says Cathy Killick.

'Let us hope. We're up for debate next week.'

'For what, exactly, do you hope, Vernon?'

'To serve my country.'

'What would it take, to do that? I don't think the country really wants this bill. We certainly don't want our legislation flapping like dirty laundry.'

'I don't write the headlines.'

'And journalists don't make law.' Killick adjusts her posture, sighs heavily, looks Vernon dead in the eye. 'Nor do they understand you, Vernon. You have pedigree and you have integrity. I need statesmen, Vernon. I need you with me.'

'In what capacity?'

'We've been talking about you.'

'*We?*'

'You know there's a reshuffle in June.'

'What are you saying?' Vernon tries to remain calm, but there is a bubble between his heart and his stomach. He barely dare listen.

'Your father was in Education.'

He nods. 'Briefly.' Beyond, he can see the splendid white fondant of Whitehall, high above the people. 'He was his own man, in the end.'

'It wouldn't do to follow. The PM wondered about Enterprise. With your connections in the City, we wondered if you might be able to spearhead our clampdown on bonuses, tighten up on derivatives, you know. Headline stuff – you're good at that.'

'Minister for Enterprise?' murmurs Vernon, not believing his own words.

Cathy Killick presses a button on her laptop and across the room a printer begins to softly hum as the laser does its work. 'Pick it up and have a read,' she says, nodding to the printer and smiling wide. 'We thought you might say something along these lines.'

Once Vernon has closed the door behind him, Cathy Killick places a hand on her baby within, says, 'Who in God's name does he think he is?' She reflects, considers her rise to this moment and all the prices she paid. How much of her is left?

Staffe watches as Alicia Flint gets to work on Petal Broome. She talks softly, touching Petal's elbow and guiding her towards a pair of chairs at the back of the Curious Cat, where they sit opposite each other, shoulders rounded, talking about what might possibly be happening to Zoe Bright. Every now and then, Petal looks across at Staffe. Alicia Flint says, 'Will, perhaps you could get us some tea?'

'Ginseng?' says Staffe. As he goes, Alicia Flint flicks him a wink.

By the time Staffe returns with the tea, Petal is shaking her head, saying, over and again, 'No. No. I don't trust you, it's a violation. A bloody violation.'

'The smallest detail could help us find Zoe. And if we don't find her . . .'

Staffe says, 'The woman in London died. They abducted her and held her for weeks, living with rats and having to shit where she lay. If Zoe was here and she heard you pontificating about "violations", what would she say?'

'And what if it's not like that? What I say would be for nothing.'

'What you say!'

'Inspector,' says Flint, standing, silently beseeching him not to undo her good work.

Petal looks self-righteous, says, 'All you need is jackboots and a black shirt.'

'What!' shouts Staffe. He feels his blood surge, something in his mind floods. He hates this cheap allusion. He breathes deep, takes a step away and measures his anger by the look on Alicia Flint's face. 'OK,' he says. 'I could spend all day explaining why you're more of a fascist than I am. But let's not bother, hey? Let's talk about your mother, Petal. I hear she is using again. And if she's using she'll be paying for it somehow – a little scam? A bit of shoplifting? Maybe benefit fraud. Good old victimless crimes in your book, I suppose, comrade?'

Petal has regained her composure. 'Go fuck yourself.'

'Who was Zoe with? Where did she hang out?' says Alicia.

'You don't fool me,' says Petal.

Alicia Flint looks up, at the roof, across to the stairs. She stands up. 'This place is a danger to the public. I'll give you till five o'clock tomorrow to come up with something, otherwise you're closed down.'

Outside, Staffe says, 'You don't mess about.'

Alicia Flint gets into the car and revs it up, says, 'But that's all I am doing. I can't touch her mother or the premises – not unless I want to be on the front page of the *Echo* and have everyone in the city knowing what we're up to. Like you said, it's a big village – and all the neighbours are nosy. And I don't need you fucking my interviews up.'

She looks over her shoulder, sees a line of traffic and curses. As she turns back, she catches Staffe looking at her. There is a car's-length gap in the stream of traffic and Alicia Flint cuts in, gets the horn and a finger from the car behind. She gives it back and turns to look the driver behind in the eye. He backs off.

Fourteen

It is with immeasurable regret that I have to consider the withdrawal of the private member's bill proposing the reduction in the legal limit for the termination of pregnancies. I remain committed to the cause of maintaining the highest standards of care for pregnant mothers and their unborn children but am concerned for the integrity of this legislative solution in the light of what can only be described as a media circus and indeed the spate of criminal activity which has appended itself to the bill.

I have been in the House for nearly twenty years and cannot stand by and watch the integrity of Parliament being compromised in this way. I have every confidence in the ability of the government to continue to represent the interests of mothers and this issue will continue to be addressed through the consultative and legislative process, unhindered by those who seek to undermine our country's revered democratic standing.

Staffe watches the television. Vernon Short folds up the piece of paper, placing it in the inside pocket of his double-breasted jacket. He smiles into camera, Big Ben beyond, and is strobe-lit by dozens of flashing cameras. The journalists call out questions but Vernon simply raises his hand and smiles some more, as if he is associated with a great success.

Alicia Flint smells of camomile and her hair falls in thick, wet thongs. She wears a short-topped, low-trousered velour track suit and her midriff is tanned and taut. She bounces Ethan on her lap, across the room from Staffe. Ethan is naked, his legs are strong. She says, 'I wonder what they have promised that sanctimonious scrotum.'

'He'll be tucked into some obscure ministry in the next reshuffle,' says Staffe.

'These are people's lives they're fooling around with. Big decisions. At least it will bring Lesley Crawford from out of her cover. That Breath of Life lot will have to respond.'

'I'm worried about Zoe. Christ, what will they do to that poor girl if there's nothing to be gained?'

Alicia puts Ethan in his baby walker and spins him round. He chortles, pushes himself up with his legs and claps his hands. She reaches into her briefcase, pulls out a stack of papers and lays them on the coffee table in front of the sofa. 'I can do this on my own.'

Staffe wants to ask about Ethan's father, how he came to abandon them – or otherwise. 'It'll be quicker, the two of us.' He takes the Zoe stack of papers and they go through them independently: copies of all the interviews and the data for Zoe and Kerry and their parents and loved ones. Alicia Flint takes the Kerry Degg pile.

'How shall we play Anthony Bright?' asks Staffe. 'We can disclose to him that we know about Zoe's termination now.'

'And the fact that we know he went with her to the clinic. But you'll need a gentler touch than you showed with Petal Broome.'

'He's lied to us and we need to know why.'

123

'Do you really think he had anything to do with Zoe going missing?'

Staffe reads through the notes which draw the profile of Zoe Bright's professional and domestic rituals. It seems she moved within a small circle. Her colleagues at the university's resource centre said she was quiet, committed, kept herself to herself. Her university email history revealed nothing untoward and her only indulgences were a penchant for second-hand book sites and literary blogs.

Staffe flicks back through his notes, goes through the inventory of the house, looks at two items: a collection of cartons for potted shrimps and ice-cream tubs. She used the former for earrings, the latter for her necklaces – bursting with bright gems. Each from a place called Parkgate.

'Where's Parkgate?' he calls through to Alicia Flint.

'Across the water. It's worth a daytrip before you head back. When *are* you going back to London?'

'You look dead on your feet,' says Pulford, pushing through the crowd, holding the drinks out to Josie. 'I got you a vodka Red Bull.'

'So I won't be able to sleep. Cheers.'

'There's a band on in the back. Fancy it?'

'We're here to see whether Cello Delaney shows, and who with.' Josie has her hair frizzed and is wearing a beret, no eye make-up but blood-red lipstick – enough to wipe her off Cello Delaney's radar.

'I'm not sure about the new look.'

'Oh, David. I'm so sorry. There was I hoping it would make you swoon. I so want you to adore me.'

This had been Pulford's night off until Josie persuaded him away and he's already had a couple of drinks. 'But I do. You know that. We have history. Remember?'

'Pulford! That was years ago and we both agreed it was a mistake.'

'Maybe I like mistakes.'

Josie turns her back on him, looks around the room. She can't see Cello Delaney, and it's already gone nine. A rhythm section starts up in the back room and she says, 'Let's try the band. Cello might be in there.'

Pulford reaches for his warrant card and Josie takes a hold of his hand, says, 'You may as well have come in a helmet if you show that.'

He pays them in and leads her around the back room as the sax pipes up, playing the opening bars of 'Night in Tunisia'. He holds onto her hand and leans down, talks into her ear. 'I'll be your cover. The things I do for the love of the law.' And he puts his arm over her shoulder.

'Don't push it.'

'Don't blow my cover,' he laughs, drinking from his bottle of Moretti and watching the band on the stage, picturing Cello Delaney from the publicity shots Josie had shown him on the way over.

He gets a nudge in the ribs and Josie reaches up with a hand, whispers into his ear, 'Bingo. Just by the stage, with the old fella. On the right.'

'Where? Aaah.'

'Let's wander round, see if I can get them in a picture on my phone.'

Pulford slides his arm from her shoulder, begins to back

away, towards the door, taking Josie's hand and bringing her with him as the sax player finishes his chorus and takes the applause, moves away to the side of the stage where he picks up his drink and raises it to Cello Delaney. Except, it's not Cello so much as the older fella the sax player is toasting. 'There's no need for a photograph,' says Pulford.

'I don't trust my memory. I can do it. It'll look like I'm taking one of the band.'

'I know him.'

The older fella is right by the stage now, chinking his drink with the saxophonist and saying something that makes Cello and the horn player both laugh. Tonight, she seems less out of it, and whilst the two men smile and nod their heads to the piano player's eight-bar solo, the smile fades quickly. She looks as if she'd rather be somewhere else.

Pulford says, into Josie's ear, 'He's Tommy Given. I came across him during my stint at the Met.'

'Rings a bell,' says Josie, on tiptoes. She likes Pulford's aftershave and it brings the better part of a memory back on a breeze. 'Why should I know him?'

'Because he's a bad bastard.'

Fifteen

Staffe takes a sharp intake, flicks a look across to Alicia Flint as he begins to glean what he can from Anthony Bright. Her hair is scraped back, clipped up meticulously into a plaited bun. Her cheeks glow and her eyes are bright. She sits erect, wearing a tailored, chocolate-brown suit. The police station is two miles from her home, a million miles from Ethan bouncing on her knee.

For some reason, he feels nervous. 'Anthony, it is time we were honest with each other. So I'll start.'

Anthony Bright's expression changes. Since they came in, he had sat with his head high and his back straight, hands clasped loosely. Now, he stiffens, looks across to his solicitor – then back to Staffe.

'I have deceived you, Anthony. I chose not to tell you that I have spoken to Zoe's parents, and I didn't tell you I have been to see Petal Broome. Soon, I will know as much about Zoe as anyone – save you.'

'Save me?'

'So you have to realise that you can't spend the next days and weeks trying to guess what we know – or should I say, what we might not know. Every day, we get a little closer.'

'You'll find Zoe, then.'

'And what took her away. Does that make you nervous, Anthony?'

'Why should it?'

'You said Zoe visited her parents every week. She didn't. Is that a lie, or do you simply not know your wife?'

'I know her all right.'

'You shouldn't feel ashamed.'

'Ashamed? Why would I be ashamed?'

Staffe smiles at him, reaches out with a hand and clasps his arm, says, 'You've had your chance. Coming clean would have helped us all.' He stands and Alicia Flint takes his seat. Staffe leans against the wall, arms across his chest.

Anthony's brow puckers, as if he is trying to solve a riddle.

'How were things between you and Zoe, you know . . .' says Alicia.

'Normal.'

'Really?'

'She's having a baby, for fuck's sake.'

'She is a curious, educated woman. Different from you.'

'Things were fine. Just fine.'

'People are complex. Zoe went away and came back. She even changed her name, didn't she?'

Staffe intervenes, 'But you didn't tell us that, either.'

Alicia Flint ignores Staffe, says, 'She was mixed up. Caught between two worlds. She didn't really know what she wanted, did she?'

'She wanted to be with me. We got married.'

'She wasn't the same when she came back from university, was she?'

'I was the first – I know that. And she's the only woman I can love.' He looks down, at his shoes, then up at Alicia

Flint. 'You probably think I'm a sad fuck, but you don't know how lucky I am. I trust you.'

'And if we don't find her – at least nobody else will ever have her,' says Staffe.

'You don't know what you're talking about.'

'She was going to get rid of the baby, wasn't she, Anthony?' says Alicia Flint.

'You went with her,' says Staffe.

'No.'

'You lied to us. Now, tell us the truth!'

'Inspector,' says Alicia Flint.

'Tell me!'

'You don't get it, do you?' says Anthony. He bites his lip, as if in pain. He leans forward, arms crossed, holding his knees beneath the desk.

'Forget your pride.'

'I have tried to love other women – like when Zoe went away. And I probably don't understand her. But I'll tell you, I'll tell you on my life and her life and the baby's life, there's nothing I can't forgive. Nothing. And that makes me hate myself, sometimes.' He leans back now and he is scratching, jabbing at his wrist. He grimaces. Anthony Bright leans further back and the whites of his eyes roll up and he topples from his chair and his solicitor gets down on her knees, screams, 'Get someone. Get someone!'

Staffe rushes across, bends to pull up Anthony Bright but Anthony's eyes have gone. He has passed out and as Staffe reaches for him, he sees Anthony has four short lengths of pencil in his hand, broken to the size of cigarette butts and taped together – sharp as nails.

Blood begins to pool on the floor, seams of red ribboning from his wrist.

He has Anthony in his arms and looks up at Alicia Flint. For the briefest moment, before she calls for help, she looks daggers at Staffe – as if this was his fault.

By the look of her, Cello Delaney had stayed the distance last night with Tommy Given and maybe the band. Her hair is all over the place and her face is puffy and grey. She smells of drink and a recent cigarette.

'What the fuck?' she says, peering at Josie and Pulford. 'Who's the boy?'

'This is DS Pulford,' says Josie. 'He wants to know a little more about the company you keep.'

'You can let us in, Cello,' says Pulford. 'I'll make you a coffee.'

'I don't have to let you in.'

'And we don't have to talk to you. I guess we could go round to see Tommy Given, ask him what it is that he gets from a friendship with Cello Delaney, best mates with murdered Kerry Degg.'

'I can see who I like.'

'If that's what you want.'

She steps back, runs both hands through her hair and rubs her temples with the balls of her hands. 'You followed me?'

'We've got better things to do, Cello. It's a question of reliable sources.'

She trudges away, down the hallway.

Today, Fleetwood Mac are sultry in her kitchen. 'Stevie Nicks,' says Josie. 'Perfect for hangovers.'

'I like rumours,' says Pulford. 'It's sometimes a way to skin a rabbit.'

'Tommy's a friend, is all.'

'In the music business?'

'Kind of.'

'And a friend of Kerry's, too, I bet.'

'They know each other. Kerry knew a lot of people and so does Tommy. This isn't such a big city, you know.'

'We were talking about Kerry and her men the last time I was here,' says Josie.

'Do you know who Tommy is?' Cello sneers.

'We can do you a favour,' says Josie. 'We can get you out of this mire you've talked your way into.'

'I'm in no mire.'

'Without you, there's no way we would have linked Tommy Given to Kerry. I suppose if he asked, we'd tell him that you led us to him.'

Cello Delaney sits down heavily in a chair at a small table in the corner of her kitchen. She lights up a cigarette and says 'Fuck,' as Pulford makes them all a cup of coffee.

Eventually, Cello says, 'How can I trust you?'

'How can you not?' says Josie.

'I don't know anything. Not really.'

'Give us what you've got and you're safe.'

'Safe?'

'Just like Sean. You're the one who said Sean was being looked after. It's Tommy who makes him safe, right?'

She nods, appraising the tip of her cigarette.

'And what about Kerry? What did Tommy Given do for her?'

'Got her that residency, is all I know.'

'At Rendezvous? Why would he do that?'

Cello shrugs. She takes her coffee from Pulford and lobs her cigarette into the sink; sparks up another.

Staffe walks away from Anthony Bright's dream home. From what Alicia Flint has told him, it was always Anthony's dream, to have a home like this. The garden suburb is where a certain sort of aspiring couple would want to be. He notices the apple blossom is out. It's too soon. There could still be a frost and then there will be no fruit.

He thinks about the row he had with Alicia Flint after Anthony's assault on himself. Whether it was a cry for help or a flight from interrogation, Alicia Flint had blamed Staffe for pushing Anthony too far, but they both know Anthony had come to the interview with his pencil device. He had come prepared.

The street is tree-lined and no two houses in this inter-war garden suburb are alike. Birds shrill and retired folk and housewives potter and stoop in their gardens, readying for the summer.

He looks at his map and turns left and right and left and right again, crossing the green and weaving a way to the outer skin of the unreality of the estate until he can see the clock tower that stands proudly at the head of Wavertree High Street, leading to the city proper. Now, he sees what he wants – his first CCTV camera. Gone are the curtain twitchers, here are the mechanical eyes. He refers to the master sketch of the security web that Alicia Flint's DC had given him and he ticks off each camera from here all the way to the railway station. Whenever and wherever possible, Zoe Bright took the train rather than the bus – as borne out by the contents of her bin and by her husband.

When he gets to the station, Staffe sees that by changing once and travelling under the Mersey, then getting a bus, he can get to Parkgate in just over an hour. He buys his ticket and calls into Flint's DC with the co-ordinates of the coded CCTV positions. He gives the date and time frame of Zoe Bright's disappearance.

He can't help feeling that the real key to this case is that unholy pair Vernon Short and Lesley Crawford. Or must he simply dig so deep into Kerry Degg and Zoe Bright's pasts that the truth will emerge – like drilled oil?

The unwelcome truth, he knows, is that sometimes you have to engage as deeply as you can on each and every front of enquiry – until a theory becomes untenable. For now, much as he is beginning to miss his own city, he gets the train, changes, and then a bus.

Zoe might have been seen on the streets here in Parkgate. She might have been with somebody that day. He takes out the cartons Zoe chose to cling onto: the potted shrimp and ice-cream tubs, somehow harking back to a previous age. A childhood in which she was never fully indulged?

His phone goes and it is an unknown number.

'Sorry, chief. They only keep the video data for three days,' says the DC.

'Shit,' says Staffe.

'You know how many CCTV cameras we have? And someone's got to watch the stuff.'

'Someone watches it all?'

'They fast-forward it. Up to twenty-four times. That's an hour to cover a day. We've got sixty cameras. Do the maths.'

'And is anything kept?'

'Too right. Just the juice, though.'

'And that day – between midday and four in the afternoon – the three cameras I told you about?'

'They're all on Greavo's watch. I can't tell if he saved anything or not. You can ask him. He's in tomorrow.'

'Get hold of him.'

'He's on leave.'

'Get hold of him and give him my number.' Staffe hangs up, looks across at the Welsh hills. There should be sea between here and them; instead, a silted estuary with marshes and sandbanks. A different country, altogether.

Parkgate's promenade is flanked on one side by a fine terrace of mid-nineteenth-century houses and on the other by wrought iron. But beyond the railings, where there should be a beach and a sea, there is only grass. The sea is gone. The pub is called the Ship and there is an old-fashioned fish and chip restaurant, a café that would have been a Lyons or Forte in its day, an ice-cream parlour and a shrimp-and-cockle shack. But no sea. Gulls are above and salt is in the air. And no sound of surf, nor the rattle of shingle beneath the tide.

The trippers have come nonetheless and they cluster against the dry breeze, stabbing their cockle and whelk tubs with thin blades of wood; they lick at ice-cream, and Staffe follows the trail, goes into the shrimp shack, checking the livery on the empty tub he purloined from Zoe's house. This is the place.

He shows the youth behind the counter his warrant card

and the queue disperses. The boy tells Staffe, 'I fuckin' done nowt. You lost me them customers.'

Staffe holds the photograph of Zoe up and sees the youth instantly clam up, tight as a live shell. 'I think she used to come here, maybe every couple of weeks, so if you don't tell me when you last saw her, I'll bring you in – all the way across the water and then you'll have no fucking customers for the whole day. Maybe longer.'

'I haven't seen her,' says the youth.

Staffe shuts the door, turns the sign around to show 'Closed' to the outside. He picks a tub of potted shrimps from the counter and leaves a fiver, sits on a low, three-legged stool and stabs the buttered flesh. It melts in his mouth, tastes of a near shore. He lets the shrimp go its own way and spears another and another, savouring each and every one. Traces of mace enrich the flesh. He takes out a tenner and takes two more pots. 'You don't know what you've got here,' he says to the youth.

'But I don't like 'em.'

'Sick of the sight?' Staffe looks up at him. 'I'm only trying to help her.'

'She's in trouble?'

'You could help save her.'

'She never says much,' says the youth.

'She come with a friend?'

The youth shakes his head. He has dry skin that flakes around his eyebrows and on his forehead and chin. 'I only seen her on her own. She looks sad.'

'She'd come on a certain day?'

'Sunday mornings, most often.'

'But not last Sunday?'

He shakes his head again.

'And not with her husband?'

'She got a husband?'

'Why wouldn't she?' says Staffe.

'He must like rollmops, then. The husband.'

'Why d'you say that?'

'She always took rollmops, wrapped. She'd have the shrimp for herself. Like you. But she said she can't abide rollmops. That's what she said.'

'Give me a couple of rollmops,' says Staffe, thinking it might brighten Anthony's day – for an instant.

Staffe's phone goes and he stands, leans on the counter and the youth takes a step back, as if he might catch something. Outside, a line of five people has formed, waiting for the shop to reopen.

'They come from miles around,' says the youth.

'Inspector Wagstaffe? It's Sergeant Greaves. I'm on leave, I . . .'

'Second of April. Between one and four o'clock. I'm looking for a woman on cameras WH 3, 4 and 5. Hang on a second . . .' Staffe takes his herrings and the shrimp and leaves the money, winks at the youth as he turns the sign back round on his way out. '. . . The woman is Zoe Bright. You'll have heard of her, I'm sure.'

'I know her all right. At least I do now.' The phone goes quiet, fills up with background chatter, as if Greaves is outside a pub, and Staffe can tell he is smoking, breathing heavily. 'What's wrong, Greaves?'

'I don't know. I can't be sure. I didn't know it was her, then. How could I?'

'You saw her?'

'I didn't wipe it. I kept it. Christ, I didn't twig it was her.'

'You kept the tape?'

'I'm sure I did. This one was with an old fella. Having a ruck, they were. A right set-to. Not to blows, like, but waving their arms. She kind of pushed him and he was trying to grab her, trying to hold her, like. That's why I paused it. Looked like it might develop, you know.'

'An old fella?'

'Old enough to be her father, I'd say.'

It has become a beautiful day and the gulls have come up the estuary to feed on what the visitors discard. A line of Scandinavians forms outside the seafood shack now, mostly wearing the red replica tops of Liverpool Football Club. They spill onto the road, like an isthmus, almost as far as the low wall of the faux prom.

Staffe wishes he could surrender to the day, let it take him like a tide and maybe book into a guest house, look out across the marshes to the Welsh hills and lose himself in a book: Iris Murdoch, perhaps. Or Toni Morrison.

He slips away from the crowd. Far away to his left, where the estuary meets what he thinks must be Cheshire, he can make out a sprawling industrial complex which rises from the distant horizon like a cold, steel city. He squints, brings into focus tall and thin tubular chimneys which expectorate. He turns back towards the Welsh hills. A long plume of mist comes in from where the sea must be. It works its way into a fold in the hills, like giant, parted thighs.

A heron flies directly towards him, its giant wings flapping slowly. It arcs away, head high, towards a copse of trees way down on a swathe of high grasses. There, amongst the trees, he sees a redbrick Victorian building. He thinks it might be a water tower – where the sea once was. How strange. And he wonders if those same Victorians had done something to drive the estuary away; whether they had gone engineering mad.

His phone rings and he sees it is Finbar, which makes his heart a little gladder.

'What's up?' says Finbar.

'I'm on the Wirral.'

'Aaah.'

'You know it?'

'Sailed past it a few times. Good sailing but it's a bastard if you don't know what you're doing.'

Staffe recalls the one time that he went sailing with Fin, a year or so before his friend's calamity. The phone is quiet for a long moment and each man decides to give that subject a wide berth.

'I've got something for that pal of yours,' says Finbar.

'Jadus?'

'You can pick 'em, for Christ's sake.'

'You met him?'

'Got one of my muckers in the post room to take a look at him. They've got something in the non-con.'

'Non-con?'

'Safe matter. Non-confidential. We have two kinds of waste here.'

'Waste?'

'It's recycling. That pal of yours can do his bit to save the world. It's only seven quid an hour, I'm afraid. That's the best I can do.'

'You're a star, Fin. I'll make it up to you.'

'I'll make sure of that. Don't doubt it. Got to go.'

Staffe is kind of sad not to talk to Finbar for longer and he feels a tug back to London, looks back towards the estuary and sees that the mist has come further up. He looks for the water tower, can't see it any more even though he squints for it. He thinks his eyes might be playing up.

The baby has been heavy on Zoe's bladder all morning and now it kicks her. She puts her hand to her stomach and swallows away a curse, reminds herself of what she owes this baby; the second chance it brought her. Not the other way around.

That happiness soon fades, is replaced by fear as to what will become of her. She tries to concentrate on what would have become of her had she not had this baby. At university, she used to think of the footprints she would leave in the sand. Then, she had gone back to Liverpool. She hadn't meant to stay, but she had bumped into Anthony again. It had seemed only a small surrender in a constant and sometimes pointless struggle. She thought she knew what she was, but that night, it had seemed easier not to be and she allowed him to tell her he loved her and always had.

A mist has come in, fast from the sea, and she watches as the heron glides away from her, swallowed up by the sea vapours that race up the River Dee.

She goes back to the big cushion and sits with her legs apart, stroking her belly, thinking the baby will come sooner than anyone thinks. For an odd moment, she wishes Anthony

139

was here, wishes she could have loved him the way he deserves. If only she could be held, for a moment or so, or a whole afternoon. If only her father was here and she was young again, before it all happened.

A sob forms in the back of her throat and she swallows it away, heaves herself to her feet, not able to keep still. She wants to be out amongst the world. She craves a conversation and reaches for the door, twists the handle but it resists, locked. 'Let me out,' she calls, banging on the door. The baby kicks again and nobody is there, save the life inside her.

Pulford hands across the free tickets that Phillip Ramone had given him. The transvestite on the kiosk flutters his thick lashes at the bashful young sergeant, gives him the knowingest of looks. 'New blood,' he purrs in a gravelly voice that comes between glazed, red lips.

'Is Phillip in?' says Pulford, trying to avoid the transvestite's look. Instead of looking him in the eye, he unwittingly diverts his attention to the thoroughly convincing cleavage.

'Oh my,' murmurs the transvestite. 'I'm afraid he doesn't take visitors.'

Josie leans across, shows her warrant card.

'Aah. I see.' He looks Pulford up and down. 'Make sure you come in uniform next time. I'm Juanita, if you need to know.'

They press against the crowd in the bar and force through onto the dance floor. Above, and in front of his office on the mezzanine, Phillip Ramone sits alone at a small table alternately sipping champagne and sucking on a replica cigarette. He looks washed out, perusing his punters like the curmudgeonly judge on a talent show.

Jimmy Somerville is belting out his version of 'I Feel Love' and Bronski Beat's furious rhythm fills the dance floor. The crowd spins round, hands behind their backs, as if they are handcuffed dervishes.

'You didn't waste any time cashing in your freebies,' says Phillip Ramone.

'Events have overtaken us,' says Josie, pulling up a chair and sitting alongside Ramone who pours them each a glass of champagne. She notices it is vintage Taittinger and can't help taking a sip. Looking down at the dancing crowd, she suddenly feels energised.

They sit close together, so the three of them can hear each other.

'Events?'

'It's a shame you didn't tell us how Kerry came to get her residency.'

'I never said my memory was perfect. Did I?'

'Somebody persuaded you to take her on. On Sean's behalf.'

Bronski Beat fades to nought and is replaced by the effortless boom of Rick Astley's masquerading soul.

Eventually, Ramone says, 'You should watch yourselves.'

'We need to hear it from you, Phillip.'

'Somebody's been shooting their mouth off. He'll find out, and woe betide the poor fuckers when he does.'

'Did they meet through you, Phillip?' asks Josie.

Ramone shakes his head. 'You're City police, right?'

Josie nods.

'And he's a west London boy, as you know. If I were you, that would be my excuse to leave well alone.'

'I'll make it easy for you,' says Josie, leaning forward, taking another sip of Taittinger. 'Was Tommy Given seeing Kerry Degg?'

Phillip Ramone appears to shudder.

'You have to tell us, Phillip,' says Pulford. 'We won't be dropping this and soon we'll be sitting down with Given.'

Ramone shakes his head. He looks down on his dancing clients but can't derive a smile from the joyous abandon. Tonight, he remains uninfected. 'He wouldn't do that to Sean.'

'He looked out for Sean?'

'That's how it seemed to me, is all I can say. And it's all I will say. Tommy's clean,' says Ramone, standing up. 'Always has been. And that's official.'

Sixteen

Michael Flanagan looks kind of defeated when he spots Staffe, waiting for him by the pond in Princes Park. He sits alongside Staffe on a bench and for a few moments they watch two young men cast their lines. They are set for the day and have a windshield and cool boxes and chairs. They chat and laugh, like old boys.

'Why didn't you tell me you saw Zoe the day she was taken?' says Staffe.

'I was ashamed.'

'You had a row. What was it about?'

'What makes you think we had a row?'

'What makes *you* think I won't do everything I can to save Zoe? Why didn't you tell me?'

'She doesn't love him, you know. Can you imagine what it must be like, to carry the life of someone you can't stand? The first baby nearly killed her. I don't care about no more grandkids. *She's* my baby.'

'She was going to get rid of her baby, wasn't she, Michael?'

'It'd be a life sentence, to bring it up when you think where it came from. A constant reminder. I can see how she saw it.'

'But you wanted her to keep the baby, even so?'

'That's because I just can't imagine her not. You know, what that involves.'

'I need to know exactly what you did that day. Where you were.'

'I wouldn't harm her. I couldn't. I just didn't know what to do for the best.' He stands up, takes a marbled blue notebook from his pocket. It has an elastic band around it and when Michael removes the band, he takes a stack of betting slips from the back of the notebook. 'It's my weakness. She thinks I don't do it no more.' He laughs: the weak satisfaction of a meaningless victory. 'I keep track, see, of what I stake and what I win.' He flicks through the pile of pink slips and picks out half a dozen. 'All losers from that day.' He reads out the names and the racecourses and the times, even the odds, from the 1.05 handicap chase at Wincanton to the 5.43 dog race at Walthamstow.

'But I had a winner.' He flicks through the notebook. 'Thrice in Bundoran. I had two quid on at fifteen to two. I ended the day a quid down. Not much, for a whole afternoon's entertainment.'

'You could have got these slips from off the betting-shop floor.'

Michael looks hurt, says, 'Ask in the shop. They know me.' He sits back down and they watch the two fishermen for a while. 'She came to me for help and what did I do? I made it worse. I said she had to let it run its course. I was worried for her. You should have seen her the last time, when she lost it. I couldn't bear the thought of her having that done to her. I was being selfish, that's what it was.'

'Anthony knew, didn't he?'

'She was scared and she came to me. He knew all right, the bastard.'

'What do you think he might have done?'

Michael shakes his head.

Staffe says, 'Anthony told me he couldn't ever hurt Zoe.'

'He did that to her, though – when she wasn't interested.'

'Do you think . . . ?'

'Don't!' says Michael. 'I can't think about that. I'd kill him. Fucking kill him.' His hands turn into fists and he bites his lip. 'I'm sorry, Inspector. I don't swear. Not normally.' After a while, Michael stands up and says, 'I turned a blind eye. It's not what a father should do.'

Josie watches DI Smethurst walking down from Putney Bridge to the riverbank. He is Smet, to his friends – not that he has many – and he's with the Met; and some kind of a mucker of Staffe's, though Josie would never put them together.

Every so often, Smet tries to hitch his belt a little higher, but it doesn't last more than a dozen paces. He sucks on a cigarette and has a sheen of sweat on his forehead and jowls. As he gets close, it is clear that he doesn't know what he's looking for, so Josie stands up from the low wall that runs between the Duke's Head and the Thames and says, 'DI Smethurst?'

His eyes light up and he can't help himself look her up and down. 'Chancellor? Have we met?'

'I was in uniform.'

'Is he here?'

'Given? He's inside.'

'You have got the all-clear to do this?'

'Yes,' says Josie, looking away, across the river.

'You spoke to Staffe. He said it was OK?'

145

'Yes.' She turns quickly, pouts at him, watches him blink.

'Good. This *is* a favour, you know.' Smethurst leads the way between the luncheon stragglers and the early bar, through the dining room and right into the front snug. There, dappled in the low spring sun, is a suited heavyweight with a steely mop of golden hair. He has an open shirt with thick gold around his neck and jewels on most of his fingers; a loose-fitting watch the size of a manhole cover. He is flanked and faced by cronies who are in tucks of laughter at something he has said. The table is littered with empty and full heavy-glassed tumblers of whisky and half-pints of lager.

'To what the pleasure?' Tommy calls to Smet, raising a glass. He doesn't see Josie straight away, but when he does, he stands, cuffs his neighbour and offers her the chair.

'Maybe not here,' says Smet.

'I'm drinking.'

Smet leans down, puts a hand on Tommy's shoulder as if they are on the same side and whispers something.

'This lot can fuck off,' says Tommy. 'Ten minutes?'

Smet nods and the cronies gather up their drinks. As one, they take out their packs of cigarettes, no doubt glad of the relief.

Josie figures that Smet must have told Tommy they were here about Sean Degg, and that Sean isn't a subject to be discussed in front of that particular group of hangers-on.

Tommy holds up his hand towards the barman and makes a rapid gesture with a twist of his golden hand. By the time Josie and Smet have settled into their seats, three whiskies and three halves of lager have been brought to the table and the occupants of the neighbouring table ushered away.

Tommy clinks glasses with Smet, then Josie. Smet necks his whisky and Josie follows suit, swallowing away her flinch.

'Didn't take you long,' says Tommy.

'You've read about Sean's wife?' says Josie.

'Who's running this?' says Tommy, swiping Josie with a sideways, dismissive glance.

'This is DC Chancellor, City CID,' says Smet. 'I'm only here for the beer.'

Tommy laughs from deep within his keg chest, says, 'Constable skirt, hey? I must be going down in the world.'

'Sean Degg has gone missing,' says Josie. 'He's a suspect for his wife's murder and we know that we'd find him in no time if people would talk to us. It seems that people won't talk about Sean, though. Some say that Sean is a low-life and would have got his comeuppance years ago if it wasn't for you.' She tries her damnedest to hold Tommy Given's look.

'Tongues wag in the strangest ways,' says Tommy.

'Maybe Sean told us about you and him.'

Tommy plays with his heavy watch and looks past Josie as he addresses her. 'You'll get to hear some fucking shit in your line of work, Constable. People might call Sean "low-life", but take it from me, he's not. He has integrity. That's a hard thing to find.' Tommy curls his lip.

'What makes you and him so close?'

'What makes a tight little missy like you want to work with scum like Smet?'

'Whoah, Tommy.'

'You steer clear. You go asking questions about me and I'll know. It's bad for business.'

'Sean's in trouble, Mr Given. He needs to hand himself in. Why do you protect him?'

'Fuck off.' Tommy raises his hand again and flicks his wrist. The barman collects the empty glasses and the hangers-on come back in. They sit close to Josie, eyeing her up and getting lewd.

Josie says, 'You're a part of this investigation, Mr Given – until you can prove we're wasting our time.'

'You just try, missy. See what happens.'

'Come on, Chancellor,' says Smet, taking her by the arm.

She wrings herself free, watches him weave his way out through the crowded bar, and then follows him – at a distance.

Staffe persuades the constable at Liverpool General to let him see Anthony Bright, dark-eyed and with his left wrist heavily bandaged. He is pale, seems to have lost much weight this past week.

As soon as Anthony sees Staffe, he can tell the inspector means business. He drags a chair up to Anthony's bed, talks fast, in a raised whisper.

'We need to go way back, to when you first impregnated Zoe. Shall we call it that? I guess we could call it a lot of things, couldn't we? How long were you with her before you realised she found you vile? Before you had to persuade her because you just didn't do it for her? You must have felt small.' Staffe brings his finger and thumb almost together, right in front of Anthony Bright's eyes.

Bright looks up at the uniformed PC by the door. He leans right back in his bed, but Staffe leans further forward – still in his face. 'It's a strange kind of love, that, isn't it, Anthony? You've got your house and that's a two-year-old car in the drive. But it doesn't count for much when your wife won't carry your baby unless you force her, hey, Bright?'

'Get away from me.'

Staffe reaches into his hip pocket, puts the parcel on the bed. He unwraps it, painstakingly. Immediately, you can smell it. The herring skin is grey and silver. It is shiny and the smell of its souse is sweet and acidic. 'For you,' says Staffe, offering Anthony the rollmop.

'Get it away from me. I hate that shit. Why d'you bring that? Why?'

Staffe reaches into his inside pocket and slams a piece of paper on the desk, followed by a pen. He turns to the uniformed officer, shouts, 'Get this bastard's lawyer in here. He needs to think again about his statement. Now!'

'I can't, sir. I . . .'

The PC looks around, shifts from the doorway, standing to one side to let DI Alicia Flint into the room. 'Inspector Staffe,' she says. 'A word.'

In the corridor, Staffe and Flint face each other.

She says, 'You shouldn't be here. Not after the other day. Not without me.'

'I got him herring. He doesn't like it.'

'What?'

'Zoe used to buy rollmops in Parkgate. They should be for him, but he doesn't like them.'

'You need to leave him to me, Inspector. You really do,' says Alicia.

* * *

Catherine Killick hangs her keys on the coat stand's hook in the Minton-tiled hallway of her fine cottage on the outskirts of the New Forest. The nights are beginning to draw out and she makes her way into the large farmhouse kitchen, listens to her security aide manoeuvre his way across the gravel drive and drive away, into town for the Chinese.

She places her red ministry box on the scrubbed pine table and kicks off her shoes. Miss Etheridge has been in and set the fires, and a smell of burning wood hangs in the house. She rubs her stomach and opens the box, flicks through the papers. She will do them first thing in the morning, knows she will rise at first light, if not before; she doesn't have to be at the hospital until ten.

Cathy wonders how the press – or, God forbid, the people – will react to Vernon Short's bill being laid to rest; and what of the missing woman in Liverpool? Will she be superseded by some different kind of news altogether?

Her husband, Alex, is in Brussels until Friday and she misses him. He should be back tomorrow, and she was quite cruel when he left. She wants to take back what she said. He is a good man, will be a good father.

The wood crackles in the grate and she eases herself slowly down to her knees and removes the guard, riddles the fire, feels its heat on her face. This baby is a long time coming. Upstairs, the floor creaks and she looks behind her. For a moment, she thinks Alex might have come home early, but then the radiators rattle and she realises it must be the house groaning as it warms through.

Cathy watches the flames and loses herself, wonders how much time she will ever have for this baby. She will be forty-two next year and when she found out she was heavy with child she had cried tears of unrestrained joy. Alex had been shocked, said he didn't know why she was so happy, said that she had never said she wanted a baby so badly; had said nothing about the baby that she could have had, fourteen years earlier when she was first shortlisted for that safe seat in East Hamlets.

She stands, heaving herself up on the brass coal box at the side of the fire, not wanting to think about that. Cathy puts a milk pan on the Aga and pours in some blue top. She watches it begin to roll, sliding it off the heat so it doesn't boil, and she thinks what a wonder it is, that she has made it so far – to here. All she ever dreamed of. She tips a wary glug of whisky into the pan and puts it on the table, lets it sit until the spirited milk forms a skin, which she will skim. She will sleep well tonight.

After the first sip, her head feels gladder, as if she is better prepared for what's coming at her.

The floorboards creak again, and again she turns around, hoping she might see Alex in the doorway and she gasps, thinks for a moment that he is here. She actually puts her tongue hard on the roof of her mouth to say the 'D' of 'Darling.'

The eyes of the man in the balaclava are wide and mad, and his lips are the red of pillar boxes. His teeth are yellow. 'Sit down,' he says, coming towards her and tapping a leather cosh against his thigh.

Cathy cannot move. The baby presses down on her bladder as the man takes her by the arm.

His breath is sweet and bad. He places the end of his leather cosh on her stomach.

Cathy misses her breath and her heart misses two. Her mouth loses its form and her lungs are empty. 'Why?' she whispers, unable to look at him.

'You know why. You can't pick and choose just to suit your own fancy.'

He touches her and she makes tiny steps as he directs her towards an armchair beside the dresser. He takes out a phone, presses a number and she hears her own tone pipe up from within her handbag. It is 'Dreams' by Fleetwood Mac and for an instant she catches a scent of that young girl. Less blemished.

The man grabs her bag and takes out the phone, then removes the battery. He throws the two parts of the phone on the fire. Curiously, Cathy calls out, 'You can't do that.' She doesn't actually know what happens if you put batteries on a fire, just that it's bad.

'You think I want to do this?' He drags a dining chair to her and sits on it. Once more, he rests the end of his cosh on her belly. It is heavy, harder than it looks and she thinks it has lead in it. She bites her lip, can easily imagine herself crying.

The man says, 'You kill babies, don't you, Home Secretary? That's what people will say. They'll say, what's so special about her baby?' When he talks his lips seem mad and out of kilter with his words. 'They'll say that you choose who lives and who doesn't, so why can't someone like me?' He presses the cosh and she shifts back, the chair hard to her spine and nowhere further to go. He follows, with the tip of the cosh.

'I don't . . .' says Cathy, unsure what she could say for the best.

'You know what I'm talking about, don't you? I'm here to speak for the ones who have no voice.' He says this by rote, like a child in a classroom. He stares Cathy in the eye. Everything is still. 'And that includes your child.'

Cathy loses her breath again. She gasps.

'You had your career, then. And now, you are having your baby. Now it suits.' He stops talking, leans back and his wet lips spread into a smile.

Cathy sees a slackening in the man's eyes.

He lets the cosh slide down and away from her stomach and he stands. He breathes deep. His chest rises and falls, slower. He envelops his top lip within his bottom, then opens his mouth, saying as slowly as he can make himself. 'We want the killing to stop but we know that can't happen, not overnight. But we can make it better. You can make it better. We get the bill, right? This way, or the other. It is our time. It's what the people want – for Vernon to change his mind, before it's too late.'

He tosses the cosh to Cathy and she catches it, just, but its tip knocks into her. She holds it, watches him go. She hears the door close, then his steps across the gravel. And she cries, and cries, holding and loving her baby – and mourning, too.

Seventeen

Staffe tips a third miniature into the plastic cup which the Metropolitan Hotel has provided for his bathroom. He is now on the brandy, having drunk the Bell's and the Glenfiddich. He should really go down to the White Star, which is his kind of pub – cloistered with panelled booths, segregated from the bar by stained-glass panes and with an array of proper beer. But here he is, sitting at the foot of his bed looking out onto the city. Between the civic monoliths he can see the top of the Liver Building, the black sky beyond, laid out above Wales.

He slowly goes over what Zoe's father had said to him and what he said to Anthony Bright, and what Flint had said to him. He knows Bright is still holding out on him, but can see that he might have gone too far. Sometimes, though, you have to go too far.

Staffe looks at the brandy and swirls it, watches it catch the light. Round and round.

The phone rings and he downs the spirit in one, feels its burn, easing into the gut of him. 'Yes,' he says.

'We've got a problem.' It is Pennington and he sounds unnerved. Pennington is never unnerved – or so he would have it.

'*You've* got a problem?'

The phone is silent. He can practically hear Pennington seething.

Pennington says, 'Jesus.'

'What is it, sir?' In the window, he can see himself looking him in the eye. He seems lost, with the waterfront city behind him.

'I'm in bloody Hampshire, man. In the middle of nowhere. This case is out of control.'

'Hampshire? Why didn't you send Pulford?'

'I'm trusting you, Staffe. This goes no further.'

'Go on.'

'I've just been with the Home Secretary.'

'Cathy Killick?' Staffe feels bilious. He should have eaten.

'She's been threatened. They said they'd kill her baby. The Home Secretary! It's a bloody disaster.'

'It must be that bill of Vernon Short's.'

'Straight to the top of the class, Staffe.'

'You need to get hold of Lesley Crawford.'

'She's gone missing. *Quelle* bloody *surprise*! You'd better get yourself back down here. *Tout suite*, man. I don't care what time you get in. You call me. And not a word of this to anyone.'

Staffe puts down the phone and packs as quickly as he can. When he is done, when he looks out on the city, glimpsing the estuary between the buildings, it feels wrong. His work here is not done and he picks up the phone, calls Alicia Flint.

'I have to go,' he says. 'I just wanted to say good luck with the case.' He can hear Ethan shouting in the background.

'You have to go?' Despite what happened with Anthony Bright, she sounds disappointed.

'Zoe went to Parkgate. She bought herrings for somebody.'

'Bloody herrings again?'

'I think it's important.'

Ethan screams.

She says, 'I've got to go,' and hangs up.

Josie sips her tea and watches Sheila Archibald go through the archway into the dining room to tend to Miles and Maya. Husband John knocked it through from the lounge himself, so they could keep an eye on the children while they had their dinner. John is proud of his work.

The Archibalds like their quiz shows and the opening titles for another programme come up on the big old tank of a telly. John watches the drama unfold with one eye as the children sit at the dining table, despite Josie's suggestion that Miles and Maya might be better upstairs.

She says to John, 'The father has gone to ground. Has he been in touch?'

For a moment, John looks confused. 'The father?'

'Sean.'

'Aah.'

'You know he's not . . .' Josie lowers her voice to a whisper. '. . . the real dad.'

'That's not our concern.'

Through the archway, Sheila takes the plates away from the children, even though they haven't touched the fish fingers or peas on their plates. The oven chips are all gone. Sheila says, 'No clean plates, no pudding.'

'I want a biscuit,' says Maya.

'Bedtime,' says Sheila.

The children slide off their chairs, looking glum. It is seven o'clock.

'We thought he might have tried to see them,' says Josie. 'You'll call if he does.'

Sheila takes the children upstairs and John Archibald looks at Josie from the corner of his eye. 'We're not involved. It's our misfortune, that's all it is. You have to understand, we won't be roped in.'

'Kerry must have talked to you about their real father. That's your concern, surely – in the children's interests.'

'She only came round once, we told you.'

Josie finishes her tea and places the cup and saucer on the coffee table. It is glass-topped and has a shelf below. On the shelf are a couple of romantic novels, a TV guide from the tabloids and a travel brochure – for cruises.

She contemplates asking John if he and Sheila are planning a trip, but decides against, instead says, 'There's the funeral to think about. We'll let you know, of course, but I can't say when it might be. I suppose Kerry's sister will be the one to organise it – now the dad's missing. The children should be there, but I'll talk to the care worker about that. She'll do an assessment.'

'We wouldn't want any part of that – the funeral, I mean.'

'No, of course not.'

Upstairs, a child cries. Josie thinks it is Maya but can't be sure.

She says good evening to John Archibald and at the door, which is panelled with frosted glass, she reminds him to let her know when Sean Degg gets in touch.

'What makes you think he will?'

'Oh, he will,' says Josie. 'He isn't a bad man and he's the closest those children have got to a real father.'

'You can't know that, though.' John looks up the stairs, follows the noise from the children and his wife. He looks like a child in a supermarket aisle, bereft of its mother.

Josie takes a step closer, softly says, 'We'll get whoever did this. We owe it to those children, don't we?'

John nods, averting his eyes. He looks down at the telephone stand by the door.

'Between you and me, John, we know who Kerry was seeing. We know who was looking out for her – or should I say, Sean.'

Upstairs, a commotion breaks out. Maya cries. Josie knows it is her for sure this time, because above the crying and the stern coaxing of Sheila Archibald, she hears the voice of a young boy pleading, 'I want my dad. I'll tell him. I'll tell him.'

Josie has heard enough and lets herself out, leaves the Archibalds to their contrived domestic. Outside, she turns right at the gate and waves to John, who watches her – all the way. She goes past her car, which is unmarked and on the opposite side of the street. At the end of the road, she turns right again and waits for three minutes, then goes back onto the Archibalds' street, texts Pulford and tells him it might be time. Then she waits ten more minutes and returns to her car.

It is cold in the car but she resists the temptation to turn on the engine and suck in the hot air. From here, she can see the Archibalds' home quite clearly. The upstairs lights go off and she tries not to dwell on what long, sleepless gloom the children face. Downstairs, the hall light comes on. Two shapes appear in the frosted panes of the front door, beside the telephone stand.

Josie texts Pulford again: 'Archibalds calling. Anything your end?'

Pulford gestures to the barmaid from the side bar of the Duke's Head and asks for another glass of low-alcohol lager. All the while, through that gap between the optics and the counter in the opposite bar, he keeps an eye on what goes on in the front snug.

Tommy Given and his entourage have been guffawing and drinking, slapping each other and taking the piss out of the barmaid, since early doors – just like Smet had said. Smet didn't have to go to a file or refer it around the Met. He knew, straight off, and he told Pulford to steer well clear and not be seen. For fuck's sake not to be seen.

Some folk have ventured into Tommy's sphere, but few have stayed. A couple of old-timers schlep against the bar, happy to be victims of the gang's chidings. They give as good as they get. They're in some kind of circle, and probably have been since the good old days.

But now, the laughter stops. Pulford leans down, gets his change, and sees that Tommy has a serious look on his face. Pulford leans further down so he can see Tommy properly beneath the optics. He sees all of Tommy for the first time, as he stands: how broad he is, how hard he is.

Tommy raises the phone to his ear and pushes one of his cronies out of his way. He has a good face – bright blue eyes and a strong jaw, a boxer's nose and big, golden-brown hair, all combed back. His skin is white, almost translucent, and he has a scar across one cheek, from his eye to the lobe of his ear. There's a big ring on each big finger of both his big hands.

He makes his way out of the bar, pausing at the door, phone still raised to his ear. Pulford can't make out what he's saying but it's bad news for somebody. He points at one of the entourage, who stands, leaves the rest of his orange juice. The driver?

As soon as Tommy is gone, Pulford turns his back to the bar and texts Josie: 'They're coming. Make scarce. On my way.'

Josie knows she should make herself scarce. Pulford had told her what Smet said about not being seen and she twirls the car keys around her finger, looks back at the Archibalds' house. The shapes in the frosted windows of the front door are gone and the hall lights flick off. She knows it will be fifteen, twenty minutes, if he comes at all. What harm can she do?

She thinks about Grace, and what it must have been like to be born like that. What kind of repercussions there will be. She's been thinking through the possibilities all day.

Josie does her hair into a high-up ponytail and pulls a baseball cap from the glove compartment, then teases her ponytail through the gap in the back of the cap. She drags a pea jacket from under the passenger seat and takes off her tailored woollen blazer, folds it neatly and places it under the seat. Josie zips the pea jacket right up and checks her watch, kills minutes by sifting the backlog of texts on her mobile. As she does it, she realises how seldom she returns messages from her friends. She can't remember the last time she saw any of them.

She gets out of the car and pulls the peak of her cap right down. There's a minimart on the corner and she walks up to it, slouching, hands thrust in the pockets of the short jacket.

It is cold, now the sun is down. There might be a frost tonight.

In the minimart, which does halal, she keeps an eye on the street. There's every chance they will come by this way – from off the North Circular. She asks for a can of Diamond Power and the owner IDs her. For a second she feels a glow of satisfaction, but has to be careful not to let him see her warrant card as she fumbles in her purse.

She loiters in the shop doorway, as if its light might make her warm. She snaps the ring-pull and takes a sip, tries not to baulk as its sickly sour zings in her mouth and throat. She moves away, realising the doorway isn't the place to be.

Josie leans on a wall obscured from the Archibalds' street by a privet hedge. She can just about see the house if she takes a step back from the hedge and, as each car passes, she raises the can to her lips, sips a little. After a while, the supercharged cider laps up to her senses, makes her feel kind of happy, optimistic about the night. Tomorrow, she will text her mates. All of them. For sure. She will be a better friend.

A car approaches. It's a Merc GL, she thinks. It rolls high and comes faster than the others did. She steps back, tight against the privet and raises the can, swigs for real. But she can't help sneaking a peek. Her heart misses a beat. Her guts feel loose. She would remember Tommy Given anywhere.

He's in the driver's seat, alone.

Another car comes: fast, but not quite so fast. It is Pulford, which makes her happy and suddenly she feels stupid for getting herself worked up. All they need is to clock Tommy Given going into the Archibalds'. Nothing more.

She lowers her can and raises the peak of her cap, so he can see her, but he is on his phone, slowing now. Another car follows behind Pulford but turns off down the side street, parks up just past the shop. She wants to wave to Pulford, but knows she can't and presses the half-empty can into the privet and moves off, towards the minimart. Tommy's car has slowed right down outside the Archibalds', its brake lights glowing red – but then they fizzle out and the car moves off. She'll text Pulford from inside the shop. But what will she buy?

Josie stops by the entrance to the shop and looks in the window. She could get some gum, or a magazine – *Just Seventeen* or something like that. This makes her smile. She hears a voice, from behind.

'Bad girl.'

Then she feels flesh on her face, her mouth; then the dullest pain, the slowest fall that has no landing. And straight away, she is in the land of Nod.

PART THREE

Eighteen

Her clothes tack to her when she tries to move. Her bones ache and her head feels brittle. She tries to move, but it hurts too much and she thinks she might have broken something. She opens her eyes and it is too bright. She blinks, squints at an oval light which has a cage around it; and she can smell excrement and bleach.

Josie raises a hand to her face and feels her chin and cheeks and eyes. She puts her other hand to the floor. Is it the floor? She pushes herself up and grimaces through the pain as she swivels, looking around the room.

She is on a bench with a mattress no thicker than a pack of cigarettes; a steel toilet in the corner and a steel basin; a thin window, high up, and a big steel door with a spyhole in it.

'Shit,' says Josie, realising where she is – that she is on the other side.

She tries to remember how she came here. She was up at the Archibalds' house and she was waiting for Pulford. Wasn't she?

Josie looks down, sees her legs swing from the bench. Her bare legs. She looks again and feels for her clothes but all she has on is a short, tight minidress that has ridden up and which is ripped across the midriff. It's not her dress. She doesn't have a dress like this.

She heaves herself up and has to lean on the bench for support. She tugs the dress down and makes her way, gingerly, to the door, pounds on it.

Eventually, a metal plate slides across and a female face appears. Josie says, 'What am I doing here? I'm police.'

'Yeah, right,' says the woman. 'You sticking with that shit?'

'My name's Josie. Josie Chancellor. DC Chancellor.'

'It's not what your ID says.'

'What?'

'You give me a shout when you're through wasting our time.'

'I want to make a call. I'm entitled.'

The metal plate slides shut, with a sharp clank. Josie's head resounds with pain and her thirst burns. She bangs on the door but it hurts her hands. She shouts at the spyhole but her throat is dry as ash.

Eventually, she eases herself back to the bench and tries to recall what happened to her, but the last thing she can remember is being held, thinking it was Pulford. And music. Was there music?

Vernon Short knows better than to drive his own car. Six months ago, after spending nine hours over lunch at his club, he was pulled over by the police just a quarter of a mile from his town house in Pimlico. He blew eighty milligrams and immediately insisted on being allowed the opportunity to give a blood sample. Then his lawyer turned up and discovered that Vernon had only been given one shot at the breathalyser. He instructed his client not to proceed with the blood sample unless he could be breathalysed again. The duty sergeant had every confidence in his bag of crystals. The second time, two and a half hours later, and having drunk an entire bottle of Milk of Magnesia, Vernon blew twenty-nine; the Milk of Magnesia, being alkaline, had defeated the alcohol in Vernon's system. He drove home, licence intact. The first thing he did next day was to hire Bob Tomkins, driver.

Tomkins waits for his client on double yellows in Berkeley Square, the engine running – to keep him warm and to present the argument that he's not actually parked.

Staffe taps on the passenger window, opens the door and gets in alongside Bob, says, 'How's it going, Tomkins?'

'I don't know you.'

He shows his warrant card and says, 'Let's keep it that way. When's your boss back?'

Ten minutes later, Vernon Short gets in the back and tells the driver to take him home. Five minutes after that he says, noticing Staffe in the front and breathing alcohol fumes all over the car, 'What in God's name are you doing here? I have nothing to say to you.'

Staffe turns round, raises a finger to his lips. 'I'll be honest with you, Vernon. I'm not supposed to be here.'

'So get out.'

'You need to tell me what Catherine Killick promised you.'

'What makes you think I'll say anything to you?'

'Because there isn't a cat in hell's chance you'll get a place in the Cabinet. She'll fob you off with some talk of a reshuffle and by the time it comes around, you'll have fucked up. It might be another driving mishap.'

'How d'you know about that?'

'Or a woman, or whatever it is that floats your boat. I bet she hasn't even told you what they've done now?'

'They?'

'They? Maybe it's you. I don't think you've got the gumption, or the balls. But you might know someone who has.'

Vernon Short looks perplexed, and is clearly a quarter cut. He rubs his temples and screws up his eyes. They practically disappear into the podgy flesh of his face. 'The balls to do what?'

'I can't tell you. It's a matter of national security.'

'You know nothing.'

'What was in the bag, Vernon?'

'Bag? I don't know anything about the bag.'

Strange, thinks Staffe, to employ the definite article. Poor Vernon shouldn't drink.

'Drop me at the end of the street. There'll be someone watching your place when you get there. You say nothing, just go in and wait five minutes then go out the back. I'll be there. You let me in.'

'Why should I?'

'Because it wouldn't do for Cathy Killick to know you've been exchanging favours with Lesley Crawford. Not after what's happened.'

'What *has* happened?'

'Honestly, Vernon, you don't want to know.'

'It involves the Home Secretary?'

Staffe raises his eyebrows.

'Sweet Jesus,' says Vernon, leaning back, blowing out his cheeks. A man out of his depth, it would seem.

* * *

Short holds a thick, cut-glass tumbler of scotch as he opens the back door and lets the inspector into his home.

Staffe mooches around the kitchen. He opens the door to a utility room and downstairs loo. The room is stacked to the gunnels with Glenlivet and San Pellegrino. But contrary to what you might expect, Vernon recycles. Of course he does. The press probably goes through his rubbish. And he puts his empty bottles in a hessian eco-friendly bag – from Waitrose, *naturellement*.

Staffe wraps a plastic bag around the handle and picks up the eco bag, shows it to Vernon. 'Whose prints do you think I might find on this?'

'What?' Vernon is incredulous. Then the penny drops, his mouth agape.

'The question is, Vernon, what was in it?'

'I'm calling my lawyer. Anybody could have touched that bag.'

Staffe weighs up his options, trying to think four, five, six moves ahead. He has his finger on Vernon's queen. Why not take it? He says, 'Put down the phone, Vernon. This is for your ears only.'

'What?'

'You have what came in the bag, don't you?'

'No.'

'I'll do you a deal. You needn't tell me a truth until I've told you a truth.'

The Rt Hon Vernon Short sits at his kitchen table, looking at the bottle of Glenlivet. Sometimes, all he really wants, has ever wanted, is an easy life and he curses his father, his family – the tradition. 'Tell me. What has she done?'

'No matter what we tell each other, Vernon, this is our secret.'

Vernon nods.

'They have made a threat – against the baby inside her.'

'Good God.' Vernon leans forward, elbows on knees, blowing his cheeks out.

'I'm your only friend, Vernon. Nobody else would tell you. You have to put your faith in me. Imagine, after what has happened to her, what Catherine Killick will do if she knows you have been in touch with Lesley Crawford.'

'You don't know that.'

Staffe holds up the bag, wiggles it. 'What was in it, Vernon?'

'How can I trust you?'

'I'm all you have.'

Staffe takes out his phone, scrolls through his numbers, knowing that the Home Secretary does not feature amongst its data. 'I will talk to Catherine Killick.'

Vernon sits at the table, puts his fat, balding head in his little hands. His nails are perfectly manicured.

'Tell me, Vernon.'

The would-be Minister for Enterprise gives the inspector a pitying, withering look. 'How did you know about Lesley Crawford?'

'I've told you my truth.'

Vernon reaches into the inside pocket of his jacket, hands two documents to Staffe.

The first is dated the second of May 1997 and is confirmation that Catherine Killick had been selected as candidate for East Hamlets. It is still, Staffe knows, the safest of safe seats.

The second document is confirmation of an appointment for a procedure at the City Women's Clinic, and dated the sixth of May 1997.

'Apparently, tennis players do it all the time, poor cow,' says Vernon. 'If she'd come clean before she was made up to the Cabinet, she would probably have been all right. But this bill of mine won't go away. You've seen the papers. If this gets out, she's finished.'

'Why wouldn't Lesley Crawford just publish this?'

'It's an ace up the sleeve. Only one ace and only one sleeve. You wait for the chips to pile to their highest. You'd do well to remember that,' says Vernon.

'You mean Lesley wants her bill back.'

'It's my bill, Inspector.'

Staffe realises that Vernon is already plotting ahead, seeing how this might come back to kiss him on both cheeks. 'If the police reveal this information, it puts your bill back in play. It will destroy the Home Secretary, but you're OK. You've just lost a leg-up in the next reshuffle.'

'I could never reveal this. You know that.' Vernon nods at the papers in Staffe's hands. 'How could I? A man of my integrity?'

Staffe meets Pulford at the end of Lesley Crawford's street in Southfields. He has picked up the long-term unclaimed car from the pound, arranged by Jombaugh, in case the Queen's men are surveilling on behalf of Cathy Killick.

'I'm sick of the sight of this bloody street,' says Pulford.

'We wouldn't be here if you'd kept tabs on Crawford.'

Pulford looks exhausted, and Staffe says, 'I tried to get Chancellor to take a turn, but she's nowhere to be seen.'

'Oh,' says Pulford, sheepish.

Staffe looks at him, sidelong. 'What's up?'

'Nothing.'

'Call her, then.'

'I've tried. She's not answering.'

'We've worked together how long? Three years? Long enough to know when you're lying.'

Pulford eases off the plastic lid to his designer coffee, nods in the direction of Crawford's house. 'We've checked the ports and airlines and issued a trace on her car, but it seems to have disappeared completely.'

'It could be anywhere. There's thousands of lock-ups in London alone. What about her family?'

'A sister in Nottingham. Her father passed away five years ago and her mother is in New Zealand.'

'What about her bank accounts?'

'I've applied for a warrant to track her use of cards but that's been blocked.'

'Who by?' Staffe knows there couldn't ever be a straight answer to that question. 'Never mind. Don't push it.'

'Are we going in?'

'Not a chance.' Staffe looks at his weary sergeant and contemplates how much he should disclose about his conversation with Vernon Short, decides that in Pulford's case, ignorance is as blissful as this case will get. 'Let's bide our time.'

'For what? You don't know how many hours I've spent on this street.'

'Not enough,' says Staffe. 'Now, tell me where Chancellor is.'

'I don't know.' Pulford looks Staffe in the eye. 'It's the truth. I'm worried about her.'

'Is this anything to do with Tommy Given?'

'I didn't say anything about Given.'

'I know. When were you going to?'

'We know he is something to do with Kerry Degg.'

'Smet told me. He's probably the one looking after Sean.' Staffe opens up his newspaper, swallows away any temptation to tell his sergeant what Short spat up earlier in the day.

He flicks through to the inside pages, doesn't have to read far before he finds an article on the withdrawn bill. There is a third-string paragraph in the editorial about the 'Unborn Rights' bill – not commenting on the pros or cons, but casting aspersions as to the erosion of the democratic process which the withdrawal of the bill would imply. And there are two letters, too, both demanding that the bill be resurrected, at least to present the argument to Parliament.

'What's this, sir?' says Pulford, pointing up the street.

Two men in dark-blue suits get out of a car outside Crawford's house. The car drives away and the men march up to the front door, are let in without knocking.

'She's not in,' says Pulford. 'I'm bloody sure of it.'

'I don't doubt it, Sergeant.'

'Who are they?'

'The good guys,' says Staffe.

'We could follow them,' says Pulford. 'If they find something and it leads them to her, we could . . .'

'Forget it. They'd have us before we got to the South Circ.'

The good news, which Staffe keeps to himself, is that Lesley Crawford is, without doubt, involved with Kerry Degg and Zoe Bright, as well as Cathy Killick – according to the most informed people in the land. And Tommy Given, too, apparently.

'Get hold of Chancellor, Sergeant. Tell her to call me straight away. Day or night.'

Nineteen

Staffe puts on his mask. Through the glass, hatched with reinforcing wire, he watches the two nurses leaning over Baby Grace's cot. The plastic bubble is gone. She will live.

The fair nurse looks up and catches his eye, she smiles and immediately whispers something to her friend – dark and altogether more serious. The fair nurse comes out, extends her hand, says, 'I'm Nurse Natalie. I haven't seen your DC Chancellor recently. You must tell her to come. Grace is going to be fine, just a case of building up her strength, getting her ready for the big bad world.' Nurse Natalie puts her hand on Staffe's arm. 'Keep your mask on. Go see her.'

'Is it OK?' He nods through the glass towards the other nurse, doting over Grace.

'That's only Eve,' and she chuckles, makes a zipping motion with her finger and thumb across her mouth, then pats Staffe on the back and goes on her merry way.

Staffe stands beside Eve. She smells of crisp laundry and fine soap. She looks up at him and smiles, barely moving her mouth; turns back to Grace and sighs, happily, like a freshly sated child.

'I've been away,' says Staffe. 'Up north.'

'Nice for you. Any burlesque up there?'

'I'm not that big a fan.'

'You could have fooled me.'

The baby has colour in her cheeks, now, and tiny, circular plasters on her wrists and arms, where once there were tubes. She looks straight above her, blinks. Staffe wonders what she makes of the world.

'She can't see, not properly,' says Eve. Her voice is brittle at its edge.

'Poor thing.'

Eve looks up at him again, shifts her body. Her eyes glisten. 'It's normal. She will see the shadow of you.' She looks down and up at him, 'But not your hair or your face.'

'If only she could talk,' says Staffe.

Grace kicks her legs, makes a grumpy expression of her face.

'She wants something,' he says.

Eve reaches for the board, hooked on the foot of the cot. 'Almost feeding.'

'Will she know she has no mother?'

'I'm afraid she'll know more than you'd want her to know. You ask strange questions.' Eve looks at Staffe a third time, enquiringly.

He says, 'She looks unhappy. Will you feed her?'

'Not my job.'

They each look at the baby, watching her kick her legs and blink at the ceiling. After a while, Grace becomes less grumpy and Staffe even thinks she smiles. Whatever it is, something has passed, something better has replaced it. One day, she will know that she has no mother and slowly, surely, he feels the full weight of the passing of Kerry and he knows he must find Sean, must discover what dragged this baby's mother below ground and into the dark.

'You look done in,' says Eve.

He laughs. 'This is me on a good day.'

'This is a very good day.'

'You should celebrate,' says Staffe.

Eve looks sad, and turns back to the baby. It is as if, suddenly, she is alone in the room.

'You have someone to celebrate with?'

Eve shrugs, and as she does, with her back to him, Staffe feels something between his heart and his stomach. It is a familiar, absent feeling that makes him sad and joyous. It makes his nerves jag. After a while, just watching the back of her, he says, 'My favourite place is just around the corner. I could, we could . . . They make great sandwiches. Proper bread. I like the corned-beef sandwich. They get the beef from an Argentinian restaurant. It's amazing.'

She turns round, looks unsure about him. 'I'm not hungry.'

'Neither am I.'

'But I'm partial to gin. Plymouth gin.'

'It's just the place for Plymouth gin,' he says.

Eve touches her fingers to her lips and places her hand on Grace's cot as she leaves the room. It is precisely the same thing that Sean Degg had done. The baby is asleep now.

'What's wrong with you, son?' says Jombaugh.

Pulford stirs his tea, down in the station kitchen where the smell of microwaved meals never quite fades to nothing. He has eaten a quarter of his biscuit, has been down here an hour.

Jombaugh pulls up a chair, says again, 'What's wrong?'

Pulford knows that Jom is the closest this place has to a trustworthy confidant – even though he's Staffe's mate. 'There's something I have to tell Staffe, but I can't.'

'Try me. I've known him fifteen years. Sometimes, I'm sad enough to know how he thinks.'

Pulford laughs, keeps looking into his tea. He is sure the only person who would be involved in anything bad happening to Josie would be Tommy Given.

Jombaugh says, 'It's not to do with your . . . you know, your habit.'

'What! How do you know about that?'

'Everybody knows,' laughs Jombaugh.

A mist descends and Pulford feels his hands move away from him, fists clench.

'We're all human,' says Jombaugh.

Pulford can't believe his gambling problems are out of the bag. 'It's not that.'

'Aah, lady problems. Well, she's a belter if you ask me.'

'What?'

'Josie. I thought it was all over between you two. But I see she's not been around the last day or so.'

'I'm worried about her, Jom.'

'I'd worry too, son.'

'She's gone. I mean, really gone. I'm sure she's in trouble.' He puts his hands to his hair. 'Shit, Jom. I think we overstepped the mark. Staffe's going to kill us. Me, at least. I'm going to have to see Tommy Given.'

'Tommy Given? Christ, lad. What have you been fucking with? You don't want him on our patch.'

Pulford weighs up whether to tell Jombaugh what he and

Josie did up at the Archibalds', but he knows they don't yet have the evidence to nail down any relationship between Tommy Given and Sean Degg, or between Given and Kerry; let alone that Tommy might be the father of Kerry's children.

Jom grabs hold of Pulford's arm and hoists him out of the chair. 'You can tell me on the way.'

'The way where?'

'If you're involved with old Tommy, I'm coming with you. Nothing like winding back the years. I'll need to change, though. This is a social call, right? It has to be.' Jombaugh smiles, which irons away the creases from all the reams of paper that are piling up beneath his desk. Suddenly, Jom looks ten years younger.

'Where is the other one?' says Anthony Bright. 'What's his name? Wagstaffe.'

'You'll be dealing with me now, Anthony,' says Alicia Flint.

'You will find Zoe, won't you? She's not . . .'

Alicia Flint watches the doubt peter out into a wordless gaze. 'We have to address the implications of what Inspector Wagstaffe was asking you, about Zoe.'

'I know!' Anthony Bright's hands clench into fists. He flinches as his stitches nip.

Alicia Flint moves her seat away from Anthony, sits in silence. She waits, and waits.

'I know your game,' says Anthony.

'If only we could ask Zoe if this is a game.'

'It was hard for her, to be with me.' He laughs, a paper-bag laugh, sadness punching through. 'Love, eh? That's a bastard. I thought when we were having the first baby it would change her. Change us.'

'Did she see other people?'

'I can't say no. Not for sure. I didn't want to know. I still don't. She did love me, you know. Once. I'm not a nutter. When we were at school, it was her who made the running, and again when she came back.'

'Was she seeing someone special, Anthony?'

He shrugs.

'What about Petal Broome?'

He laughs. 'That dyke! Jesus. No way.'

Alicia Flint has checked all the numbers that Zoe called from her contract phone and the landline, and the calls logged to her extension at the university. 'Did she have two mobiles?'

'Two?'

'You ever had an affair, Anthony?'

'Aah,' he says. 'You don't know what it's like. We'd go months without, you know . . .'

'What made Zoe want another baby?'

Anthony is ready for this question. It's the one that keeps him awake and his response, as far as Alicia Flint can tell, is the unmodified truth. 'Our first baby, the one that died, was blocking us, everything we did. Zoe wanted to do something with her life. That dead baby was stopping us. It was stopping her going forward. I knew she had to have another and she had to have it with me. I said I'd love that baby and look after it, no matter what happened and I still will.' He looks at the floor, puts the palms of his hands to his face, says through them, 'I still fucking would, no matter.' He looks up. 'Said on the radio that baby in London's going to be fine. They saved her, that Baby Grace.'

'But not the mother.'

'I asked if you were going to find her.'

'Did you force Zoe, Anthony?'

'She was cruel to me. She made me feel like I was nothing.'

'And then the baby came.'

'Are you married?' says Anthony.

'No, thank God. I have a child, though.'

'You reckon that's the best way?'

'I need to know about the phone, Anthony. Zoe's other phone. The one with just the one number in it.'

He nods. 'She loved her garden, you know. Always in it.' Anthony laughs. 'Check the bird table. Check in the feed. It's springtime now. The little birdies have been pecking. She never knew I knew. How sad is that?'

Nurse Eve has the rest of the afternoon off. She sips her Plymouth gin slowly. This is her second glass and she has stretched the first tonic.

April winks at Staffe from behind the bar of the Hand and Shears, gives a thumbs-up. Eve can't see her. Staffe takes the drinks back to the tiny snug with the fire.

'So you've nothing to do with the Degg baby,' says Staffe. 'Not directly.'

Eve shakes her head. 'I was in the hospital when she was admitted. I do some liaison work but I'm in pre-nat.' She smiles, reservedly. 'I never drink in the afternoon.'

'There's cause for celebration.'

'You're a bad influence.'

He spots her looking at his hands. He looks at hers – no significant rings. Her Claddagh ring is the right way up, if you were interested. 'It must be hard, working with expectant mothers. I bet you've got some stories to tell.'

'It gives you hope, no matter what the parents are like or how they carry on.'

'Doesn't that make you worry – for the children? How to break the cycle.'

'We make sure they are as healthy as they can be, give them the best shot. And I pray they rise above. Some of them do.'

'You pray?'

'I'm not religious. Are you?'

Staffe shakes his head and finishes his drink, wishes he could stay for another, but he needs to get back into Kerry's life. He needs to peer long and hard at Tommy Given, now.

'I should get your number,' he says.

'And why should you do that?'

'Because I'm going to want to talk to you again.'

'Really?' For a blink of the eye, two, Eve looks worried.

'And I might need to talk to you about Grace, too.'

'Aah.' Her smile is broad and her eyes sparkle in the fire glow. 'I barely know you.'

'That's why you should give me your number.'

'It's not something I do. Not often.'

'I don't ask often.'

'I bet you don't.' She finishes her drink, pulls on her coat, says, 'It's not a good time for me. Thanks for the gin. It takes me back.'

'Back where?'

'Mainly a bad place.'

He watches her go, sees that April looks glum as she watches Eve leave, without so much as a backward glance.

Staffe gets out his notebook, jots down names in a ring around the name 'Kerry'. He writes: Phillip Ramone, Tommy Given, Bridget Lamb, John and Sheila Archibald. Then he flicks back through his notes, finds the name of the teacher from Kerry's poems, writes: Troheagh. Outside the circle, he writes: Eve.

Lesley Crawford looks up at Nottingham Castle, across the Trent from the university lawns, and fondly remembers picnics here. She thinks back to her first tutorial group and pictures the students' faces. Clear as bells, and all girls – for some reason.

Her phone rings, and from the ringtone, she knows immediately that it is the wrong phone. How could it be?

Lesley scrambles in her bag and pulls out the bog-standard Nokia. The battery sounds as if it is about to die, and that name is on the screen. It makes Lesley want to shiver. The name is untrue, now. It fades as the battery dies.

Lesley walks towards the river, takes out the sim card – although it only holds one name – and throws both the handset and the card into the waters, wondering who the hell was using Zoe's phone to call her.

Twenty

Jombaugh whistles when he sees Tommy Given's place, at the end of a hundred-yard track and through a five-bar gate. This is the posh side of Cobham. A breeze shimmers in the tall elms and yews. A dog barks.

The house itself is old and stone, with low, leaded windows and mullions. Out front are a new-plated Merc GL, an old and clearly rehabilitated Alfa Spyder, and a knackered short-wheelbase Land Rover with large mounted spots like frog's eyes and a horse box hooked up. Round the side are four newly built stables in dressed stone.

The dog bowls up, snarling. Some kind of bull terrier with a head like an anvil and shoulders like hams, a tiny arse and slobbering chops. Pulford gasps, takes a step back, but Jombaugh goes down on one knee, as if meeting royalty, and pats the dog, slaps its shoulder and holds its muzzle with both hands, playfully shaking it left and right.

Pulford takes a step away as the dog howls with joy.

'Not lost it, Jom!'

Jom stands up and the dog jumps up at Pulford, snarling.

'Sarge,' whimpers Pulford.

'All right, Tommy? A long time,' says Jombaugh.

'Good for both of us.'

'Sarge!' calls Pulford.

Jombaugh clicks his fingers and pats his thigh and the dog comes to him. 'It's not the dog that bites,' says Jombaugh. He stabs a finger at Tommy Given. 'This one'll poison you.'

'Very funny,' says Tommy. He looks at Pulford as if he might recognise him. 'Not so funny, is why you're here.'

'We need to eliminate you is all,' says Jom. 'Just tell us where you were last night, Tommy.'

'Why should I?'

'Let's not make a fuss, in front of your family.'

'Fuck that, Jom. You can ask my wife. I was in the Duke's Head early doors. There's six of my mates can vouch for that, and the bar staff.'

'But just your wife after that?' says Pulford, looking down at the dog, who growls up at him.

'And my daughter. And the guy from the Thai restaurant. He came round with a takeaway at half-eight. Why? What's up?' Tommy turns his back, walks away round the side of the house, through a loggia with honeysuckle climbing all over it. He pauses, takes a bud between his big thumb and forefinger. 'These are too early. I don't know what's going on in the world.'

Jombaugh and Pulford follow him. The dog has its head against Pulford's trouser bottoms.

A woman appears from a conservatory at the back of the house. A swimming pool is covered with blue tarpaulin. She wears a kaftan and has her auburn hair up in a careless bun. She is beautiful, delicate and with a young child. She says, 'Hello,' in a foreign accent. Probably French.

'This is Sabine,' says Tommy. He says her name in a perfect, soft accent. 'These men want to know where I was last night,' he continues, in his thick and wide London accent.

'Ahaa. Like the old days.' Sabine laughs. Her voice is fine as porcelain. 'He was here, with me and our daughter.'

'I didn't know,' says Jom. 'Congratulations.'

'Giselle is napping,' she says.

'Maybe next time,' says Tommy.

'I'm not so sure you're telling the whole truth,' says Pulford. 'You were with my DC.'

Tommy nods at his dog, who jumps up at Pulford.

Pulford steps back, bangs into the loggia.

Sabine laughs and Tommy looks at her, adoringly.

Tommy says, 'Come in and I'll show you my receipt from the Thai. Then you can be on your way – once you've told me what I'm supposed to have done.'

Jombaugh smiles at Sabine, says, 'That won't be necessary.'

Tommy whispers to Pulford, 'One word from me and that dog will rip out your throat.'

Pulford wants to tell Tommy that he saw his car last night, that he knows exactly where he was. But he bows to the better part of valour.

As they make their way back to the car, Jombaugh says, 'It looks like you're going to have to tell Staffe we appear to have mislaid a detective constable.'

Anton Troheagh is biscuit thin, a ginger tom in his lap and a long, thin joint hanging from the corner of his mouth.

'I am police, you know,' says Staffe.

The joint jiggles and the ash spills as Anton talks. His eyes are vague and watery, his speech lazy. 'I take it for pain.'

'Pain from what?' asks Staffe. Beyond Anton, through the bay window of his first-floor flat, a thick band of

Brighton's beach lies between the balustraded promenade and the sunless, cloudless sky, the colour of kaolin and morphine.

'I'm dying,' he says, matter of fact. 'Is this about Kerry?'

'You remember her, still?'

'You know, I'm amazed I don't remember more about my children. But you couldn't forget Kerry. She demanded to be known. Not much to look at, but you couldn't take your eyes off her. She had mischief, you know. It made you want to be her. She didn't give a toss.'

'And that's what Sean saw in her, is it?'

'I remember him. Some of the teachers were concerned at one stage, but he wouldn't harm her.'

'He preyed on a schoolgirl almost half his age.'

'It wasn't like that. I knew Sean. I was in a theatre group. Just did the pubs, round Islington and Camden, you know. It was just before I left teaching and he was good to me.'

'Because you were Kerry's teacher?'

'It was she who chased him.' Anton Troheagh coughs. He doubles up and holds his ribs, wheezing, reaching for a glass and sipping, holding his throat as he swallows, slowly leaning back, resuming his position. 'She was a minx. Before Sean, there was a man who'd pick her up from school in a car, but she set her sights on Sean Degg the minute he started seeing her sister.'

'Bridget? Sean Degg went out with Bridget Lamb?'

'Lamb? She got married, then. I always knew them as the Kilbride girls. It made us laugh. Kerry would kill the bride to get to the groom – even if it was her own sister.'

'She got her man,' says Staffe. 'And this man who would

come to pick Kerry up from school. Was he a gangster? Do you know Tommy Given, Anton?'

'I'm dying, Inspector. But I don't have a death wish.'

Enough said, thinks Staffe. 'Bridget has done very well for herself – living in Surrey with a doting husband,' he says.

'And children?'

'She can't have them.'

'It wasn't always thus.'

'What?'

'Ask Sean.'

'Bridget had a baby with Sean?'

'She left school as soon as she started to show. I heard she went the whole term and lost it right at the end.'

'Is that when Sean left her?'

'God only knows, but the minute Bridget left school, he was there at the school gates for Kerry. It was summer and Kerry never came back after the holidays. She could have done anything she wanted to, you know.'

'I read her work.'

'That's how you got hold of me?' Anton looks proud. Staffe tries to work out how old he is, reckons they must be the same age, even though Anton's drawn and pallid face is thickly riven with lines and his hair is all shorn away. His eyes are dark, hollow as two halves of an egg's shell.

'If there's anything you want to tell me, anything you remember about Kerry and Bridget and Sean; about Tommy Given – you should give me a ring.' Staffe stands, hands Anton his card and laments the life unlived. He makes his way back out through the book-lined hallway: floor to ceiling with thoughts and memories; stories and theories. How many has Anton read? he wonders. How many unread? Lying on its back, atop a line of Bruce Chatwins, is *Beloved*.

When he was done with Anton, Staffe had stomped down Brighton's pebble beach to the shore. It was heavy going and as the pebbles rattled and shifted beneath him, his muscles had begun to burn. He couldn't remember the last time he had some decent exercise. So he had walked all the way to the pier. When he got there, the sun was disappearing down beyond the playboy beach houses that stand high, silhouetted on the pale road to Hove. He treated himself to oysters in the Regency and was pleasantly surprised that the place was much the same as he remembered it. Then he drove back against the traffic, took a call from Pennington who had asked where he was going. He told him and the DCI said he was to steer clear of Tommy Given. Pennington had received a call from the Met. Tommy was their man. Always had been, and it would stay that way.

Now, Staffe puts down his pint and looks out of the enormous plate-glass window onto Harrow Road, the walled enclosure of Wormwood Scrubs in the background. Each time a lorry trundles past, the window rattles.

'Tell me what your deal is with Given, Smet,' says Staffe, pushing away his empty glass.

Smethurst wraps his fat fingers around his own glass and takes a mouthful. A third of the bitter disappears. 'Do you really think that's how we operate?'

'He knows Kerry Degg. He helped get her a residency at one of Phillip Ramone's places.'

'Why not have a chat with him?'

'I've been warned off.' Staffe unfolds a piece of A4. As he reads from it, he wonders if Tommy Given might somehow be in the Met's pay. The biggest grass in all of London town? 'He did six months of a three-year in 1978 when he was just a pup. Since then, he's only been up in court twice and neither went to trial. He's one of the nastiest bastards in all London and we haven't got so much as a DNA swab.'

'You've got his dabs.'

'That won't prove he's the father of a murdered woman's child.'

'I should be careful who you say that in front of. He's got some mighty fine lawyers – so I hear.'

'I thought we were mates, Smet.'

'And you'd be right. As long as you're in City and I'm at the Met, it'll stay that way.' Smet laughs, but the truth is raw enough. They spent six years together and didn't always see eye to eye. Each of them knows that either would help the other at the drop of a switchblade – so long as it didn't harm themselves.

'All I need is a whisper where Sean Degg is. Forget Tommy Given, I'll find some other way to cook that bloody goose. You must have heard something.'

'You tried Ross Denness?'

Staffe says nothing, wondering how Smet would know about Ross Denness. He's on Staffe's patch, supposedly. All Staffe has to work out is: has Smet slipped up, or did he mean to let him know he had been told about Denness? He watches Smet finish his pint and tug at his belt, look at his watch. Smet purses his lips and makes the smallest shake of his head.

'Shouldn't you be concentrating on that Crawford woman? It's in the papers again, you know. That bill of Vernon Short's is on the rebound. Now, there's a real fish to fry.'

'What are you doing here?' says the nurse, Eve, to Staffe in the reception of City Royal's antenatal unit. She puts on a stern face and looks around, as if he might be tarnishing her in some way, but when she sees they have the place to themselves, she allows herself a smile.

'I don't have your number. Remember?'

'Something tells me this isn't a social call.'

'Does it have to be one thing or the other?'

'What do you want from me?'

'The time you spent in the hospital, with Grace, did anybody else come to see her?'

'There was the policewoman. The pretty one who found her.'

'Anybody else?'

'The police had someone there the whole time – to keep the press away, they said. There were other mothers there, of course, and their families. You should ask Natalie.'

'The other nurse? Is she a friend of yours?'

Eve laughs. 'More than that. We're from the same part of Yorkshire, we were in the same hostel when we first came down to London.'

'Yorkshire, hey?' says Staffe. 'Which village?'

'A place called Appletrewick,' says Eve.

'Aptrick,' he says, smiling.

'That's what the locals call it. You've been there?'

Staffe recalls a weekend in the Yorkshire Dales with Sylvie.

'You're not here to chat about the Dales,' says Eve, turning towards him. Her mouth is set, but her eyes sparkle.

'I'm here to coax something out of you.'

'Anything in particular?'

'Kerry's sister. She's called Bridget.'

'And nothing alike, if I remember. I was with her, but you should ask Natalie. She made Natalie pray with her. I saw them together, kneeling by Grace's cot.'

'Did she come more than once?'

'Not that I know. She was stuck-up. I didn't like to think of Grace as being her niece. That sounds awful, doesn't it? The father, he looked right with the child, but I didn't take to that sister. Something seemed wrong, even though you could tell she loved them.'

'Loved them?'

'You had to look hard, but yes, she loved them all right, the baby and the mother.'

Staffe hands her his card, then puts a hand on Eve's shoulder, squeezes it gently. 'Thank you. You've been a great help.'

'I don't think so.'

'Let me buy you dinner.'

'I can buy my own dinner, thank you.'

'Let me eat it with you.'

Eve laughs and flicks his nose with the card he had given her. 'Maybe I'll call you. Maybe you can pay. You can afford it.'

'What?'

'I spoke to your friend, the policewoman. I'm not sure how happy she would be, you chatting me up.'

'Am I?'

'Have you taken her out to dinner, Inspector Wagstaffe?' This time, as she goes, she looks over her shoulder. Her eyes sparkle and her teeth show, pearly white.

He watches her go and he wonders what the hell she was talking to Josie about. And come to think of it, where has she got to? He calls Jombaugh, but he's not in the station. Jombaugh's always in the station. What's happening to the world?

Twenty-One

Sean Degg looks down on the Regent's Canal. From here, he can see everybody who comes: from the bus stops up and down the New North Road, and along the towpath. The only blind spot is out back, through next door's garden. Because of the fixed, frosted window in the bathroom, he can't see next door's garden properly. Next door the other way is just fine.

He knows that if they are to find him, they'll come the back way, whether they're the filth or the filthier – they'll know what they're doing. Does he have the stomach for this? Can he dig in and fight to his last breath? He's got Grace now, but she seems a million miles away. That kind of a life – one they might forge together, the way he always dreamed – seems impossible. He looks at the photo he has of her on his phone.

Sean goes to the fridge. He has a half-drunk can of Tennent's left and a swallow of vodka in the bottom of the bottle. He has eight tins of Big Soup and two loaves in the freezer and a multipack of Jaffa cakes. He has a quarter-ounce of dried-out Drum and two spliffs short of an eighth.

He wonders if he should phone. He's going mad in here, but they told him not to call. It's a funny feeling, being nowhere; having no one. He doesn't register on any kind of radar, which ought to be a good thing.

Sean goes through to the back bedroom, hangs out of the window and checks next door's garden. The days are drawing out and the sky is hues of orange and coral where the sun is trying to set, way behind Canary Wharf's oblongs and prisms of glinting glass. And then he realises that by hanging out of the window he isn't helping himself, so he slams the sash frame down, pulls the catch across, and picks up his phone. His finger hovers over the green, but he chucks it onto the bed and counts his cash. He's only got twelve quid left and he can't go to the machine. He can't leave that kind of a trail, not yet; not until it all plays out. He doesn't know quite what that means.

He waits for the sun to drop and the last of the dog walkers to drift away from the canal, and he puts on his coat. He hasn't been out for two, or is it three days?

As he pulls the door behind him, Sean's fingers tremble and his bowels shift. He feels loose inside, feels kind of alive.

Staffe takes the record from his turntable. It was his father's LP and not exactly his cup of tea. He prefers the later works: Miles and Coltrane; Mingus and Ornette. But he can see now, hear now, that his father was right about Ellington being the master. He puts the needle back to the first track and listens again, this time intent upon following the sweeping lines of Jimmy Hamilton's clarinet. But by the time he has popped his coffee back in the microwave for ten seconds and settled back into his American spoonback, his mind has flitted across Eve and all the way back through to the moment he first set eyes on Kerry Degg down in the tunnel.

The tendrils from this case go all over the place. He needs something to focus on – like a magnifying glass, put to the sun, that burns a hole when the clouds roll away.

He picks up the data sheets for Zoe and Kerry, and Cathy Killick, too, looks at the thinly populated central core of the Venn diagram. The only thing that unifies the women is that they were twenty-four weeks pregnant when they disappeared (or were threatened, in the case of the Home Secretary).

Jimmy Hamilton's clarinet meanders. Occasionally, and fleetingly, he swims with the melody. Staffe looks at the data reports for the three women, then works his way through the list of names that are in his head, looking for connections – a job for Pulford, rerunning the data fields for everyone in this case: victims, witnesses and suspects alike.

The orchestra swoons and rolls, and Ellington picks out strands of the melody with a few choice piano chords – just so much that you can follow him, like someone almost out of sight, giving chase in the half-light of dense woods.

Staffe reaches for the telephone, to tell Pulford to spread further the data matches, but as his fingers touch the phone, it rings.

'Inspector?' It is a woman's voice: calm, lofty, distinguished. He recognises it immediately, from the radio.

'Mrs Killick, you shouldn't call me here. Your people won't be happy.'

'The line is fine. We checked.' She pauses and he suspects her hand is over the mouthpiece, thinks she might be talking to somebody else. 'This isn't an official call, you understand. We are not having this conversation.'

Staffe considers what he discovered of her past from Vernon Short.

'I need this case to be solved, Inspector. The other women disappeared at my stage, and as you know, there are people who want Vernon's bill back.'

'I can't do as much as I would like – as you know. Can you arrange for me to have access to Lesley Crawford's house?'

'What I am about to tell you is absolutely confidential, Inspector.'

'You shouldn't tell me, then.'

'I have to.' Her voice cracks. She lowers her voice, almost whispering. 'They have been in touch again. They said that they have no choice.'

'Was it a man or a woman?'

'A woman.'

'Was it taped?'

'No.'

'And did you recognise the voice?'

'No. I'd like to say it was her, that Crawford woman – but I can't.' Cathy Killick's voice is tremulous.

'Tell me about Vernon Short. What might the future hold for him?'

The phone falls silent.

Staffe tries to imagine what the scene might be on the other end of the line.

Eventually, she says, 'There's someone who could make way for him. There's always somebody wanting to spend more time with their family.'

Staffe is quite dizzy at what is at stake here and, although he knows it might not advance his own cause, he feels a compulsion to tell Cathy Killick what he knows Vernon knows. 'Mrs Killick . . .'

'Yes?'

He falters. 'Have you offered Vernon a Cabinet post?'

'I can't say any more.' She laughs weakly, trying to break the tension. 'I'd have to kill you.'

'Can you get me into Lesley Crawford's house?'

'How might that help?'

'Why call me? You have your own people,' asks Staffe.

'I will arrange what you want, Inspector.'

'Mrs Killick . . . ?'

'Yes?'

'Nothing.' He hangs up.

The record has come to its end and the needle scratches away in the runaway grooves at the end of the final track. As Staffe flips the record over, there is a knock at the door and he checks his watch. Who could it be, this time of night?

Pulford looks sheepish and, immediately, Staffe knows that the news must be bad. He invites his sergeant in and they sit opposite each other at the kitchen table in the flat which, earlier in the year, they had shared.

'It's Josie, sir. You know we were onto Tommy Given.'

'We've a problem with that. He's the Met's man. Anything to do with Given, we have to pass through Pennington.'

'We didn't know that.' Pulford looks at his hands. He can't keep his fingers still.

'What's happened?'

'I don't know, sir. I've not seen Josie since . . .'

'Since when?'

'You know Josie spoke to Cello Delaney, that friend of Kerry's.'

'What's happened!'

'She told us about Tommy Given and so we – well, Josie – went to see the foster parents, the Archibalds. And I went to Given's local. Josie wound the Archibalds up and they phoned Given. I followed him. We wanted to see him going into their house, that's all. It's the connection we need.'

'And they saw you following them.'

'I don't think so.'

'And where was Josie?'

'That's it, sir. I don't know.'

'You haven't seen her since then?'

'We think it's Tommy Given, sir.'

'We?'

'Jom came with me.'

'With you?'

'To Given's spot, down in Surrey.'

'My God, Pulford.' Staffe stands up, paces the kitchen. 'What have you done about it?'

'I've checked all the A & Es and I've called Josie's folks . . .' Pulford looks up at Staffe, appears to be close to tears. 'I don't know what to do, sir. It's a right mess.'

Staffe sits heavily in his chair.

'Have you knocked on, in the Archibalds' street?'

'Not yet.'

'First thing in the morning, Pulford.'

'And in the meantime?'

'When was the last time you phoned a DCI at home? Call it staff development.' And Staffe tosses Pulford his mobile.

199

'Then, you can do something constructive. I take it you're in no mood for sleep.'

Sean puts down the phone, fearing the worst. He shouldn't have even come out tonight. From the phone box, he looks along the canal, then back up at the window of the flat he is holed up in. You would never guess. There is no outward clue as to who or what might be within.

Now, though, he is out. It is done. He may as well make the most of it.

In the off-licence on the New North Road, he counts his change again, keeps his phone money separate, in a coin bag, then gets himself a quarter-bottle of an obscure brand of vodka with an implausibly eastern-bloc name. All set, he slips in the side door of the Nags.

There's only two others in – sitting separately and each sucking hard on the house doubles. One chases it down with a half, the other a pint. The place smells of toilet. The Pogues track on the CD keeps jumping. It's the one about whisky on Sunday and tears on your cheeks. He thinks it's called 'The Majestic Shannon'. Kerry used to love it. Kerry . . .

Nothing seems real.

He looks around the place and tries to think of something not Kerry, tries to block out the sound of Shane's cracked and bleeding throat. It's a place you'd come if you took pubs but left people. It suits, down to the ground, for tonight.

Sean orders the premium lager. The barman weighs him up, as if he might be a threat, and when Sean says, 'You all right?' he smiles and nods, looking as if he has decided he knows Sean won't present a problem. The phone goes and the barman goes out back, and Sean, deft as a thief, slurps a sixth of his pint, pulls the vodka from his pocket and glugs half the quarter-bottle of vodka into his pint. It comes up nicely to the rim and Sean smiles at a job well done. One of the others catches him at it and gives him a look of admiration. Sean takes a drink and immediately feels the full whack. It fuels a softening inside him and a vial of optimism unfurls. He settles back in his stool and watches Sky Sports News with its looping tales of sacked managers and sub-continental cricket.

The barman comes back in, eats his freebie chilli at the bar. He winks at Sean, as if to say he knows his sort. When he turns away, Sean empties the rest of the vodka in and takes a slug. It is almighty powerful now and his eyes water a little. When he gets towards the bottom, he orders a half, hears the words of his request tumble softly into each other. The barman smiles, but instead of pouring a half, he takes the pint from in front of Sean and fills it right up, just asks him for the one-eighty for the half.

Sean begins to picture a better outcome. The prospect of it flows slowly in his blood. He wonders if he might approach Phillip Ramone. Technically, he is due a commission, still. Kerry's contract had been signed. And he wonders also if simply considering this makes him a bastard. He thinks of Grace, knows he has to provide for her, somehow. God knows how, if he's holed up like this. But this can't be for ever.

If Phillip coughed up and he could get to Grace, he could take her out of London altogether until things settle down. Which they will. He tries to remember who had assured him everything would 'settle down'. His head is fuzzed. Soon, his pulse quickens, his mood darkens. He needs another drink. Just one. He takes a final and almighty gulp of his strange brew, feels the stool beneath him waver.

The fellow who was chasing with pints sups up and heads for the door, pulling a fag from his black pack of cheapo cigs. Sean looks for the other punter, but he's gone. Now, he's all on his own. He looks at his pile of change and thinks he hasn't quite got enough for a final half. He doesn't want to leave just yet. He could dip into his phone money, his lifeline.

The barman says, 'Another?'

'I'm not sure . . .' Sean looks at his pile.

The barman raises a finger to his lips and says, 'Pay me next time.'

Sean necks the remainder of his pint in one go, but has to stop himself gagging on the viscosity of the booze. It's like winning on a long shot after a stewards'. The barman hands across his glass then goes out back again, leaving Sean to his good fortune, his head soft and his heart lifted.

As soon as the barman goes, a hand appears upon Sean's shoulder. It feels neither unusual nor familiar, and Sean recalls that the last time he touched or was touched by another human was days, maybe a week, ago. He had pressed the sole of his boot to the wrist of that prostrate newsagent.

'Hello, Sean,' says his new companion. 'We should go. I have what you asked for.'

'Why don't you stay? Just for one.'

'We can't be seen. Come on, there's plenty where we're going.'

* * *

Pulford taps away on his laptop at Staffe's kitchen table, whilst Staffe ploughs through the case notes and statements, calling out slivers of information for his sergeant to enter.

The computer does the hard bit and Staffe takes a break, cuts them each a slab of Cornish Yarg and a chunk of bread, serves it up with spoonfuls of spring chutney and a handful of salad leaves growing on his window-sill. 'Do you want a glass of beer?' he asks.

'Wait!' says Pulford, peering into the laptop's screen. 'Lesley Crawford went to Sidney Sussex College, Cambridge, from 1984 to 1987.'

'Same as Vernon Short,' says Staffe.

'Hang on. I need to style these correctly or the computer won't pick up the match.' He types in Cambridge, then the dates, then the college, into three separate fields – just as he had for Vernon Short and Zoe Bright.

'I knew that. I'm *sure* I knew that, from somewhere,' says Staffe. 'Am I going mad?'

'No. Vernon was there eight years earlier. They wouldn't have met.'

'When can I look at this? On paper, I mean – not on that damn thing.'

'We're nowhere near done, sir.'

Staffe wants to bomb straight up to Cambridge, to talk to the tutors who might still be there, who knew Crawford and Short. Absently, he reads out more details regarding Lesley Crawford, pausing, habitually now, for Pulford to input the data. As he talks, his mind wanders. 'First house, Argyll Street, Wandsworth, 1992 to 1998; next house, Paternoster House, Battersea, 1998 to 2005; then her Southfields place, from 2008 till now.'

'What did she do between '05 and '08?' says Pulford.

Staffe flicks through his notes, then through Josie's jottings on the photocopied cuttings. 'I don't know.' He flicks back and forth, loses himself, half his mind still on the Sidney Sussex connection.

'She was at university. I'm sure she was,' says Pulford. 'Here, give it to me.'

Staffe pats his sergeant on the shoulder and looks at the dense grid of rows and columns and text, wondering if they are helping or hindering.

Twenty-Two

Josie is cold and the rough blanket scratches her legs. They have brought her a cup of tea and some cold toast, spread with bright yellow marge. She wolfs it down, then bangs at the door again, complaining that they haven't made the phone call yet. Her head thumps and her mouth is still dry. She feels as if she could drink a bathful of water and still be thirsty. She slumps to the floor, runs her hands over the rough scabs on her knees.

They said she had tried to glass a police officer in a night club. Hence, the treatment.

She skews round and uses the tray to bang on the door for five, ten minutes. She loses sense of time, but eventually, the metal plate slides across the spyhole and she recognises the dark eyes of the sergeant who brought her food.

'I'm sorry about what happened, but I want my phone call, Sarge.'

'You've had it.'

'Who did I call?'

'Your dad.'

Josie doesn't get on with her dad. Her dad is a treacherous, selfish, vain pig. She hasn't called him in a year. She knows they are lying.

She brings her knees up to her breasts, holds herself and wonders what state she must have been in. But the door opens.

The duty sergeant stands over her. 'What did you say?'

'What did I say to him, Sarge? I'm curious. We don't get on, me and my father.'

'You called me "Sarge".'

'I'm one of you. I'm one of us, I mean. I told you that. Can I have some water?'

'Not according to your ID.'

'Who am I?'

The sergeant crouches down, says, 'You were off your tits. You punched out a nineteen-year-old girl and you tried to glass one of my WPCs. It took four officers to get you out of that club.'

She looks down at what she is wearing, tries to cover herself up. She puts her hand on the sergeant's knee and twists round, looks into his eyes, smiling. 'Then you should charge me.'

'What?'

'Sounds like a Section 89.'

'What?'

'Surely, you know your '96 Act. Or maybe she wasn't in uniform, so you're worried about mitigation. At least hit me with a Section 39. That would be the '88 Act.'

'Christ,' says the sergeant.

'What the hell did they give me?' Josie stands up. 'I need to be tested.' She pulls down her skirt but its lycra content is too high and it recoils. 'Let's go.'

'You're going nowhere, young lady.'

'What?'

'I've had the wool pulled over too many times to fall for that.'

'Call Leadengate and ask for Sergeant Jombaugh or DS Pulford and check me out. Tell them what I look like.'

'Is that really what you want?' says the sergeant, allowing a smile and closing the door behind him as he goes.

It is early morning and although the sun is bright, it is still low in the sky. A pewter dew lies across Thames Ditton's Green. Staffe is on his way down into Surrey whilst Pulford organises the knock along the Archibalds' street. Seeing as how he was on the A3, and bearing in mind what Anton Troheagh had told him about the Kilbride sisters, he thought it only polite to call in on Bridget. And he had wanted to pull off the A3, to see if the knackered blue Beemer followed him. Looking around now, he can see no trace. Is he becoming paranoid?

A frost had missed by the barest degree and the house of Malcolm and Bridget Lamb is pretty as a picture. Pretty as a picture of a chocolate box.

Staffe knocks on the door and the sight of him is enough to bring a frown to Malcolm Lamb's fresh face. Nonetheless, Malcolm can't suppress a whole life of decency and he invites Staffe in.

Bridget is in the living room, sitting in her pyjamas with her knees tucked up in a bergère chair beneath a standard lamp and flicking through a soft-furnishings magazine. She says, 'It would be nice if you had called. I suppose it's one of your tricks, to catch people unawares.'

'Why would I need tricks?'

'I told you what I know.'

'You didn't tell me you went to see Grace.'

'I hadn't been, when I saw you.'

'I can check the dates. And I will. You'd want me to check, wouldn't you? To find the person who killed your sister.'

Bridget removes her spectacles and closes *Country Home*. She sighs. 'You obviously have something to say.' Turning to Malcolm, she says, 'You have to prepare, love. You can leave us.'

'Where are you going?' says Staffe.

'He has a church group,' says Bridget. 'Druggies.'

'They are lost,' says Malcolm.

Once Malcolm has gone, Staffe says, 'I went to see Anton Troheagh. Mr Troheagh, to you, I guess.'

'Kerry was his favourite.'

'And you were Sean Degg's – until Kerry came along.'

'He was a predator.'

'He loved her, though, didn't he?'

'I judge a tree by its fruit, Inspector. I don't see much love in that fruit.'

'This isn't the best analogy, is it, Bridget?' Staffe perches on the edge of a library chair, clasps his hands together. 'Anton Troheagh told me you were expecting a baby while you were at school.'

'It was a long time ago.'

'But you must still resent Sean – leaving you in that state.'

'I was weak, for a while. Time heals.'

'It doesn't heal everything, though, does it?' Staffe wants to say more, but holds himself back, speculating that it must have been the dénouement of her pregnancy that had wreaked some kind of havoc on Bridget, preventing her from being a mother, now and for ever.

She says, 'I have learned to trust in God's will.'

'It must have been hard for you not to hate the two of them.'

'Hatred is not in my repertoire. I can only live as good a life as I can, and I have been rewarded with more love than poor Kerry ever brought on herself.'

'Tell me about when you went to the hospital, to see Grace.'

For a moment, Bridget looks befuddled, as if she is trying to remember that day, what she might have said and to whom. 'I can't remember. I was upset. Surely you can understand that.'

'I'm trying to understand why you wouldn't tell me that you once carried Sean Degg's child.'

'It was a long time ago.'

'What did you see in Sean?'

'I was a different person.' She forces a smile. 'I see it as a step on the road to salvation.'

'Has he been in touch since I last saw you?'

'Why would he?' Bridget looks confused.

'You're his sister-in-law. He's an only child and his parents are dead. His children are in care. You are as close a relative as the poor man has.'

'They're not his children.'

'Grace is.'

Bridget bites her lip and her eyes glint. A weaker person might show a tear, but all Bridget does is open her magazine. Without looking at him, she says, 'I don't care for the way this is going. She was my sister, you know. My damned sister.'

'I'll show you out,' says Malcolm, standing in the doorway with a light mac over his arm even though it is a fine day. 'Please, there's only so much she can take in one go.'

Staffe nods. On the way out, he looks back at Bridget. She is staring into nowhere, as if she can see something that is coming to get her. At the door, he says, 'This won't go away, not unless we can get hold of Sean.'

'He's still missing?' asks Malcolm.

'Without trace. Anything you or Bridget can tell us, and I wouldn't have to be round here so much.'

'He won't be able to stay away from the babies, surely.'

'Babies?'

'You know,' says Malcolm, opening the door. The day floods in. 'He's got the others, too.'

Miles and Maya aren't babies. Perhaps they are to Malcolm. Babies, Staffe thinks, and he feels the gap in Bridget's life – and Malcolm's, too.

Pulford looks through the spyhole, scarcely believing what he sees. 'That's her,' he says. 'For fuck's sake, what have you done to her?'

Josie sits on the bed below the high, barred window, shivering. Her knees are scabbed, her hands red raw, the knuckles scuffed. She is wearing a thin, red dress that barely reaches the top of her legs and the bodice of the dress is torn, revealing a black bra. Her make-up is smudged and smeared. Her hair looks big and brittle and broken.

'Get her some clothes,' Pulford says to the WPC behind him.

'Where from?'

'I don't care. She's one of us. Why the hell have you let her stay in this state? Let me in and then get her some clothes and a hot meal.'

'She had a go at one of our WPCs. Tried to glass her – so you can get fucked. She's a right bitch.'

'Get her the bastard clothes!' Pulford glares at her and hisses, 'Have a word with your sarge. He's in on the picture.'

When the bolt shoots and the door swings open, Josie sees Pulford and gasps. Pulford wraps his arms around her. Gradually, her body becomes less taut. He remembers when they were briefly together. She smells of drink and stale cigarette smoke. She doesn't smoke. He says, 'What did they do to you?'

'What *did* they do to me?' she asks.

'You were drinking cider. Strong cider, according to the shop owner, by the Archibalds' house. You were supposed to make yourself scarce. Remember?'

'Not really.'

'Then you ended up in a place called Scotty's, out in Southend.'

'Scotty's? Never heard of it. Am I in trouble?'

'We need to get you looked at. Tested, you know, and see what they gave you.'

'Did I do what they said?'

'You laid out a girl in the night club but she's OK, and you went for a WPC.'

'Oh, my God.'

'But we need to know how you got there. Can you remember anything?'

Josie shakes her head. 'I got the cider. I remember that. I was waiting.' She looks up at him. 'I was waiting for you, and then you drove by. I wanted to wave, David.' Josie surrenders to him again, says over and again, 'You should have looked,' like a little girl.

Suddenly, Pulford lets go of her. 'Oh, God!'

She looks up, afraid. 'What is it?'

'I've got to call Staffe. He's on his way to see Tommy Given. He's going to shake it out of him. Wait here.'

'Where would I go?' she says, curling up on the bed, a soft smile smudged on her face now. By the time Pulford gets to reception, she is asleep.

Staffe recognises the type immediately. The suit is blue and his eyes are covered by a pair of Wayfarers. Leaning against Staffe's Peugeot by the Green, the man flicks his cigarette into the gutter and stands erect.

'What have I done now?' says Staffe.

'I'm taking you to Southfields.'

'You're not. Not now.'

'I was told you were desperate to have a poke around.'

'I am, but I'm going the other way.'

'We'll take your car. It's best.'

'I told you, I'm . . .'

The bonnet of his own car and the powdery sky and then his bonnet again swirl. Then his face is cold, on the metal of his Peugeot, and the side of his face is compressed. He is looking across the bonnet towards the Green and a searing pain is shooting down his shoulders and through his head. He tries to move, but he can't. Now, he feels pressure behind his ears and he thinks he is going to black out. Just as he does, it is as if he is landing on feathers and when he opens his eyes, he is in the back of his own vehicle and the houses around the Green are moving, as if he were on a fairground horse. There is a deep voice alongside him, telling him he has a call.

* * *

As they come up over the cusp of Kingston Hill, Staffe has recovered his bearings, has absorbed the news that Josie Chancellor is being released from prison and that charges will not be pressed. And he has been told, by Pennington, that he is, under no circumstances, to go west along the A3. Tommy Given, for now, is still off limits.

'I take it Crawford won't be there,' he says to the man in the blue suit, alongside him. He can't work out if that is the one who assaulted him, or whether it was the driver. They both wear Wayfarer sunglasses.

'We'll catch up with her,' says the passenger, clearly taking her continued absence to heart.

Staffe wonders whether his companions know anything of the ace that Lesley Crawford has put up Vernon Short's sleeve. And is Lesley Crawford necessarily behind the threat to Cathy Killick?

Once in Southfields, the men in suits remain outside and Staffe is given the run of the house. He can have as long as he likes.

The kitchen is in keeping with the unspoiled, early Edwardian ethos. What was once the scullery still sports a gleaming, renovated black range, and it is clear that Lesley Crawford has lavished much love on the place.

Working his way from the larder, round the cupboards and sideboards, Staffe finds nothing of interest at all and moves to the dining room, then the lounge. It appears that Lesley Crawford keeps all her paperwork in an inlaid, deco secretaire. She maintains a modest credit balance in her current account and has the maximum in her ISA account. Her income seems to flow from a trust and yields her two thousand pounds per month. A copy of the trust document shows the estate is that of a Lieutenant-Colonel Bruce Crawford, and that Lesley has been the recipient for five years.

Staffe checks in the airing cupboard and under the beds, at the back of her drawers and every level of her three wardrobes. There is not an item out of place in this pristine and orderly house, not a thing to suggest that Lesley Crawford has any connection with any political cause, nor even the faintest interest in the plight of the 'unborn population'. There is an invitation bearing the embossed crest of Sidney Sussex College inviting her to a Victorian Society dinner at the beginning of June and from the tick she has struck through 'RSVP', it would seem she has accepted. Staffe takes note, will check with the secretary if Vernon Short is also on the guest list.

He clambers up into the loft void, using the telescopic ladder. The loft is boarded and lit by a single, bare bulb. There are several suitcases, all empty, and boxes of *History Today* which go all the way back to the early sixties.

And there is a small tidy-box, the film of dust undisturbed on its buff-coloured cardboard. Staffe sits cross-legged, places the box in his lap, knowing this is his last hope of a connection between Lesley Crawford and Kerry Degg – or Zoe Bright.

He lifts the lid and goes through the contents, item by item. It is a museum of Lesley's life, from the plastic nameband for her wrist when she was born, through certificates up to grade seven in piano and violin, all the way to her O and A level, BA and MA certificates, to a letter congratulating her on gaining her Doctorate of Philosophy, from the Vice-Chancellor of Nottingham University. The subject of her PhD: 'Midwifery and the sexual politics of the Victorians.'

Staffe tries to recall if anything else had suggested that she lived or studied in Nottingham, but he can't. The letter is dated June 2008. Zoe Bright was at Nottingham University from September 2005 to June 2008.

He notes down all the details and checks the rest of the box, hoping there might be letters, and then he goes back down below, checking everything again.

There is not the faintest draught of Breath of Life in the house.

Sometimes, on a blind search, you have a subconscious agenda. The brain can't help but prescribe what the eye is looking for. So he goes through everything again. This time, he even checks behind all the books on the shelves of the inlaid, two-door Stickley case. It is a beautiful piece and surely beyond the means of what he has seen of Lesley Crawford. It must have belonged to Lieutenant-Colonel Bruce, he thinks, replacing the last stack of books, pushing the spines straight, his finger lingering on a hardback of *Beloved*, by Toni Morrison. It makes his heart miss. He removes the volume, looks for an inscription, sees only that it is a signed and dated first edition.

Immediately, he calls Petal Broome who is brusque with him. 'What the hell do you want?'

'Tell me more about Zoe's reading. I'd like to know what books she liked.'

'Find her and she could tell you herself.'

Staffe bites his tongue, says, 'If you tell me, I might be able to find her. *Catch 22*?'

She gets the joke, laughs sarcastically. 'Very funny. There was a Hemingway, *Bell Tolls*, I think.'

Staffe checks the shelves. No Hemingway. 'Go on.'

'There was a Katherine Mansfield.'

'*Collected Short Stories*?' says Staffe, looking at the spine of Lesley's book.

'Of course. And Virginia Woolf.'

'*To the Lighthouse*?'

'How do you know?'

'Carry on. Please.'

'Anne Tyler.'

There are four Anne Tyler novels on Lesley's shelves and Staffe decides to flip the roles, begins to read from the spines of Lesley's books. '*Enduring Love*?'

'No,' says Petal.

He goes for something more obscure. '*Limestone and Clay* by Lesley Glaister.'

'She loved Lesley Glaister.'

There are seven Glaister novels in Crawford's case. Staffe looks for what he thinks might be the most obscure of all her novels. '*Cradle To Grave*, by Gareth Creer?'

'Yes.'

'Thanks, Petal. I owe you one,' says Staffe, elated, hanging up. He calls Alicia Flint straight away and tells her of the connection between Lesley Crawford and Zoe Bright. It seems strange, to hear her voice again. When they are done, she says, 'I'm glad you've kept me in the loop, Staffe.'

He looks out of the front window, sees the men in the front seats of his car. One of them is leaning forward, appears to be faffing about with his shoes. 'Don't tell anybody, will you?'

'Why not?'

'I'll send you everything I've got on Crawford, but keep it to yourself.'

'Why?'

'Because we have to find Crawford before anybody else does. She will be able to tell us where Zoe is.'

'Find her first? Who else is looking for her?'

'Dead birds don't sing. That's all I know.'

'Any luck with the herrings?' says Alicia Flint, laughing.

Staffe says, 'What? Hang on.' He goes into the kitchen, opens the door to the fridge and sees a tub of rollmops. 'You beauty.'

'Who?' says Alicia.

'The herring is a beautiful thing,' he says.

'You're going round the bend, Staffe.'

'I told you there's something about Parkgate. And they met at Nottingham University, too. Maybe we should meet.'

'It's half-way,' says Alicia.

Staffe says goodbye and leaves the house, wiping the smile off his face.

'Any luck?' says the man.

'Not a sausage,' says Staffe.

'I told her,' says the man, smiling. The mat in the passenger footwell, beneath the man's feet, is an inch out from the line of dirt around it. It has been moved.

Staffe says nothing.

Twenty-Three

'There was a residue of Rohypnol in her blood,' says Pulford. 'The clothes are from Topshop and there's no trace on them apart from Josie herself.'

'When can I see her?' asks Staffe.

'When she wakes.'

'What exactly did happen on the night?'

'Like I said, she was supposed to have got right away from the Archibalds'. I called her to say what car Given was in and I followed. I followed Given all the way and he just drove round and went back to Putney. There must have been another car behind, following me.'

'So you still can't prove Given knows the Archibalds.'

'But we know he does.'

'What use is that?'

'It's the truth, sir. We can always prove the truth.'

Staffe is trying to stay annoyed with Pulford, but he can't. 'The truth of the matter is, we don't know any more than before you allowed DC Chancellor to put herself in danger.'

'No, sir.'

'And you'll take it on the chin, Sergeant?'

'How will we get to Given, sir?'

'Let me worry about that. Just remember, it's all the more reason to stitch him up with decent evidence. Thank God you took Jom down there with you.'

He remembers being a young lad – about Pulford's age and fresh in the force. Jom had just passed forty – the same as Jessop. He wonders if he will go the way of Jombaugh – ground down by the job. Will he ever go the way of Jessop: once his mentor but tempted too far. Would he ever take it into his own hands? There will be a case out there with his name on it. And he will be shown a way to mete justice, beyond law. It could be this one.

Outside, whilst he is busy examining his Peugeot, Staffe gets a missed call. It makes him happy in the pit of his stomach. He feels light in the head and loose in his loins. Against his better judgement, Staffe returns the call, then says precisely what he thinks. 'Eve. I'm glad you rang.'

'Really? You said to call.'

'Are you working today?'

'Not until tonight. I start my ten-six shifts tonight.'

'How about an early lunch? It will help you sleep the afternoon.'

'That's thoughtful of you, Inspector,' she says, jokingly.

'There's a place I want to try. It's called Menage.'

'Will there be just the two of us?' She laughs, throatily, and he glimpses a different her – one with the guard down. Getting to know her . . .

Staffe is on his knees. In the car park at the back of the City Royal, beside his Peugeot, you might think he is answering a call to prayer. Appropriately enough, he finds what he is looking for. In the footwell of the passenger seat, he holds the tiny device between finger and thumb. It is no bigger than the decade bead of a rosary.

'She's asked for you.'

Staffe twists round, feels a nerve pinch. Pulford looks down at him.

'I've a job for you.' He gets to his feet and puts a finger to his lips, hands Pulford the device, knowing his sergeant embraces the continuing aspects of his professional development in a way that Staffe does not.

Pulford carefully takes the device from him, examines it and – holding the offending article tight in his fist – whispers, 'It's not police issue, but if I had to guess, I'd say it's a hybrid. A tracking device and a bug. It tells them what you're saying and where you are when you're saying it.'

Staffe whispers, 'Put it back where it was. Under the mat.'

'Why?'

'Now we know it's there, it's our device. Wait here.'

Josie is in the raw. They have bathed her and dressed her in a paper gown. She sits up with her hair combed back off her face. Her eyes are tired but there is blood back into her lips and she manages a shallow smile that soon collapses.

'I'm sorry, sir. I was a fool.'

'Shush. Don't be silly.'

He sits next to her, takes her hand in both his and squeezes a little. He looks around the room, sees there is nobody and leans forward, puts his lips to her forehead. He lets the soft kiss stay there for a count of three, four.

'Thank you, sir,' says Josie. Her eyes are glassy.

'I don't know,' says Staffe, his voice beginning to crack.

'Don't know what?' A broader smile is on Josie's mouth. Seeing her this way, she could be sixteen or thirty-five.

'I don't know . . . what I'd do.'

She nods her head and clamps her mouth shut, for fear she might say something she would regret. 'Sit with me, will you?'

He nods, holds her hand, still.

'Just a while.'

And after a while, she falls back into sleep, with her mouth turned up. He waits a further while and slides his hand from hers, puts his lips on hers, so they barely touch.

'In five minutes, ask me how I got on at Crawford's,' whispers Staffe beneath the revving engine as they drive away from the City Royal.

'Aah,' says Pulford.

Five minutes later, Staffe answers his sergeant, by reporting that nothing whatever had turned up at Crawford's house and he's pissed off with this case and they've no chance of catching up with whoever is responsible and maybe they should just leave it to Cathy Killick and her bloody people who seem to have all the resources and unrestricted access.

For twenty minutes, they drive slowly out to the Old Street roundabout and leave the car parked up between the Limekiln and Flower and Dean. It's where you'd park if you were staking out Sean Degg's place. Staffe leaves Radio 4 playing low and then they get a cab to the police morgue.

'Why are we going there?' asks Pulford.

'Have you met Miles and Maya Degg?'

'Kerry's kids? Do they have Sean's name? That seems odd.'

'What else would you call them?'

'Kilbride? Archibald? I don't know how these things work.'

'But you wouldn't call them babies.'

'They're three and five, right? I've not met them but I've read the reports.'

'You know about babies?'

'My sister had them. They're not babies once they can walk.'

'Even to the uninitiated, like you and me, Sergeant. Thanks.' He slaps Pulford on the shoulder and leans back, watches Whitechapel come at them, with its fruit and fish and dodgy boozers and its off-piste City folk and mothers and children: some walking, some babies being pushed.

Pulford brings them coffee through from Janine's kitchenette, off to the side of her half-basement theatre. High windows let weak light seep down from the Raven Lane pavement into the world of the pathologist. They sit in a midday twilight because the buzz of the operating lights drives Janine berserk.

Pulford pauses at the waxy white corpse in the corner, spills some of the coffee.

Staffe says, 'Would you have checked for twins? Could Kerry Degg have had twins?'

'She *could*. But it's a bit late now. It would have helped if we could have looked for that when she was still alive.'

'Wasn't she too weak?'

'Yes, I suppose so. But we could have checked before the post mortem.'

'It would have shown up in the post mortem, though?'

'You would have to be looking for it. And the elapsed time was too great, bearing in mind how traumatic the birth was. There was no collateral evidence either. Maybe if we'd known straight away.'

'What about the placenta? What I found in the tunnel.'

Janine shakes her head. 'Twins can share a placenta, or have separate placentas, or the placentas can merge to form one. What makes you think she was having twins?'

'Something I heard.'

'What difference does it make?' says Janine.

'They only left us one baby.'

'Sometimes, they don't both survive.'

'You'd have to know what you were doing, surely – to cope with that, to *administer* that, even if both the twins didn't survive.'

'It would have been more problematic,' she says. 'There would have been more signs to clear – at the scene.'

'And imagine, if there is another baby out there – if Grace's twin is out there.'

The three of them contemplate that: the skills required, the additional twist and nuance of motive, the trail of consequences.

Pulford says, 'If Grace has a brother or sister out there, it would be a crime for them to be kept apart. Who'd do such a thing?'

'What exactly did you hear, Staffe?'

'Kerry's brother-in-law said something about Sean's babies. He said "babies".'

'He's got other kids,' says Janine.

'They're not babies,' says Pulford.

'They might have been last time he saw them. That's how he might see them.'

'Hmm,' says Staffe. 'But they're not Sean's.'

'Even if you're right, it seems to me, this doesn't change anything. It's still an abduction that turned into murder.'

'Same crime, different motive. Different motive, different suspects,' says Staffe.

'Did you check the records, at the clinic?'

'As far as I could,' he says. 'I've just come from there. There was no mention of Kerry having twins. I asked the duty doctor whether, if Kerry was having twins, the last consultation would have spotted it, and he said it would have, for sure. But there's no notes from her last consultation.'

'All I can say is, there's nothing to suggest she wasn't carrying twins. Except . . .' She looks sad.

'Except what?'

'Except we only have one baby.'

'We're looking,' says Staffe.

'Have you checked all the paediatric wards?'

'As we speak,' says Pulford.

Staffe turns his mind to who might want the baby. He can't get past Bridget Lamb. But he has been to her house twice now. Not a whimper from upstairs, nor the slightest trace of a nappy. Not a grain of SMA. And Malcolm? Could Malcolm be a party to such subterfuge? He loves her enough, that's for sure. Or he might have said 'babies' in all innocence. 'You have to take babies to be weighed, right? They have to be monitored.'

Janine says, 'Surely, if you don't register the birth, nobody would know it exists – provided it's healthy. As long as you get some ID by the time they go to school or got poorly, nobody would ever ask where a baby came from. If you moved away, people would assume it was yours.'

'I know this place. Or should I say I've heard of it,' says Eve, looking down the lunch menu. Occasionally, she issues low moans. 'I'm hungry now.'

'The portions are starter-sized. If the French did tapas, they would do them like this.'

Eve closes the menu and smiles at him. In the soft light, she appears different. Her face is for the night. She has picked out her cheekbones with rouge and softened her eyes with Touche Éclat. A thin line of kohl makes her eyes seem brighter, more sultry, too, and he sees for the first time that she has a dimple high on her right cheek. Her hair is half-up, half-down, teased to make it look as if she hasn't made the effort.

As they order, he watches her eyes light up and then pinch together as she has to choose whether her ribbon of lemon sole is to be grilled or pan-fried. Her hair is the same colour as Sylvie's – but her face is fuller, her eyes bigger. Her nails are French-manicured and she wears the Claddagh ring on one hand, a large-stoned diamond on the wrong wedding finger of the other.

Once he has ordered, Eve says, 'It's my mother's ring.'

He is embarrassed.

'Did you think I'd been left standing at the altar?'

'No.'

'Liar. But people our age don't come without a little bit of scar tissue around the vital organs, do they?'

'I don't think we're of a similar age.'

'Inspector! You're not trying to get me to disclose, are you?'

'You'd be surprised what I know about you,' he says, immediately realising he has said the wrong thing.

'You checked up on me?'

'Can we say "checked you out"?'

Eve adjusts her expression – as if not to spoil lunch. She frowns, but it is playful.

'So tell me. Who am I?'

'You're not what you seem. A trained vet who gave up on animals to concentrate on humans.'

'You think I must be mad.'

'It can be a dirty business, that vet malarkey,' he jokes. He feels relaxed. 'Pushing pills and screwing owners into agreeing to futile operations. Playing on love and hope.'

'My God. How do you know these things?'

'I knew a vet once.'

Eve raises her eyebrows, as if to pry.

The waiter brings the wine and, even though she didn't order it, a gin and tonic for Eve. She looks surprised and then winks at him as if to say she didn't know how he did that, but she's glad he did.

For a stretch, they each say nothing, but the silence isn't awkward.

'Usually, it's not good when our worlds collide,' he says.

'We'll have to see.' Eve takes a lusty sip from her gin and says, 'But this is a good start. Plymouth gin, too, hey, Staffe.'

'How do you know people call me that?'

'Did you go to see Bridget, the sister? Grace's aunt.'

'I didn't say I was going.'

'Come on. You're a copper and I've spoken with the victim's sister. Fire away.'

'You know her?'

'I know she loves that child.' Eve finishes her gin and pours herself a small glass of wine, tops up Staffe.

As she leans forward, Staffe sees that she has no foundation on. Her skin is pale and smooth as china.

She says, 'I went to see Grace as soon as I heard. It's only across the way from my unit. But as much as I love children . . .' The waiter brings their first dish and Eve lowers her voice. '. . . As much as I love them, it's not the same.'

'The same as what?'

'It's not blood. When I was with Grace, saying my kind of a prayer for her and not wanting to be anywhere but there at that time, it wasn't the same as what that poor woman was feeling. I wasn't going through anything in comparison.'

'She said something to you?'

'She couldn't. She was catatonic.'

'Catatonic?'

'I put my arm around her and it was like hugging a rock. She was frozen. She didn't dare move – as though, I don't know, if she did, the baby might stop breathing.'

'Catatonic?' repeats Staffe. For a second, he forgets where he is, struggling to lend some order to the theories of Bridget: respectable wife and almost a teenage mother; sister of Kerry and spurned lover of Sean.

'If someone was having twins, one of your patients, I mean – you'd record it, wouldn't you?'

'Of course. They need a completely different antenatal regime. And we record everything.'

No, you don't, thinks Staffe. His telephone rings and he apologises to Eve, says he has to take it.

When he has finally done with the call, he comes back to the table, sits down heavily.

'What's wrong?' She reaches out and wraps her pale, small hands around his clenched fist; he doesn't respond. 'Don't say. If you can't tell me, I understand,' she says.

But he knows that no matter how relationships start off, in the end they never understand.

Staffe tries to evaluate the situation. He looks Eve in the eyes and says, 'They've found Sean Degg.'

'That's good.'

'Behind the gym at Notre Dame School, in Hackney. It's where he used to pick Kerry up at the end of the day.'

'That's odd.'

'He overdosed. Enough speed to stop a bull in its tracks, apparently.'

'He's dead?'

'Oh, yes. Of a splattered heart.'

Twenty-Four

Nick Absolom manages to catch Staffe's eye as the DI reaches the line of uniformed officers at the back gates of Notre Dame School. This is Hackney, where Kerry and Bridget Kilbride were each schooled and were courted by Sean Degg. Sean came back, a last time.

Clamouring photographers use stepladders to peek above the fence and they hold their cameras high – the opposite of meerkats looking for distant predators – hoping they might capture a snatch of what lies within the screened rectangle in the shadow of the gym.

'Are we expected to believe that this is an overdose, Inspector?' asks Nick Absolom, holding his dictaphone by his side. 'An act of grief? A desire to be with his poor, departed loved one?'

'Who told you that?'

'It's the word. It's what muppets will print unless advised otherwise.'

'And what will you print, Nick?'

'That depends on what you tell me.'

'Imagine I'm going to tell you nothing.'

'I'd imagine why Breath of Life would do a thing like this.'

'Because Sean had evidence to pin Kerry's abduction on an individual within the organisation.'

'Hence Lesley Crawford is in hiding,' says Absolom.

'So you're not going with the suicide theory?'

'I'm in the business of selling newspapers. Murder or suicide? It's no contest.'

'What about jeopardising the case?'

'If I wanted to jeopardise the case I might speculate why you might have been questioning Kerry Degg's sister. The husband didn't seem too pleased with your visit.'

'What?' hisses Staffe.

'I wouldn't mention the Lambs, of course, if I had something decent to run with.'

'People's lives are at stake here.'

'Really?'

Staffe grabs Absolom by the sleeve of his coat and pulls him through the line of officers, where they can't be overheard. Absolom can't keep the smug look from his face as he regards his peers, the other side of the line and looking daggers. 'You'll get first run. When it's time to release the information.'

'You have information for me?'

'We haven't found the woman in Liverpool. We have to keep her interests uppermost.'

'But there's something else. Let me have a whiff of it. I won't print anything. I swear.'

Outside the screened area, two women and a man, all dressed casually smart, mill around, shaking their heads. Staffe guesses they are teachers. The oldest one, a woman with steel-grey hair, has clearly been crying.

Can he trust Absolom? He looks at the other journalists peering this way, and he realises that they are his enemy, and Absolom's enemy, too. He can use that. 'Take that smirk off your face. Look disappointed and keep your mouth shut until I say you can run this.'

'OK.' Absolom already looks pissed off. The supreme deceiver.

Staffe takes a copy of the *News* from his pocket. It is open at Absolom's latest article, on the resurrection of Vernon Short's bill. It has a quote from Breath of Life. 'Just where did you get this quote from?'

'I can't say.'

'We have to scratch each other's backs.'

'So you give me something.'

'There is another child involved. A small child.'

'Degg's orphans?'

'It's all I'm saying.'

'A baby?'

Staffe thinks how her association with the spreading misery will suit Lesley Crawford. It will keep the orphaned Grace on the front pages a while longer. Long enough to resurrect Vernon's bill once and for all? 'I'll give you more, as soon as I can.' He grabs Absolom, makes a scruff of the lapels of his jacket. He whispers, 'Keep Bridget out of this. You hear,' and pushes him back through the line of police.

Absolom calls him a 'Fucking jerk!' for all to hear. Each man looks angry; each enjoying their part, in different ways, to different ends.

Behind the screens, freestanding boards show photographs of Sean Degg. He had died in a pile, head slumped to his chest and arms outstretched, hands clenched into fists. There is a close-up of a bump at the base of his skull. Behind the ear, a line of dried blood.

'There's only one sign of needle intrusion that I've seen so far,' says Janine. 'I'll be going over him back at my place later, but he had been drinking, for sure. I think it was circulatory collapse, and there are signs of convulsions. A little vomit, but I need to open him up.' She taps a photograph of Sean's face – eyes wide open and pupils like pinpricks.

'He took a load of speed, is what I heard.'

'A planeful would be my guess.'

Pulford comes across, opening his notebook. 'I've got Smet getting verification of Given's whereabouts for the time of death, sir. And I spoke to Ross Denness.'

'What about Bridget Lamb?'

'Are you serious, sir?'

'Too bloody serious.'

Staffe turns to the SOC officer, asks what was found on Sean Degg's person. 'Person' – an odd term for a dead soul.

'A quarter-bottle of vodka, empty. A few crumbs of rolling tobacco and half an eighth of resin, and two hundred-mill wraps of MDMA. There were four empty wraps and a syringe, too. It looks like crystal meth and we found some ice on him.'

Janine comes across, says, 'From the pre-theatre inspection, he's no meth mouth. It doesn't seem to add up. And no tracks on his arms. Just the one mark.'

'Anything else?'

The SOCO says, 'One pound eighty in twenty pences in a coin bag in his back pocket, Yale keys and a book. Here.' The officer hands Staffe a clear plastic bag with a notebook in it. On the cover is a pen and ink drawing of an angel in a basque.

'Kerry's,' says Staffe, recognising it from his visit to Flower and Dean. 'There's a receipt from an off-licence down on the New North Road. The time was 19.43.' He turns to Pulford, says, 'Check that out and make sure you speak to the person who served Degg and get them to describe anybody else who was in the shop at the same time, or just before and just after.' He turns to the SOCO. 'Let me see the money.'

The SOCO shows him the plastic bag of twenty-pence pieces.

'See if there's a phone box nearby. Whichever phone is closest to that off-licence – in each direction – I want the details of all calls made two hours either side of when Degg was in the off-licence. Run the numbers through the case data filter.'

'I thought you wanted me to bring in Bridget Lamb?'

'I'll do that.'

When Pulford is gone and the SOCO has returned to his painstaking documentation of the scene, Staffe whispers to Janine, 'That injection. Was it administered in a professional way, would you say?'

'It's a perfectly clean entry and no signs of tourniquet shadowing. But all kinds of people are expert in IV these days. Why do you ask?'

'No reason. Not really.'

Pennington rubs the corners of his mouth with thumb and forefinger. He hasn't spoken since Staffe came to his office. He sighs.

Eventually, he says, 'This Sean Degg thing, Staffe. You know, it does stack up as a suicide.'

'Of course it could, sir. His wife died, in awful circumstances. There's overwhelming evidence that he loved her.'

'I said "does", not "could".'

'I've looked into Sean Degg's life as deeply as I can and I know the man was a scumbag, but nobody has ever mentioned that he was into speed. And he has just become a father – the first time. He actually had something to look forward to.'

'He was on the run. Some might say he had plenty to feel guilty about, don't you think?'

'Are you suggesting he might have killed Kerry, sir?'

'There's more than enough circumstantial. Just try presenting the argument – for argument's sake.' Pennington laughs at his quip.

'And maybe he took off with Zoe Bright. And fired off a threat to Cathy Killick?'

'You know we don't have to conflate that case with this.' Pennington leans back, looks Staffe in the chest as he says, 'At least present the argument.'

'It seems you already have, sir. Perhaps you can tell me who sold him the speed.'

'He moved in those circles.'

'We'll need to know precisely who. Evidence, sir.'

'You know where to look. Be sure you take DI Smethurst with you.'

'Given? You want me to shake that tree?'

'Keep Smet in the loop, Staffe.'

'If I'm doing this, I need to know what exactly it is that grants Given his immunity.'

'I don't know he has immunity.'

'We know he has an alibi.'

234

'Test it,' says Pennington. 'And you'll need to scratch around. He doesn't get his hands dirty.'

'I'll need a warrant – for a DNA test.'

'Present the argument and it's yours.'

'You've changed your tune, sir.'

'If Given had anything to do with what happened to Chancellor, we'll fuck him over with all our might. You can count on that.'

'Thank you, sir.'

'Do you really think he is the father of Kerry's first children?'

'Sean was protected by Tommy Given. They had some kind of pact.'

'Under pain of death?'

'Sean was in hiding. They would have needed to know where he was. It would have been someone he was talking to.'

Pennington folds his arms. 'Let's imagine it wasn't suicide. For argument's sake. Just who do you think did kill Sean, Staffe?'

'That's easy, sir. Same as whoever killed Kerry. Someone with the irrepressible need.'

As Staffe drives down to Cobham in blossoming Surrey, he thinks about how he would like to swerve into Thames Ditton and call on Bridget Lamb, then take things up with Eve. The thought of that conversation makes him nervous.

Smet is smoking out of the window and reading the *News*. When he's not smoking, he is reading the *News* and scratching his balls. Coming off the A3, he happens upon an article about Vernon Short's bill and how church groups in Reading and Plymouth, Wolverhampton and South Shields have put petitions together supporting the resurrection of the change in the statute governing abortion. There is talk of a national campaign and even a march on Parliament. A spokesperson for Breath of Life says, according to Nick Absolom, that if a country can march to save a fox, they can march to save a human life.

'The way they put it – it seems to kind of make sense,' says Smet.

'I spoke to Absolom and asked him who his source is. He wouldn't disclose. Sometimes, the bloody law's against us, not with us.'

'And did you read the bit about the woman in Liverpool?'

For the briefest moment, he considers telling Smet about Lesley Crawford having tutored Zoe Bright. 'There's nothing happening up there.'

'They've got that Flint woman working the case, I heard.'

'Flint woman?'

'Oh, yes. I know her, all right. Had to mentor her when she came down for her assimilation training. She made inspector a couple years ago. A bright cookie. But you know that, don't you, Staffe?'

'What do you mean?'

'I heard you've been to Beatleland. She'd suit you, that one.' Smet laughs.

Staffe looks at him, not amused.

'Just your type.'

'What's my type supposed to be? I don't have a bloody type.'

'You do.'

'So what is it, my type?'

'I'm not saying.'

'I'd tell *you*,' says Staffe, looking across to Smet who is delving beneath his belly, scratching at his balls.

'I don't have that problem.'

He thinks about what it must be like, being Smet. Are his chances all behind him?

Smet says, 'I'm no student of relationships. Christ, none of my mates have even had a sniff in years, but . . . no, forget it.'

'Go on.'

'It just seems to me, you go for women who you know won't work out. And who can blame you? Just enjoy it.'

'Piss off, Smet.'

'Suffer for the rest of us. Pull in. We're here.'

Staffe pulls off the road and stops in front of Tommy Given's electric gates. He stares up the driveway, watches Smet talk into the videophone and as he does, Staffe's phone goes. It is his sister, Marie. Which won't be good news, he's sure. He lets it ring out, prays it's nothing bad about Harry. He loves his nephew; the closest he's got to a child of his own.

Smet gets back in and as they drive up towards the house, gravel grinding beneath, he says, 'If you want relationship advice, you should ask this pillar of the bastard community. Have you met his wife and kid?'

'Why would I? You're the one who looks after our friend Mr Given, eh, Smet?'

'Look after? What's that supposed to mean?'

'Just saying what I see. Is there anything you want to tell me?'

'Just that I don't come here a-prying. I've had no need.'

Staffe gets out of the car, sees the dog coming. It is a killer dog, and the ground resounds as it bounds up, spittle spraying the air.

'Shit,' says Smet.

Staffe makes himself limp and goes down onto his knees, holds his arms out and lets the dog bowl onto him. It licks his hands and face, and Staffe stands, rubbing its skull, scratching at its neck. 'You getting out of the car, Smet?'

'Is it safe?'

'I'd say you're safe.'

'Nobody's safe,' says Tommy Given, walking up to the car, frowning, his first gambit gone awry. 'Not from police molestation. What the fuck are you doing here?'

'You didn't call ahead?' says Smet, to Staffe.

'Why would I?'

'I'm sorry, Tommy. I thought he had called.'

'We're not here to apologise. I've just come to drop this off.' He hands a sheet of paper to Given.

'What is it?'

'It requires you to provide a sample of your DNA. Quite painless.'

'Why the fuck do you want my DNA?'

'Sean Degg is dead, Tommy.'

'I heard. I've told you where I was.' Tommy is thoroughly convincing with his grieving expression. He even appears to be a shade of pale.

His beautiful wife, Sabine, appears in the porch with her young daughter beneath a trellised arch of honeysuckle. She rubs her hand on the pronounced bump of her unborn child, looks a million euros, maybe more.

Tommy says, 'Go into the house, *chérie*.'

Sabine looks at Tommy as she does as she is told. For an instant, they are locked in an exchange of togetherness. She twinkles her fingers and the little girl clutches at the tight calf of her leggings.

Tommy must see the look of surprise on Staffe's face because he says, 'Preconceptions, Inspector. They can be bad for the health.'

'We've not come to cause a scene, Tommy,' says Smet.

Staffe says, 'And we're not here for the good of our health, or yours. This is a murder investigation. A double murder investigation and another woman missing. In your language, Tommy, we're not here to fuck about.'

Given turns his back on them and walks away, around the side of the house, past the stables and with a single, light pat on his thigh, his killer dog bounds up to him, snaps playfully at his heels. The horses each take a step back, their heads disappearing into their boxes.

Staffe and Smet follow him and Tommy points to a paddock. 'This isn't mine. I lease it. The neighbour is a farmer – old school. But we get on. His daughter is at the Sorbonne. Sabine helped them out a little.'

'The country life suits,' says Smet.

'You could just tell us about Kerry,' says Staffe. 'It might rule you out of contention for Sean's passing. A bit of information is all we want.' Staffe goes into his pocket for a pair of disposable gloves, then tears open a small paper parcel, produces a swab. 'If you don't mind.'

Tommy looks back towards the house, which is obscured by the stable block. He says, 'My wife gets one whiff of this and the law won't help you, Wagstaffe.'

'Easy, Tommy,' says Smet.

Given opens his mouth and Staffe steps forward, sticks in the swab, runs it up the inside of the cheek. While Given is unable to speak, Staffe says, 'We don't buy your bullshit alibi for one second. We'll be getting each and every one of your arse-licking hangers-on to cough you up.' Tommy's eyes are wide and wild, and Staffe pokes the swab right up into his mouth, thinks Given might bring his teeth gnashing down on his fingers any moment, but Given is more switched on than that. Not in front of another officer. 'And if you had anything to do with what happened to my DC, you'll be going down.' Staffe pulls the swab out of Tommy's salivating mouth and holds it up towards the house, hoping Sabine might be watching.

'Don't try to embarrass me.'

Staffe pops the swab into a sample bag and seals it, says, 'We can only embarrass you if there's something to be embarrassed about.'

'You're a prick.'

'Sean was a friend of yours. What kind of bastard kills a friend?'

'Sean didn't have friends but I was probably as close as he had. You'll hear plenty of shit about him, but he was a good man – I could see that. And you come here, treating me like this . . . accusing me . . .' Tommy looks past Staffe to a line of trees on the far side of the paddock. His eyes glaze over and he looks back to Staffe, says, 'I hope you feel proud of what you do.'

Twenty-Five

Staffe knows he has to make the call on Bridget Lamb himself. Pulford is working on the off-licence and payphones down on the New North Road. He needs to dig deep into Bridget, where she is most tender. But he had to drive past, get Given's DNA sample to Janine, and also to end the flickering of his phone.

Marie has called him twice more, has messaged that she has to see him, that she's waiting in for him.

He pulls up outside his old house in Kilburn, which he rents to Marie for two hundred a month plus bills. It's a three-storey, four-bedder and the two hundred is half what he has to pass onto the Western Shires Building Society; a round two grand less than he would clear each month on the open market. It gives him a tax loss that he can offset, and this is what makes it not charity.

By calling on Marie, rather than speaking on the phone, he will have some kind of an upperness of hand. It is the nature of their relationship that this is something he wishes to hold over a sibling. He speaks to his nephew Harry at least once a week, but seldom to the boy's mother. It is a dead cert that, after months of silence, Marie wants something.

Marie opens the door and her mouth shapes into a widening, spaced-out smile. She holds out her arms and says, slow and wasted, 'My brother. I called you. Just today, I called you.' She leans forward, puts her hands on his hips and kisses his cheek. 'Wasn't it?'

'Where's Harry?'

'Broken up, for Easter. He's with his dad.'

'Paolo?'

'No. Silly. Paolo's here. With his *real* dad.'

'But he's a wanker.' Not, of course, that Paolo isn't a wanker, Staffe iterates silently.

Marie lets go of him and takes an unsteady step away. 'Paolo and I have a plan. We need to be together much more. A proper family. It's why I called you.'

Staffe thinks, Oh, shit, poor Harry. What's in store for the boy now?

As she leads him through his house to the kitchen, he feels a wash of nostalgia for the few months he made this his home. They were good times, he thinks – until Jadus Golding. Until Sally Watkins and that awful case. Briefly, he thinks of his old boss, Jessop. He corrects himself. Those times were a mess.

They pass the open door to the drawing room which seems to be tidy. The kitchen is orderly, with only a light dusting of condiments and unwashed mugs. Paolo is out back in the tiny garden, where he drags, chilled, on a joint.

'We've something to tell you, Will,' says Marie, beckoning Paolo in.

He takes a long, last toke, and stubs the half-smoked spliff out in his fingers. His eyelids are heavy and his lips are malleable as he says, at the very limit of his powers, 'Will. Dude. How's it going, man?'

'Shall I tell him?' says Marie.

'Tell him,' beams Paolo.

'I'm pregnant, Will.' Marie actually jumps clean off the floor and claps her hands like an infant.

'Shit,' says Staffe. He says it out loud and instantly apologises, but it's too late. The damage is well and truly done. Marie is utterly crestfallen.

Paolo tells him his herb business is going 'Gangbusters, fucking gangbusters, man.'

The reason he came, rather than call her on the telephone, was to catch her unawares, not be caught out like this. But, like an idiot, he says, 'If there's anything you need. Anything – you know – I'll see what I can do. At least you've plenty of space here. And your landlord's not going to kick you out. He's not a complete bastard.' He laughs and she does not.

Eventually, she smiles. Then she hugs him, saying into his chest so she can't see his expression, 'It's all right, Will. Everything's forgotten. I know you love me, and especially Harry. And there's going to be a new little person. A niece for you, or another nephew.' She unlocks the hug and leans away from him. 'And as it goes, there is something.'

'What is it?'

The front door swings violently open and a tumbling resounds from the hallway, and then a scream. They each turn towards the sound and Harry enters, dressed as a Native American, his chest bare and war-paint smeared all across his face. When he sees his uncle, the young boy drops his bow and arrow and runs full pelt at Staffe, launching himself at his uncle's midriff. Staffe catches him and lets Harry wrestle him to the ground, sit on his chest. When he looks up, Marie says, 'Paolo's got him watching westerns. He knows the cowboys are the bad guys, of course.' She turns to Staffe, rests the flat of her palm on her bump. He can see it, now, the new life. Flat on his back, with his nephew bouncing up and down on him, he thinks how peculiar, that she should fall pregnant now.

She says, 'We've found a nest. They call it El Nido.'

Eve is wearing a dressing gown. Staffe touches her arm and knows immediately that it is silk. They are in the doorway on the fourth floor of her mansion block on the Castelnau, where that grand thoroughfare meets the river. Staffe knows this building of old. He looked at buying here once and knows what it is worth. He knows, roughly, the salary of a nurse on the NHS. In isolation, the two things don't equate.

He says, 'Did I wake you?'

'It's afternoon.'

He knows there could be a dozen reasons to explain the mismatch: inheritance, crazy banks, a fractured relationship. 'You're on a ten-six.' Her eyes are puffy and her hair is down and dishevelled. 'Have you had your night's sleep?'

'How did you know I was here?'

'It's where you live.'

'I didn't tell you.'

'I wanted to see you. So I found you.' He takes a step closer, puts his hands on her waist. They slide a couple of inches to the soft ledge of her hips.

She smiles. Her lips are plump. 'What can I do for you?'

He smiles, looks over her shoulder and into the flat; thinks he can smell a meal just made. 'Like I said, I wanted to see you. Is it OK? Do you have someone here?'

'You can see me. Of course you can. When would you like to do that?' Eve rubs her face, as if something has irritated it.

'You were with Sean at the hospital. Grace's father.'

She turns her back on Staffe, goes into the apartment, saying, 'This is your work, right?'

He reaches, takes a light hold of her wrist, just to stop her moving away from him. Her wrist is warm and thin and she turns on her heel. Even though she is barefooted, she moves like a dancer, smooth as breeze. Her big eyes are wide, now, and close to his. He puts a hand on the narrow ledge of her hip again. They fit. She moves a half-step towards him and he watches as her eyes dim, then close. Their lips come together. She presses her mouth tight to his, keeping it shut, but her hands are in his hair and she moves a quarter-step closer – as far as she can. She opens her mouth, ever so slightly, and he tastes menthol. She is cool, wet, and their heads slant the opposite way. His hands find the small of her back and the hollow of her neck. The tips of their tongues touch and she pulls away.

'Tell me what it is,' she says.

He can't take his eyes off hers. 'It's nothing.'

'What happened?'

He shakes his head.

'Come in and sit down. I'll make us a drink. Then you can tell me.'

The living room is painted warm lemon and pale orange and she has a couple of Georgia O'Keefe prints; Moorish rugs on the floor. He says, 'How do you know something has happened?'

In the kitchen, which is knocked through to the living space, American style, she puts an Italian coffee pot on the hob then comes alongside, slumps back into the sofa. 'You're here, aren't you?'

He is flummoxed, says, 'I went to see his body.'

'God.' Eve hooks her arm through his and curls her feet under her bottom, rests her head on his shoulder and wraps her free arm around his waist.

They stay like that a long while.

He thinks about Kerry's visits to the hospital that were never recorded. How could that be? And then the child is born in such a manner. And the father falls victim to an expertly conceived and precisely administered ingestion of high-octane narcotics. And Eve's mournful presence by Grace's bed. Her large, dark eyes. Who said to keep your enemies close?

She squeezes his hand and murmurs, 'That poor child. No parents, now. What will become of her?'

'Imagine, if she had a sister, or a brother, and they never met.'

'What?' Eve unravels herself from Staffe and sits up.

'Have you ever come close to having children?'

'It's early days, Will.'

He puts an arm around her, can't bring himself to look her in the eye. 'I'm sorry. I ask too many questions.'

'It's your job,' she says, standing.

'I can still be sorry.'

'You can see to the coffee. I'm going to get dressed.'

'Don't.' He reaches out, takes a hold of her thigh. The dressing gown rises slowly across her skin. Her legs are brown from winter sun. He doesn't even know where she was. She leans down, her hair tumbles between their faces as she stoops, finds his mouth and sits across him. 'Let me.'

And he does.

Afterwards, as soon as he hears the shower run, then the noise slowly dampen from a closing door, Staffe takes the burned coffee pot from the stove. The handle scorches his hand but he manages not to drop it. He wraps a folded tea towel around the handle and pours a cup. The liquid is soupy, over-brewed. He looks for milk in the fridge and sees that Eve has none, then wonders if she might have a reserve of UHT or creamer in the cupboards. The first one he opens, he sees a round tin of powdered milk: the image of a baby being doted on by its mother. SMA Extra Hungry Infant Milk.

The shower is still running. With an eye on the door to her bedroom, Staffe opens Eve's handbag. He closes it; sits and stares at it.

Still the shower runs. He hates this job, sometimes; despises the person he becomes.

When Eve comes into the living room, she is brand-new. Her hair is wet, but she has on a cream, angora sweater that leaves a seam of her tummy showing. Her midriff is brown and he could ask where she collared her winter sun, but he doesn't. His mind has turned, to Bridget Lamb, and to the final question he has for Eve. There's no easy way. He pours her coffee and immediately she says, 'I take it black.' She drinks it down, doesn't grimace.

'If Kerry was having twins, wouldn't you have known about it?'

'We have three and a half thousand babies a year through pre-nat, so of course I wouldn't know about it. I've told you before, everything's computerised.'

He looks at his watch.

She looks hurt and she takes a deep breath, as if she might lay into him, but she catches herself, steps into her shoes and slings the handbag over her shoulder. 'I'll come down with you. I need to get bread and milk.'

Once he is through the Richmond gates of the Deer Park, passage along the meandering tracks is slow. Because it is Easter, the holidaying children are out in herds, some with working mothers stealing a day; others left to play on their own by chatters of au pairs. The deer are hither and thither, mainly on the fringes of the woods on the high slopes.

Wending to Kingston Gate, he runs the conversation with Eve one more time. They had kissed in the common hall of the mansion block – her harder than him, and when they had pulled away, the look in her eyes made him feel warm, then immediately cold. He can't get it out of his head. Was she afraid? Or was she warning him with her pouted glare?

More tangibly, why – when he looked into her handbag – had he seen, written on the back of an envelope from Thames Water, 'Sean', followed by Degg's number? Had Sean called Eve with one of his many twenty-pence pieces?

He blows out his cheeks and says 'Damn!' aloud. He tries to think of something else, but can only divert himself as far as his sister; as if simply living under the auspices of an alien tongue will solve her problems. He fears for Harry in this new start, how he will cope in such new conditions.

Paolo, it seems, has a friend in a place called the Alpujarras, in southern Spain. It is supposedly the real Spain and land can still be had for tuppence. Paolo, genius that he is, has been wised-up to an old *finca* with twenty hectares where he can grow herbs. Also, there is a poplar wood which they can plunder and plant for beams for the building trade, They can make a little money, make like heaven on earth. Paolo's words.

The whole thing will only take a year and Paolo and his friend will do the work on the *finca*. When it is done, half of it will be Staffe's, naturally. All he has to do is stump up eighty thousand euros for the land and materials. When it is done it will be worth a quarter of a million, 'all day long,' according to Paolo the loafer, the occasional gardener; the master builder with his trowel under a bushel. And Staffe's Spanish will help, too, according to Marie. The thought of brushing up makes him sad, reminding him of how and where his parents were murdered.

Staffe had seen the unuttered desperation on his sister. She had taken a hold of his hand and placed the palm on her swell and he had called his broker, asked if he could draw the eighty thousand euros against his Kilburn house. 'It might take a week,' he had told Marie, and she had burst into happy tears. Paolo rolled a fresh one.

Malcolm Lamb has a haunted expression. He shows Staffe through to the morning room, overlooking the garden where Bridget is kneeling amongst a crescent of meadow flowers that run across the right side of her lawn. Malcolm calls her and she waves, smiling. Then she sees Staffe and the joy evaporates, like dew. She pushes herself up and shrieks, looks down at her hand, which is bleeding.

Malcolm mutters, 'My God. Oh no, my good God,' and rushes out.

* * *

249

Staffe picks the last of the china splinters from Bridget's hand. She had pressed down on the saucer as she stood, and lost barely a half-teaspoon of blood, but Malcolm had become apoplectic, repeating how he can't bear to see her suffer.

She is upstairs changing and as they wait, Malcolm says, 'You know, Bridget hasn't a bad bone in her body. She's nothing to do with any of this, Will. She keeps a brave face, but don't let that deceive you. This is breaking her heart. First Kerry, and now Sean.'

'But she had no time for Sean.'

'It's a human life, someone she had been close to.'

Bridget comes down and throws her bloodied dress into the utility room. Malcolm goes to get it, but she says, 'Leave it, Malcolm. Just leave it.' The smile she forces dies under its own weight. 'Please.'

Staffe says, 'I need to know precisely where you were, and with whom, the night before last. All evening.'

'I was here.'

'From six till midnight – every minute?' He glances at Malcolm. 'And you, too.'

'We were here. Together,' says Bridget.

'Did someone phone the house?'

Malcolm sits down, puts his head in his hands. When he looks up, his face is quite grey.

Bridget says, 'That's when Sean died. Am I right? You're asking these questions because you think I might have killed him.' Her voice tremors. She tries to catch a look from Malcolm, but he studiously looks at the floor, begins to talk. 'We were at a meeting, in Kingston. There were plenty of people there. It will be easy to verify. We went at seven-thirty and stayed until gone ten, then we gave someone a lift home, to Petersham. We got back here at around eleven.'

'We got the end of *Newsnight*,' says Bridget. 'I can't abide him, that Paxman, but it was the girl. The Jew.'

'Who did you give the lift to?'

'The point is, we couldn't have done it,' says Bridget. 'We have people who can vouch. Isn't that enough?'

'I don't understand why you would be reluctant to tell me.'

'They are good people. We are good people. It isn't right, that's why.'

'What was the meeting?'

'It was our church,' says Malcolm.

'Which is?'

'It's not a church as you would think of one,' says Bridget.

'Look, a man has been murdered, not to mention your sister. Your niece was in intensive care, for Christ's sake.'

'There's no need for that,' says Bridget.

'Tell me!'

Malcolm says, 'It's the House of the Holy Innocents.'

'We were worshipping, for crying out loud,' says Bridget, standing.

'Don't get upset, darling.'

She goes to the sideboard, hands Staffe a leaflet. At the top, it gives an address, on Norbiton Road. At the bottom, the Reverend Laurence Hands has signed the newsletter.

'What was the meeting in aid of?'

'What does that matter?' says Malcolm.

Staffe says, 'You must understand, the more you evade my questions, the more likely I am to think you have something to be ashamed of.'

251

'Ashamed?'

Staffe stands.

'Where are you going?'

'To see the Reverend Hands.'

'Don't,' says Malcolm. He stands, but is unsteady and totters back to the sofa, lands heavily, groaning.

'What's wrong?' says Staffe.

'It's his levels,' says Bridget.

'Levels?' he says, as Bridget goes to the sideboard and opens a leather pouch. 'Ah, insulin.' A shabby memory emerges. Strange, how deep and dark the mind can make its recesses. Staffe looks at the floor as Bridget calmly tends her husband. They were thirteen, he and Malcolm. Staffe was just one of a gang and Woodsy had got hold of Malcolm's bag and stamped on the kit inside. Malcolm hadn't grassed Woodsy up, but neither did Staffe, not even when the ambulance came for Malcolm because he hadn't got his insulin fix.

'I'll tell you about the meeting,' gasps Malcolm.

'That's all right, Malcolm. It's not necessary. Not now.'

'Did you remember something? You look peculiar,' says Malcolm. 'So long as you don't feel sorry for me, Will. Don't you dare do that. It's too late.' He flinches as Bridget feeds him his drug.

'I remembered when Woodsy . . .'

'I was at your house when your parents were killed. The police came and Marie was at home. My father saw the police pull up and he went round. We looked after Marie when your parents died. And you went off the rails, I remember. And look at you now. Look at us both.' Malcolm laughs, at himself, it seems – or perhaps not.

Twenty-Six

The House of the Holy Innocents is a down-at-heel, turn-of-the-century chapel which looks Methodist or Congregationalist. Nowadays, from the outside at least, it doesn't conform to what you would expect of a holy house. The windows are cracked and the chimney is crudely pointed. Beneath the patched-up roof, the running boards hang down, rotten and flaking.

Out front is a ten-plated Mercedes with a silver fish of Saint Peter on its tail. Thirty-five grand's worth of chariot.

Inside, the House is high non-conformist. On three walls, hand-fashioned quilts hang, and Staffe suspects that this is a place where they clap happily, where guitars strum all over the hymns.

From a back room, a dog-collared man in a red track suit strides boldly towards Staffe. He reaches out with a big hand and beams a yellow-toothed smile. 'Laurence Hands.' His shock of russet hair struggles against a damped-down parting. 'You need not beat around the bush, Inspector,' he booms, as if addressing a packed congregation. 'I am here to uphold the law of the land. And God's law, too.'

'Which would you choose – if you had to?' says Staffe, wondering how the Reverend knows he is police. A call from the Lambs, perhaps.

'The one should represent the other, don't you think? I am

answerable to God, just like you, Inspector.'

'And Sean and Kerry Degg?'

'Baby Grace, for that matter. Oh, yes, we have been offering up our prayers for that innocent soul.' The Reverend sits on the end of a pew and beams at Staffe, as if his smile is sculpted.

'The Lambs said I was coming?'

'I can vouch for them.'

'Reverend, would you go beyond prayers, to save an abandoned soul?'

'This is a church.'

'Who prays with you, besides Bridget and Malcolm Lamb?'

'There are many fine people.'

'Do you subscribe to the beliefs of Breath of Life?'

'Of course. "You knit me together in my mother's womb." We are God's work from the get-go, Inspector.'

'And what of their methods?'

'I know Lesley Crawford. Why would I pretend that I don't? She has a great mind, a lively mind. If you have ever heard her speak, you would understand.'

'Do actions speak louder than words?'

'You won't get me to judge her. We have a Lord for such things.' Laurence Hands' smile grows impossibly wide. He shows his scarlet gums.

'I will need to see a list of your congregation. And affiliated churches. Is there a denomination as such?'

'You could say we are independent.'

'The list, please.'

'I'm not sure we have such a thing.'

Staffe looks around the church, sees nothing that might

help him. But Hands doesn't know that and he rubs his chin, nods to himself. 'You're a charity, right?'

The Reverend's smile falters. 'What?'

'If you're a charity, you will have benefactors. You will account to the Commission for your income and expenditure. *All* your income. Your Mercedes. It's a nice one. A brand spanker.'

'It's a year old.'

'I'm curious. Would that car belong to you or to the church? If it was the church, I suppose you would have to declare it as a benefit in kind.'

'As you said, it's not really your business.'

'You've heard of the Crown Prosecution, Reverend? Well, we sing from the same hymn sheet.'

'You can't intimidate me.'

'Is that what you call it, when a policeman takes an interest in the statutes of the land? I have to say, we do see the world in different ways. I suppose we *are* answerable to different deities, after all.'

The smile is back. 'Mine is not an adversarial system.'

'And mine is not necessarily so. I only have to dig so far. When I get what I want, I stop. Do you think there might be a list, Reverend?'

'I can look.'

'I'll come with you.'

Janine has a mischievous look on her face as she sits down opposite Staffe in the back snug of the Hand and Shears. It's an expression you'd never see when she has her forensic hat on.

'What's amusing you?' he says.

'When you give me something, I can tell what you want the outcome to be.'

'The outcome will be what the outcome is. That's the beauty of your job. It's a science. You don't know how lucky you are.'

'So's yours.'

'Until people get involved. They usually crop up somewhere along the line.' Staffe taps his glass against Janine's large merlot and, drinking from his Virgin Mary, says, 'A little early.'

'I'm done. I was in at six. A rush job for some inconsiderate types I know.'

'Damn them. And I suspect the news is not good.'

'Tommy Given's DNA is conclusive, Staffe. He's not the father of Miles or Maya Degg.'

'What?'

'You'll have to look elsewhere for the father.'

'Are you sure?'

'It's a scientific fact.'

Staffe downs his tomato juice and stands.

'Charming,' says Janine. 'I'll just drink this on my own then, shall I?'

'We'll go for a drink tomorrow, if you fancy.'

'A little birdie told me you were seeing someone, kind of a colleague of mine – in a roundabout way.'

'There's some big-mouthed birdies around.'

'Are you off to see our friend Mr Given?'

'Maybe.' Staffe knows he has to meet Alicia Flint up in Nottingham, is calculating whether he has time to make a diversion.

'If you can get him to cough up some sperm, I could check if he's able to be any kind of father.'

'I wasn't expecting it to be that kind of a visit.'

Janine laughs. 'You can be rather persuasive, when you want. Give it a whirl.'

'Fortunately, I know my biology, and he is able. He has a daughter.'

'Which might insinuate that he and Kerry weren't lovers. She seemed to get knocked up easily enough.'

Which sets Staffe thinking.

As he drives down to Cobham, to call on Tommy, this time without Smet, he looks down at Laurence Hands' list of members on his passenger seat. He is growing tired of the A3, doesn't even look at the City towers, receding in his rear view, finally disappearing beneath the cusp of Kingston Hill.

The benefactors of the House of the Holy Innocents include Lesley Crawford and Bridget Lamb. Most surprising of all, though, is the name of a Thomas Given, of Cobham.

His phone goes and he sees it is an unknown number, which probably means it is the station, so he takes it, but hears a weak, vaguely familiar voice.

'Sir?'

'Yes?'

'It's me. Josie.'

He wants to say that she sounds terrible, but refrains. 'You should be resting.'

'I was going crazy in there.'

'You've no business discharging yourself.'

'Too late, sir. Where are you?'

'I'm going to see Given, but keep it under your hat.'

'Can you pick me up on your way? I can meet you at Whitechapel Tube.'

'I'm out west,' says Staffe.

'I need to get back into the swing, sir.'

'Tomorrow, Chancellor.'

'Give me something to do.'

'Run the numbers again that Sean Degg called from the payphone.'

'How do we know which were his calls?'

'You don't. I've got the obvious numbers. There's just one we can't match – to a mobile.'

Tommy Given's brow is crumpled, his mouth downturned. He jigs his leg double time and thumps his big clump of a fist up and down on the arm of his Lloyd Loom armchair in the conservatory. Away across the paddock, his beautiful wife is leading his beautiful daughter out on a cloud-white miniature pony.

'I owe you an apology, Tommy.'

'You'll owe me more than a fucking apology if you haven't pissed off by the time my wife is back. What the fuck, exactly, are you sorry about anyway?'

'About Miles and Maya.'

'Kerry's kids?'

'I thought you were the father.'

'You sad bastard.'

'Who is?'

'How would I know?'

'What was your relationship with Kerry?'

'There wasn't one.' Tommy's leg stops jigging and he puts

his hands together, begins to wring them, staring into a middle distance, somewhere between Staffe and his loved ones.

'You took care of Sean. You made sure he was safe.'

'That's your opinion.'

'Does Ross Denness work for you?'

'He's a Bow Bells fuckwit. You should know your geography.'

'But so was Sean. What makes Sean different? And why would you have a hotline to Miles and Maya's foster parents?'

'That's shit.'

'And because Sean was safe, I'm thinking there must have been something between you and Kerry. And I'm thinking, I can't see Sean getting Kerry that residency at the Rendezvous. Not on his own. So that leaves me with the impression that you and Kerry were close. And if you were, and you're denying it – then, that's pretty dodgy. You can see that, can't you?'

'I don't need to see anything. I'm not involved. Does Smet know you're here?'

'You lost that kind of immunity when you fucked with a police detective.'

'You know that's shit. You should have called him.'

Staffe takes out his BlackBerry, scrolls to the attachment to Pulford's last email. It lists the calls from the payphones down on the New North Road. 'The last thing Sean did before he died was get wasted. The last thing he did before that . . .' He looks at the bold items on the call log. '. . . was call Ross Denness. Within three hours, he'd committed suicide. Supposedly.'

'Why aren't you talking to Denness?'

Staffe is looking at the data, keeping to himself the small lie he has just told. Sean did call Denness, but it wasn't his last call. That was reserved for the unknown mobile. He looks up at Tommy. 'I wanted to see the organ grinder.'

'You're full of shit.'

'How do you think we found out Sean was in your keep?'

Tommy's leg jigs again.

'Why did you give the word to have him taken out of the game?'

'You're trying to stir things up. Well, I'm not having it.' Given stands up, towers over Staffe. 'You're out of your jurisdiction, Wagstaffe, and out of your depth. Get the fuck out of my house.'

'It's not just Kerry, though, is it? How about Bridget?'

Tommy takes a hold of Staffe's jacket. He scrunches it tight with one hand and lifts Staffe out of his chair.

Staffe looks Tommy in the mad eyes and fears that, should Tommy decide to kick off, there would be little he could do. He tries to swallow, but can't, is on his tiptoes now, tasting the angry breath of the man of the house. The dog barks and bounds in from the dining room, it jumps at Staffe and takes his trouser leg in its bludgeon muzzle. Staffe wheezes, 'And the Reverend Hands. Let go of me. Fuck that dog off. I'll have you in. Your wife, too.'

Tommy's mad eyes go wider, but his grip slackens, ever so slightly, and Staffe takes the opportunity to suck in deep, get some air. 'You're in the Holy Innocents. I know. So is Lesley Crawford.'

'That's crap.'

'You're in the shit, Tommy. You have to start talking.'

'You shouldn't be here.'

'I'm here for Kerry, and Sean, and Grace.'

Tommy shakes his head.

'Is Giselle yours?'

Given takes a hold of Staffe with his other hand, clasps him around the neck and lifts him clean off the ground.

His eyes bulge and his head is light, his face bursting with fluid. He can't breathe. Tommy's face becomes paler and paler. Staffe whites out, feels the air all around him, then the wicker crackle of the sofa. The ground slaps him heavily, all along one side.

A dog snarls and he can feel the lick and spray of its spittle. Somehow, he manages to say, 'I'm on to you.'

'Tommy, what's going on?' Her voice is soft and unmistakably continental.

'Nothing, *chérie*,' says Tommy.

'I hope not,' says Sabine.

The dog moves away from Staffe who sits up, his back to the sofa, and says, to Sabine, 'We were messing about. I bet Tommy the dog couldn't get me to the floor without biting.' He takes out a tenner and hands it to Tommy. 'You win. I'll get you next time, though.'

'He bites, for sure,' says Sabine. 'Why are you here?'

'It's about the Holy Innocents, Madame Given.'

'The what?'

'Just give us a minute or so, *chérie*,' says Tommy. He takes Sabine by the arm and stoops, brushes her hair behind her ear and kisses its lobe. He might be saying something, but Staffe can't hear. The infant Giselle, meanwhile, is playing with the killer dog's head, as if it is a rag doll.

Sabine walks away, trailing her hand in his as she goes, until they are apart. At the door she says, 'You should tell him, Thomas. You have nothing to be ashamed of.'

They look each other in the eye, clear as day that they are in love. It seems that the trust in each other is unbreachable; seems also that, together, they have something to fear from the world.

Tommy offers Staffe a hand and he accepts it, is pulled to his feet. He and Tommy stand toe to toe, neither quite sure who holds the upper hand. He looks out across the paddock, hangs his head. 'You should know, I won't let anything harm Giselle and Sabine.'

'And the new baby.'

Tommy nods. 'That's right.'

'Your new baby?'

'It's mine all right, you prick. Don't you worry about that. Now, get out.'

'Tell me about Kerry. What was she to you? Tell me and I can leave you in peace.'

'Kerry!' He laughs. 'Christ, that girl.' Still looking across the paddock. As if in a trance, Tommy says, 'I loved her, you know. She'd drive you berserk, but I loved her.'

'Loved her like . . . ?'

Tommy looks as if he is coming round from anaesthetic. 'She's my sister's girl. Me and my sister, we weren't that close, you know. I was young and she killed herself. She left Bridget and Kerry and I did fuck all to help. And when I'd grown up enough to realise what I had done, it was too late.'

'You're their uncle? You're the great-uncle of Miles and Maya?'

'They don't know who I am, or what I am, so you don't say a word. So help me God, you don't utter a fucking word to Bridget or them kids.'

'You go to the same church as Bridget. She must know who you are.'

He shakes his head. 'You've got to be joking. She's not got a loving heart, that one. And that might be my fault, but I don't care if she calls herself a Christian, or what. There's no way she'd ever forgive me.'

'And Kerry?'

'Kerry was everybody's favourite, and it ruined her. She could be a monster. A real monster.'

'That's why you helped Sean out?'

'That man was a saint. Don't you listen to what anybody says.'

'And Miles and Maya's father?'

'He's fucked off. Knows what's good for him.'

'Did you kill him, Tommy?'

'As if I would.'

'Maybe I should ask Smet.'

'Maybe I've told you enough and you should be fucking grateful and let just this one sleeping dog lie.'

'How come you forgave Sean, for what he did to Bridget?'

'She lost that baby, is all. It was bad fortune, but he loved Kerry. God knows, he loved those kids, too, even though they weren't his.'

'Who killed Sean, Tommy?'

'Sean killed Sean. You believe it. It's what I want to believe, and that's the truth.'

'Where's Lesley Crawford?'

'How the fuck would I know?' He takes Staffe by the arm, leads him to the front door. 'That's me done. You leave my family out of it, you hear. I've co-operated, but that's the end of me. Got it?'

Twenty-Seven

Staffe sees her anew, as if for a first time. Her hair is down and he thinks she might have straightened it. Her back straight, she looks elegant. But this time, he doesn't feel any kind of flutter around the heart.

As she brings him up to date with her end of the case, he tries to work out why he isn't remotely attracted to her. The answer is unwelcome, and all about Eve.

Alicia Flint says, 'We've checked the cameras all the way along Zoe's route, and at the railway station.' She senses that she doesn't have his undivided attention so she touches his elbow. 'You were right.'

'Right?'

'We interviewed at Wavertree railway station to see if anyone remembered Zoe. But we didn't ask at the other end.'

'We didn't actually know where she was going.'

'I assumed it was Parkgate – like you said.'

'There's no station.'

'The nearest station is Neston. Nobody knew her. But she'd have to get a bus.'

'What about the bus driver?'

'Bingo!' says Alicia Flint. 'She went to Parkgate the day she disappeared.'

Alicia gets into a large car outside Nottingham railway station and he gets in alongside. She unfurls a laptop and navigates her way to the file she wants, taps a button, says, 'This is from Wavertree station', points at the screen and plonks the computer on his lap, begins the drive to the university campus.

Looking at the screen, Staffe says, 'That's Zoe. Who is that with her?' He squints, angles the screen and peers at the image. 'It's . . . it's Anthony. When was this?'

'The same day. The day she disappeared. It's twelve minutes after the argument with her father.'

'But he's hugging her.' On the screen, Zoe Bright looks around, nervously, as if she might be looking for snipers on a skyline. She clocks the camera and pushes Anthony away. He holds out a hand to her. She takes it. 'Is that a package? What is he giving her?'

'We had the frame digitally enhanced. What do you think it is?'

Staffe peers at the screen again. 'A book?' He feels a smile pool upon his face. '*Beloved*?'

'Clever boy.'

'That means he knew she was going away. Maybe he was expecting her not to come back. What has he said to you about this?'

'We can't ask him. His solicitor is saying he is in no fit state to be questioned.'

'That was no suicide attempt.'

'He was provoked.'

'You mean I provoked him,' says Staffe.

'They could get litigious. My hands are tied.'

Staffe tries to fathom why Anthony Bright would bid his wife farewell, the day she disappeared, seemingly knowing that she was about to be taken, and catering for that by handing her a favourite book. And then refuse to co-operate in the investigation of her disappearance – indeed, go to extreme lengths to prevent the police questioning him.

'Have you ever heard of the House of the Holy Innocents?'

Flint shakes her head.

'No cranky religion in Anthony's life?'

'We stripped his house and there was nothing like that. In fact, nothing much at all. You saw their house.'

'She was a reader with no books.'

'And no DVDs. Only a few photographs on the walls. No albums.'

'As if it had been wiped clean?'

'You think Anthony's our man,' says Alicia.

'What do you think?'

'I'm thinking Lesley Crawford. She's why we're here.' Alicia Flint turns into the driveway of Moore House, where the Dean of the Faculty of Culture, Letters and Thought has his office. It is a neo-classical building but with Edwardian bay windows. Clematis gropes at the upper storeys and students gaggle and smoke on the lawn that slopes out front.

'Zoe and Crawford know each other. They read the same books – I mean, precisely the same books. They were here at the same time, involved in the same subject: one an undergraduate, the other a research student.'

'Surely that means Crawford wouldn't abduct Zoe,' says Alicia.

'Zoe knows and trusts her. It would be easy, wouldn't it?'

'But the closer we get to Crawford, the more danger we could put Zoe in. Have you considered what Crawford might do, to protect the path back to her?'

'Of course. Sean Degg might have paid that price.'

'She knew Degg?'

'She's a member of the House of the Holy Innocents, that crackpot church I told you about, and so was Bridget, Kerry's sister. Bridget and Sean used to have a thing.'

'Jesus.'

At reception, they are taken straight through to see the Dean: Professor Robert Flanders. He sports a full, jet-black beard and wild, silvery hair. He wears a crusty old suit and Hush Puppies, and stands with his arms pointing out, his feet planted east and west, a befuddled look on his face, as if he is disturbed in the middle of building new logic.

He offers sherry, which Staffe and Flint decline, then calls through for some coffee, pours himself a large schooner of *fino*.

Staffe says, 'We told you that we are trying to discover whether a Doctor Lesley Crawford ever taught an under-graduate called Zoe Flanagan. Doctor Crawford was here writing up a DPhil between 2005 and 2008.'

'I summoned the class lists.' Flanders hands pieces of paper to Staffe and Flint. 'This is Miss Flanagan's transcript. It shows all the modules she took. I have checked with human resources and Doctor Crawford didn't ever teach on these modules.'

'Are you sure?' says Alicia Flint.

'Why would I say this to you, were I not sure?' Flanders smiles, drinks lustily from his sherry. 'However, Doctor

Crawford did supervise some dissertations on Miss Flanagan's programme of study.'

'She supervised Zoe?'

'We can't tell. We have two and a half thousand students in this faculty.'

'Wouldn't the programme leader remember her?'

'Probably not. And in any event, she's moved on.' Flanders drains his sherry and points to three large boxes under the window. 'I took the liberty of requisitioning these from our archive. All the dissertations from 2008.' As Flanders leaves the room, bottle of *fino* in hand, he says, 'The building closes at seven during the vac.'

They each take a box and begin by checking the carbon covering sheets with the tutors' faded, barely legible comments.

Twenty minutes in, Flint holds a copy aloft, waving it in the air. 'Ahaa. We have a signature of the esteemed Doctor Crawford.'

Staffe takes a copy of the letter from Breath of Life and compares its signature to that on the comment sheet of the twenty-page dissertation. 'Yes. That's her.' He looks at the paper, sees that it is submitted by a Suzanne Byrne, and its title is *Jane Austen, mother of chicklit: a blueprint for the inevitable demise of feminism.* 'Quite the reactionary, our good doctor.'

'I don't know,' says Flint. 'I think the bra-burners have got something to answer for. Here am I – got a 2:1, got a career, not seen my son for two days and I feel like a worthless harlot.'

They race through to the bottom of their boxes looking for a reprise of Crawford's signature, and then, having failed to find a paper for Zoe, share the contents of the third box. Half an hour later, Staffe finds another script with Crawford's signature on it. He checks the name of the student and sighs, puts it on the pile and looks at the next. He is tired. Too tired.

Then it hits him. 'Zoe!' he says.

'You got it?' says Flint.

'No.' Staffe goes back to the last paper. 'But I've got Anne-Marie. She changed her name.' He brandishes the paper.

'We'll need to get her deed poll papers.'

'Crawford knows Zoe Bright, and now we can prove it,' says Staffe.

'And it looks as if she was one of the chosen ones. Look. She got a 74. That's a First,' says Alicia.

He looks at the script itself, sees the title: *Feminism can damage your health: the malnourished mother and the malevolent manifestos of the seventies.*

Flint leans back and sits cross-legged, her arms wrapped around her knees. 'What now?'

'We can issue an order for Crawford's arrest. But how does Anthony fit in? He can't be in cahoots with Crawford, surely.' Staffe writes a receipt for the Anne-Marie Flanagan papers. 'You have to speak with Anthony again.'

Staffe follows Alicia Flint down the wide staircase from Flanders's office and into the bright hallway, licked by the low, setting April sun. Particles of dust dance in the golden shafts that beam in through the weeping willows outside.

His mind flits.

He is thinking how grand Lesley Crawford's scheme might be. He thinks also of his sister, Marie, and Cathy Killick, too. And if the future bodes ill for some who cross Lesley Crawford's path, then what of the past? He says, 'The past.'

Alicia comes towards him, says, 'You all right?'
'Just tired.'
'You need a lift, to the station?'
He nods, already elsewhere.

Twenty-Eight

On the return to London, Staffe had considered what he had failed to see. Clearly, Crawford had known Zoe Bright for years. Clearly, Crawford could easily have known Vernon Short for many years.

He has been pointing the wrong way. He should be facing the past.

Now, he regards Bridget Lamb, 'How long have you been in the House of the Holy Innocents, Bridget?'

They are in Leadengate station and Bridget's bottom lip is red and ragged. This business has well and truly caught up with her and whilst she has managed to stifle tears, she has chewed at her lip non-stop for half an hour.

Staffe recalls that her sister, Kerry, had done precisely the same, though in a more extreme fashion.

'Should we take a break?' says Pulford, feeling Bridget's distress.

'As soon as I'm satisfied that Bridget has told us everything about Lesley Crawford.'

'I don't know the woman. I keep telling you,' says Bridget.

'And I keep telling you, I don't believe you. Until I do, you're staying.'

'Fine,' says Bridget, crossing her arms, resteeling herself.

'There's a woman in Liverpool about to have a baby. Do you want her to go through what happened to Kerry?'

Bridget stares at her feet, crinkles her nose.

Staffe says, 'She'll be just like the others. Crawford tells them one thing and does another.'

'The others?' says Bridget, her eyes wide.

'You don't have to say anything,' says Bridget's lawyer.

But it's too late.

'You know about the others?' says Staffe.

'What others?'

'You thought you were the only ones, did you? Did Lesley tell you that she could save your unborn flesh and blood? The life that was knitted in the womb.'

'What?' Bridget looks confused.

'Grace is the closest you will ever get to having your own bloodline.'

'No.'

'Did Crawford make you feel special? Well, you're not, Bridget. You're just one of many.'

Bridget shakes her head, looks at her solicitor who drags her chair closer, whispers confidences straight into her ear. Pulford says, into the tape machine, 'Interviewee's legal representative providing confidential counsel.'

'Did Lesley Crawford tell you she had done it before?'

'I don't understand,' says Bridget, to her solicitor.

'My client is tired. We need a break.'

'Did Lesley talk about Vernon Short to you? Did she mention his bill? Is that what made the difference, for you?'

'That's God's will. It will stop the suffering. Anybody with a soul can see that.'

'How many were there, before Kerry?'

Bridget shakes her head.

'I suppose Lesley showed you the babies she had saved; not so different from the soul you lost.' Staffe and Bridget gaze awkwardly at each other. 'I'm sorry, Bridget. I can see how it would hurt, to learn what Kerry was going to do, simply because it didn't suit.'

Bridget focuses, as if appraising him for truth.

He waits for a sign, but she becomes expressionless. For a moment, Pulford and the solicitor look at their notes. Staffe and Bridget are in a cocoon. As if alone in the world. He whispers, softly, 'Were there others, Bridget?'

'How should I know? Why should I care?'

'Because you know how precious life is.'

She smiles, as if coming round.

'Was Kerry having twins?' he asks.

'What makes you think she'd tell me if she was?'

'I wonder,' says Staffe, smiling back.

When Staffe sees Josie in the back snug of the Hand, he gasps. Somehow, here in the soft, dancing light from the hearth, Josie's injuries seem so much worse. The flesh beneath her right eye is puffed up and plum-coloured, and her knuckles are bruised and grazed. He tries not to be too sympathetic, knows that would make her feel worse, but he can't help putting his arm around her. He lets the hug linger, for an extra moment.

She winces, says, 'I'm a bit tender. Any chance we can finger Tommy Given for doing this to me?'

Staffe shakes his head. 'No forensics. No witnesses, and half a dozen sworn alibis. He was with his beautiful wife, don't you know?'

'Bastard.'

'We'll get him one way or the other. Get this, he's Kerry's uncle.'

'What?'

'Kerry didn't know he was.'

'So he's related to Grace.'

Staffe nods, pensive. 'And Bridget. But Bridget doesn't know.'

'Aah.' Josie takes out some papers. 'That reminds me. You wanted me to check those numbers from the booths on the New North Road. Guess what?' There is life in her eyes now and they sparkle in the fireside glow. 'I cross-checked the unidentified mobile number to all the other numbers on the case data universe. That same mobile number Sean Degg called, three hours before he died, appears on Malcolm and Bridget Lamb's landline records.'

'So the mystery mobile is a friend of Bridget's?'

'Or a foe she keeps close.'

'I could kiss you,' says Staffe.

'Don't,' says Josie. 'I'm embarrassed enough about facing that lot in the station. I'm a laughing stock.'

'No, you're not.'

'You don't mean that.'

'We'll laugh about it one day. Now, how do you fancy some evening work?'

Josie puts down the phone. It is the last of the calls on her list. The sun had dropped low and the computers gloam in the Leadengate dusk. Josie, Staffe and Pulford have the place to themselves.

'It's a blank, sir.'

The Givens, it seems, aren't registered at any of the clinics within eight miles of Cobham.

'And how about the adoption agency, Pulford?'

'They're getting back to me, sir.'

'Tonight?'

'They promised.'

'So let's employ the time well.' He points at the boxes of missing-persons files. 'You take those, Pulford. Arrange them in date order. And Chancellor, shout out the medical appointments, clinic by clinic – in date order.'

'I couldn't get them all, sir.'

'We'll take what we've got. And we'll start with City Royal.'

Pulford and Josie look at each other, behind Staffe's back, neither quite sure whether he has lost it or not.

Three hours later, it is dark and Leadengate echoes with the silence of absent police. Pulford's missing-persons files cover two desks in piles the size of wine cases.

Josie is looking through the admissions records of City Royal Hospital and all the other antenatal clinics in the City that they could requisition. Nine out of sixteen complied with the request for their appointments data. None would release patient records without the requisite court orders.

Staffe paces the room, wondering what to do with his theories. Sabine Given wasn't on the radar of any of her local clinics. One of them – the Orchard in Stoke D'Abernon – said that their general practice showed a record of having treated a Giselle Given, though they would not say what it concerned. And yes, they recalled that the mother was pregnant. A beautiful-looking woman. They remembered mother and daughter well. No, they didn't think it odd that the mother wasn't registered there for antenatal treatment.

The phone rings and Pulford reaches across the paper piles. He takes the call, standing. It is the adoption agency and he checks his watch, sees it is gone ten.

The poor administrator on the other end sounds crotchety. She says, 'The result is positive.'

'Really! The Givens made an application?'

'Three years ago. I can't say any more.'

'All I need to know is whether they were accepted.'

'I can't say.'

'Look. If I need to use this, as evidence, I will come back to you with the authorisation, but a child is involved here. Can you give me any kind of indication?'

'Not really.'

'A new-born baby is missing. You're part of that investigation.'

'Oh, Christ.'

'I won't breathe a word,' says Pulford.

'The application didn't see its fruition. It's all I can say.'

'Thank you. Thank you very much.' Pulford returns the phone to its cradle and claps his hands together. 'Given applied to go on the adoption agency's books three years ago. But they declined him. They can't say why.'

'Too old?' says Josie.

'Too bloody evil,' says Staffe.

'Why would he apply for adoption if he's got a daughter?' says Josie.

'He didn't, then. Giselle isn't three yet.'

'They must have had her soon after.'

'Or not.'

'Is Sabine the type to have an affair?'

'I don't think she'd risk it,' says Staffe. 'And from what I've seen of them together, she loves him to bits. God knows why.'

'I don't get it.'

'We need to crack on with the data match.'

'We're only half-way through.'

'I'll get coffees, shall I?' says Staffe.

'How noble,' says Josie, putting the pad of her index finger in the margin where she left off and running down to see the pattern of attendance of each woman in the register. When the woman reappears only once or twice, Staffe checks the name against registered births. If there is no registered birth, Pulford checks to see if the woman appears as a missing person.

As Staffe comes back with the coffees, Josie says, 'Soraya Constantine: last appointment February 2009.'

Staffe scans through the births register. 'Son, born twelfth of May. Father's name: Emmanuel Constantine.'

Josie sighs and leans back, scrunches her eyes shut to try to find some perspective. She reminds herself that every name that results in a birth is a thing to rejoice. 'Thank God.'

'What?' says Pulford, looking across. 'Aaah, I see. Right. But don't go thinking you've moved into the good news department.'

The night outside is a deep indigo and they can all see themselves reflected back in the windows, by strip light.

Staffe fails to find the next name in the births register, nor is the mother-to-be in Pulford's missing-persons stacks. This is what Staffe has designated a 'possible' and will have to be followed up, should the inspector have his application for overtime granted.

Pulford says, 'Another needle for the bloody haystack.'

'They're not needles, Pulford. They're lives.'

'I know, sir.' Pulford walks along the piles he has made, each for a three-month period, going back five years. Twenty stacks.

'Bagshot,' says Josie. 'Have you got an Emily Bagshot? Last appointment at City Royal, July 2008.'

Staffe checks the births. 'No birth,' he says, waiting as Pulford drags the relevant stack onto his lap. He has lost count of the number of times they have done this.

'She'll have got married and changed her name, or not gone the full course . . . Aah.' He stops, squints at the page in his hand. He holds it up, closer to his face. He stands, and the pile that was on his lap falls to the floor, scattering everywhere.

'Pulford!'

'Bagshot,' he says, quiet as a scolded child.

'Emily . . .' says Josie.

'Emily Mae. Born 1990, reported missing eighteenth of July 2008. Last known address, 33 Bevin House.'

'The Attlee estate,' says Staffe, moving towards Pulford, reading the paper over his sergeant's shoulder. 'Report filed by a Robert Hutchison, born 1987 and of the same abode. Case open.' He goes to Josie, who is standing with the extract from the City Royal's appointments register held out in front of her. Frozen to the spot, she looks at the scant information on the hospital register. He says, 'Can you get down to the City Royal, see if our Emily had a consultation about a termination?'

279

Slowly, Josie shakes her head. 'I don't want to, sir. I mean, I don't think I can. Not now.' She is pale and done in. She reaches for the desk, sits heavily in the chair, blowing out her cheeks. 'You don't think . . .'

'You come with me, then. We'll make a call on this Hutchison fellow.'

'I'll check the hospital,' says Pulford.

Josie says, 'Do you think there'll be others?'

'God knows.'

'If it's anything like Kerry Degg, there won't be any records of her appointments,' says Pulford.

'For her sake, then, let's hope there are. And let's pray we find her and Hutchison curled up like love's young dream up on the Attlee.'

'And if they're not? What if she's not there?'

But Staffe has turned his back, is disappearing out of the door.

PART FOUR

Twenty-Nine

Staffe looks across the Attlee estate, can see into the flats on the Bevin's lower decks, opposite. It's where they had found Bobo Bogdanovic last year, hoisted from the neck by his foes. People die all the time in these blocks and anything sinister usually crosses Staffe's path. No matter what he does, the harm that man wreaks on man still comes. But you can save one life. In his time, he has done more than that. He counts back. But sometimes, the closer you get, the more damage you can do.

Josie knocks again and a shadow scrolls across the living-room window. They each take a fraction of a step back.

'Robert Hutchison?' says Staffe as the door opens.

'I've done nothing. Don't owe nothing neither.' He is wearing jeans and his chest is bare.

Josie shows her card, says, 'Can we come in?'

'It's late. I've got company.'

'Emily?'

Hutchison's eyes flit and he takes a step out, even though he is barefoot. 'No. It's not. She fucked off.'

'With your baby?'

'Rob!' calls a woman, distant within the flat.

'Where is Emily?' hisses Hutchison, pulling the door almost closed as he steps fully onto the deck.

'Was it your baby, Rob?' says Staffe.

'The fuck you want?'

'Did she go of her own accord?' says Josie.

'Look. I never done nothing to that girl. She was carrying my baby for fuck's sake and she said fuck all, she just left one day and then I never saw her. I reported her missing. I done all the right things.'

'Was she going to keep the baby, Rob?' says Josie.

The door opens and a woman in velour bottoms and a grey bra appears behind Hutchison. 'What baby?'

'Fuck off,' says Hutchison. He turns round and snarls, in the woman's face, 'Just fuck off, go on.' He steps back into the flat and says to Staffe, 'I said I'd marry her. I would tomorrow.' In the light of the flat, Josie can see he is a handsome man with fine features and expensively cut, mod hair. He's skinny-rib and his jeans are crazily low, showing tufts of hair, the hollow indent of his loins.

His latest girl looks him up and down as she brushes past, the top of her velour trackie under her arm.

They go inside and sit down and Hutchison runs through the last days he spent with Emily Mae Bagshot. He swears blind he hasn't seen her since the fifteenth of July 2008 and he doesn't know she had ever signed up to not follow through with the birth. Josie asks him about the two visits Emily had made to the City Royal's antenatal unit – as verified by his own statement in the missing-persons file.

'I'd have gone – like a shot – but she never wanted me to.'

'Was she looking forward to the birth?'

'Mostly.' Hutchison stands, goes into a cupboard and pulls out a framed photograph. 'That's her. Something else, eh?'

Josie takes the photograph: a beautiful girl with almond eyes and a shock of honey-coloured, ringlet hair, smiling the broadest smile, straight into camera. 'She was going to get rid, wasn't she, Rob?'

He shrugs. 'She was messed up. She was cool and then she wasn't. Don't get me wrong, I loved her, but she'd have been fuck-all use as a mother. I'd have brought the baby up. I told her that. I love kids.'

'More than the mother?' says Staffe.

'What do you mean?' Hutchison looks up, stares Staffe in the eye. 'Hey! Not like that. I'd never have forced her, fuck me, not like that poor cow they found the other week.' He sits down. He talks to the floor. 'Jesus. It's not one of them. It can't be. Not Emily.'

'Tell me about her appointments at the hospital. She went to City Royal,' says Staffe.

'I didn't go.' His voice cracks as the ends of his words fail. 'The first time, she liked it. I remember. She came home and she was buzzing. It was a good day, for her. She didn't always have good days. You think she's all right, don't you?'

'What did Emily say about the hospital?' says Staffe.

'She said the nurse was nice to her.' Hutchison wrings his hands, frowns, searching for the memory. 'She sat there.' He turns to Josie. 'Where you are now. She'd been worried about going, said she felt ashamed.'

'So she was going to end it.'

'Like I said, she couldn't make her mind up, but this nurse made her feel like what she was doing would be all right.'

'Did she say anything else about the nurse?'

'Said she was pretty.' Hutchison smiles to himself, lost in a good thought. 'She always said when she thought a girl was pretty. She was like that. And she knew her.'

'Knew her! What was her name?'

Hutchison shrugs. 'They weren't mates or nothing.'

'Try to remember.'

'I can remember, exactly. Emily said, "I'm sure I know her." I asked her where from and she said she didn't want to talk about it. She was dog tired. Simple as.'

Staffe stands, whispers something to Josie and goes into the hallway.

'What you doing?' says Hutchison.

'I have to make a call.'

'Oh, my God,' says Hutchison. He leans forward and his shoulders twitch. 'You think they took her? You think she's down there?'

'I don't know, Rob,' says Staffe. 'DC Chancellor's going to ask you some questions, about Emily. We'll do whatever we can to find her.'

Staffe steps out, calls Jombaugh, who says he'll get hold of forensics, and Staffe gives him Asquith's number, tells him to get the underground historian down there, pronto. And then he asks Jombaugh to get hold of Pulford. He says, 'Tell him to check the nurses' rota for the days and shifts when Bagshot had her appointments. Tell him to look for a Nurse Delahunty. Eve Delahunty.'

Pulford sits in a steel-framed chair and feels the knots in his lower back tighten. It is well past midnight and there are only a couple of nurses here. The duty sister quite literally groaned when he said he needed to see the files of a patient going back three years. But she had gone off, wearily, checking in on beds along the ward as she went.

286

He watches her come back, pausing by a bed with a blonde, smiling nurse he recognises from when Baby Grace was in her pod, struggling for life. As she approaches him, the sister shakes her head. 'No record of her being here. Are you sure she didn't transfer to another clinic? They often do. This is such a big place. Not everybody's cup of tea.' She manages a smile, but soon remembers who she is.

Pulford refers to his notes. 'Emily Bagshot. She came here on the sixth of June, and again on the fifteenth of July – 2008.'

'That's odd. We went computerised way before then and there's nothing on file. She *must* have transferred to another clinic.'

'There's no birth registered.'

'That's sad, but it happens all the time,' says the sister.

There is no need to tell her about Emily going missing. Instead, he says, 'I'd like to know who was on duty the afternoon of the fifteenth of July 2008. Can you show me the rosters?'

'Why?' The sister looks at him warily.

'We'll need to talk to the staff – see if their memory is better than the computer.'

Which makes the sister smile. 'You know we have three and a half thousand births a year here. I'll get the roster up, but then you'll have to come back when we have more cover if you want to talk to the nurses. That's if they're still here.'

As they go, the blonde nurse smiles at Pulford. Her teeth are good and her eyes sparkle. She closes one of them, slowly, and makes Pulford laugh. As he goes, he half turns, catches her looking him up and down. It brightens his night.

In the sister's office, the overhead lights fizz and the computer screen glows. Her office faces onto the Victorian bricks of Raven Lane. It is a skyless aspect and he wonders how long the staff might go without seeing natural light.

'Duty sister was Underwood. She's gone. Nurses Redpath and Gilligan are gone, too.' She clicks onto another screen. 'But Stafford's still here. She's on tonight, actually.'

'Is she blonde?'

'I can't spare her. Like I said, you'll have to come back. And there's Nurse Delahunty, too. That's it.'

'Eve Delahunty?'

'Yes. How do you know her?'

'From the Baby Grace case.'

'Aaah yes. She got attached to that one.' The sister shakes her head, suddenly looking stern. 'I'll show you out.'

Staffe takes his final step down the ladders into the Smithfield tunnel. Unlike the last time he was here, the tunnel is ferociously lit, revealing a cavern that had been intended as a passenger hall. Within fifty yards or so, the cavern forks into two separate conduits.

Staffe stands at the confluence of the two tunnels, walks backwards towards the entrance, looking left and right. The entrance curves round towards the bottom of the ladders and you can barely see into the left-hand tunnel. Kerry was found in the right.

From the left, emerging from their blind spot, a group of SOC officers in white, disposable overalls march into view. The gang on the right are following the historian, Asquith. As soon as he sees Staffe, Asquith tacks an extra clip to his stride, holds his hand aloft, as if this is his world, Staffe merely a guest.

Staffe looks beyond Asquith, into the brilliantly lit, carved tubes, going nowhere. The Victorians had cut into London's clay these perfect cylinders – except at the bottom, where they had carved shelves for the two platforms and below that, troughs to take the rails, except you can see now that they are not perfect, on account of what Asquith had called Quaternary river terrace deposits. This is the sand and gravel from the course of the Thames, and it rendered this tunnel unstable. Elsewhere, in this part of the network, they would cut and cover.

Kerry Degg had been at the end of the right-hand platform and the detritus from the birth had been recovered further along, up what Asquith called a service spur.

Now, in this light, it seems perfectly plausible, and not quite so inhumane, to be tended down here, but Staffe reminds himself of that first scene he discovered, when Kerry had bitten almost clean through her lip. And he begins to wonder where the hell they might have put Emily Bagshot.

Asquith says, 'I've taken them every navigable yard of the system and there's nothing.'

'Are you sure? What about the spurs, where we found the placenta.'

'Am I sure?' says Asquith, pulling his beard. He looks at Staffe, quite nonplussed. 'Am I sure? Do you have any idea how much research I have conducted since our last trip? I have spoken with the London Transport in-house historian. I have consulted with engineers at Imperial College. I have cross-checked the mappings of the water, gas and electric companies, and the cable communications cartographers.' His eyes sparkle and his lips are wet with his passion for this subterranea. Above, the tunnel roof glistens with percolating moisture. 'I know this place. I know this place like nobody else alive.'

A strange phrase, thinks Staffe.

Asquith takes a step closer. Behind him, the SOCOs are packing away. A light shuts down and the electric fizz goes down a notch. Kerry's tunnel goes back to black.

Staffe feels a chill jag through his blood.

Asquith whispers passionately, up close now so Staffe gets a gust of the bearded man's supper, 'Is there another woman? Were we looking for a body?'

'Mind your own damn business.'

'You invited me to make this my business. I'm part of this.'

'What made you come down here the night we found Kerry Degg?'

'*I* found her.'

'What *exactly* made you come?'

'I had planned the visit for months.'

'You had no permissions. What if you had discovered something of value? That would be theft, as well as trespass.'

'You're not proposing to betray me, Inspector?'

'Answer me. Why that night?'

Asquith looks away.

'You had seen somebody coming down here, hadn't you?'

'No.'

'Was it a man?'

'I've told you.'

'How about a nurse?'

He shakes his head.

'Which tunnel did you go down?'

Asquith turns, says, 'The left.'

To his back, Staffe asks Asquith, 'And did you hear anything? Anything at all?'

Asquith doesn't move, nor does he say anything.

Staffe taps him on the shoulder.

Asquith spins round, smiling and tapping his ear. 'Sorry. A little hard of hearing.'

'You saw nothing down here?'

Asquith shakes his head.

'You wouldn't want to obstruct the truth. You're an historian, for crying out loud.'

Which makes Asquith smile. 'I have nothing to be ashamed of. And as for obstruction, my actions have been quite the reverse.' He holds his head high and walks away, towards the constable at the bottom of the ladder. As he gets to the uniformed officer, he has to pause, waiting for somebody else, descending the ladder.

'Don't talk to him!' shouts Staffe. Asquith and Nick Absolom stand just feet apart. Each of them looks bemused and as Asquith climbs, Absolom approaches Staffe, wide-eyed, like a child in the grotto of all grottoes. He looks around in wonder, says, 'How could this be here and nobody know?'

'I've done my bit, Absolom,' says Staffe. 'Now, you tell me what you know.'

'We have our deal? Can I take photographs?'

'No.'

'Who was that I just passed? He looked weird, but not a suspect, right?'

'You're here. Nobody else.' Staffe is uneasy about this pact he has made with the devil's own, but he has a pro quo in mind, so extends his arm with a sweep and points the way to the tunnels. 'You can have a look round. I'll even show you the spot we found Kerry Degg. Now, what is it you said you could tell me?'

Absolom says, 'I've had contact from Lesley Crawford.'

'I knew it,' says Staffe. 'She'd been in touch when we were at the Sean Degg scene.'

'And since. She saved another baby, in 2008. The mother and baby survived.'

'My God,' says Staffe. 'How do you know she's not bullshitting just to get this bill of Vernon Short's resurrected?'

'The mother is Emily Bagshot.'

Staffe stares into the deep-set, dark eyes of Nick Absolom. 'I need to know how you know this.'

'Am I in?'

Staffe nods.

Absolom produces a piece of paper from the top pocket of his suit jacket, hands it to Staffe who reads it in silence. 'It checks out.'

'What was the postmark?'

'It was hand delivered.'

'You have CCTV.'

'A motorcycle courier delivered it. We tracked him down, but he said he was paid in cash to deliver it by another courier.'

'Did he know him?'

Absolom grins. 'No. And he kept his helmet on. You've got to hand it to her.'

'Have you run a story yet?'

'Are you kidding? Vernon Short's bill is making a comeback. I had to run something.'

'Did you mention Bagshot?'

Absolom shakes his head, which tells Staffe that Absolom needs more. He will drip feed what Crawford has told him over the course of the next two or three days, hoping that the story develops, that he can garner further details.

'You scratch my back, Absolom, and I'll give you more.'

'Like what?'

'Tomorrow, you'll be planning to name Emily Bagshot, right?'

'Maybe.'

'That's fine. You'd like a picture of the baby, though, wouldn't you?'

'Too bloody right. Do you have one?'

'Oh, yes. So tomorrow, you tell your readers about Emily and her baby.'

'Baby Bagshot.'

'Is that what you're calling her?'

'Her? I didn't say it was a girl. The note doesn't mention it's a girl. You know it's a girl?'

'I'm damn certain. You should tell your readers that you're about to acquire a picture. You should include that in your next copy. As soon as you can.'

'What's in this for you?'

It is Staffe's turn to grin. He slaps Absolom on the shoulder and says, 'Come with me. We don't have to need opposite things, Nick. Not always. Sometimes, what's good for you can be good for me. Vice versa.'

'Vice bastard versa,' says Absolom. 'Now, where did you find Kerry Degg, exactly? I can have a photograph, can't I? Just the one.'

'Later. First, let's see what you're made of.'

Thirty

Tommy brings the suitcase downstairs, sets it by the front door and calls, 'Sabine! It's time.'

In the lounge, he pulls a drawer all the way from its housing in the Dutch dresser and he empties the contents, turns the drawer upside down and pulls away a taped passport inside a plastic bag. Tommy removes the secreted identity from the bag, trousers it and puts the drawer back, loads it.

'Do I really have to go, *chérie*?' says Sabine. Giselle is by her side.

'I want mama,' says Giselle.

'We'll have a special time,' says Tommy, sinking to his knees and hugging his little girl. He whispers, 'Go to your room, my *petit singe*.' He tickles her under her chin and she giggles freely. In her eyes, you can see she has already forgotten that she was upset. Giselle nods and skips out of the room.

Sabine sobs. Tommy sits on the edge of the sofa and pulls her towards him. He listens to Giselle, playing upstairs, and runs his hands up his wife's legs; all the way, under her loose-fitting Karen Millen dress. He bought it for her. She swears blind it is her favourite. He rests his head on her lump and says, 'We've wished it so. We've wished it so long, *chérie*. Be strong. For Giselle and for me, be strong.'

She puts her hands on his face and he looks up, into her eyes.

He loves her so much and with his hands busy inside her clothes, he unclasps the hooks from the eyes on the rigmarole beneath her fine dress. Sometimes, people stop Sabine in the High Street and say they don't know how she does it – to look the way she does when she is so pregnant. So elegant. To which Sabine smiles coyly, almost embarrassed.

Tommy continues to fumble, but he gets there in the end. With a final release and a gentle tug, he relieves Sabine of this sham burden. He pulls the lump down and she runs her hands over her flat stomach and sighs. They each look down at the bump that Tommy has placed on the floor. His tailor had run it up, had expanded it – once each month, for the last five months – to get her showing and to keep it that way.

Tommy hands Sabine her passport, equally false. He says, 'When you come back, Giselle will have a baby brother.'

'Your blood,' she says, her eyes flitting as if there is so much to be wary of. 'How is he?'

'He's in good hands. As healthy as you like.'

'I wish I could see him.' She runs her hands in Tommy's hair. She does it roughly. He is such a big man. She can be rough as she likes and he doesn't feel it. But that's only half the truth. 'We need to talk about him, Tommy. He'll never be whole, not without his sister.'

'He'll have the perfect life, just you see.'

'But I can't see.'

'Soon, they'll be together. We'll all be together. It's a natural law. This is meant to be.' He holds her by the hips.

She grabs his hair, tighter, and stoops down, kisses him on the mouth.

In the heart of the kiss, he says, 'Did I ever let you down?'

'No, never.'

Tommy thinks how, on God's earth, will he be able to accomplish this beautiful thing, from the monster he has created.

'Why do we need to see him?' says Pulford.

Staffe raps the window again and recognises the tattooed man who walks slowly, squatly, to the entrance of the Rendezvous. 'We need to know everything we possibly can about Kerry's state of mind; how she was behaving in those last days, before she disappeared. I've a feeling those who loved her most turned against her.'

'Who are you talking about? Bridget and Sean.'

'And others. She had an uncle.'

Pulford clocks the door opening, over Staffe's shoulder. He points and as Staffe turns, to see Phillip Ramone waiting as the minder unlocks the door, he whispers, 'Tommy?'

The door opens. 'We'll go out, have some tea,' says Ramone.

'What's wrong with your office?' asks Pulford.

'Don't want us coming in a third time, hey, Phillip? Do you really think you're being watched?'

'What if I just want some air?'

'It's a free country,' says Staffe, following Ramone through the alley that leads up to Berwick Street market where vendors shout and vans rev their engines, parp their horns, trying to squeeze between stalls.

Ramone weaves through the crowds, his silver, bouffant head raised high. Every few steps he nods at stallholders and punters alike, until just before the Blue Posts on the corner of

Broadwick Street, where he goes through a door to an unmarked shop. Inside, the lighting is low and the air thick with smoke. In the far corner is a tiny counter with a giant urn. All along one wall, men sit in fours, playing cards and smoking and drinking tea. An aroma of whisky swirls in the smoke.

'They're smoking,' says Pulford.

'It's someone's home,' says Ramone. 'They're allowed.'

They sit in the window and watch the busiest of life chug on by. Their tea is brought already sugared in thick china mugs. It reminds Staffe of being very young in a Lyons tea shop. His grandfather would take him and he would scoop knickerbocker glory from a tall, ridged glass with a long-handled silver spoon. His grandfather would tip whisky into his tea and smoke the whole time. Ladies would pinch young William's cheek and pat down his parting, and whisper to his grandfather. He tries to remember what his parents were doing, for him to be out with his grandfather.

'Tell me about Tommy, Mr Ramone. And all about Kerry, too – in those last days.'

'You're a dog with a bone. You want to kill a dog, you can give it a bone. One you've treated.'

'Was she going off the rails?'

Ramone takes a sip of his tea. 'This is good.'

'Her family turned on her.'

'You reckon she had a family, Inspector?'

'My guess is Tommy helped her get that residency with you. But that was before he knew she was pregnant.'

'Why would Tommy stick his neck out for a girl like Kerry?'

'Don't shit me, Phillip. You know. I know you know.' Staffe gives Pulford a nod.

'Even I know,' says Pulford.

'What do you know?'

'That Tommy Given is Kerry's uncle.'

'Was,' says Ramone. He puts out a cigarette, sips his tea and lights another. 'I'm very fond of Tommy. He's a better man than anyone gives him credit for, and I don't believe it's a crime to help out your flesh and blood.'

'What did he do when he found out she was pregnant?'

'He told me to pull the residency. Said it wasn't right. Tommy knows right from wrong all right.'

'And did you?'

'We'd signed the contract. It was a tidy sum. I tried, but. . .' Ramone shakes his head, takes in a lungful and a half, coughs up, like an engine that can't catch the light. 'She laughed, when I said to hand the contract back. She had a nasty laugh – like a knife. You can tell a lot about a person by their laugh. You can tell if they're weak, or cocky, or if they don't love themselves as much as they ought. And you can tell if they don't know what life's worth. But if you're asking me if Tommy would harm a hair of that girl.' He looks at Staffe, then back at Pulford, shaking his head, coughing again, and getting it to catch this time. 'It's a sad, sad world. But it's not that sad. I hope to God.'

'Did Tommy come round when he knew she was having twins?'

'Twins?'

'I know, Phillip.'

'He wanted the best for her, is all I know.' Phillip drags

heavily on his cigarette and tips a glug of whisky into his tea. He drinks it down and looks out at his corner of London clinging to a better past. 'This is some town, hey?'

'Did you ever meet Kerry's sister?'

He shakes his head. 'Nor hair nor hide of her. Knowing what I do of Kerry, I'm amazed they didn't break the mould.'

Staffe regards his own finger, a millimetre from the protruding plastic that is the bell. He also regards all the things he knows that he didn't know the last time he was here, stood outside the mansion block on the Castelnau, a kidney-stone's throw from the wrought Hammersmith Bridge.

If he presses the bell, she will come to him and the words will begin to spill. He could let someone else do it. Would it be such a cowardly route to take?

Staffe pulls his hand away. There had to be a nurse down there – in the tunnel: someone who knew how to usher new life into the world. And now, a baby is missing. There is powdered milk inside this place.

If he closes his eyes, which he does, he can see her in the half-light. At the height of their lovemaking, she had stopped, for an instant, and looked him dead in the eye, said, 'I could.' He had said, 'What? Could what?' and she had said, 'I don't, not yet. But I could.'

It could be love, he had thought. And then she had pulled him close to her, deeper inside her. Her skin was soft to the touch, but hard to the press. She tasted of nothing whatsoever but afterwards he could run his tongue around his mouth and find her again, like the smoke in your sweater after a bonfire.

He steps back, looks up and hopes that she is not in. He takes out his phone to call her, but sees he has a missed call, from Jasmine Cash. It seems as if it might have been a week or a month since he last met with Jasmine. He knows it will not be a good thing. But he makes the call.

'I'm worried about Jadus,' says Jasmine, without a 'Hello' or 'How are you?'

'He's still holding that job down, isn't he?'

'It's what I'm worried about.'

The line peters to silence and Staffe looks up to see if Eve's curtains twitch. But there is no sign of life. 'Go on,' he says. 'There's something you have to tell me?'

'I can trust you, right? I've called in confidence.'

'I want Jadus to make it, you know that. Now, is there something you have to tell me?'

'I have to tell you? I said I would. I promised.'

Staffe remembers. Jasmine said the promise and then said she didn't need to. And now it is her that is broken, not the promise.

Behind him, the syrupy grunt of a taxi draws close and its brakes squeal. Staffe turns. From the taxi, Eve steps out and when she sees him, she smiles. Her instinct is to be pleased, but she must then see something in his face that makes a frown quickly assert itself.

'Staffe?' says Jasmine.

'I have to go, Jasmine. But I'll see him. I'll call round.'

'I think something's going down. In fact, something *is* going down.'

'Hello,' says Eve.

'I'll see him tomorrow.'

'Promise?'

'Promise.' He hangs up.

They kiss. His hand on her hip. He doesn't mean to, but he can feel her underwear beneath. A tiny clog of kohl has gathered on that bud of membrane in the corner of her eye. It's called the . . . He can't remember. Sylvie had told him what it is called and now he has forgotten.

'This is a pleasant surprise,' says Eve.

'Pleasant?'

'Maybe we can do better than that.' She puts the key to the door.

'Is it OK if I come in?'

'Why wouldn't it be?' She smiles at him and puts a hand to his face. She seems confident.

He follows Eve in and they go up. He waits in the kitchen whilst she changes out of her uniform, can hear the ghost rustle of clothes through her imperfectly closed bedroom door, then the draw and clasp of furniture. The shower runs. He mooches around the flat. Everything looks normal, sustainable.

It is painfully easy for him to imagine being a part of the domestic here. He can picture himself kicking off sheets, preparing them both a fast breakfast, reading her mood. He reaches for the cupboard, opens it. The powdered milk is gone. He rummages to the back, tries another cupboard, then another, looking over his shoulder.

He looks under the sink but there is not so much as a grain of SMA. He hears the gurgle of plumbing and tiptoes through the lounge and into the bedroom.

A child was here. He is sure. Yet now, his assumption seems quite preposterous. She has laid out bra and pants and thick tights on the bed, a white lambswool crew top and a short kilt, and he can see she will look just so inside it. On hands and knees, he looks under the bed, then hears the shower stop. His knees click as he stands, retreats, closing the door to its precise degree, and forming sentences of what he might say to her.

As he waits, sitting on her sofa, he can't shake the clarity from his head.

'What's troubling you?' She bends to kiss his cheek and her dressing gown falls open. She grabs it, quite coy, and takes a step back.

He looks at the slim rise of her legs but quickly averts. He knows he is about to forfeit that.

'What's wrong, Staffe? Something's wrong.'

'The powdered milk is gone.'

'What powdered . . . ?' She moves away. 'You've been looking. The last time you were here . . .'

'Why was it here? And now it is gone.'

'You're a bastard.'

'I'm not. Tell me why.'

'You don't have the right.'

'Rights have been removed. There's no such thing when people are murdered. A baby's life is at risk here.'

'What baby?'

'Tell me about the milk, Eve.'

'You're in a world of your own. What use is it, whatever I say?' She smiles, weak and trembling. 'You're wrong.'

'You had Sean Degg's number.'

'I felt sorry for him. It's a normal emotion. I don't know how this happened to me. How did I get here?'

He takes a step towards her, reaches out and she lets him rest his hand on her shoulder. 'We should get you a lawyer.'

'I don't understand.' She looks at him with half-closed, weary eyes.

Thirty-One

'This is a first,' says Pennington. 'Bringing your girlfriend in for questioning.'

'She's not exactly my girlfriend. And we need to check where she was when Kerry Degg's babies were delivered.'

'Just how long have you thought there were twins?'

'The paperwork at the hospital is non-existent, so we can't be sure.'

'Hence you think your nurse was involved.'

'Not *my* nurse.'

'If you're right, we need to find this other baby. Do you think your girlfriend . . . ?'

'Miss Delahunty. I found powdered milk in her house. And then she hid it.'

'When was this?'

'The other day. We're getting close, sir. Bridget Lamb and Tommy Given are part of the same church. Not a church, as such, it's called the House of the Holy Innocents.'

'Christ.'

'And Lesley Crawford is in the group, too. I'm sure Given must know Crawford. If anyone knows where she is, I think it might be him.'

'You want to rock the boat?'

'Are my hands untied?'

Pennington nods, reaching for the phone. 'Will you bring

him in?'

'No. I want him to take me to Crawford.'

'Can't we take the simple option for once?'

'And risk not finding Zoe Bright? I wouldn't want that on your conscience,' says Staffe.

Tommy Given travels light and throws the holdall into the back of the Merc. For her part, Giselle is much more the seasoned traveller. She toddles across the gravel, tugging her small suitcase on wheels behind her. It keeps getting snagged and toppling over. The case is bright pink and the size of one volume of the OED. It is adorned with the image of Sleeping Beauty and Tommy comes across, scoops her up in one arm and lifts the case with two fingers of a giant hand.

Smet says, 'You get it?'

Pulford squints into the eyepiece of the camera and squeezes, like a trigger, and the motor drive kicks in, louder than he thought, the shutter capturing four images per second through its three-hundred-millimetre lens. 'Let's go,' he says. 'Before he sees.'

'That's it?'

'Staffe said not to follow him,' says Pulford, walking up the lane, getting into the car. He is tempted to see where Given goes, to see if he might lead them to Kerry and Sean's orphan twin, Grace's sibling. Should there be such a person.

'He hasn't the guts to interview me himself.'

Josie weighs Eve up, seeing how she would appeal to Staffe. It is the first time she has seen Eve in civvies and she isn't what Josie had expected. She is wearing a print top that Josie had admired in Whistles, but couldn't afford, and a pair of wide-flared, jersey slacks; heels that would send her immediately overdrawn. 'Inspector Wagstaffe is out of the City. We're a team.'

Eve looks Josie up and down, smiles faintly. 'I feel an idiot.'

'Tell me what drew you to Grace. I remember you calling in a lot when she was in intensive care.'

'You were there, too.'

'The sooner you account for everything, the sooner you can go.'

'Everything? What exactly is it that you are saying I have to account for?'

'You had powdered milk in your apartment.'

'So?'

'Why would you have such a thing?'

'Is it a crime?'

'You can't verify where you were when Kerry Degg gave birth and we have reason to believe a nurse was with her.'

'A nurse wouldn't abandon a woman like that?'

'If you thought she was doing wrong, by putting herself before the baby.'

'You think I'm one of them? Jesus. Would you abandon a woman like that? Could you?'

'Listen. I found Grace. I'm not sure what would have happened if I hadn't. That's why I stayed with her. And now I know she is going to be fine, I have to find out who left her there. Whoever did it would feel guilty. It would haunt them.'

Eve presses her fingers to her cheeks and sighs. She avoids Josie's eye.

'Especially if there is another baby.'

'Another?'

'Twins, Eve. A child is missing and the mother was left to

306

die. At least Grace was delivered to us, but it all went wrong down there. Were there complications?'

'I really don't know what you are talking about.'

'We have a warrant. As we speak, we're going through your place with a fine-tooth comb.'

'You can't do that.'

'Did you think it would help, attaching yourself to Inspector Wagstaffe the way you did?'

'He made the first move. I'm the one who was dragged in. Ask him.'

'You have Sean Degg's number in your handbag.'

'He snooped on me. Staffe. He looked in my bag.'

'Why would you have his number?'

'We were with Grace, together. We said if she made it we'd celebrate. I felt sorry for him.' The whites of Eve's eyes are pink and she blinks fast as she fleetingly looks at Josie. 'What makes you so sure a nurse would be involved? Childbirth is the most natural thing in the world. Hundreds, thousands of babies are born every day under a mother's own steam.'

'Not underground, and finding their way out of a tunnel and into our car park. And there's something else, Eve. There was another one. At least one. Three years ago, Lesley Crawford took another woman. We know.'

Eve seems lost in thought, as if trying to recall something. Her face is grey-white.

Jadus Golding waits for Jasmine Cash to leave their flat on the Limekiln estate. She has Millie in a papoose, facing outwards. Jadus knows that Jasmine prefers to have Millie facing towards her, likes to cup her bottom and hug the baby close into her bosom, whispering to her. But Jasmine says it is better for the baby to look out, to be fed the world.

The instant the door closes, Jadus puts the snick up and shoots the bolt, then he watches until Jasmine and his daughter cross the tenemented Limekiln enclave, fading onto the City Road.

He goes to the baby's bedroom and sinks to his knees in front of the wardrobe. He took art classes when he was in Belmarsh and when he got out, had painted a frieze of dolphins around the bottom of the wardrobe. He removes the boxes of toys and slips the hook from its eye at the base, lifting up a false bottom and reaching right to the back, pulling out his Browning Forty-Nine. He doesn't want to use it, or even carry it; he still finds it an ugly weapon. He'd rather have to carry a Glock. He can't help it, but a Glock makes him feel good about himself.

Jadus checks the clip, puts the pistol down the back of his jeans. There's no safety on the Browning but the trigger pulls the best part of ten pounds – heavy enough to be safe.

Today, because he is carrying, he wears a belt and has his jeans hoisted a few inches higher than normal. He pulls on his Sean John jacket, suitably long, and then makes the text to Carlyle.

Within a minute, Jadus has the response he requires. The poor bastard Carlyle is shitting himself.

He makes his way across the Limekiln quadrangle, reminding himself how good his eGang had been whilst he was inside. Jasmine has her X5, still. Baby Millie wears only Monnalisa, and her Grandma Rose was flown over from Trinidad for the Christening. And now, he has to reinvest.

As if he had a choice.

Jadus has to chip in. They had given him this gun. This gun, whose steel he can feel in the crack of his arse, had been pressed hard into his jaw just three days ago when he had said he wanted out. When he had placed one foot outside the circle, they had treated him like the enemy and now that treatment is going down the line, towards Dan Carlyle.

Dan is thirty-six and is waiting for Jadus in the disused underground car park round the back of Peerless Street where they are knocking down an old block. Dan is smoking. Jadus didn't know he smoked, but there is plenty he doesn't know about Dan, who is a director of Devere Chance, the firm that saved Jadus's arse by giving him a job in the post room. What Jadus does know about Dan is that he has a beautiful wife who doesn't need to work and three beautiful children, one of whom, Luke, has cerebral palsy. Dan loves Luke the most, which makes Dan sad. Lately, many things have been making him sad. And to comfort him, Dan has a friend, called heroin.

'You got it?' says Jadus.

Dan is standing by a pillar in the middle of the car park. Above, the ground shudders with the demolition work going on next door. He nods and produces an oversized chequebook from a Waterstone's bag.

Jadus takes it and flicks through. 'Shit, man. They say these are good for fifty grand. Each. I'll get it back the day after tomorrow.'

'No. I need it back tomorrow. Before four o'clock. It's what you said.'

Jadus reaches behind him. He takes a step towards Dan,

pulls out his Browning and kicks out at Dan's midriff at the same time. Since he was four, Jadus has done karate. It's the one thing he has to show from having had a father. He pins Dan to the pillar and aims the Forty-Nine. He can feel his pulse change its beat and his blood courses fast. He has a good feeling which he knows will pass but he puts the gun to Dan's left temple. He turns it ten degrees to his right and makes the almighty squeeze. It's the most power a man can exert and the sound is fat and sharp and Dan Carlyle screams.

He closes his eyes tight shut, then opens them, waits for the life to pour out of him and onto the car-park floor. He is trembling and Jadus watches his ear, waits for it to bleed and it does. A thin, viscous stream emerges from the folds of hard membrane. Jadus reaches out to Dan, grabs his tenderest hair, above the ear and when Dan can't help but scream, he pushes the hot, cordite-reeking barrel of the gun into Dan's mouth, says, 'Day after tomorrow. Right?'

Dan closes his eyes, slow, to nod 'Yes'.

'You've got the authorised signatures, too?'

Dan closes and opens his eyes again.

Jadus removes the gun and wipes it against the shoulder of Dan's jacket to remove the spittle on the barrel. 'You meet me here, day after tomorrow, four o'clock, then you can have your book back.'

What Dan will receive is an extremely competent forgery of the book, down to the feint and the watermark and the serial numbers. Drafts aren't used so much these days and this book is the next but one in line. The plan is, no one will notice until the original drafts are presented for payment, which they will be. They'll all land the same day and that night, at close of business, the books won't balance.

Dan will have to make up his own story, but he's senior enough to survive. He'll have to come up with some whipping boy.

Soon, Jadus will deliver the banker's drafts – so many licences to print money, provided you get them precisely right. But he feels low, feels all the hope for a different life making its way to the ground beneath, sticking between his toes like sharp sand. He leaves it behind with each step as he goes.

Out on City Road, he smokes a joint and by the time he gets to Shoreditch for the drop, he feels less bad. He is dulled, but the ghost is there. He felt this way after what he did to the postmaster, but can't see himself doing any more time. He can't go back in there and pretend, every minute of each day, that he can fly his bird like a true soldier. Truth is, Jadus doesn't feel like a soldier any more. Outside the back of Cutz, he finishes the joint. He knocks on the door and when they open it, he can smell the oil of Dax Wax. It's a whiff of the Caribbean, a blast from when his dad took him to have his hair cut, to when he used to walk back to his mother feeling brand-new, his Short and Neat making him feel a million dollars.

Staffe watches Jadus disappear through the gate that leads to the back door of the barber's shop.

As soon as he had seen the restraint to Jadus's low-slung, backward-sloping gait; as soon as he saw the jeans a little high, he had suspected something was awry.

Earlier, he had watched Jadus light up his spliff and he had waited to see what else emerged from the underground car park. An expensively suited man transpired, every vestige of colour gone from his face and holding a bloodied handkerchief to his ear. He knows that he has to get to the bottom of whatever Jadus plans to do with that poor man in the expensive suit.

Staffe contemplates whether to go into Cutz, or wait. And he plots the sequence of actions that will enable him to discover who the suited man is. He will start with Finbar Hare. Or will he? He doesn't want to pull the plug on Jadus if there might be something innocent, by way of explanation.

His phone goes and he steps away from the gate, walking round the corner. A gaggle of City boys suck on cigs outside The Nelson between the strippers' acts. He can remember when The Nelson was for locals, when the old boys played doms and the young boys played pool while the girls took their clothes off standing on a little round table by the ladies. Who can say which is the better world?

'Pulford?' he says into his phone.

'Given's on the move, sir.'

'Shit. Already?'

'We let him go, like you said.'

'Oh, God.'

'You said to, sir.'

Staffe wonders if he is too sure about Crawford; about where Tommy might go. 'It's OK. Does he have the little girl with him?'

'Yes. They're packed for an overnight stay by the look of things. Should be easy enough to keep track of – he's in the Merc.'

'You got the photograph of her?'

'I've emailed it in. They're doing it now.'

Staffe is outside the front of Cutz. Jadus has his feet up in a barber's chair and looks at himself in the mirror with more than the usual weight.

He wants to intervene, to stop this playing out, but the call is from afar and it cannot wait.

Thirty-Two

The two women unclasp from their hug. It had lingered, had involved Lesley whispering assurances that everything will be just fine, that they will have to adapt. It may not be exactly what they had planned, but an impression will be made upon the world, for the better.

For her part, Zoe Bright says nothing.

The baby kicks and she reaches out for Lesley Crawford's hand, places it on her bump. The baby kicks again and the women look at each other in dead earnest. This joyous thing makes neither woman smile, and Zoe's recent convictions are reconfirmed afresh. All that matters is this baby. She has to bring it to the world safe.

'You said that the police are onto Given,' says Zoe.

Lesley Crawford looks out of the window, follows the flight of the heron across the marsh. 'He'll look after himself. We must do the same.'

'I was shown a newspaper.'

'I'm sorry you were kept like this. It had to appear this way. It had to convince – for your sake. It gave you a way out.'

'*Gave* me a way out?'

'What did the paper say?'

Zoe considers what Lesley Crawford might have meant when she said it *gave* her a way out. Have her plans changed?

'They mentioned Emily Bagshot, and Vernon's bill, too. It seems that the public are with us.'

'It's democracy. The only kind that's left.' Lesley Crawford sits on the edge of the threadbare sofa that Zoe had pushed under the window. The sun is slanting in, low, shaved by the Welsh hills. She rests the pads of her fingertips lightly upon her knees, together. 'There's no such thing in Parliament. Those thieves and liars will do only what lines their pockets or plumes their power. So you have to offer them power. Sometimes, the outcome can be democracy.'

'But will the MPs vote for the bill?'

'They'll vote for what the electorate want. And that's in hand.'

'Have the plans changed?'

'We have to adapt. It's the way of things.'

'It can't be good that Given is cut adrift. You know what he's capable of.'

The heron swoops low. It moves fast but its wings are slow. 'He came to us by chance. Chance was never going to be sufficient. Our interests fused, but nothing is for ever.'

'He'll kill us.'

Lesley Crawford looks quite demure as she turns to face Zoe, saying, with utter calm. 'No, my love. It was me who let the cat out. He'll kill me. If he can.'

Staffe closes down the image on his phone. The artist's impression of Baby Bagshot, as Absolom insists on calling her, is in pen and ink and pictures the infant by a five-bar gate with an idyllic cottage behind. Appearing from the right, the lower arm and hand of a parent – probably her father – rests on her shoulder. The wrist is wrapped in an oversized watch. The likeness, obscured here and there and duly vetted by the solicitors at the *News*, will send Tommy Given berserk. Staffe can only pray that he and they can cope with the consequences.

Jombaugh has issued alerts to all airports and the ferry terminals, but Staffe reckons they will draw blank. His money is on Tommy having made a trip north – to either Nottingham or the Wirral. Either way, he'll be in a hurry to catch up with Lesley Crawford for having made contact with Nick Absolom and the *News*. Right now, Staffe is unsure quite who is prey.

He raps the door. It is dusk and he has been told that Vernon Short was not in the Commons today and nor did he visit his club. Perhaps he is busy mulling the final words of his resurrected bill. Not so much resurrected as a nulling of its withdrawal. It comes before the House the day after tomorrow.

When Vernon opens the door, it is plain to see that the statute book is far from the forefront of his mind, for Vernon is not his dapper self. His hair is ruffled and his eyes are heavy. His shirt is three buttons undone and the collar is frayed, the sleeves rolled up and his moleskin trousers are bagged at the knee. He looks as if he might have been gardening, except, when he says, 'Oh, you,' a pall of booze hums forth. He turns his back and pads into his home, along the Minton floor and into the kitchen.

They sit at the table and Vernon pushes a bottle of Glenlivet in Staffe's direction, then a tumbler. Staffe pours himself a modest one, not wanting it, but neither wanting Vernon to feel as if he has to drink on his own.

'Your bill is finally upon us.'

'Like a bloated body in the Thames.'

'I thought you'd be pleased, though I have to say I'm surprised. How does the Home Secretary feel about it?'

'After all these years in politics, nothing surprises me any more.' He forces a smile and lights up a Rothmans. 'Time was, we did what was best. Parliament was trusted to govern.'

'And your pro quo? Is that secure?'

'You take what you can, but really, the forces are irresistible. You can't impose your will on the people any more. There was a time when we believed in something; something different from the other side and you wouldn't give a toss if somebody disagreed with you. In fact, it was a good thing. That was the point of it all. It lit the fire in the belly.'

'In your father's time.'

'There was an acceptance that we knew best. It's why we were in the club and the man in the street was in the street. Now, it's a kowtow to the press. Today's dish is my bill. That's all it is.'

'And your place in the Cabinet?'

He shrugs.

'Your father would be proud.'

'My father.' Vernon pours himself another and stubs out the cigarette, just two drags into it. 'I don't smoke. I keep them in the house for visitors. Remember?' He looks at Staffe, trying to weigh him up. 'I'm older than you, but not that much. When people called on our parents, you'd offer them cigarettes and a gin and they'd ruffle your hair. It was a different time. But you didn't come to humour me, Inspector. What do you have?'

Staffe thinks about what Declan Hartson had said about Vernon not having the balls. He thinks how none of what Vernon has done this last month fits. He tries to find a not unpleasant way of saying this, but he can't. He does his best. 'You don't really care about the bill, do you, Vernon? I mean, you don't care about twenty or twenty-four or twenty-eight weeks any more than you care about the war or Eldercare or nailing benefit frauds, and if you did, you'd keep it under a bushel.'

Vernon lights another cigarette. 'Go on.'

'I'd like you to tell me exactly why you put yourself behind the bill in the first place.'

'I'm not going to do that.'

'You gave Lesley Crawford what she had to hold against the Home Secretary, didn't you?'

'I would never do that. And anyway, you said she gave it to me.'

'You arranged for the details of Cathy Killick's abortion to fall into her hands because you had no choice. She got a bag with that in it and we got it the wrong way round. And you got behind the bill because you had no choice.'

'I was going to water the lawn. The sun is down. It's the best time.' Vernon finishes his drink and stands up, takes an almighty drag from his cigarette and holds it in.

'What does she have on you, Vernon? What was in the bag that she gave to you?'

'Nobody has anything on me.'

'Lesley Crawford has a hold on you and I need to know. This has to stop. She has to stop and you know it.'

'What do I know?'

'It's out of control and Lesley Crawford is going to do something. She doesn't care about you or about Kerry Degg or Zoe Bright, or Tommy Given any more.'

Vernon blinks, twice. His Adam's apple rises and falls and he reaches for the whisky, pours himself another and tries to inhale his cigarette without removing it from his lips, but this makes him splutter. He punches his chest, twice.

'You know about the threats that Cathy Killick received?'

He shrugs; has the decency to look ashamed. 'The strangest things can suit a cause – especially in my game, Inspector. Sometimes, you have to look a little deeper.'

'Crawford will say it's you who spilled the beans on Killick and her abortion all those years ago. She'll ruin you, but if you tell me what she knows about you, I can manage the information. If I have to dig around, everybody's going to know. I will ask whoever it takes, whatever it takes. But I don't want to do that. Honestly, I don't.'

'I swear on everything that is dear to me that Lesley Crawford has not one iota of information against me.' He looks Staffe in the eye. His eyes are milky. 'Not a jot.'

And Staffe believes him. He says, 'I believe you.'

'Thank you. I'm going into my garden. You can show yourself out.'

Staffe watches him go, fiddling with the concertina security grille that keeps the unwanted from trespassing. He opens the door to his garden. 'Who, then?' says Staffe.

'What?' Vernon looks back at him, as if he has gone for his wallet and come up blank.

'Who does she have the dirt on?'

'I said I'm going to water my lawn.'

'And your father's lawn before you.'

Vernon turns his back, walks into his garden with his head down, looking older, much older, than his years.

'You were on duty the day Kerry Degg went to City Royal for her final consultation. The records from that consultation have conveniently vaporised. And you refuse to provide an adequate explanation for the powdered milk.'

'I told you, a friend came to stay. She left it and I threw it out.'

'Give me her name.'

Eve looks stronger, now. Her resolve seems stiff and her breathing and speech are even. She has refused a solicitor, saying innocent people don't need solicitors.

Staffe says, 'It was convenient, us becoming friends. A coincidence. I don't believe in coincidences.'

'You seduced me.'

'It didn't feel like that.'

Eve smiles, knowingly. She runs her tongue across her top lip. 'It looks as if you were abusing your position of authority. Was I always in your frame? Did you fuck me for information, Will?'

'You know I didn't.'

'I know I had nothing to do with the events that preceded the birth of Grace Degg.'

'You sound different.'

'Different from what?'

'If you tell me everything, you could leave here.'

'Even if I am guilty?'

'You say you are not. And I believe you.'

'Then release me.'

'This isn't about you, Eve. Or me. It's about Grace and Kerry and Sean. And it's about Grace's twin sister, or brother.'

'How can you be sure of that?'

'And it's about Emily Bagshot.'

'I saw something about that.'

'She visited City Royal two and a half years ago and three days later her boyfriend reported her missing. The baby's birth was never registered.'

'There was another?'

'And you saw her. You were on duty the day Emily Bagshot went to City Royal to say she wanted to end her pregnancy. And you told Lesley Crawford.'

Eve's mouth is open but she says nothing. Her face turns pale and she doesn't blink. 'Not me,' she says.

'Do you know Tommy Given?'

She shakes her head, slowly and slightly, as if she fears her head might topple.

'You're in it deep, Eve.' He stands up, pauses by the door and watches her nod. 'And I didn't seduce you. It suited you, to be with me, didn't it?'

Eve looks Staffe in the eye. As he leaves her, he thinks that perhaps she has something to be ashamed of.

Outside, Staffe tells Jombaugh to keep her in the interview room and to allow no food or drink in. If she calls, he is to ignore it. The walls are thick and nobody is next door.

He goes up to the incident room and sits down alongside Josie. He pulls out the bottom drawer of her desk and rests his feet on it, leans back, blows out his cheeks.

'Not going so well?' says Josie.

'She's digging her heels in.'

'It must be weird for you, having to interview her.'

'Do we have any of Bridget Lamb's photos?'

'I've got her wedding photograph, from the *Kingston Advertiser*.'

'Perfect.'

'I'll talk to Nurse Delahunty again, if you want.' Josie pulls the image of Bridget Lamb from a file. The bride beams into camera on the happiest day of her life, the arm of her husband around her shoulder and him looking as if he might have done too well for himself.

'Let her stew,' he says, taking the photograph from Josie. 'Do you have the rosters from City Royal there?'

Josie flicks through a different file and hands him a sheet.

He says, 'This is for the day Kerry disappeared. What about the earlier one, from when Emily Bagshot went in?'

Josie flicks again and hands him another sheet.

Staffe looks at one and then the other, then back again.

'You want copies?'

'No.' He hands the papers back and picks up his car keys.

'Where are you going?'

'To find out who killed Sean Degg.'

Staffe parks his Peugeot 406 outside the off-licence on the New North Road. He flicks the key fob, but it has died and the doors don't lock. He should get a new car, but this one suits. Locked or not, nobody is going to steal it. And it's not a car which a police inspector would drive.

From here, he can see the payphone that Sean Degg used the night he died. From there, he called a person who used the very same mobile phone just moments later to call the Lambs' landline. It occurs to Staffe that the telephone in Bridget's home might be the very one that Malcolm Lamb would have used when they were at school together. Every now and again, Staffe's dad would come back from the Angel and say he had seen Malcolm Lamb – Malcolm's dad, that is. He would ask Will why he was not friends with Malcolm and when Will shrugged, he patted his son on the shoulder and said, 'His father drinks halves of shandy. *Shandy!*' He would say it in the manner of a confidence.

Staffe takes out the photograph of Malcolm's bride and breathes in through his nose and mouth at the same time, turning to the off-licence and going in. He waits for the manageress, Maisie Dixon, to finish serving a child a pack of ten Mayfair. He knows it is Maisie Dixon because he phoned ahead. Maisie was on the night Sean Degg came in.

He closes the door behind the child and flips the sign to show 'closed'.

'Oi!' says Maisie. 'I got an alarm. I got a fuckin' alarm an' fuck all in the till.'

Staffe says, 'I'm DI Wagstaffe.'

Maisie squints, as if she's trying to read film credits. 'You're no copper.'

He approaches her, shows his card and Maisie eyes him up and down. She smiles, says, 'I done nothing. I told you on the phone I done nothing.'

'You were working on the fourteenth, right? In the evening.'

'I work every fuckin' evening. It's shit. My mother is charging me rent. To live in my own house. Is there a law against that?'

Staffe takes out the photos. He is careful not to mix them up and he shows her the image of Sean. It is Sean a year or so ago in a Hawaiian shirt at a free concert in Victoria Park. In the background it says: *Sing Haiti. Dance Haiti*. 'Did you serve this man, on the evening of the fourteenth?'

'What he do?'

'Did you serve him, Maisie? It's important.'

'He could come back. Do for me. I'm not saying nothing.'

'He won't come back. I promise you. He's dead. You served him, didn't you?'

'Dead?' She nods. 'Cheap fuckin' vodka. He started payin' me in coins then changed his mind. I remember him all right. He gave me the creeps. How'd he die?'

'And this person?' Staffe takes the photo of Bridget on the happiest day of her life. He folds it, to focus Maisie's attention.

Maisie squints again. She shrugs and then her face screws up, like a flower, her nose the centre. 'Aah, right. That's it.' She nods up at the top shelf where there are three glass sweet jars. They are misted up and the labels are scratched away at the corners. Humbugs on the left and sherbet lemons on the right. In the middle, a jar half-full of tubes of Parma violets.

'Parma violets?' says Staffe.

'How d'you know?'

'I'm a copper, aren't I?' he smiles.

Maisie smiles back, quite radiant.

'You've been a great help, Maisie.' He hands her a tenner. 'Treat your mum to a fish supper tonight, and cut her some slack. And try not to serve fags to the children, hey? It'll kill them in the long run.'

Thirty-Three

'I know who the friend is – the one who came to stay with you. The one with the powdered milk.'

'You can't hold me here indefinitely,' says Eve.

Staffe says, 'I have to go away soon. They won't release you without my say-so. I could be gone a few days.'

'I want a solicitor.'

'You were offered one.' Staffe feels relaxed. He thinks he might see how everything makes sense. What he has been working with, throughout this case, are many separate pockets of nonsense. People's lives don't make sense. The things we do are difficult to fathom. We act illogically. Put the nonsenses together and the sense rises to the surface, like subjecting silver nitrate to light and then immersing it in chemicals. It tells the story of what happened at a moment in time: a marriage, a death, a birth.

And the more he feels relaxed, the more unease he can detect in Eve.

She says, 'What are you smiling about?'

'Look at this.' He takes out a piece of paper. He is deliberate, wants his hand to be neat. He writes two dates, side by side. Beneath each date, he writes two names. The names are the same. He turns the paper around, so Eve can read it. He rests his pen above the second date, 6 January 2011. 'You know this date.'

Eve nods. 'When Kerry disappeared. You keep asking me about it.'

'And the other?'

She shakes her head.

'Just another date. Why would you remember it? And I don't need to ask you about the names, do I?'

Eve shakes her head. She looks disconsolate.

'Nurse Eve Delahunty, Nurse Natalie Stafford. Nurse Eve Delahunty, Nurse Natalie Stafford.'

'I can read.'

'Nurse Eve Delahunty, Nurse Natalie Stafford. Nurse Eve Delahunty, Nurse Natalie Stafford.'

'Stop it.'

'Nurse Eve Delahunty, Nurse Natalie Stafford. Nurse Eve Delahunty, Nurse Natalie Stafford.'

'Will, please.' Eve can't look at him and she wraps her arms across her chest. Her shoulders tremor.

'Two nurses in London. They each came down from a village in Yorkshire.'

'Stop. I asked you to stop.'

'You can't separate them. So much so that they were the only two nurses who were on duty on both the night that Emily Bagshot was abducted and the night Kerry Degg was abducted.'

'I don't know anything about an Emily Bagshot.'

'That's bad luck. Do you think we take heed of bad luck in this business? You're going down for this, Eve. It's conspiracy. It's withholding evidence. It's obstructing the course of justice. It's almost as bad as if you had been the one who took them. And you looked after Grace's twin, didn't you? You fed it.'

'I'm a damned nurse, Will. What could I do?'

'You could have saved Kerry Degg's life. Sean needn't have died. And God knows what the hell happened to Emily Bagshot.'

Eve looks up at Staffe, her mascara is melting down her cheeks and she bites down on her bottom lip. 'It's a boy.'

'Grace has a brother? You know where he is?'

She shakes her head.

'Where is Natalie? We sent cars round to her house and the hospital. She's not there. You could text her, arrange to meet her. We could make things easy for you. You could save Zoe Bright.'

'You keep talking about a woman called Bright. I don't know her.'

'What about Emily Bagshot?'

She shakes her head without looking at him. 'I'd only be guessing.'

'You shouldn't have to serve time, Eve. Your instincts were good: to protect a friend, to save a baby – two babies. We could keep you from going to prison.'

'I'm scared.' Eve is trembling, now. 'Would you hold me, Will?'

Staffe says, 'Interview ends,' and flicks off the recorder, fumbles in his pocket and finds a stick of Wrigley's. He sucks on it and presses it into the spyhole on the door of the interview room and he goes across to Eve. He sinks to his knees and wraps his arms around her. Despite everything she has been through, she smells of barely anything at all. He whispers, 'Tell me about Natalie. What happened to her?'

'I told her, you can't bury the truth.'

'Tell me.'

Eve talks against his neck. Her breath is warm. She presses her ear against his, tight, and he thinks that maybe she might have liked him a little; that perhaps she was not using him, entirely. He banishes this, listens as her softly spoken story drums lightly in his head.

'We were only fourteen. We'd go into town the first Saturday of every month, just me and Nat. My dad would give me a fiver and so would my mum. Nat only had a dad. Her mum ran off. She only ever had a fiver but we'd share my mum's fiver, but this one time, we got on the bus and the driver said to Nat, "You again?" I said, "What d'you mean?" and he said, "She's always off into town," and Nat pulled me down the bus and shouted at him to watch his tongue, that customers had privacy rights. She said "Privacy rights".' Eve laughs softly at the memory. 'But that was the end of the line for our Saturdays.

'As soon as we got to town, Nat said she had to do something and she'd meet me at the station for the ten past five. I knew her dad always waited for her at the stop in Grassington. He'd run me home, too, so Nat needed me to be on the bus with her. Her dad loved her enough for two. He's a lovely man.' Eve exhales and it tickles Staffe's neck. 'I let her go, but I followed her round town. I almost had to run to keep up, so I knew it was something she was excited about. I knew her better than a sister and round the back of Vickery's, I got scared for her. She was meeting a boy. But he was a man. He had a sports car, an MR2. He kissed her full on and put his hand on her and she patted it away. They both laughed and she got in his car. When he got in, he wasn't laughing. He had that look. I could see he was intent. I should have stopped them.'

'You couldn't,' whispers Staffe.

'He ruined her. Years later, she told me exactly what he did to her. He had a friend who came along later.'

'She got pregnant?' says Staffe.

'I met her at the bus station and we went home on the bus, as if nothing had happened, even though she could hardly walk and she had her coat tied around her waist to cover the blood. Her lip was cut and her eye was puffed up. She tried to cover it with make-up. Her dad knew the minute he saw her and he dragged her along to the police. They did nothing.'

'She can't have children now?' says Staffe.

'Her solicitor said we shouldn't have got the bus home. He said it as though getting on the bloody bus was the crime.'

All Staffe can say is, 'It wasn't your fault.'

'Can't you let her be?'

Staffe pulls away from Eve and brushes strands of her hair from her cheeks where it tacks to her tears. 'Did she tell you how she came to meet Lesley Crawford?'

'Can't you see, she's a victim?'

'The only victim is the victim. It would make a difference, if you could tell us Crawford approached her.'

'Crawford approached her.'

'You're just saying that.'

'Nat knew Emily Bagshot. Emily is from Otley, right?'

'Yes.'

'Nat and Emily played netball together. Years later, Emily turns up at the Royal saying she wants an abortion. It was me who saw her. If I'd kept my mouth shut . . . Nat didn't say anything to me. Not at the time.

'Every now and again, the last couple of years, Nat goes down to Cornwall. She doesn't tell me. But I worry about her, so I checked in her handbag once when we were out together and she was in the loo and I saw the tickets. She went to Truro. It was an open return. There's a bottle of ginger mead in her cupboard from a cider farm. Lizard Cider, it says.'

'You think Emily Bagshot is living in Truro?'

'I don't know. I'm not *supposed* to know anything. Nat said it was better that way. It would protect me.' Eve looks up at him. 'I thought you would protect me.'

'Is that why we were – the way we were?'

'I'm no different from anyone else. I'm just looking to be loved, a little.'

He wants to be able to say he could, given different circumstances. Instead, he says, 'If the law can protect you, it will. I promise you that. You tell me everything you know and I'll have a word with the Crown. The CPS. Will you try calling her again for me?'

Eve nods and punches in the number, to no avail. She shows Staffe the screen.

'Can you write down all the names and addresses of everyone Natalie knew well enough to take refuge with?'

Again, she nods, says, 'I should have known better.'

Staffe goes to see Jom, who calls up Evidence, gets the herring and Zoe Bright's dissertation brought down – sealed and signed for.

Zoe is on all fours, breathing in and out and gasping for air as if she has just been rescued from the deep. Lesley Crawford kneels beside her, is told, time and again, 'Don't touch me. Just get me a doctor.'

And time and again, Lesley says, 'I've made a call.'

'Just get an ambulance – a doctor – for God's sake. Please! Do it for the baby.' Zoe twists, looks up at Lesley Crawford. She snorts when another contraction comes. In reality, as opposed to the story she spun to Doctor Fahy, she is thirty weeks. It's the same time as the last one came, and she fears she will lose this one too. She knows that these circumstances are no chance misfortune. The blame weighs like a stone slab.

'Call Anthony.' She blows her cheeks out.

'What use is he?'

'I don't know.' Zoe blows her cheeks out again and walks backwards with her hands so she is kneeling up.

Lesley Crawford says, 'Is it better? Is it getting better?'

Zoe nods and Lesley helps her to her feet, supports her as they walk across to the sofa. She eases Zoe down and kisses the top of her head. She kneels between her legs and rubs her hands up and down along Zoe's thighs. 'Better?'

Zoe nods.

'I've made a call and she's coming.'

'Natalie? You're sure she can help me?'

'She's delivered thousands of babies.'

'You won't let me lose it.'

'We *can't* lose it. We've come too far.'

'I want this baby,' says Zoe. She feels the mist rise now and she breathes deep, feels the baby low on her. It feels almost out of her, as if it is further along than the last one. Dare she hope?

She looks down on Lesley Crawford, knows that something is afoot; a change to proceedings. Lesley is always a step ahead, but now she is unsettled, constantly looking at her phone and her watch and down along the thin track that leads to the Strand. Today, it seems far, far away. It is deadly quiet again. The Easter weekend has come and gone, and now there is not a soul in any direction.

Zoe says, 'Will Natalie come alone?'

Lesley Crawford hesitates. 'Yes. I'm sure she will.'

'Why wouldn't she come alone? Lesley? Please look at me.'

Crawford turns away from the window. She looks stern. 'There is the other child, too. The boy.'

'Oh.'

'There is plenty to think about.'

'Is it time?' asks Zoe, putting both her palms on her swollen belly.

'It can't be far away.'

'You *will* tell me. I have to prepare. Mentally as well as physically. I have the baby to think about. Don't let me lose it, Lesley.'

Crawford looks hurt. 'How could I? We need the baby to come, now it is showing the desire.'

Thirty-Four

Pennington wasn't best pleased about releasing Eve Delahunty from custody. It had seemed perverse to him that the very statement which confirmed her as a conspirator was also grounds for releasing her – that she may bait the principal perpetrator. And the thought of the press getting hold of his DI's relationship with the nurse made him shiver. In the end, and despite himself, he was persuaded of the benefits.

Staffe watches her come back down the path. They are in Marlow, which is where Nurse Natalie's favourite aunt lives. Eve has been here many times and Auntie Barbara wasn't remotely surprised to hear from her niece's friend.

'She wanted me to stay. I couldn't get away,' says Eve, sitting in the passenger seat. She smells of marzipan. 'We had tea.'

'Natalie isn't there?'

'No.'

'You'd tell me if she was.'

'I said I would.' Eve looks sad, the realisation that her friend is destined for incarceration only just fully dawning.

'Has Natalie been to see her?'

'She was here yesterday morning. She had the baby with her. Barbara said the baby was called Samuel. She said that Natalie was looking after it for a friend.' Eve laughs – nervous. 'She said she had a suspicion it was mine.'

'Where was she going?'

Eve shakes her head. 'And I didn't get the impression Barbara thought anything was wrong. Nat's always been a good liar. I should know.'

Staffe calls Jombaugh, tells him that they can stop surveilling the hospital and Natalie Stafford's home. There's no chance that she will turn up, not with the child back in her keeping. But they should step up at the airports and ferry terminals.

'Where now?' says Eve.

It is Staffe's turn to shake his head. 'Yorkshire?'

'As good a place as any,' says Eve.

'Or Cornwall?'

'Because of what I said about Emily Bagshot? All I know is Nat got the train to Truro a couple of times. How would we know where to look?'

'Yorkshire. Cornwall. They couldn't be further apart.' Staffe looks along the high street, past the green. North or west? 'If you'd come clean straight away, we'd have been here in time,' says Staffe, unable to help himself.

Eve says nothing. Perhaps she still doesn't know if trapping Natalie is a good or a bad thing. 'Well?' she says.

'Vernon Short's bill is coming up before the House tomorrow.'

'They're going to vote? At last. It seems to have taken for ever.'

'He tried to withdraw it but now the government want it. At least want the vote – so they said the withdrawal was unconstitutional. Which way do you want it to go?'

Eve shrugs. 'You can't have that kind of opinion. Not in my job. But I wouldn't want it to be driven underground.

And twenty weeks, I don't know. How many people change their mind after twenty weeks? You're backing people into a corner. I'm just glad I don't have to make decisions like that.'

'I think we shouldn't rush this,' says Staffe. 'How about we drive across towards the M40? It's a good spot to start from. And I know somewhere for lunch.'

'That feels weird,' says Eve. 'Lunch. Us?'

'I can do weird,' he says. He feels an upperness of hand in the air, can't be sure which way it will blow.

Tommy walks the long, gentle path up from Demorna Cove. He carries Giselle, cupped in one arm, as easy as if she were a sweater he had taken off. The sun is hot on the side of his face and as he rounds the final curve by the lone ash tree, he sees the house. There is nothing romantic about the building itself: a rendered, blockwork bungalow with grey slate roof and a dormer window poking up, but it has a garden that peters to a slim paddock which in turn runs quickly to the cliffs. The cliffs here are two hundred feet above the ocean – sheer. The wooden fence between the paddock and the cliff edge fails in places, and because of the way the sea has met the land for millennia, Emily can enjoy views all the way along the coast from north to south. Her plot is on a promontory and she can see all the way from Kelsey Head to Navax Point on a good day. And on a bad day, all she can hear is the rush of the sea and the gulls above.

Tommy has done all right by her.

Emily stands at the garden gate to meet them. She sees Giselle three times a year, when Sabine Given goes visiting her mother in Rouen. Sabine doesn't know Tommy brings Giselle here, nor can she ever. The trouble is, Giselle is now of an age when she will begin to tell tales. It has to stop. Giselle's development prohibits her seeing her mother ever again, from today. Of this, Emily knows nothing.

Tommy holds Giselle to the sun, like a trophy, and he brings her quickly down, presses a thick kiss into her pudgy cheek. She smells of ice-cream. He holds her out to Emily, says, 'Has Natalie called yet?'

Emily nods.

Giselle says, 'Nattalilly.'

Tommy says, 'You didn't tell her I was going to be here?'

Emily shakes her head, ruefully. She looks guilty. Or is she ashamed? Either way, to comfort herself she pulls Giselle close to and squeezes her, says, 'Auntie Emily loves you.'

'Calm it,' says Tommy.

'So much,' whispers Emily, turning, carrying Giselle to the house. It's enough to make her cry. What actually makes her cry is the truth of the matter: knowing that Tommy has every right – knowing that if it wasn't for Tommy, and Nat, she wouldn't even have these stolen days. Regardless, it doesn't make it enough. People can change their minds. 'Let's make a cake,' she says to Giselle.

From the kitchen, Emily watches Tommy drag on a cigarette. Her stomach won't be still. It is not too late to tell Natalie not to come. Why would Tommy not want Nat to know he is here? That's something to fear in itself. Time was, Tommy and Nat were kind of friends. From what Nat had said, that bond is well and truly on the fray.

* * *

Tommy stands at the bottom of the paddock and flicks his cigarette over the edge. He looks out to the sea. It is calm, but you can hear the waves crash. There is a precipitous sheep track down to a sea-locked cove directly below. They call it Deadman's Cove. He has done the descent once, but it scared him half to death. There are two sections of scree where you have to go on your backside and clutch onto tufts of grass where you can.

Here, you're a long way from everywhere. Nowhere is half a mile down the road. The other way, the village of St Agnes is a mile off. He turns ninety degrees and picks out the stamen brickwork of the tin mines. You could hide someone away for ever down those.

He is far away, here, but perversely it seems there might be nowhere to run. Sabine would say a cul-de-sac, but the place has served its purpose and purposes change. His ears prick.

From the direction of St Agnes, a car rumbles. He legs it across the paddock to the house and down into the snicket where Emily keeps her wheelie bin and recycling containers. His Merc is in the garage. There is nothing to say he is here. He should get Giselle, just in case, but it's too late.

He waits. The tyres grind gravel. The engine stops. The handbrake grates. Then silence. He waits for the slam of a car door or the flip of a boot. But there is nothing. The engine ticks a while, then only the gulls and the sea.

Staffe hangs up his mobile and picks at his lunch. He has rack of lamb but the flesh of the meat is overdone and the dauphinoise potatoes are gloopy. He looks across at Eve who is eating a piece of sea bream daintily. It reminds him of someone playing the game Operation! Trying not to make a false move.

They are in the garden of a pub by the higher reaches of the Thames, which appeals to him very much. It makes him feel connected. All his life, he has never been far from this old father: in Surrey and when he was at Merton College up in Oxford and now his office in the City. From his flat in South Ken he can run it in five.

He checks that his phone is turned on. Alicia Flint had said that there was no sign of Tommy Given's Merc. Merseyside Police are watching the obvious roads onto the Wirral peninsula, both from the city and also along the trunk roads up from Chester and the M56; the major junctions, too. He thinks he might have upset her, by asking was she sure that she had taken the particulars correctly. He had repeated all the germane information to her and she had sighed.

Digital tones sing a tune he can't name and he reaches for his phone, but Eve holds out her hand and with the other drops her fork. She reaches into her bag, panicking. 'My God,' she says.

He realises Eve must have different ringtones for different people and says, 'It's her, isn't it? It's Natalie.'

Eve looks at her handset, as if it might detonate.

'Answer it!' he says. 'Is it Natalie?'

'It's a text.' She presses a couple of buttons with the perfect nail of her thumb and she nods.

'We have to call her. She's got her phone switched on.' He reaches for the phone but Eve leans away and says, 'Let me read it, at least.' Her eyebrows pinch together and her lips move ever so slightly as she reads the text.

'Here.' Eve hands him the phone and picks at her fish with her fork. She does it harshly and takes a big mouthful, has to reach into her mouth with her fingers, for a bone.

Staffe reads:

u must tell them wht u need 2. Ill be fine. Don't worry. This is wht I have 2 do. U know. U know me! Am in cnwl 4 now but fone going off. This is my peace, e. I luv u.x .

He says, 'What does she have to do?'

Eve shrugs. 'What do you think?'

'She's in Cornwall. Where?'

'She's never told me.'

'But she knows you know she went there? She's with Emily Bagshot.'

'I don't know.'

Staffe works his way out of Messages, clicks through the menu that offers him the opportunity to call Natalie Stafford. He presses, waits and hears that the device is turned off once more.

'She won't answer.'

'And you won't tell me where she is.'

'Believe me. If I knew, I would. She never says she'll be fine. She always says the worst. I'm afraid for her, Will. What shall we do?'

'How will she find peace?'

'Peace for Emily, maybe?'

'Or peace for herself. From what you say, she's never got over what happened.'

Eve stares towards the river. 'I dread to think what she might do. Sometimes . . . sometimes, she's so full of hate. Full of something not her. Perhaps she's getting rid of that.'

Staffe trawls the reasons Nurse Natalie might go to Cornwall, to see Emily Bagshot, the girl she knew from Yorkshire and the girl she helped to abduct, that her child be placed in the custody of the hitherto childless Tommy Given. Or is it so many red herrings? What he knows for sure is that once you are within the compass of Tommy Given, you dance to his beat. You stay put, should he say so.

He calls Josie and gives her Eve and Natalie's mobile numbers and the time of the call, and Eve's network, tells her to get a trace on Natalie's mobile then liaise with the nearest CID. He feels helpless, thinks north for Yorkshire and north-west for Merseyside, thinks south-west. Suddenly, his world is larger, even more unnavigable. The Thames flows by, the same as it ever did, and he puts his knife and fork together, with no choice but to go with the flow.

Thirty-Five

Natalie puts her phone in her pocket and leans towards the windscreen and looks up at Emily's house, sees that the light above the porch is on even though it is daylight. It is the sign that Tommy Given is still here and for a moment, this makes her afraid. She reminds herself that there is no other way. The world has to be put back the way it was, but even so, her hands tremble. She must be strong, for Emily; for that atonement.

She checks that the back seat is left down a little, to allow air to pass into the boot, where baby Samuel Degg is wedged in tight, in his Moses basket, just the tiniest dose of Fenergen in his last feed. He sleeps soundly, silently.

Everything she could prepare is done. In the pocket of her loose-fitting jacket are a scalpel and a syringe. In each of her trouser pockets she has a small canister of Mace. She takes a mobile phone from the glove compartment, bought at the services in Bodmin and honed for emergency services, just requiring a single, light press of the green. She leaves the keys in the ignition.

She steps out, smells the ozone. The sea air gusts her hair.

The front door is slightly ajar, as Emily said it would be. They have taken all reasonable precautions, have secured an element of surprise, but that is all. She knocks and goes into the hallway with one movement and Emily appears from the kitchen with Giselle in her arms. They each have flour on their arms and Giselle's hands are gooey with cake mix.

Natalie says, in a stage whisper, 'Aah, this is how it should be. Where is he?'

Emily hugs her one-time friend, her one-time captor. Natalie is a few inches the shorter, has an angelic face, but Emily is, as ever, afraid of her. It's the way it has always been, since what happened to Natalie. Nat only recently told her all about it. It's what softened Emily's heart almost enough to completely forgive. Emily whispers into Natalie's ear, 'He's out in the garden. Over by the cliff. Can't we just go?'

Natalie looks beyond Emily, her eyes opening wide, as if she is seeing a ghost.

Tommy Given is in the doorway, holding up the keys to Natalie's car. He says, 'You should be more careful. It's a criminal world, you know. Even here.'

Giselle reaches out from her mother, holding her hands towards Tommy, saying, 'Papa. Papa.'

Natalie feels peculiar as she goes across to Tommy. She makes it appear that she is happy to see him; goes up on tippy toes and kisses him on the cheek. And she is, actually, pleased to see him. This feels right. It feels as if it is the end of a chapter – a whole story, perhaps.

She takes Giselle from Emily, the way only a nurse can, and she hands the toddler to her supposed dad, rubbing her nose into the infant's neck *en passant* and making the beautiful little girl giggle hysterically. 'Pleasant surprise, Tommy.'

'Have you got Samuel?'

'I've got the kettle on,' says Emily. 'Giselle and I were making cakes. They've just gone in the oven.'

Tommy says, 'You didn't tell me you were coming to see Emily.'

'I tried you. You're a hard man to get hold of.'

'I don't have any missed calls.'

Natalie raises her eyebrows and flicks her head backwards, as if drawing a line all the way back up the A30. 'It's turned into a damn mess. And that's for sure.'

He goes into the kitchen and sits on a bar stool at the breakfast bar, appears to relax. 'I've handled worse. It just requires a little direct action. I asked you about the boy?'

'Samuel?' says Natalie. 'He's with Lesley.'

'What!'

'Who else could I trust? But he's fine. He's ready to go, just as soon as you say.' She smiles at him, as if she might be about to tell him they have found a little something but that the prognosis is not all bad. 'Nobody knows about him, still? He is a secret – right?'

Tommy looks at Emily as if he might be determining her fate. 'I'm getting a bit concerned about Crawford.' He reaches into his jacket and pulls out a copy of the *News*. On the front cover is a remarkable likeness of Giselle. It is a pen and ink rendition and the child has a hand upon her shoulder. The wrist to the hand has a fat Rolex wrapped around it. As Tommy holds up the image, his Rolex slumps, heavy. 'Who's that look like?'

'It could be any three-year-old little girl,' says Nat.

'Yeah, right.'

Above the photograph, the headline is: 'Do You Know This Child?' And in smaller print, above the article: 'Who breathed the life into this girl?'

Tommy says, 'There's been nobody snooping, has there?'

Emily shakes her head, like a scolded child. 'I swear, Tommy. Not a dicky bird. I keep myself to myself down here. They don't even know . . .'

'Know what? There's nothing *to* know. You're not a mother. You . . .' He transforms his voice to a hiss, turns Giselle away and puts a hand over her ear, 'You didn't want this life. Remember?'

And this is all it takes, to turn Emily to tears. Her shoulders shudder and she reaches for the work surface. She says, 'I . . .'

Natalie goes to her, tut-tutting at Tommy. She wraps her arms around Emily and her suspicions as to why Tommy came here are confirmed. 'Let's not upset Giselle, hey, hun.'

Emily says to Tommy, 'Thanks for bringing her to see me. Really, I mean it.'

Natalie rubs Emily's back.

Distantly, a faint cry emerges. The cry is painfully young, and muted. Natalie freezes, stops rubbing Emily's back.

'What's that?' Tommy raises a finger to his lips. 'What the hell is that?' He walks quickly out of the kitchen and the two women, holding each other, listen to him leave the house, going towards the car.

Emily whispers, 'Oh, my God. Why did he come? Really, why did he come? Do you know something?'

'You have to do what I say, Emily. Exactly what I say.'

'He said no harm would come to me, ever. He promised me.'

'Everything's closing in, Em. We have to do what we said.' Natalie takes out a tiny canister, the size of a mouth spray. 'Get it into his eyes. Don't hesitate. I'll say, "For the love of God".'

She takes Emily by the shoulders and shakes her. ' "For the love of God", ' and then you do it. You don't hesitate, right?'

Emily nods, wiping her eyes. She takes the Mace from Natalie and looks around. 'Where's Giselle? Where's he taken her?' Emily's face is drawn and bloodless. She looks as if she might faint.

'He's gone to the car. The boy is in the car.'

'He's taken Giselle.'

'He'll be back. You have to concentrate. If you hear "For the love of God", you do it. You hear!'

Emily's eyes glaze over, lose all focus. She drops the Mace and her knees go. She slumps to the floor and Tommy comes in, carrying the boy, Samuel, swaddled in a crocheted blanket. Natalie had made it with her own hands.

'What the hell were you thinking?' shouts Tommy, coming into the kitchen, holding the baby boy, and leading Giselle: his family, a kind of flesh and blood.

Natalie says, 'I had to bring him. Aren't you pleased?'

'Why would you lie? He was in the boot, for the love of God.'

Emily looks up, startled. She mouths the words, 'For the love of God', and tries to stand but she falls back to her knees, slipping on some cake mix. She looks up from the floor, holding up the canister of Mace, her finger on its top.

'No!' shouts Natalie.

Tommy is holding the boy. He pulls him close to his chest and lets go of Giselle's hand. He stares at Emily, who is holding the Mace, looking at Tommy, then Giselle. She reaches out for her daughter and pulls her away from Tommy.

Giselle screams, 'Papa!'

With the baby Samuel in his arms, he advances slowly towards Emily, saying, 'What is that? What the hell have you got?'

Emily shakes her head, tries to talk but cannot. She staggers to her feet, her hand held out before her, pointing the Mace at Tommy's face. With her other hand, she keeps a tight hold of Giselle.

As calm as sun rising, Natalie advances towards them, saying quite serenely, 'Emily? What on earth are you thinking?' As she gets to within a yard of them, Tommy gives her a sidelong glance.

Emily says, 'I'll do it.' Her finger is on the button of the spray. 'All I care about is my baby. Just her.'

'Papa!' cries Giselle.

Tommy holds Samuel, his large hand splayed on the baby boy's chest, his other hand reaching into his pocket.

In this moment, Natalie feels calm, as if the breath in her lungs is ice. What she does next reels away from her, as if she is someone else; as if it is also not just Tommy she is doing it to.

Fast as a card sharp, and with a peacemaking smile broadening across her mouth, Natalie flicks her right hand from its pocket and sprays a fine jet at his face. Samuel squeals and Tommy puts a hand to the boy's eyes. Natalie takes another step and sprays a longer blast straight into Tommy's eyes. Tommy screws up his face and steps back, holding Samuel's face to his chest and pulling a knife from his pocket.

Emily clutches her daughter to her bosom, edges away as Natalie moves closer to Tommy, reaching into her pocket.

Tommy blinks manically and forces his eyes to stay open. He gets Emily firmly in his sights. 'Say goodbye.'

'Watch the child,' shouts Natalie, moving out of his eyeline and stooping behind him. She holds the scalpel as firm as she can, swipes at the back of his knee. She can hear the material of his trousers being scored, then the ping of his tendon being cut clean through.

His knee gives way and Tommy slips towards the floor, like a drunk.

Natalie monitors his movements, calculates her next move. She could go for the other leg, the way she planned.

'Papa,' says Giselle, softly, confused.

Tommy is on one knee and blood streams down his leg, beginning to pool on the floor. His face is flexed in agony and his eyes are blood red. He draws back his knife, trying to turn to face Natalie, but she keeps moving, arcing away from him, reaching into her pocket again.

Natalie takes a firm hold of the syringe, pulls the plunger and sizes up Tommy's neck. As he twists round, flailing with his blade, still holding Samuel, she stabs the needle into his neck. He swivels. She goes with it, pressing the plunger in. She looks away from the syringe and watches as he topples back. She looks into his eyes, can savour this moment. She has stopped the big, strong bully of a man in his tracks. Little old her has brought the ogre down and she takes a half-step closer, like a matador in the eye of a kill, watching him writhe. His eyes grow heavy. The evil smile evaporates from his face and he slumps back to the ground, lies on his back, still holding Samuel, his flesh and blood, to his chest, until his grip releases and his arms flop by his side.

'Get the children to the car.' Natalie picks Samuel up and hands him to Emily. She takes her car keys from Tommy's pocket and tosses them to Emily. 'I'll be there in a minute.'

Emily says, 'Thank you.'

Natalie turns on each of the four gas hobs. 'Hurry!'

'We're even, Nat.'

Natalie says, 'No. We can never be even.' She watches Emily go and waits for the gas to hiss and fill. She closes all the windows but leaves the door from the kitchen to the hallway open. At the bottom of the stairs, on the window-ledge beside the front door is a church candle, just as Emily had said. She lights it, says a prayer for the souls of the children and Emily and herself, then she closes the front door behind her, careful that there is no draught.

PART FIVE

Thirty-Six

Lesley Crawford holds Zoe. They are on the sofa beneath the window that looks out across the marshes to where the estuary once flowed free and wide. Zoe is running a temperature.

The baby has knocked out the last seal between it and the world. Now, it is a question of the baby's will versus the membrane and muscle of its mother. Zoe is pleading to be taken to the hospital, but Lesley knows best. She really does. The vote is coming and they can stay put. They must.

Lesley Crawford strokes Zoe with a steady rhythm, running her fingers through the young woman's hair. In her other hand, she fingers the buttons of her phone, flitting between Natalie Stafford and Nick Absolom.

It is her time.

She presses for Natalie and when it is answered, she says, 'You must come quickly, the baby is on its way. She has had her show and the waters have gone. Yes I know. I know. If anything happens to this baby, we will all be ruined. Trust me.'

Natalie says, 'We are done here. He is gone.'

Lesley Crawford says nothing. She knows you can't be too careful, but as she hangs up, she gasps. The delight is deep and true, like nothing else she has known, ever.

Natalie hangs up her phone. The baby-blue Beetle is parked up on a C-road verge above the tin mines between

St Agnes and Porthtowan. It is pointed towards the road to Truro and the A30. In two hours, with a following wind, they can be on the M5.

Emily is alongside her, holding Giselle, who has stopped crying. Natalie holds the orphan Samuel, who – like his baby sister, Grace – has survived his parents, Sean and Kerry. Together, they see a flash of light. Behind it is the mighty roar of the bungalow, beside the sea. A giant, mythical lick of smoke plumes the Cornish air and flames emerge.

Natalie empties her pockets and regards the syringe and scalpel – instruments designed to save a life. She wipes them clean and tosses them into the hedgerow, but as she does, another roar rises from the field beyond. The diesel fumes of a tractor poison the air and the machine drives along the edge of the field, the farmer taking a peek.

They get in the car quickly, will drive sedately to the A30 and then they'll floor it – all the way to Merseyside and a more northern shore.

'I'm afraid,' says Emily.

'Frayed,' says Giselle, who has stopped crying now and looks up, adoringly, at her mother. But her eyes flit. For a moment she appears lost. Then, found again.

'But I'm alive. I feel alive,' says Emily. 'Did he see us, that farmer?'

'I told you, Lesley will save us. This is what she has planned. It's her life's work.'

'Is she as clever as you say?'

'Oh, yes,' says Natalie.

* * *

Staffe is paying the bill for lunch. Eve has kicked off her shoes and has turned her chair so she faces the sun, away from him. His phone rings and he sees it is Absolom. He stands and walks towards the bank of the river, as calmly as he can.

'Why can't I hear?' says Eve.

He ignores her and says softly, into the handset, 'What is it?'

Absolom is plainly excited and even from here, Staffe can tell that the reporter is choosing his words carefully. 'I'm on my way up to Merseyside. She's called. Something's going to happen.'

'The vote on Vernon's bill is tomorrow.'

'Everything adds up.'

'Where did she say for you to go?'

'She didn't. She'll call again, is what she said.'

'We had a deal. Remember?'

'You know as much as I do. But she said not to call the police, and I feel bad even talking to you, Staffe. But we had a deal. I'm honouring it.'

'Listen . . .'

But the phone is dead.

He calls Alicia Flint, tells her to get her plain-clothes men up to Parkgate. He doesn't know exactly where. And they should redouble their surveillance of the roads. All he can say is that they need to look out for Tommy Given's Merc. He is aware that his information is vague, not exactly up to date. 'Hang on,' he says, walking back to Eve. 'What car has Natalie got?'

'It's a Beetle. The new sort. It's blue. Baby blue.' Which he relays to Alicia Flint.

He calls Jombaugh, tells him to search for Nicholas Absolom's vehicle details. He recalls being followed down to the Lambs', and says he thinks it is a T-plate Beemer, and he gives Jombaugh the number of Alicia Flint, tells him to call her first with the vehicle details. It could not be more urgent.

When he looks back, Eve Delahunty has stood up. She is stepping into her shoes, ready to go. He gets to the Peugeot first, reaches under the mat and removes the tracking bug device, scuttles to the patio of the pub and pops it under a plant pot.

Dan Carlyle sits in his favourite chair in the upstairs room he calls his study. His wife, Lovena, knows not to come in here. He stares blankly into the tree-lined street. This is Fulham. This is where, for £1.1 million, you can live in a terraced house not so far from the seedier realities of London town. If Dan were to look in the third drawer down of his reproduction writing desk, he would see that the building society had statemented his debt on this place at seven hundred thousand. In troubled times, this makes his shoulders stiffen. At the back of the very same drawer, he keeps his kit: his needles and his tourniquet and a couple of bags. He wants it now.

In the morning, the banker's drafts could be discovered missing.

He can hear Lovena at the other end of the landing. Even though it is only six o'clock, she is persuading Luke to sleep. She told Dan earlier, when he came home unexpectedly early, that Luke has had a good day. Dan had held his beautiful boy who will never be right. Lovena was in the kitchen, preparing the paste for a Thai green curry. The other children were in the family room, between the kitchen and the landscaped garden. Luke had looked up at his father and squeezed him tight, had planted a kiss on his father's cheek. It was the moment when Dan had decided to get clean. To come clean.

The noises from along the landing subside and he stands, opens the door to his study and turns his chair to face out of the room. He sits, waits for his wife. When she emerges, he says, 'Vee,' and raises his index finger to his lips. Lovena smiles and she mimes a tiptoe, comes towards him. His heart beats fast. Outside, it is sunny. The whole evening is ahead of them.

Dan has calculated all his options. He can afford to take a small place in Acton, or maybe further out while the dust settles. This house will need to be sold. Lovena can take the equity and buy a smaller place. He doesn't know if he will ever get another job. It is the end of his gifted life.

'What is it?' she whispers.

He reaches out, pulls her onto his lap.

'This is nice,' she says. She kisses him on the mouth. 'A nice surprise.' She puts the flat of her palm to his cheek and says, 'Sometimes, I feel like I'm losing you. Like you're somebody else.'

He swivels on the chair and reaches down, pulls open the third drawer down.

She looks down, sees the mortgage statements. 'We don't need such a big place.'

He reaches to the back of the drawer and pulls out a syringe, the tourniquet and the two bags.

Lovena gasps.

'You can have the house,' he says.

'What are you talking about?'

'I'm in trouble, Vee. I've done something stupid.'

'Don't tell me.'

355

'I'll lose my job.'

'It's not a woman?'

He thinks, Christ, if only it was.

'No, it's not a woman.'

'I won't let you go.'

'You don't understand.'

'But I can.' She reaches across and picks up the syringe, the tourniquet and the bags. 'This isn't the problem. It's what it covers up. We can fix that.'

He nods his head. 'But it's too late.'

'Tell me. I'll help you.'

He doesn't dare look at her. He presses his face against her breast and squeezes her tight. She rubs his back, tells him it will be fine, just fine, as if he is a child.

When he has told Lovena everything, Dan Carlyle says he will phone his boss. He says he wants to do it here, in his study, alone.

'Oh, no. I have to be here when you tell him.'

He nods and makes the call. It rings and rings. He thinks it is too late and will ring to answerphone and maybe this is God telling him there is a chance for second thoughts.

'Hello,' says Finbar Hare.

'It's Dan. Dan Carlyle.'

'Can this wait? I've only just got in. I've a shower running.'

'No.' Dan's head is fuzzy and he doesn't know how he will be able to find the words. 'I've been an idiot, Fin. Someone found out I've been an idiot and . . . Christ, it's a mess.'

'Is this to do with work, Dan?'

'You'd call it blackmail.'

'What have you done?'

'I use.'

'What? Like crack?' laughs Finbar.

'No. Heroin.'

'What? What the fuck! What have you done, Dan? Have you done something for them? Is it a dummy account?'

'It's a lad from the post room. Christ, Fin, I think he's a gangster or something.'

'Jesus!' The line is deathly still. When he talks again, Fin's voice has changed. He sounds like a parent, like a small miracle might have happened. 'Tell me everything and we'll see if we can fix it. You're one of us, Dan. You're not the enemy. He's the enemy and we're the ones in the bloody gang. Our gang wins, right?'

With this, Dan can't say anything at all. The words he wanted to say clash in his head, collide in the top of his throat.

Lovena takes the phone. She says, 'Mr Hare? This is Lovena Carlyle.'

'What's he done, Lovena?'

'There's a book of drafts gone missing. Dan says they are going to be used tomorrow. He says you can put a stop on them but this young man has them. He's new and he works in the post room and his name is . . .'

'Jadus,' says Finbar. 'Jadus Golding.'

'Should we go to the police?'

'No. Leave that to me. Tell Dan to come in tomorrow, like nothing happened. Tell him to come see me at half-nine.'

'Thank you, Finbar.'

'Look after him, Lovena. And prepare for the worst. That's always best.'

Knutsford Services is like any other. Staffe brings back the coffees, passing through the cordon of smokers. Eve is leaning against his car.

'How far?' she says.

'I got you a white with one sugar. You were asleep. I didn't want to wake you.'

She says, 'It's how I take it.'

'We're an hour away.' He looks for the sun. 'Should still be light, with a bit of luck.'

'Where will we stay?'

'There's a hotel.'

'And it's by the sea? Should be nice.' The smile disappears from her mouth. She must remember the situation she is in. The coffee working.

Staffe's phone goes and he answers, expecting it to be Jombaugh with Absolom's vehicle details.

'A right fine mess.'

'What? Fin?' Staffe backtracks quickly to what he thinks he might have witnessed yesterday in the vicinity of Peerless Street. 'It's not Jadus, is it?'

'Christ alive, Staffe. It's a whole fucking portfolio of things, but yes, Jadus Golding is up there in the bastard van.'

'How?'

'He's blackmailing one of my directors. He's got hold of a book of banker's drafts that could cost us a bucketful and . . .'

'What is it, Fin?'

'I'd take care of this myself, Staffe, if I could. I really would. I've put a stop on the drafts but I have to let the police know, the Fraud Office, you know.'

'Of course.' Staffe watches the wagons thunder up the M6. It is rush hour and the traffic flows free, but dense. So much going off in the nation: hither, thither. Jadus, amongst so many lost souls. 'I'm sorry.'

'I don't want it to be embarrassing for you, Will.'

'What?'

'I can let the Fraud Office know. I'm going to do that right now, but you should come round. Come and have a drink. I need a couple of men to watch my director's house.'

'Really?'

'This Golding. He's blackmailing my man.'

'Oh, shit! I'm up north, Fin.'

'I can't put this under the carpet.'

'I know. I know.' Staffe looks at the wagons again. They go both ways, trundling north, trundling south.

Natalie had let Emily take the wheel, from Gloucester, but she had taken it back again before they got onto the M6. She is tired, but it is more fatiguing to be the passenger. In control again, she feels free, less prone to chance.

Lesley Crawford made another call, to see where they are. The Bright woman's waters have gone and Natalie can't help herself dwelling upon the rights and wrongs of that case. Nonetheless, Natalie will bring the child into the world, will make it survive.

'How come you're so calm, Nat?' Emily has seen the first sign for Liverpool.

'There's nothing to worry about. Not now he's out of the way. It will come to fruition, that's what Lesley says. She likes "fruition".' She turns to face Emily, her eyes open wide as if it is, truly, a good thing she has done.

Emily wants to believe that, after all this time, what she suffered those years ago will be irrefutably for the good. What they have done today and will do tomorrow will be for the better. 'Is the baby going to be fine?'

Natalie nods her head. She pats Emily on the thigh and turns the music up a little. It is a song from a few years ago by Lauryn Hill. 'This is "To Zion". Do you know it?'

Lauryn, baby use your head
But instead I chose to use my heart.

'I don't like it,' says Emily. 'It's too deep.'
Natalie turns it off.
Emily turns it on again. 'But it's good. And you like it.'
'We'll go this way,' says Natalie, taking the M56. 'It's the junction for Ellesmere Port we want. Keep an eye out.'

Above, a souped Volvo sweeps down onto the slip road, slots into the middle stream of traffic three cars back from Natalie Stafford's baby-blue Beetle. In the passenger seat, the DS removes the monocular from his right eye, says, 'Looks like two women. And two baby seats in the back. Occupied.'

Thirty-Seven

Nick Absolom's clapped-out Beemer roars past junction nineteen in the fast lane. Staffe boots his Peugeot down the slip road and Eve says, 'Where's the fire?'

He says, 'We're about to find out.'

The second item on the news round-up reminds them both that tomorrow, Vernon Short's controversial bill is up before the House.

Eve says, 'How could Natalie be mixed up in something like this?'

He thinks of something his father once said to him. 'Things that go away by themselves can come back by themselves.'

'What?'

'It's like most crimes. There's an irresistible force. Sometimes, there's too much love, too much hate. Sometimes, people just need the money or are caught up in situations that won't go away. Usually, there's no choice.'

'I had a choice.'

'Did you?'

They are up with and following Absolom's Beemer and now the reporter cuts across two lanes. His brake lights glow red in the early dusk. He is taking the M56. Staffe backs off, lets him get two cars ahead. He calls Pulford, is told that he is down in Fulham with Josie and they have an eye on Dan Carlyle's house.

The instant he hangs up, Staffe receives another call, from Alicia Flint.

'Our car has followed Natalie Stafford into Parkgate. We're on standby, but there's no sign of Given. I'm sorry. Hang on. Our car's calling in. You want to hang on?'

Staffe waits for Alicia Flint to take her call, says to Eve, 'I think Natalie is up ahead.'

'Staffe?' says Alicia Flint. 'They're in Parkgate – parked up on a track that leads to a disused water tower. It's all locked up, but it seems as if the driver knows where there's a key. She's letting herself in through the gate.'

The line goes silent.

'They're driving in. My team is holding back. There's no track beyond the tower. There's no way out of there.'

'Are you sure?'

'One hundred per cent.'

'I'll be there in half an hour.' Up ahead, Staffe sees the sparkly afforestation of the towers of the Stanlow oil refinery, lit up like something from James Bond in the gathering dusk. The smell of petrol is overwhelming: sweet, tacking to the nostrils.

The main news runs Vernon Short's forthcoming bill as the lead item. There has been minor skirmishing at Breath of Life marches in Swansea and Sheffield. 'We should be working on the Degg case, not stuck here,' says Pulford. 'We need to track Tommy Given down, and get Bridget Lamb in again.'

'I know,' says Josie. 'But Staffe was adamant. He said . . .'

'I know. Our bloody lives depend on keeping a lid on this Carlyle bloke. He works for that firm Staffe's mate runs.'

'I still don't get it,' says Josie. She switches the radio off and follows a set of headlights coming towards them. The car is a Jeep and it slows to a crawl, even though there are no other cars coming down the residential street. 'Look, Pulford,' she hisses. 'It's slowing down.'

The Jeep pulls up outside Dan Carlyle's house and Pulford reads out the number. 'YG10EGB.'

'Someone's getting out.'

Though the car is still moving, the passenger door opens and a man in a hooded track-suit top steps into the road, running alongside the car. He reaches back with one hand, then hurls something at the house. The downstairs window smashes. The man is back in the car and three fresh lights come on in the house.

'Shall we follow the car?'

The Jeep's tail lights fade. Pulford's car is facing the wrong way. 'Let's make sure they're safe. We'll call the plates in. Come on, let's see what they threw, but take it easy.'

As they advance slowly towards the house, a neighbour comes to her door and Josie shouts for her to get back inside. More lights come on in the Carlyles' house and Pulford is at the door, knocking. He calls, 'Police!'

A desperate-looking man opens the door. He looks afraid. He seems broken and walks heavily into the room where the window is smashed. At the top of the stairs, two children peer around the newel post.

In the lounge, a woman is on her knees, a piece of paper in her hand. Beside her a house brick is on the solid oak flooring. Glass, like diamonds and blades, is all around her.

'Be careful. Don't move,' says Josie, reaching out for the

piece of paper. It says, 'LOSE YOUR NERVE. LOSE YOUR BOY', written in marker pen.

The woman looks up, towards her husband who is standing in the doorway. She says, 'Dan. What have you done?'

Natalie parks the car as close to the water tower as she can. Hawthorn bushes have overrun the driveway and Emily struggles to get through to the front door without scratching herself or Giselle.

She waits for Natalie, who has padlocked the gate behind her and is putting the key back in its place. Natalie reaches into the car for Samuel and she carries him with the nonchalance of a professional towards the front door, which opens.

'At last!'

Emily starts, turning quickly, afraid.

Lesley Crawford stretches her arms out towards Giselle. Emily holds the little girl's hand tighter.

'Let her come,' says the woman in the doorway. Her hair is cut in a severe bob and her make-up is too harsh, quite inexpert. Her eyes are kind.

'Let her,' says Natalie.

'What's happening?' says Emily, holding Giselle away from the woman in the doorway.

'I am Lesley. I helped save her.' Crawford steps down from the doorway and puts a hand on the back of Emily's head. She strokes her hair. 'Some might say I saved you, also.'

For a reason she cannot understand, Emily ushers Giselle towards the woman, who takes the child in her arms and turns, goes into the building, talking to the girl as if she were an adult. 'It is a little cold in here, but we'll get you wrapped up warm. You can see the sea and the hills, and there's a heron. Do you know what a heron is?'

Giselle shakes her head, quite vociferously, in precisely the same manner as her mother.

Natalie takes Zoe Bright's temperature, then tells her that she needs to remove her pants.

Lesley Crawford sits beside Zoe, leaning back on the sofa. She rests the baby Samuel on his chest, on her bosom. The boy is strong and he breathes evenly, on the edge of sleep. At her feet, Giselle stands inquisitively with her hand on the baby's bottom. She has been quietly chastised for poking him in the ribs and face. Now, she understands he is weaker than her, that she must help the other women protect him. If the baby were left to its own devices, it would soon come to harm. 'Not like you. You're a big girl,' Lesley Crawford had said.

All the time she has been here, Emily Bagshot has barely said a word. Fate has put her in this room with the two women who made her captive those years ago. But her daughter is here, too. Chances are, they can remain together now. What, precisely, are the chances? She tries to calculate, but it is too complex.

'She's fully dilated. It's coming,' says Natalie.

'The contractions are all there,' says Lesley, pointing at a sheet of paper on the floor besides Zoe. Her phone beeps text.

'What happens now?'

'You're thirty weeks, right?'

Zoe nods. 'It's too soon?'

'It's a strong foetus. We'll be fine.'

'I need help. I need to be in a hospital. I keep telling her.' Zoe grabs Natalie by the arm. She hisses, 'You're a nurse. Tell her. Tell her!'

'We know what we're doing.' Natalie smiles at Lesley. 'It is nearly time.'

'He's five minutes away.'

'Who is five minutes away?' says Natalie. 'What's happening?'

'We're going to show the world, is what's happening.'

Baby Samuel writhes in Lesley's arms. He arches his back, his legs stiffen and he roars. He roars with a deep voice and stretches out his arms, punching Lesley in the face. He looks around, with half-closed eyes, and slumps back to her bosom, to his slumber.

'Now, tell me what happened to Given.'

'Let me do this,' says Natalie. She is on all fours, peering at Zoe. Zoe clutches her stomach and cries out and Natalie quickly kneels up. 'We're good to go, Zoe.' She squeezes Zoe's hand. 'I'll be damned if we're not.' She smiles. 'Remember the breathing?'

Zoe nods. She whispers, between deep breaths, 'I want Anthony to be here.'

'No!' says Crawford. 'I told you, this has to be my doing. He'll let the cat out and then you'll be for it. Remember?'

She nods.

Under her breath, Crawford says, 'You don't even like him.'

'That's not the point.'

Crawford's phone rings and she answers, saying, 'The key is under a rock by the left-hand gate post. You have everything?' She hangs up, says, 'My God, it's going to happen.'

Staffe has the handset pressed to his ear, watching Absolom's lights get further and further away until they glow a brighter red and stop. He can see the outline of the water tower, which is on an escarpment at the end of the track that runs down by the side of the Marsh Tom Hotel. You can't see it from the Strand or from any point on the Neston Road. Absolom's Beemer is just fifty yards from the tower.

'Did you hear me, sir?' says Pulford.

'Go on.'

'We've got a couple of uniforms staying with the Carlyles overnight. Dan Carlyle says they'll find out tomorrow that their scam won't work.'

'What time?'

'Not before ten. Not long after.'

He hangs up and says to Eve, 'This is it. You'd better book into the Marsh Tom. It will be a long night.'

Thirty-Eight

Alicia Flint and her entourage of sergeants and constables are in the games room of the Marsh Tom, down at the bottom of the beer garden. From here, if you walk just a few yards to the barbecue area, you can see the water tower. An officer, clad in black, is looking through a pair of serious binoculars, mounted on a tripod and hooked up to a laptop.

Inside the games room, they are wired up with internet and Alicia Flint is standing in front of a pinball machine by an interactive whiteboard, holding court. Staffe shows his ID and slopes into a seat at the back, listening to the briefing talk and fixing eye contact with her.

Alicia Flint continues, 'Natalie Stafford is in situ and we have to accommodate the possibility that Bright's baby might have been born. Stafford is with a woman we believe to be Emily Bagshot, who may have been abducted by Lesley Crawford and Natalie Stafford three years ago.' She looks across to Staffe. She could say, 'Thanks to our colleagues at City Police for this information', but she doesn't. Rather, she reiterates the positions they hold, the fact that they have no reason to believe that either Crawford or Stafford is armed. The priority is to preserve the well-being of Bright and her baby. 'One thing we must keep at the forefront of our minds is that, whether Crawford suspects this or not, she is cornered. This is the end of the line for her and as a result everyone in that tower is in danger. Crawford is capable of anything and we know there are two children and three women in there with her. Their safety is paramount.'

For a moment, Staffe allows himself to think of how he has let down his friend, Finbar, who is now up to his eyes with the latest grand plan of Jadus Golding. He feels a fool, but knows he has to hold his nerve. He checks his phone to see if there is further contact from Pulford but there is nothing.

An officer rushes into the games room. 'Ma'am. There's another car drawn up at the tower. It's a man alone. He has a large bag and he looks as if he knows where the key to the gate is. What's your call?'

Alicia Flint becomes still. She says nothing. After several beats, she says, 'Can we intervene?'

'Yes, ma'am. We have forty seconds. Our men are thirty yards away.' The officer presses a finger to his ear. 'He has the key to the gate.'

Staffe feels himself standing. 'No!'

'What?' says Flint.

'He's five eleven and ten stone, long dark hair and probably smoking a roll-up, dressed as if he's in a band.'

The officer turns to look at Staffe. 'Yes.'

'We have to trust him.'

'Twenty seconds, ma'am.'

'He's a reporter. He's not with them.'

'So he could be in danger,' says Flint, glaring fiercely.

Staffe puts his head in his hands. He was expecting contact

from Absolom before he went in. But even so, he should know what to do. All he can think of is Giselle Bagshot and Grace's twin. He hasn't figured . . .

'Inspector Wagstaffe!'

. . . quite how he can use Absolom yet. He prays he can.

'He's going, ma'am. He's through the gate and parking up. We could still stop him,' says the officer.

'No!' says Flint. 'Keep our cover.'

The officer says, into his mouthpiece, 'Stand down.'

Alicia Flint says, 'Inspector Wagstaffe? A word!' She strides out into the night.

Jadus Golding holds Millie close. Jasmine is clearing the dishes away, serving up ice-cream. It is Phish Food and Jadus's favourite. He is seldom in for dinner, and when he is, he never sticks around for pudding. Tonight, he doesn't want to go out at all. 'Just stay in. Like a family,' he had said.

It made Jasmine want to weep and it is what has made this feel like a Last Supper.

Tonight, Jadus holds Millie, whispering the story of Chicken Licken to her. It has lulled her to sleep.

Jasmine brings the ice-cream.

'Put mine in the fridge a while. I like it soft on the outside.'

'I didn't know you knew Chicken Licken.'

'Didn't know myself,' he says. They exchange a look as she comes back with her ice-cream. He thinks, she's thinking about the sky falling in.

Later, when Millie is properly put down, they make love. Jadus is tender and afterwards, he gets her to spoon and he falls asleep with his hand on her belly. Jadus can sleep anywhere – even on the eve of something like this. He doesn't feel Jasmine become progressively more rigid with fear.

Staffe took his medicine from Alicia Flint. She was furious he hadn't told her about Absolom and he explained his pact with the reporter and how indebted they are to the fact that Crawford had targeted him. If he had divulged his source, Crawford wouldn't have used him. It is down to Absolom that they knew she was on Merseyside, and his presence in the tower could be to their advantage, still.

Outside, he looks up at the black outline of the tower against the indigo sky. He thinks he can hear the sea, but knows it must be the breeze across the reeds.

There is a light on the second floor of the tower. He looks through the field glasses and homes in on the shape of Nick Absolom. The journalist reaches up above the window, reaches as high as he can. Only when he brings his hand down – empty – does Staffe realise what he was placing there. He thinks hard. He thinks of the thing that Lesley Crawford and Nick Absolom would have most in common, and he realises that Lesley Crawford is not here to hide. This is not the dead end that Alicia Flint thinks it is.

Now, Absolom stands with his back to the window, pointing. He brings a camera to his eye, then lowers it. He points some more. He is directing.

Staffe calls Absolom. He listens as his phone rings and he watches the window, waiting for Absolom to reach up for his phone. But he doesn't. He pulls one up from his hip, puts it to his ear.

'I can't talk.'

'What are you up to?'

'Waiting on Crawford.' Absolom looks out into the night. He raises a hand and for an instant, Staffe's heart misses. He thinks Absolom is waving to him so he ducks, but when he looks back, listening to Absolom say, 'She said she'd call me,' he realises the journalist is only shielding the reflected light from his view through the window and into the dark, empty night.

'We still have our deal?'

'Of course.'

'Do you have anything to tell me?'

'Not yet.'

'We had an agreement, Nick.'

'You don't call me Nick.'

In the background, Staffe can hear a hullabaloo, can see Absolom turning inwards, moving away from the window.

'Where are you, Nick? Can I hear children?'

The line is dead. Absolom comes back towards the window and points some more into the room. He holds the camera to his eye again and when he is done, he looks back into the night.

The phone perched on the frame above the window is not a phone.

Staffe makes his way back inside the games room. As he does, he feels an echo from a previous case. It zags in at him through the ether, lightning-fast. He feels wired up, has a clear picture – at long last.

* * *

Vernon Short shakes the Home Secretary's hand. She wishes him well for tomorrow and looks him square in the eye as she says it. 'Really, Vernon. I mean it. You've had a rough ride.'

'Thank you, Home Secretary.'

'Cathy,' she says and her mouth widens. She shows her teeth. He hasn't noticed before, but she has good teeth.

He goes out into Whitehall. The light-grey stone of the buildings looks almost white tonight against the indigo sky. Earlier, his father had telephoned. His father only ever calls him on his birthday and when they are short for the drag hunt. Today, his father had called him to say 'well done'. He hadn't even said 'well done' when Vernon had secured the deal to save the family firm in the winter of 1987. Today, his father had asked him to come up to the club, for supper.

Vernon had almost fallen off his chair.

As he makes his way up Pall Mall, towards Saint James's, his pace slows. After all this time, he doesn't want to arrive. The clubs line Pall Mall like so many sentrymen with their high ceilings and stuccoed frontages and extravagant balconies, as if their arms are crossed tight across their chests, backs straight. Hearts of stone.

He pauses as he climbs the steps and looks left, up to Clarence House and a cool breeze seems to come along the street. He feels cold to the bone recalling what Lesley Crawford's people had told him they knew about his father. Vernon wonders if he will have the courage to bring the matter up over supper.

Vernon is shown up to the smoking room where nobody is smoking, but still they sit in fours on low-slung armchairs around card tables drinking ancient malts from thick Irish crystal. Empire remains, in these four walls.

Edward Short raises a hand, stands and leaves his four. He walks with a stoop but is still an imposing figure. He is taller than Vernon and has always been more handsome than his son. His hair is dapper long, to his collar and combed back in thick, grey-black slicks. Easy to see he would have been popular in the highest, the very highest, circles – not so far away.

As they eat turbot, Edward talks easily about his day and the party down at the farm last weekend and how Vernon really should find time to visit more. Especially now. His mother would like to see him.

'My mother? Do you think of mother, when you are in town?'

Edward neither blinks nor stops the tiny circles he makes in the mastication of his fish. He swallows. 'You know, it's not important what is in this bill. The statute book is written on paper. It's the musculature of what precedes. That's what is important.'

'Father, I know the worst.'

Edward raises his eyebrows. 'These things can be forgotten as quickly as they are found. We're in the secrets business, after all. The important thing is that you keep your eye on the ball.'

'It matters to me.'

'It was a long time ago.'

'But it's preposterous.'

'Don't worry about me. Or your mother.'

'They hold it to my head. Not yours.'

Edward sets his knife down, alongside his fork and even though Vernon is no more than half-way through his supper, a waiter comes. The plates are removed. He says, to his son. 'You look well on it. Look well tomorrow, regardless of the outcome. It's what people will remember.'

Vernon leans forward, whispers, 'I don't even want this bloody bill.'

His father stands, pats him on the shoulder and says, 'Have pudding if you want or the stewed cheese is excellent. I'm done.'

Staffe is exasperated. Alicia Flint and her DS crowd him, pointing at the screen. For twenty minutes, he has been pumping keywords into all the major search engines. He comes up blank.

Alicia Flint says, 'What makes you think there'll be something on the internet?'

Staffe tries 'Breath of Life' for a third time, this time on Yahoo! He flicks through the 231,456 results, getting little of promise. 'There was a case a few years ago. Absolom will remember it, and so would Crawford, I bet – it would have been around the time Emily Bagshot went missing, too.'

'Was this your case?'

Staffe can tell what is coming. He nods.

'Isn't that a little . . .'

'Egocentric? Probably. But Absolom covered that case. He'll remember, and he's got a device up there. A receiver for a modem, if I'm right. He had to put it up high, by the window.'

'Lesley Crawford, as far as we know, is here to put a stop to the trail that leads to her. She has Zoe and the nurse, and she has Emily Bagshot. God knows where Given is. Imagine if he showed up.'

'Crawford is in the business of saving those children, not harming.'

'Believe me, that's the only thing that has stopped me going in there already.'

'We can't do that. Can't you see?'

'Something terrible could still happen in there tonight. It's no time for high-falutin theories. What exactly is it that you think is going on?'

Staffe has an idea. Something more obscure. Something that Crawford may not think he knows about. 'She *wants* to be found out. But maybe not straight away – and not by us.' He types in 'House of the Holy Innocents' and gets millions of responses.

Most of the results to the search are seemingly religious. Some relate to a Chilean novel, some to a Swedish heavy metal group. 'Why would she get a journalist up here if I'm wrong?'

'Maybe he got a lead?'

'He knew where the key was.' Staffe punches in 'Breath' and 'Innocents'.

'This is a blind alley. We need to focus.'

Staffe scrolls down the first page. He double-clicks. 'Focus on this.'

Alicia Flint leans close, stares at the screen, her cheek practically pressed against his. 'Fuck,' she says, looking at an image of Lesley Crawford standing between Natalie Stafford, who is holding a baby just a few weeks old, and Emily Bagshot who is holding an infant, kissing the cheek of that daughter. They are all smiling. In front of them, sitting in a low sofa, is Zoe Bright. Her face is flushed red and she is covered in a sheen of sweat. Her eyes are wide and full of fear. On her swollen belly are the words, 'Let the Innocents Breathe', written, it would seem, in lipstick.

Thirty-Nine

'What can you tell us of Zoe's condition?' Alicia Flint asks the police doctor.

He scrutinises the printouts of the photographic images posted on the internet. 'We need to go in.'

'I should go in,' says Staffe. 'I know Absolom. I have the nurse's best friend with me.'

'You can't endanger her.'

'She is a nurse, too, and it will save her, not endanger her. She has signed a consent form and an indemnity.'

'They're not worth the paper.' Alicia Flint scrutinises Staffe. There is a flicker of something in her eyes. It could be pity. 'I can't let you have her on your conscience.'

'My conscience is the last thing to have on yours.'

'And what about Zoe? I'm not going to do anything to endanger Zoe Bright.'

Almost every element is known. The principal doubt is Tommy Given. Staffe takes the examination paper from his jacket pocket, wrapped in a plastic evidence bag. He unfurls it as though it might be the map of a desert island. He taps the top of the front sheet.

'And we know Crawford's books matched Zoe's,' says Alicia Flint. 'You're going to tell me about herrings, now.'

Staffe pulls out a tub from his hip pocket. It too is in a clear evidence bag. 'Rollmops, actually. You said I was going round the bend.'

'If you go in there and something happens to Zoe or the others, that's the end of your career.'

He nods. 'I'm worried about Zoe. You saw the look on her face.'

'She's afraid.'

'She's supposed to look afraid. Crawford doesn't know we have the two of them connected. She's supposed to have been kidnapped. But that expression – it's real. That's why I have to go in. I will take Eve Delahunty with me. Nobody else.'

'Don't take her.'

'It will save her, and it might save her best friend. How could I not take her?'

'On your head,' says Alicia Flint. She nods to one of her officers, who presents Staffe with a document. 'To cover me, you understand.'

He signs it. 'I wouldn't have it any other way.' His heart beats faster and his breath becomes shorter as he goes to collect Eve, fearing the worst now, not daring to hope.

'Where is the nurse?' says Bridget Lamb. 'The smiley one with the golden hair.'

'Natalie?' The nurse lifts Baby Grace from her cot and hands her to her aunt. Bridget's face comes to life the moment she touches her niece. Her eyes are soft, her gaze locked. 'We're so short today. I don't know where she is. Sick, I guess.'

Grace blinks and looks around, but her glassy gaze eventually settles upon Bridget.

Malcolm stands alongside her and puts his arm around Bridget. She brings the baby higher, rests its head in the hollow between her jaw and shoulder. The baby is warm. She feels Malcolm kiss the top of her head. He tells her that he loves her. She always hoped she could love him back. Now, she knows that it is better to love than to be loved.

'She will come to us,' says Bridget.

'She must,' says Malcolm. 'It's what is right. God's will.'

Still nestling Grace's head in the crook of her neck, Bridget looks up at Malcolm. She sees him in a new light. 'I feel like this is what my life has been for; the path we have been on. It has been the right path. Good has come of it, Mal. Hasn't it?'

The instant Staffe eases shut the gate to the tower, its front door creaks open.

'My God,' says Lesley Crawford. She looks from Staffe to his companion. 'There is no point coming here. We are innocent people. There have been no crimes committed here.'

He says, 'This is Eve Delahunty, a friend of Natalie Stafford.'

'What are you doing here? Do you have a warrant?'

'You're trespassing.'

'I am here by invitation. I have the papers to prove it.'

'I'll come in while you show them to me.'

'You can't change anything. It is time.'

'Time is the operative word, isn't it, Lesley? I've seen your site. I suppose the plan is to make an announcement in the morning, to publicise the website then, just as the MPs are chomping on their kedgeree.'

'How is Natalie?' asks Eve. 'I'm a nurse, too. I can help with Zoe's baby.'

'If anything happens to that baby, you're ruined,' says Staffe. 'You're ruined anyway.'

Lesley Crawford looks at Eve quizzically, biding her response. 'That remains to be seen.'

Eve holds up the canister of oxygen she has brought. 'This will help. We need to secure a healthy birth.'

Crawford nods. 'Natalie can tell you herself.'

Staffe walks into the entrance of the tower. As he passes Crawford, he hisses, 'If you don't tell me the truth, I'll go for Zoe Bright. Or should I say Flanagan? Anne-Marie Flanagan as she was when you were her tutor.'

Lesley Crawford's mouth opens. In her eyes, he sees the briefest flicker of uncertainty.

The room on the second floor is wide and long, improbably lit all the way to its high ceilings and out to the night. The brightness casts shadows across everybody's face, makes them like gargoyles. When he sees Staffe, Nick Absolom conjures the decency to look embarrassed, if not ashamed. Emily Bagshot is lost in her child, with whom she crouches, trying to distract. She is clearly confused by everything around her. On the floor, a baby lies in its Moses basket. Staffe goes onto one knee, says, 'Grace's brother.'

'Samuel,' says Natalie. Her eyes flit and she scratches her chin, rubs her eyes. She is calculating something and regards Eve only briefly.

'I'm sorry, Nat,' says Eve.

'What are you talking about?' Natalie looks across at Lesley Crawford, then Staffe. 'I had no choice.'

'They forced you?' says Eve.

Beyond Natalie, Zoe Bright breathes dramatically, through a pursed mouth. Her knees are slightly raised. On a blanket beside her chair is a stack of brilliantly white towels.

'We should get her to a hospital,' says Staffe.

'You can't take her,' says Crawford. 'Not yet. We have a nurse. In fact, we have two nurses.'

'You had a nurse in the tunnel,' he says. 'But it all went wrong, didn't it, Natalie? What happened? Did you have Samuel taken to Tommy? And with Grace, you were disturbed. It was Asquith, the historian.'

'I don't understand,' says Natalie, to Lesley Crawford. 'Why did you bring him here?'

Zoe Bright sighs, loudly. Then she grunts.

Natalie says, to Staffe, 'I don't know what you're talking about, or why you are even here. This is my job. It's what I do.'

Lesley Crawford makes calculations of her own.

'What's happened to Tommy, Natalie?' says Staffe.

'Don't say anything,' says Crawford. 'We'll get you a lawyer. The best. We have a baby to deliver.'

'A lawyer! I don't want a lawyer. You never said anything about a lawyer.'

Staffe says, 'When Emily Bagshot came to City Royal, three years ago, you told Lesley, didn't you, Natalie? You started all this.' He looks at Crawford. 'How did you two meet?'

Crawford looks at Natalie, imploringly. 'You'll be fine. I'll make sure you are fine.'

'You're going to prison, Natalie. Rest assured. All of you are.' He looks at Emily, says, 'Not quite.'

'All of us?' says Zoe Bright.

382

'He means me, and Natalie,' says Crawford.

'What!' says Natalie. 'It's all right for you – you want to be a martyr.'

'What did you do to Tommy Given, Emily?'

'Say nothing, Em,' says Natalie.

'I was with Giselle. She's my girl, my little girl. We were making cakes.'

'Tommy brought her to you?'

'It was an accident,' says Natalie. She begins to fidget in her pockets, stepping from foot to foot, but working her way towards the Moses basket.

'No!' shouts Staffe, but it is too late.

Natalie Stafford has the baby, Samuel, in her arms. She has a scalpel in her hand and a look of utter desperation in her eyes. 'I can't go to prison.'

Zoe Bright grunts again, louder. She pulls at her hair and squeals. 'It's coming. For God's sake. It's coming!'

'Put down the knife, Natalie.' Eve is standing in the doorway. 'He's a baby. We save babies.'

'*I* saved this baby. She is betraying me. *You* are betraying me.'

'Help me. Please, help me,' groans Zoe.

Absolom takes a photo and Lesley Crawford goes across, snatches the camera. 'When I say!'

Eve takes a step towards Natalie, but she moves the scalpel an inch closer. 'No,' says Eve.

Zoe Bright pleads, 'Please. My baby is coming.'

Eve takes another step.

Natalie puts the scalpel to the blanket by Samuel's neck, where it is pulled up to cover his head. Her bottom lip is quivering. 'Let me out. Just let me out.'

'We have to help the new baby, Nat.' Eve reaches out.

Natalie says, 'No. You have to help *me. Me.*'

'Nobody helps us, Nat. Remember? Remember what we said, when we got the bus back? That night from Leeds. We said we have to help ourselves, look after ourselves.' Eve takes another step towards Natalie and reaches out. She puts her hand on her friend's hand, which holds the handle of the scalpel. The two friends regard each other, as if they are alone in this room. 'Come on, Nat. I'll help you. Let's help the baby, together.' They intertwine their fingers and Eve slowly pulls her hand away, holding the scalpel.

Staffe watches the two friends hug each other. When they are done, Eve leads Natalie to Zoe Bright.

He says to Crawford, 'This is over, Lesley. Give me the camera.'

'No. This is mine. A moment of history – how can you not allow this to be documented?'

'Nothing will happen until after the vote, tomorrow.' He looks at Absolom. 'Nothing.'

They each look across at Zoe Bright, supported by Eve, who administers gas and air whilst Natalie is on her knees, between Zoe Bright's glistening calves. Natalie says, 'Push, Zoe. Come on, sweetheart, push!' lost in these moments.

Staffe takes a hold of Crawford's arm and pulls her into the kitchen. 'This is the transcript you marked for Anne-Marie Flanagan.' He reaches into his pocket and pulls out the rollmop tub in its evidence bag. 'And this has your prints, and Zoe's. We know she has been complicit in this and she will become as involved as we want her to be. So you play ball, you understand – for Zoe's sake!'

'There's more at stake than that.'

He holds her by the shoulders and turns her to face into the room. He whispers, heavily, into her ear. 'These people each have a life. A life has to be lived, not just given. There's no point bringing them into the world and abandoning them. And that's what you do, Lesley. You use people. You undermine yourself. You think you are God. You can't make decisions for everyone.'

Natalie reaches out, towards Zoe. Eve helps the mother sit up, her hair matted and her face coated with sweat. She reaches out towards Natalie. Between them, with blood on her head and her mouth agape, is Zoe's baby. It is a daughter. She tries to roar, but something is trapped inside her. She can't breathe.

Zoe cries out, 'What's wrong? Is she dying? Have I killed her?'

Eve picks up the baby and feels her neck. She looks at Natalie, eyes wide and full of fear.

Natalie takes the baby from Eve and whispers into her ear, then she holds the baby high, the umbilical cord almost taut as she tilts the baby and pulls one hand away. 'No!' shouts Zoe. Natalie raises her free hand, flattens it and angles it to the shape of a karate chop and fast as a flash she brings it down, tilting the baby and tapping her back.

The baby roars.

'You have to let people choose,' says Staffe to Lesley Crawford. 'And they will, tomorrow.'

Forty

'When was the last time you slept?' asks Josie.

'Are they in there?' says Staffe, peering through the reinforced glass panel of the small room. It is off the main ward, to keep germs at bay and contains two cots.

'Can't this wait, sir? They're going nowhere,' says Pulford.

Staffe runs his hands through his hair and blows out his cheeks. He summons images of his last meeting with Sean Degg, can't escape the bad thoughts he had of him, the accusations levelled. All he did was love a woman too much.

He reaches for the door, pushes it, takes a step closer to what he has to do.

Bridget Lamb has Baby Samuel in her arms. The baby looks up at his aunt and, hearing somebody enter, turns his head. The infant's faculties seem to have advanced in the day since Staffe last saw him, and Bridget looks different, too. Her husband sits opposite the two of them and doesn't look up. He has Grace in his lap. Staffe thinks that Malcolm might know what is coming and he has another flash memory of the young Malcolm, miserable at school.

He pulls up a chair and sits alongside Bridget, who says, 'You know, I can see Kerry in him. And something of myself in Grace.' She rocks the baby now, but it is a disguise. Staffe can see that her hands are shaking.

'And Sean?'

'There's nothing of him,' says Malcolm Lamb.

'We can't say that,' says Bridget. 'But it's not what I see.'

There is a window beyond the cots. They are three floors up and there is nothing between them and the ground. Outside, in the main ward, Pulford and Josie are waiting. There is a uniformed WPC there, also. At the main entrance, another two uniformed officers wait, and two more by the service entrance just in case.

'If only Kerry could have seen. If she'd have known better,' says Bridget. 'She should have talked to me. I could have helped. This could have been arranged properly.'

'Properly?' says Staffe.

'They will come to me, these babies,' she says.

'We have spoken to a solicitor, and she has consulted the authorities,' says Malcolm. 'Bridget is their aunt. She will be a wonderful mother to them now. It's in her blood.'

Staffe and Malcolm exchange a look and Staffe's heart sinks as he says, 'I'd like a few words with Malcolm.'

'Of course,' she says, smiling at Samuel, her thumb lightly upon the baby's cheek.

Staffe nods for Josie to come in. 'Alone, the two of us,' he says to Bridget.

Josie comes in and takes Grace from Malcolm.

'Why?' says Bridget, suddenly concerned.

Josie ushers Bridget towards the door, says, 'They should get to know each other – brother and sister. We'll have some tea.'

Staffe says, 'I need to talk to Malcolm about when we were young. He was there with my sister . . .'

'When your parents were killed. He told me. I'm sorry.'

'I'm sorry, too,' says Staffe, watching Bridget go, Samuel in arms, and Josie beside her, holding Grace.

When the two men are alone, Staffe takes out the wedding photo of Bridget. He can see now that it is probably no longer the happiest day of her life. 'I went to see a young woman, out east a little. It's where Sean was for the last days of his life. He went into a shop to buy something. Earlier, he had made a telephone call.'

'I thought you wanted to talk about when we were young,' says Malcolm.

Staffe looks at the photograph of Bridget, Malcolm beside her. She is beaming into camera and he is looking at her, a frightened smile creasing in his face, as if he can see that one day he might have to do anything for her.

'Sean called a mobile number. And that mobile phone then made a call to your home.'

'I don't understand,' says Malcolm.

'You have a mobile phone, don't you?'

Malcolm shakes his head.

'You'd do anything for Bridget, wouldn't you? You can't give her children, though. But you could help her have Kerry's.'

'I'll support her however I can.'

'Sean ruined her.'

'I don't know what you're driving at.'

'That young woman in the shop who served Sean remembered him. She remembered who else was in the shop just afterwards. I have her statement here.' He holds up the photograph. He puts a finger to it. 'She remembers you going in.' Staffe looks at Malcolm, says, 'I remember that time at school, Malcolm. When the ambulance came.'

'You were there. You could have stopped that bastard.'

'You know how to inject. You have done it all your life. And you work with druggies, down at the exchange that the church helps with. You could get your hands on it.'

'Hands on what?'

'Sean called you on that mobile phone you say you haven't got.' Staffe pulls a phone from his pocket. The device is sheathed in an evidence bag and Malcolm's eyes hood down. 'You called Bridget from this mobile, Malcolm. There are some bastards out there who are paid by the government to get convictions. They look for accessories in crimes like this. They don't like loose ends.'

'I called to see how she was, that's all. Bridget knows nothing. She knows nothing at all about this.'

'If you're saying you did it on your own, you'll have to tell me how.'

'How? How is easy, Will. If you love somebody – have you ever? If you love somebody and somebody hurts them . . . you get a hate. You get a hate as big as the love. That's how it works and you can't do anything else.'

'You killed an innocent man.'

'I brought peace to a beautiful woman, an innocent woman who had her inner being, her holiest element, taken away from her. She can be complete.'

'I thought Sean was guilty, once. But I was wrong. You killed an innocent man, a father.'

'You said you wanted to talk about when we were young.'

'They killed my father, my mother, too.'

'I know, and I'm sorry.'

'And I don't doubt they had their reasons.'

'It's not the same.'

'It's always the same, Malcolm. It has to be. It can't be any other way. How could I bear it if they didn't have a damned good reason?'

Malcolm leans heavily against the wall. He looks through the window in the door, watches Bridget and her family. 'Can I be with them, a little longer?'

'I'm afraid not.' As he says it, Staffe feels a little less decent about himself.

The uniformed officers take Malcolm Lamb away. His wife is not with him as he is led away – at his insistence. Staffe cannot help speculating what his father might make of him and the things he has to do.

'If only that was the end of it,' says Josie. On their way out of City Royal, she hands Staffe a bound SOC printout of the forensics down at Emily Bagshot's bungalow on the Cornish coast.

'Where is Emily?'

'She's had the tests – to prove she's Giselle's mother – and now she's with social services.'

'They've released her from custody?'

'We have a scalpel and a syringe found less than a mile from Emily's bungalow – both taken from City Royal. Natalie Stafford has admitted to it. Her prints were on them.'

'And what do the Crown say about Natalie?'

Josie shakes her head. 'It'll be murder, sir.'

'And people talk about innocence,' says Staffe. 'What about her innocence?'

'She's as guilty as they come, sir. Conspiracy, abduction, concealment and destroying public records as well as murder.'

'And finally, Emily will be with her daughter.'

'And Rob Hutchison. They're together. You should have seen them.'

'The happy family. But . . .'

'Sir?'

'But for Natalie's interventions.'

'There's something else, sir.'

Staffe watches Malcolm Lamb being manhandled into a police car on the hospital forecourt and he thinks about when the police came to see his sister Marie and how he wasn't there when she was told her parents were murdered, but Malcolm and his father were. 'What is it?'

'It's the bank draft fraud, sir,' says Josie. 'We can deal with it.'

'No!'

An ambulance roars up the approach road and screeches to a halt in front of them. The siren stops and from within the vehicle, a scream cuts the city afternoon. They are asked to stand aside.

When the man is wheeled past, blood proliferates, from the chest of what some people would call a patient. To others, he is a victim. It could be a knife wound, or gunshot.

'Tell me,' says Staffe. 'Did they catch anyone with the banker's drafts?'

'Nearly, with the first. They used it to try and buy a car out in Ilford. After that, they must have got word round the gang and it looks like they dropped the scam.'

'Any prints on the cheque?'

'No. But we've got a definite ID on the one who presented it. He's got a record and it's the eGang all right. But they've gone to ground.'

'Have you checked Jasmine Cash's flat?'

Josie nods.

'How was she?'

Josie says, 'We can do this, sir.'

Staffe watches the bloodied victim disappear between the automatic doors of the hospital. 'Fine.'

'What?' says Josie, and she watches as Staffe walks away from City Royal, but in the opposite direction to Leadengate station.

Staffe is a little worse for wear. He tried to sleep and knocked back a couple of stiff nightcaps, but his brain couldn't stop ticking and now he feels even worse, needs to do something. He had called Finbar and is waiting for him now. It is one of their haunts, of old.

He drinks from his bottle of Moretti and twists on his stool at the bar of the Boss Clef. The performer is singing 'Lili Marlene' and has a crimped bob of golden hair and blood-red lips, is wearing a basque and a tight black skirt, split all the way to her hip. It has a scarlet lining. The place is all dark, save a single shaft of light from above that picks out her sway of the song.

With her golden hair, the singer reminds him a little of Natalie. Poor Natalie, who has borne the brunt of the charges that the CPS have brought in the abductions of Kerry Degg and Emily Bagshot, the manslaughter of the former and the murder of Tommy Given. For her part, Lesley Crawford is copping conspiracy charges and, according to the CPS, who are talking to her brief, Jasper Renwick, she is probably facing as little as two years. She might even get the lot suspended.

Her attachment to the abductions was opportunistic, superficial and political. Renwick has sufficient argument to pin the abductions to dead Tommy Given and the stunt with Zoe Bright is political, also, and conducted with the absolute consent of Zoe, according to the wily Jasper. Because of Crawford's testimony, Zoe Bright will probably be charged with conspiracy.

When Staffe had called Alicia Flint, she had said that Lesley Crawford was cold as ice. It had made her blood boil and when she visited Zoe, Anthony Bright had been there, holding the baby beside the hospital bed that Zoe was chained to. Alicia said, 'If you looked at them quick, you might think they were a family. It shows how much we know.'

The applause for 'Lili Marlene' subsides and Staffe recognises the opening chords of 'Shir Hatan'. The singer introduces the song over the piano prelude and he is sure he has heard these spoken words before. It is a homage to Dietrich and he is sure Kerry had done this also, back in the winter when she was Lori Dos Passos and he had chanced upon her – little knowing. He could swear she had.

The words drift into a verse of animals crying because they are hungry. The child cries, too, because he is lonely. Staffe closes his eyes, pictures Zoe Bright chained, her baby in the arms of Anthony Bright. He wonders if his love of Zoe is diminished now.

He looks around the audience as the chorus belts out in Hebrew. From the dark, some of the audience join in.

'Penny for 'em.' Finbar Hare draws up a stool alongside Staffe and orders up two more bottles of Moretti and large Laphroaigs.

'I'm so sorry, Fin,' says Staffe.

'Don't ever apologise to me, old boy.' They clink. 'You were only trying to help someone, so don't beat yourself up about it. There's others can do that.'

Staffe feels a smile spread across his face. It feels alien to him, seems as if he is a long way from himself.

Fin talks across the music and drinks quickly, playing catch-up, draining his malt and ordering another for himself – a 'hollow legs', as he calls it – and three songs further into the set, he begins to muse on how he would like his evening to pan out, unable to take his eyes off the singer. He raises a glass to her and she winks at him. Staffe doesn't know how he does it, but when he turns to the bar to take a swig of his Moretti, he sees the barmaid undressing the foil from the neck of a bottle of Veuve Clicquot, and Fin miming the action of putting it on ice. When he catches Staffe watching him, he says, 'That poor bastard Vernon Short, eh? You were involved in all that, weren't you?'

Vernon's bill had lost its vote by three bodies. He had stepped down, immediately, with a smile upon his lips and – the first time Staffe had seen this in him – a glint in his eyes. He looked like a different man. Nothing like his father. He had said he was done with Parliament and was going to see if vines would take on his small parcel of land in Puglia. When the interviewer had asked him about Lesley Crawford and was he involved with her political activities, he said, 'Of

394

course not. She's a maverick and the laws of slander prevent me from being candid.' The interviewer persisted and Vernon had said, 'The beauty of stepping down is I don't ever have to give fools like you the time of my day. I suggest you stuff yourself.' He had thrown back his head and laughed, then walked away. As he went, you could hear the crew guffawing.

'What's happened to Dan Carlyle?' Staffe asks.

'We're looking after him. He's booked into the Hermitage for as long as it takes for all this to die down. Rehab's the best bastard place in the world to hide.'

'I'll catch up with Golding, I promise, Fin.'

'Don't knock yourself out. We didn't lose a penny and the chances are it might have saved Dan Carlyle's marriage and career in the long run. You know he was hooked on heroin?' Fin drains his third large Laphroaig and slams the glass on the counter. 'Fucking heroin. For the love of God.'

The singer finishes the first half of her set and comes to the bar, sits on a stool between Staffe and Finbar and the barmaid brings across the chilled Veuve Clicquot.

'I'll leave you two to it,' stays Staffe.

'Don't go,' says Finbar.

'I know you from somewhere,' says the singer to Staffe. Fin has a hand on her hip.

Staffe thinks right back to the beginning of this case. Some have passed and some been born. He says to the singer, 'You know *The Blue Angel*?'

'Of course. I just sang something from that.'

Staffe says to Fin, 'Thanks for trying. We're even.'

'No!' says Finbar. 'I'll never be even. Not with you.' He

takes his hand from the singer's hip and grips Staffe's shoulders. 'And that's the bastard truth.'

The night is quiet and as the door of the Boss Clef closes behind him, the music from inside shuts to almost nothing. Staffe skirts around the Old Street roundabout, making his way past Peerless. He looks up to the Limekiln Tower beyond. Jasmine is there, with Millie, her man on the run and hopes all gone to dust.

For some reason, he walks on up towards Flower and Dean. It is warm and his thoughts won't slow. Nor can he impose any order on them. The melodies, the staccato rhythms of Brel and Schultze, the ghosts of Dietrich and Lori Dos Passos, stay with him, snagged.

On New North Road, he pauses outside a row of shops. The line about the lonely child who is hungry and cries in the night swirls like wind in a cove. He stops and he looks, feels a familiarity. These shops are run down, but they serve. There is a fruit and veg shop, a newsagent's. Then two carcasses, a caff and a bookie's. Finally, a hairdresser's. Cutz. He knows this place, and the familiarity takes shape. The reason he has, subconsciously, brought himself here becomes apparent.

Above the shop, a dim light glows within, presumably from a room at the back. He crosses the road and works his way round along the narrow road that runs along the back of the shops. He counts the units as he goes and, right enough, there is somebody in an upstairs room at the back of Cutz.

He calls Jombaugh and gives precise instructions, saying he wants a 10–39 to Cutz on the New North Road.

Jom asks what is wrong and Staffe tells his sergeant it is a matter type five. Under no circumstances must the officers get out of their car. He hangs up and waits. He thinks of what Finbar had said to him about them never being even and how he might have changed since that sequence of events, those years ago. For sure, Finbar has changed and Staffe wonders what perverse circumstances can contrive to make a sad man happy.

The squad car's response is quick and as he hears the siren grow gradually louder, like a first movement, he wonders if he is correct; how prepared he really is.

He positions himself by the back gate and he waits. His muscles harden and his breathing deepens. The blood pumps faster and only now does he fear the worst.

The police car is out front already, wailing, and the light in the upstairs back of Cutz flicks to black. A couple of beats and he hears the back door open and then a curse and heavy footfall. The bolts on the other side of the gate are shot and the door opens inward.

'Jadus,' he says.

'Fuck.' Jadus smells of coconut oil and his hair is slicked back. The moon catches it, silver and black. He closes and opens his eyes, slow; makes an ironic and disparaging slow shake of his head. 'You shouldn't have.'

'The officers out front aren't coming. Don't worry. Don't do anything stupid – it's just me and you. I want to be the one.'

'Not you,' says Jadus. 'Not you, man.'

'It has to be,' says Staffe.

Something glints in Jadus Golding's hand. 'You're not taking me. Not you. Not any fucker.' He sounds like a boy, a frightened boy.

The gun rises and Staffe takes a step back. All he can think to say is, 'Please.'

'You going to let me go?'

'I can't.'

'You have to.'

'You can't do that, Jadus. You can't do that to Jasmine, or Millie. Put it down. Come of your own accord.'

Jadus shakes his head again. He is rueful, resigned.

Staffe recognises the look. He thought he knew him.

The sound is fearsome. He feels the sound and it is all he feels. And then another.

He was wrong.

The street comes to meet him and he can't feel the bang to his head, just the worst stitch you ever had in your chest. He looks up and in the indigo sky, sees a constellation, close. He tries to keep his eyes open, but he can't. He feels himself being lifted and held: the warmth of a fellow man. And then he falls back to ground, but the ground doesn't come.